INVADER ZIM

VOLUME 3

Created by
JHONEN VASQUEZ

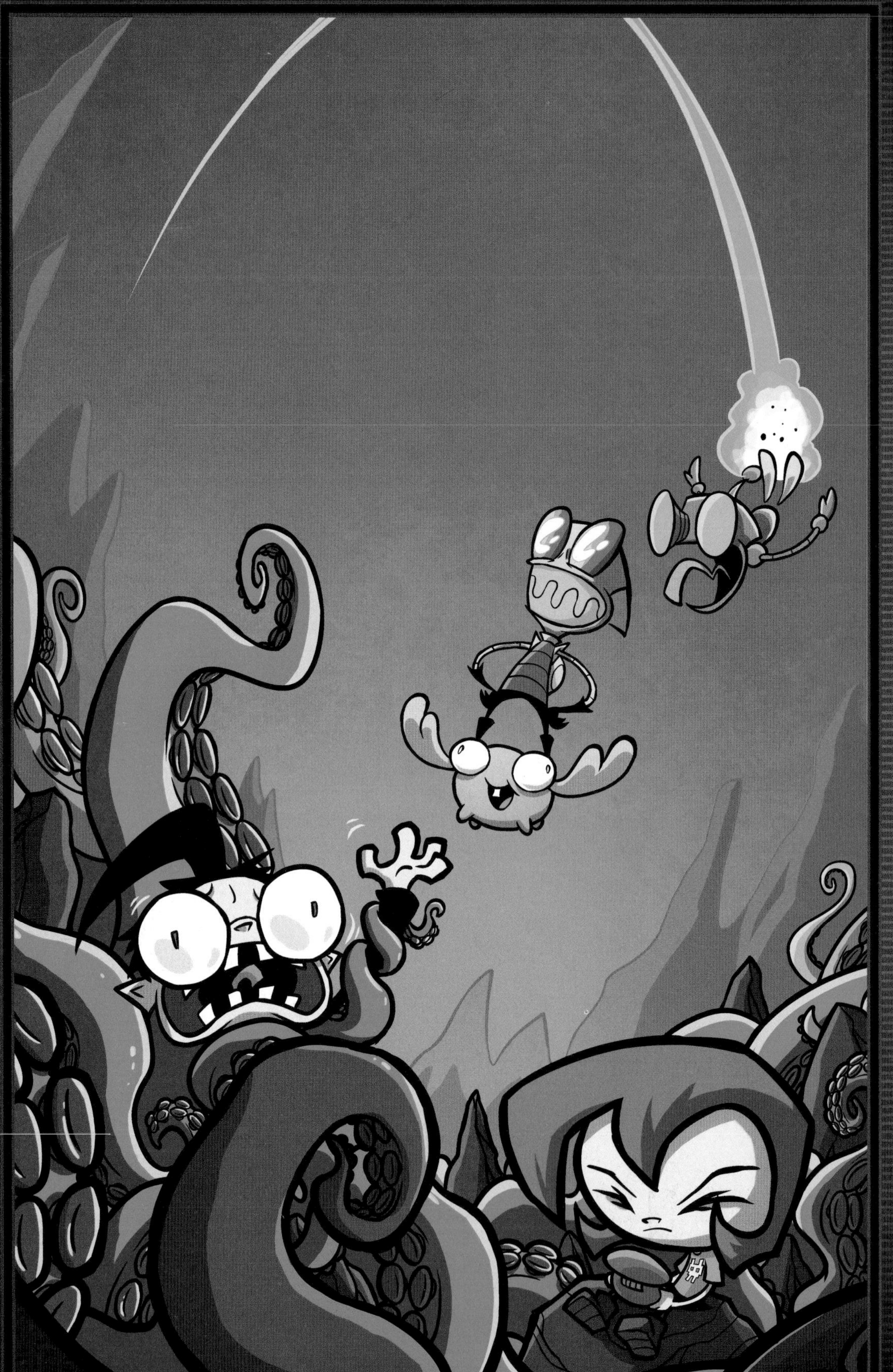

INVADER ZIM

VOLUME 3

Writer and Illustrator, Chapter 1 **SARAH ANDERSEN**

Writer, Chapter 2-5 **ERIC TRUEHEART**

Writer, Chapter 5, "The Evil Ms. Bitters" **DANIELLE KOENIG**

Writer, Chapter 5, "Sweetheart Bitters" **JAMIE SMART**

Writer, Illustrator, Colorist, and Letterer Chapter 5, "Bitters and the Witch" **KC GREEN**

Writer and Penciller, Chapter 5, "Bitters the Bug" **IAN MCGINTY**

Layouts, Chapter 2 **AARON ALEXOVICH**

Illustrator, Chapter 2-5 & Letterer, Chapter 1-5 **WARREN WUCINICH**

Colorist, Chapter 1 **KATY FARINA**

Colorist, Chapter 2-5 & Inker, Chapter 5, "Ms. Bitters' Bugs" **FRED C. STRESING**

Inker, Chapter 5, "Ms. Bitters' Bugs" **MEG CASEY**

Retail cover by **WARREN WUCINICH**

Oni Press variant cover by **JHONEN VASQUEZ** and **J.R. GOLDBERG**

Control Brain **JHONEN VASQUEZ**

AN ONI PRESS PUBLICATION

Special thanks to **JOAN HILTY** and **LINDA LEE**

Designed by **KEITH WOOD**

Edited by **ROBIN HERRERA**

Published by Oni Press, Inc.

publisher **JOE NOZEMACK** editor in chief **JAMES LUCAS JONES**

v.p. of marketing & sales **ANDREW MCINTIRE** sales manager **DAVID DISSANAYAKE**

publicity coordinator **RACHEL REED** director of design & production **TROY LOOK**

graphic designer **HILARY THOMPSON** digital prepress technician **ANGIE DOBSON**

managing editor **ARI YARWOOD** senior editor **CHARLIE CHU**

editor **ROBIN HERRERA** editorial assistant **BESS PALLARES**

director of logistics **BRAD ROOKS** logistics associate **JUNG LEE**

This volume collects issues #11-15 of the
Oni Press series *Invader Zim*.

Oni Press, Inc.
1305 SE Martin Luther King Jr. Blvd.
Suite A
Portland, OR 97214
USA

onipress.com • facebook.com/onipress • twitter.com/onipress
onipress.tumblr.com • instagram.com/onipress

First edition: December 2016

ISBN: 978-1-62010-371-5 • eISBN: 978-1-62010-373-9
Oni Press Exclusive ISBN: 978-1-62010-372-2

nickelodeon

Library of Congress Control Number: 2015950610

1 3 5 7 9 10 8 6 4 2

PRINTED IN USA.

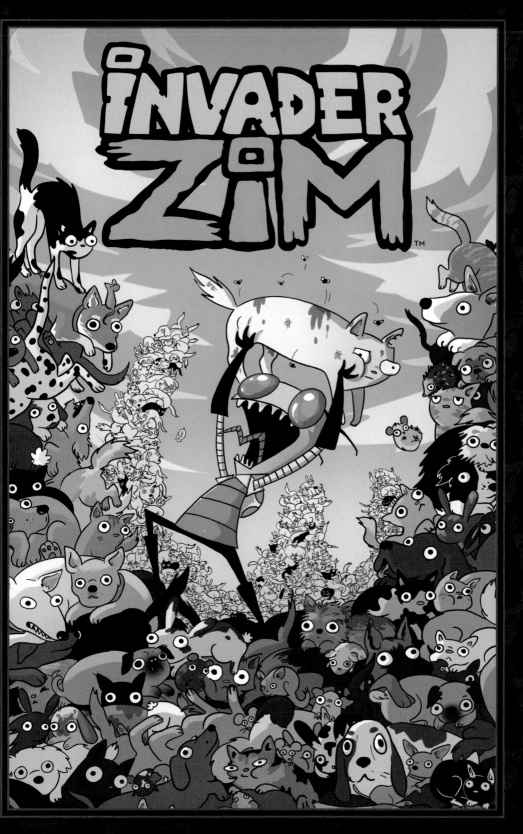

 CHAPTER: 1

illustration by SARAH ANDERSEN

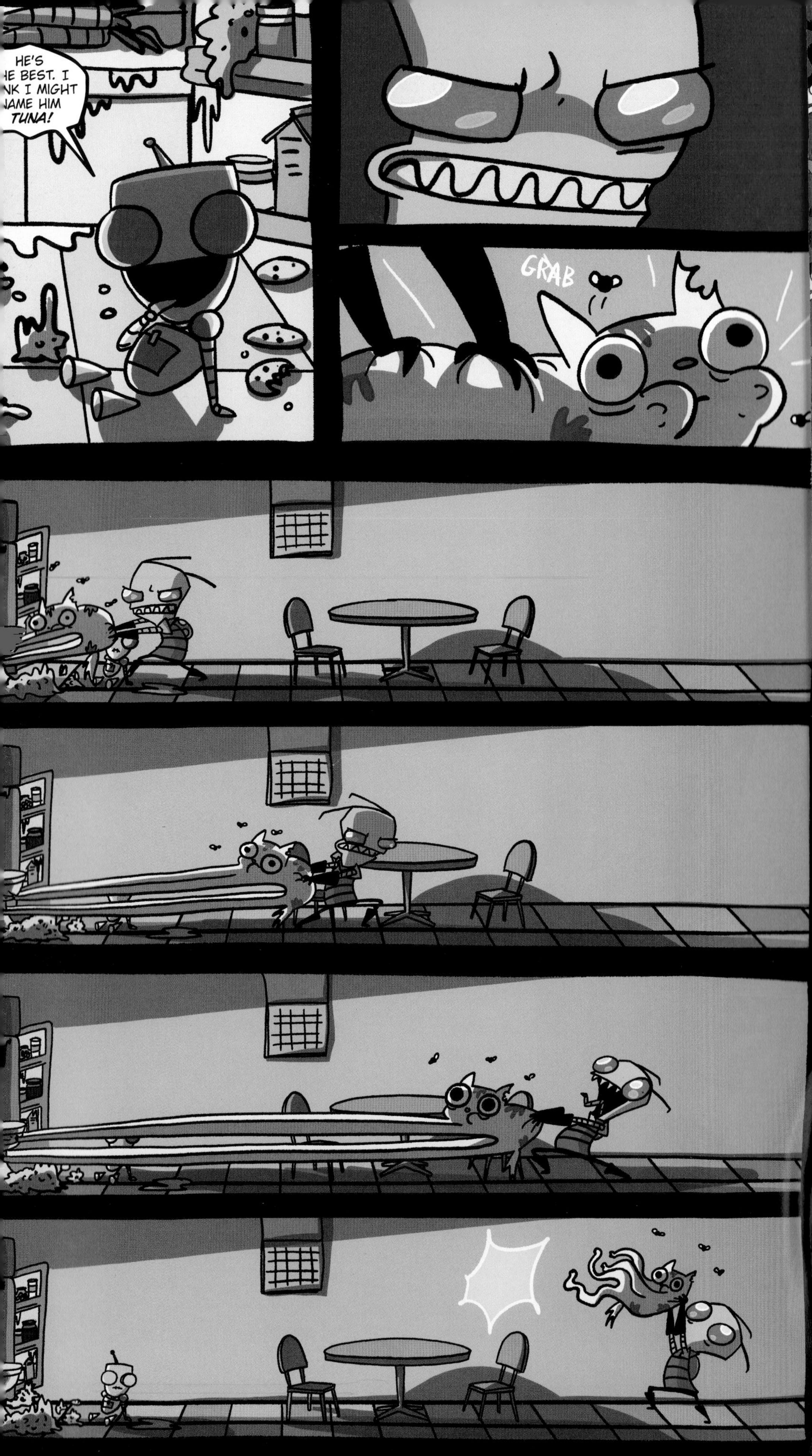
HE'S
E BEST. I
NK I MIGHT
AME HIM
TUNA!
GRAB

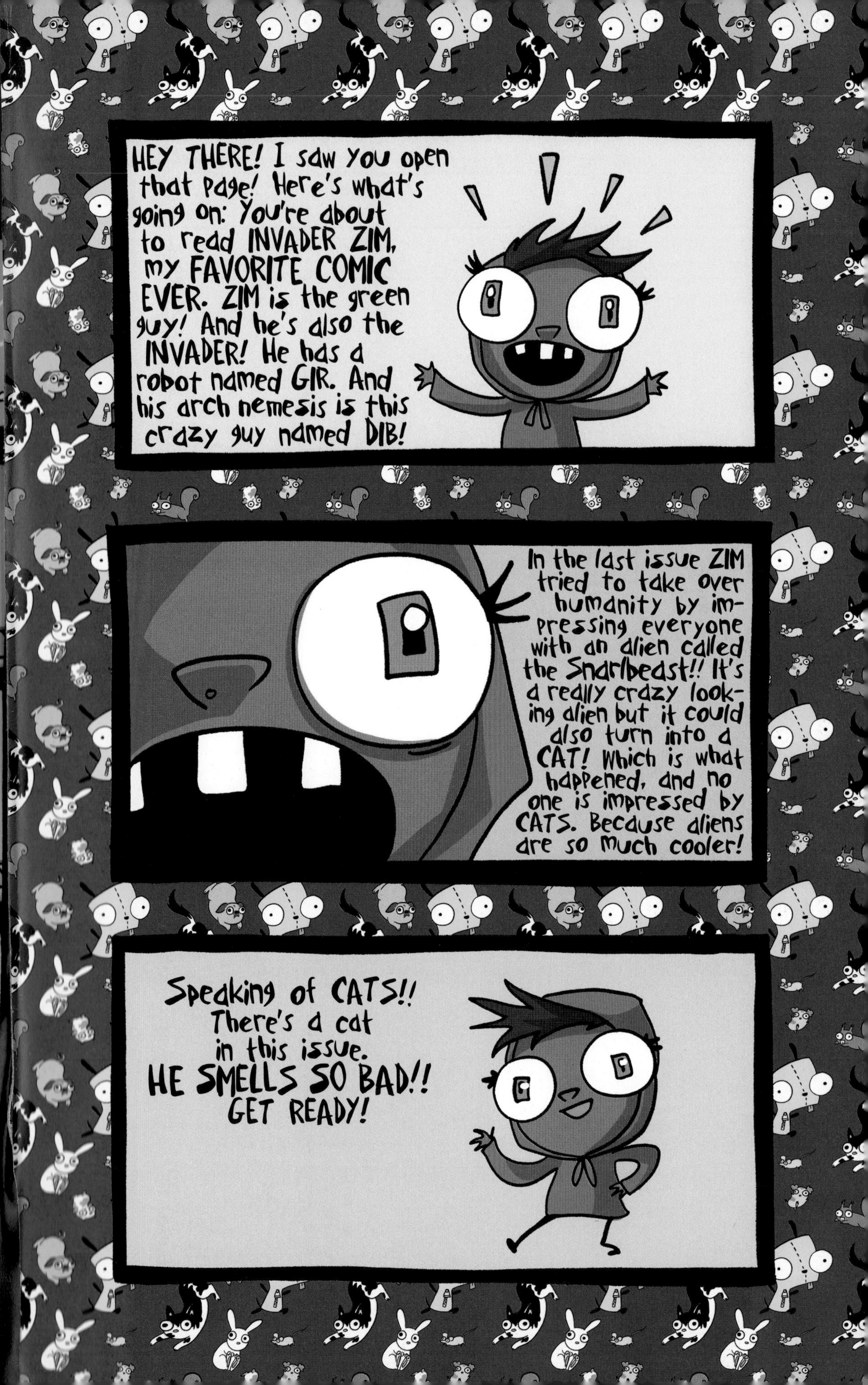
HEY THERE! I saw you open that page! Here's what's going on: You're about to read INVADER ZIM, my FAVORITE COMIC EVER. ZIM is the green guy! And he's also the INVADER! He has a robot named GIR. And his arch nemesis is this crazy guy named DIB!
In the last issue ZIM tried to take over humanity by impressing everyone with an alien called the Snarlbeast!! It's a really crazy looking alien but it could also turn into a CAT! Which is what happened, and no one is impressed by CATS. Because aliens are so much cooler!
Speaking of CATS!! There's a cat in this issue.
HE SMELLS SO BAD!!
GET READY!

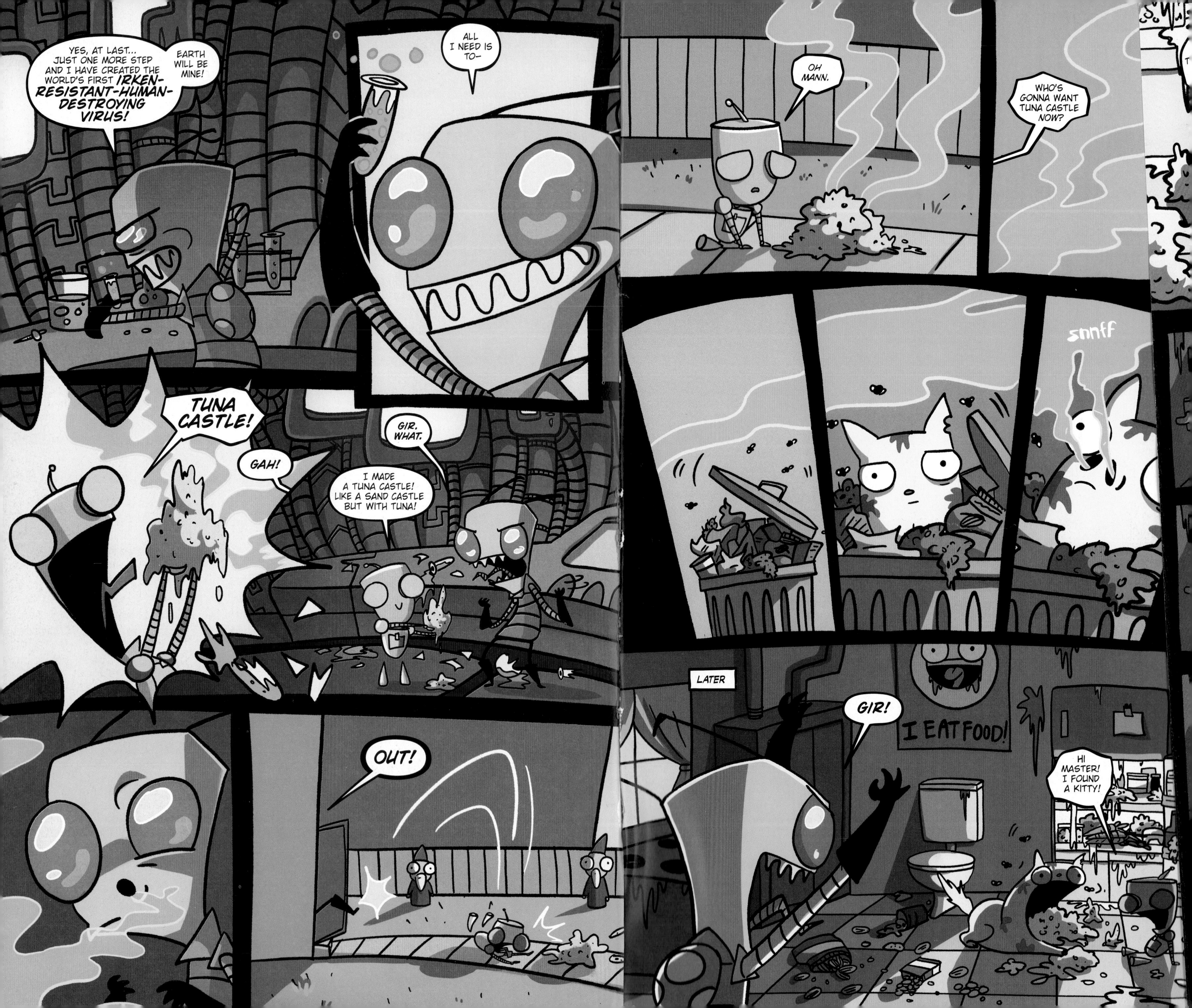

YES, AT LAST... JUST ONE MORE STEP AND I HAVE CREATED THE WORLD'S FIRST IRKEN-RESISTANT-HUMAN-DESTROYING VIRUS!
EARTH WILL BE MINE!
ALL I NEED IS TO—
TUNA CASTLE!
GAH!
GIR. WHAT.
I MADE A TUNA CASTLE! LIKE A SAND CASTLE BUT WITH TUNA!
OUT!
OH MANN.
WHO'S GONNA WANT TUNA CASTLE NOW?
snnff
LATER
GIR!
I EAT FOOD!
HI MASTER! I FOUND A KITTY!

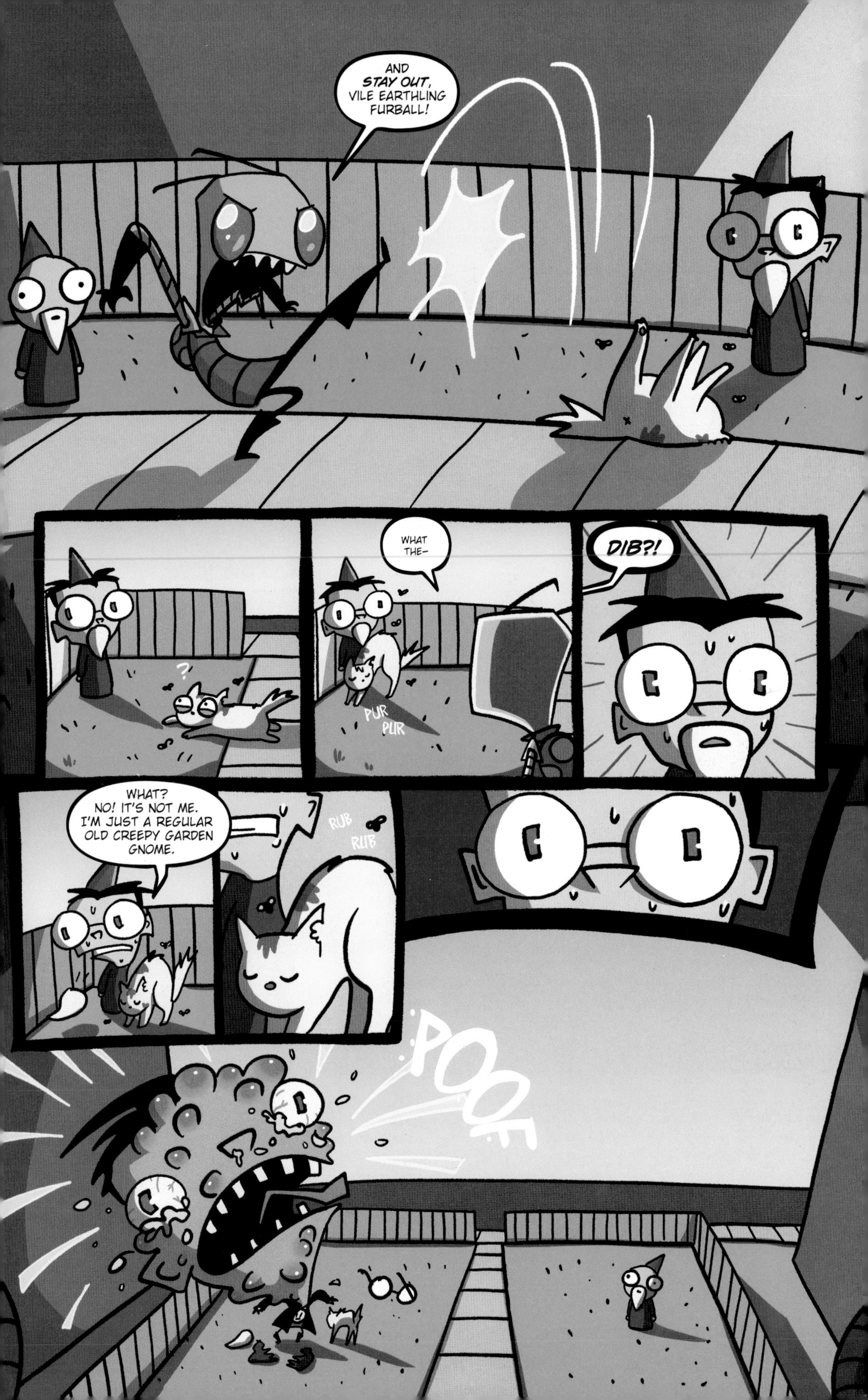
AND STAY OUT, VILE EARTHLING FURBALL!
?
WHAT THE-
PUR PUR
DIB?!
WHAT? NO! IT'S NOT ME. I'M JUST A REGULAR OLD CREEPY GARDEN GNOME.
RUB RUB
POOF

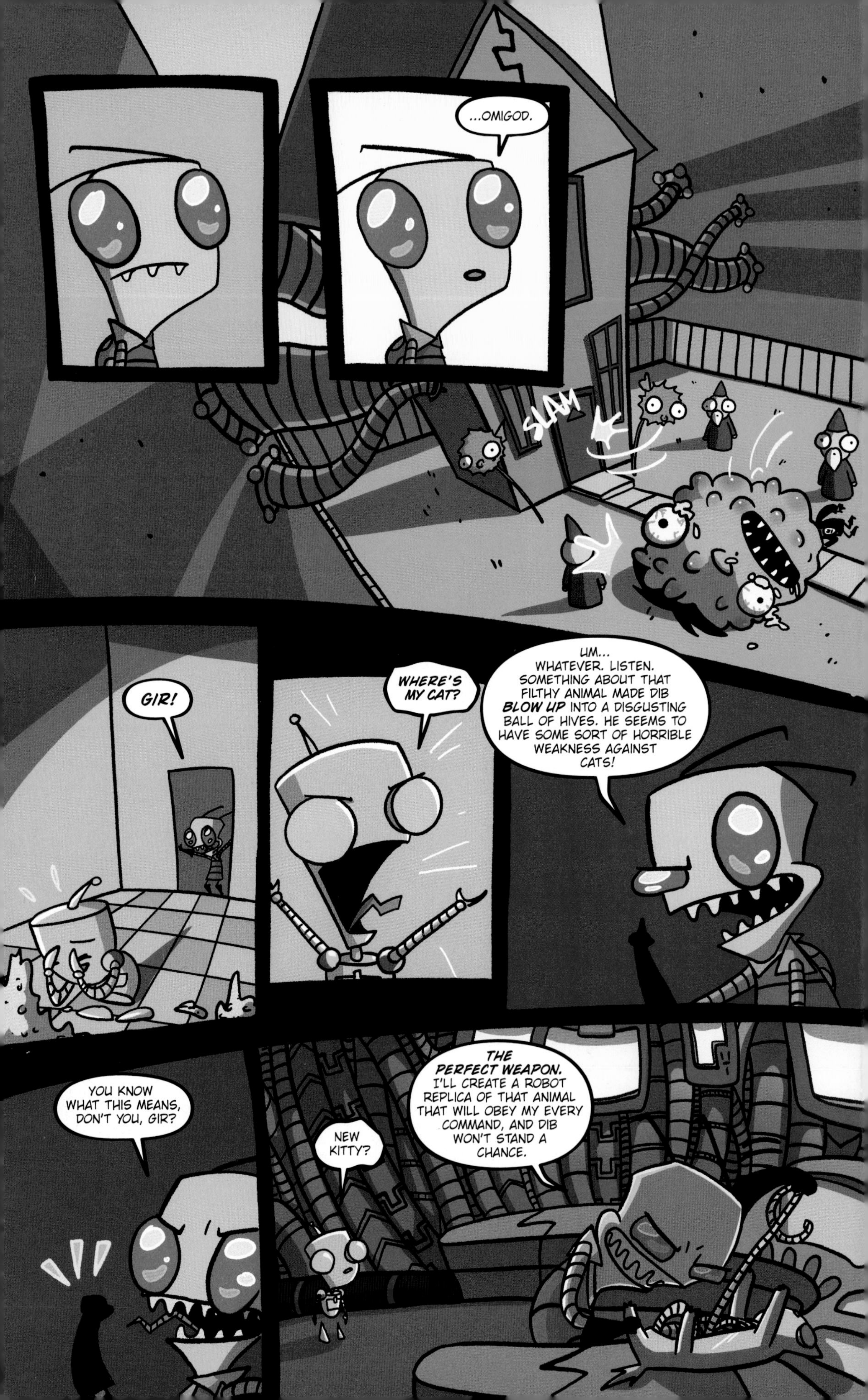
...OMIGOD.
SLAM
GIR!
WHERE'S MY CAT?
UM... WHATEVER. LISTEN. SOMETHING ABOUT THAT FILTHY ANIMAL MADE DIB *BLOW UP* INTO A DISGUSTING BALL OF HIVES. HE SEEMS TO HAVE SOME SORT OF HORRIBLE WEAKNESS AGAINST CATS!
YOU KNOW WHAT THIS MEANS, DON'T YOU, GIR?
NEW KITTY?
THE PERFECT WEAPON. I'LL CREATE A ROBOT REPLICA OF THAT ANIMAL THAT WILL OBEY MY EVERY COMMAND, AND DIB WON'T STAND A CHANCE.

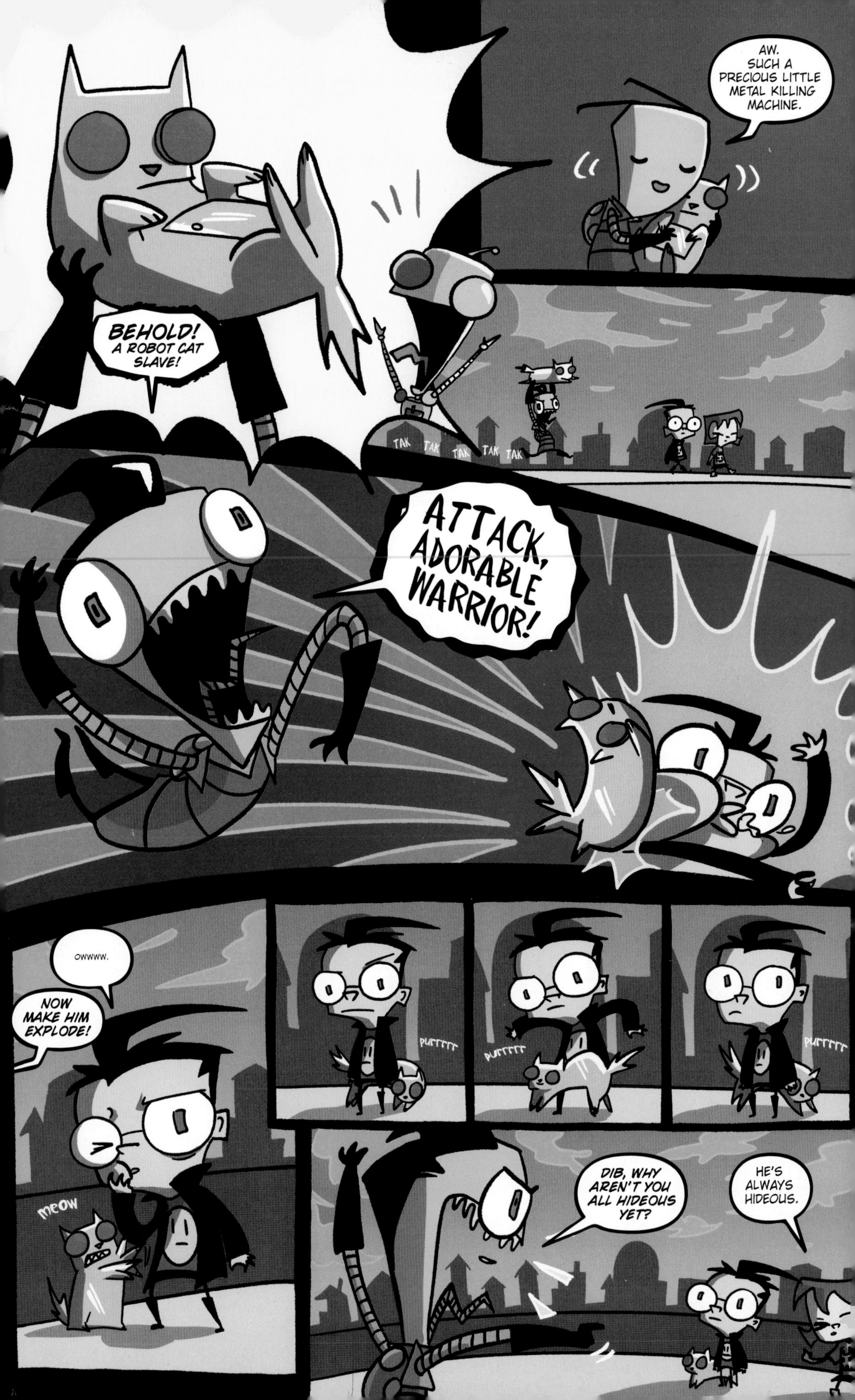

BEHOLD! A ROBOT CAT SLAVE!
AW. SUCH A PRECIOUS LITTLE METAL KILLING MACHINE.
TAK TAK TAK TAK TAK
ATTACK, ADORABLE WARRIOR!
OWWWW.
NOW MAKE HIM EXPLODE!
MEOW
purrrrr
purrrrr
purrrrr
DIB, WHY AREN'T YOU ALL HIDEOUS YET?
HE'S ALWAYS HIDEOUS.

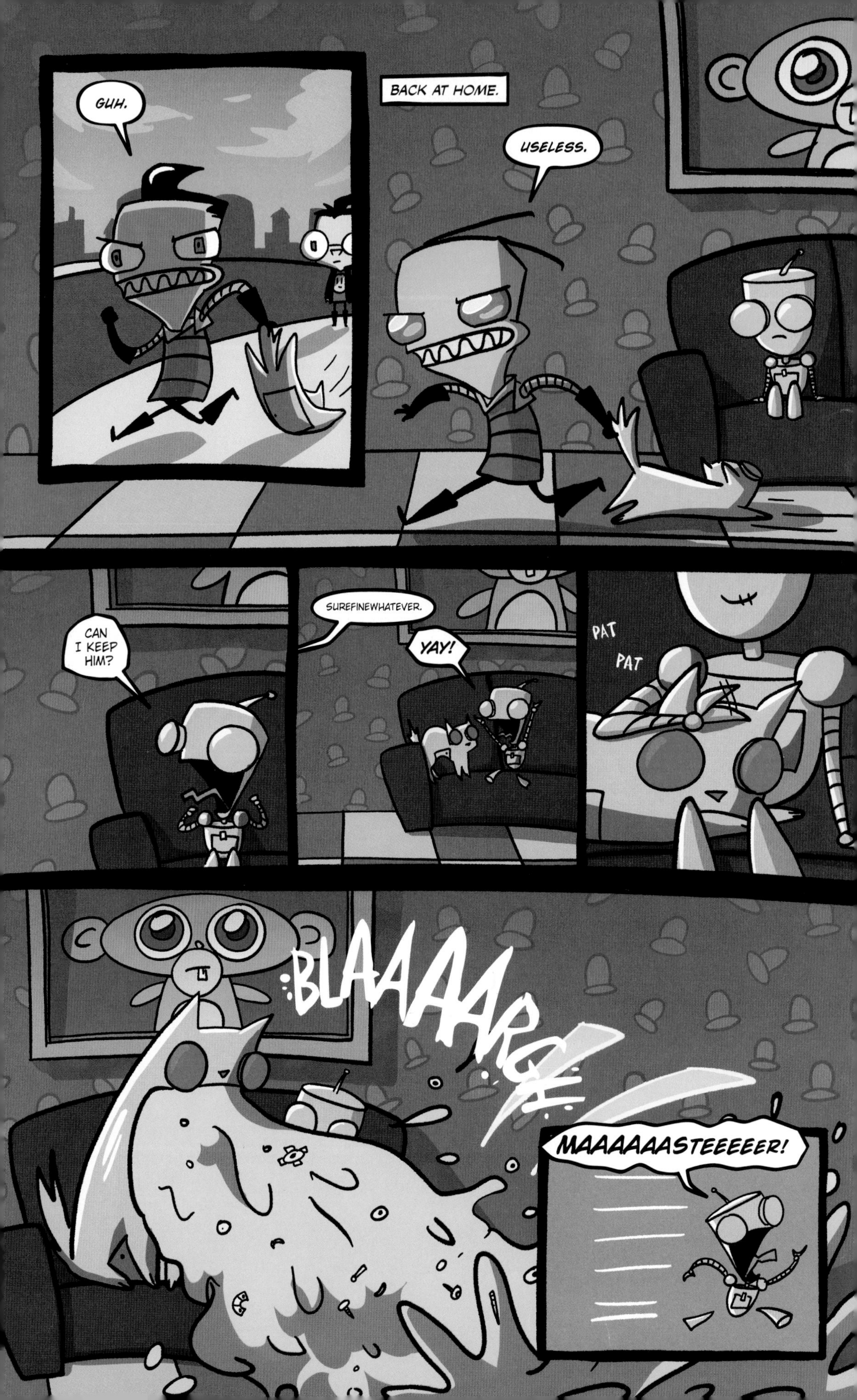
GUH.
BACK AT HOME.
USELESS.
CAN I KEEP HIM?
SUREFINEWHATEVER.
YAY!
PAT
PAT
BLAAAARGH
MAAAAAASTEEEEER!

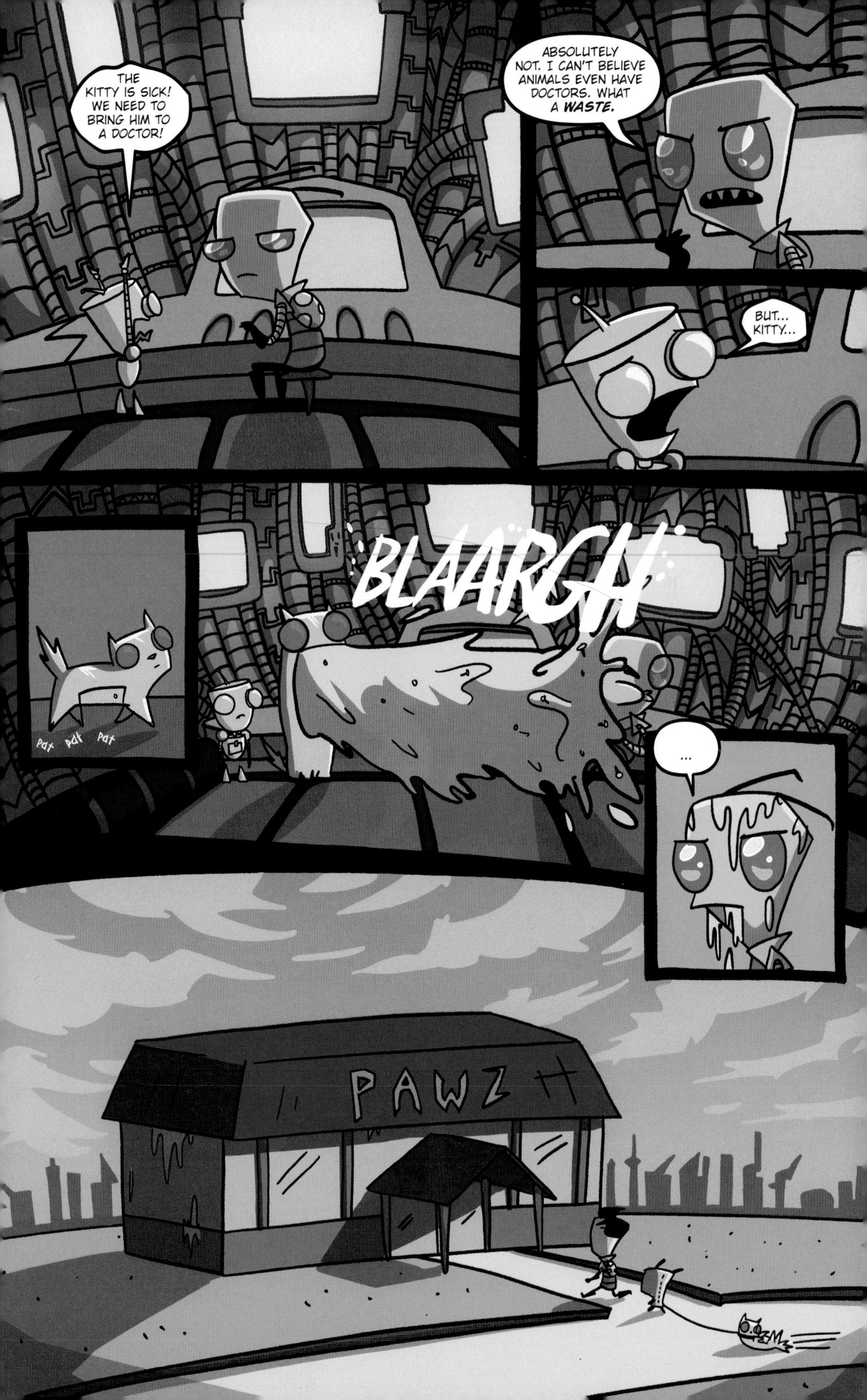
THE KITTY IS SICK! WE NEED TO BRING HIM TO A DOCTOR!
ABSOLUTELY NOT. I CAN'T BELIEVE ANIMALS EVEN HAVE DOCTORS. WHAT A WASTE.
BUT... KITTY...
pat pat pat
BLAARGH
...
PAWZ

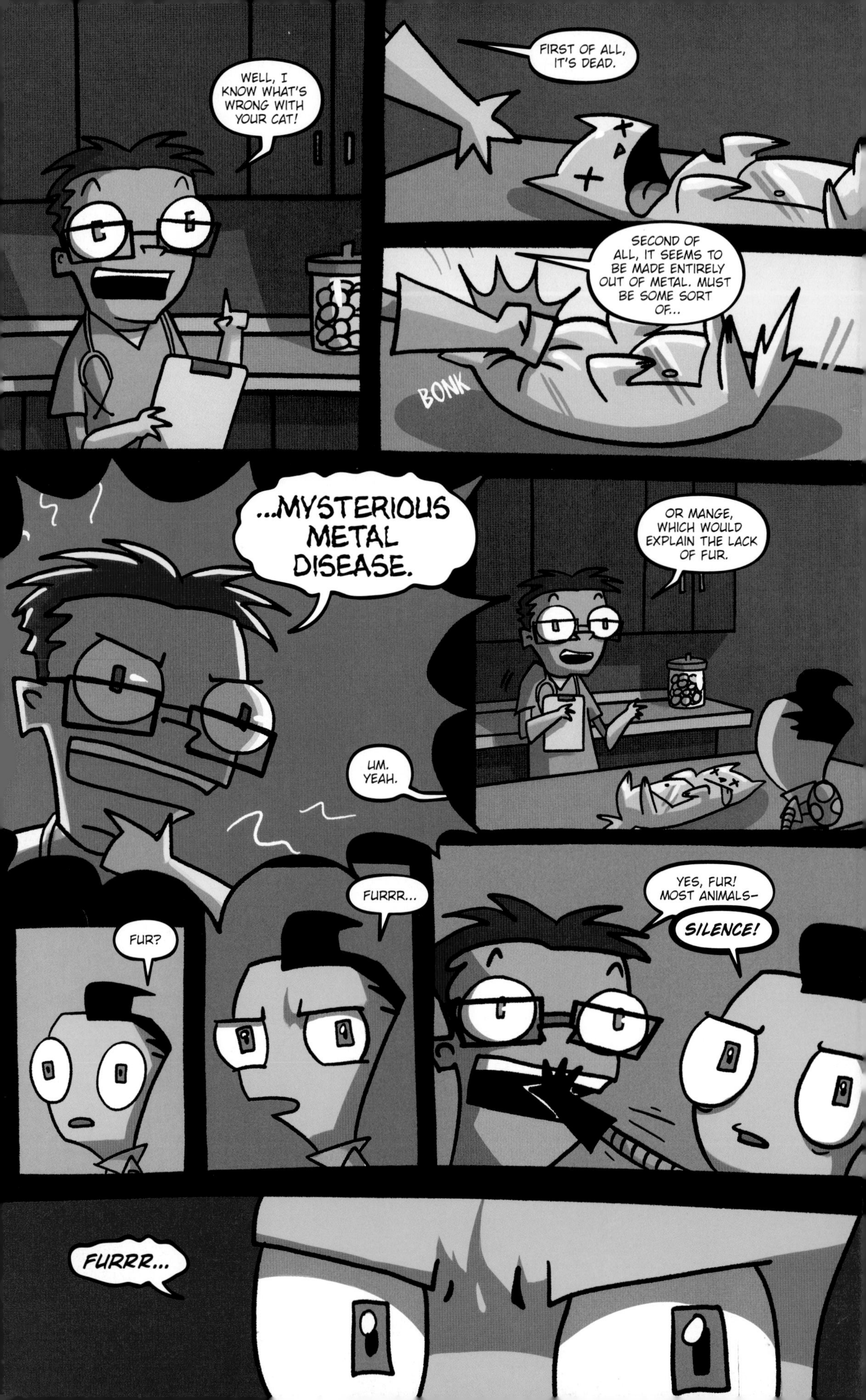
WELL, I KNOW WHAT'S WRONG WITH YOUR CAT!
FIRST OF ALL, IT'S DEAD.
SECOND OF ALL, IT SEEMS TO BE MADE ENTIRELY OUT OF METAL. MUST BE SOME SORT OF...
BONK
...MYSTERIOUS METAL DISEASE.
UM. YEAH.
OR MANGE, WHICH WOULD EXPLAIN THE LACK OF FUR.
FUR?
FURRR...
YES, FUR! MOST ANIMALS-
SILENCE!
FURRR...

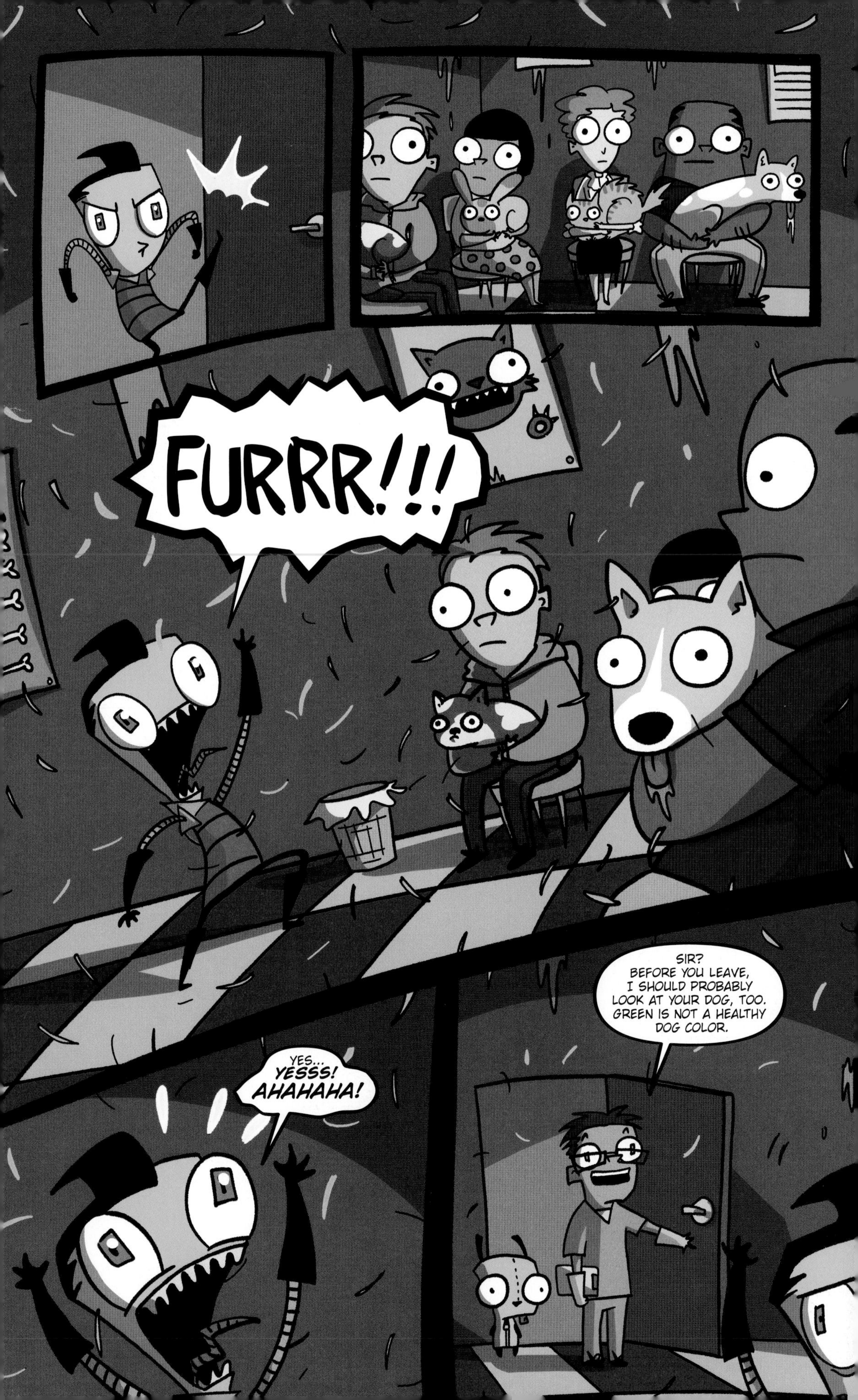
FURRR!!!
YES...
YESSS!
AHAHAHA!
SIR?
BEFORE YOU LEAVE,
I SHOULD PROBABLY
LOOK AT YOUR DOG, TOO.
GREEN IS NOT A HEALTHY
DOG COLOR.

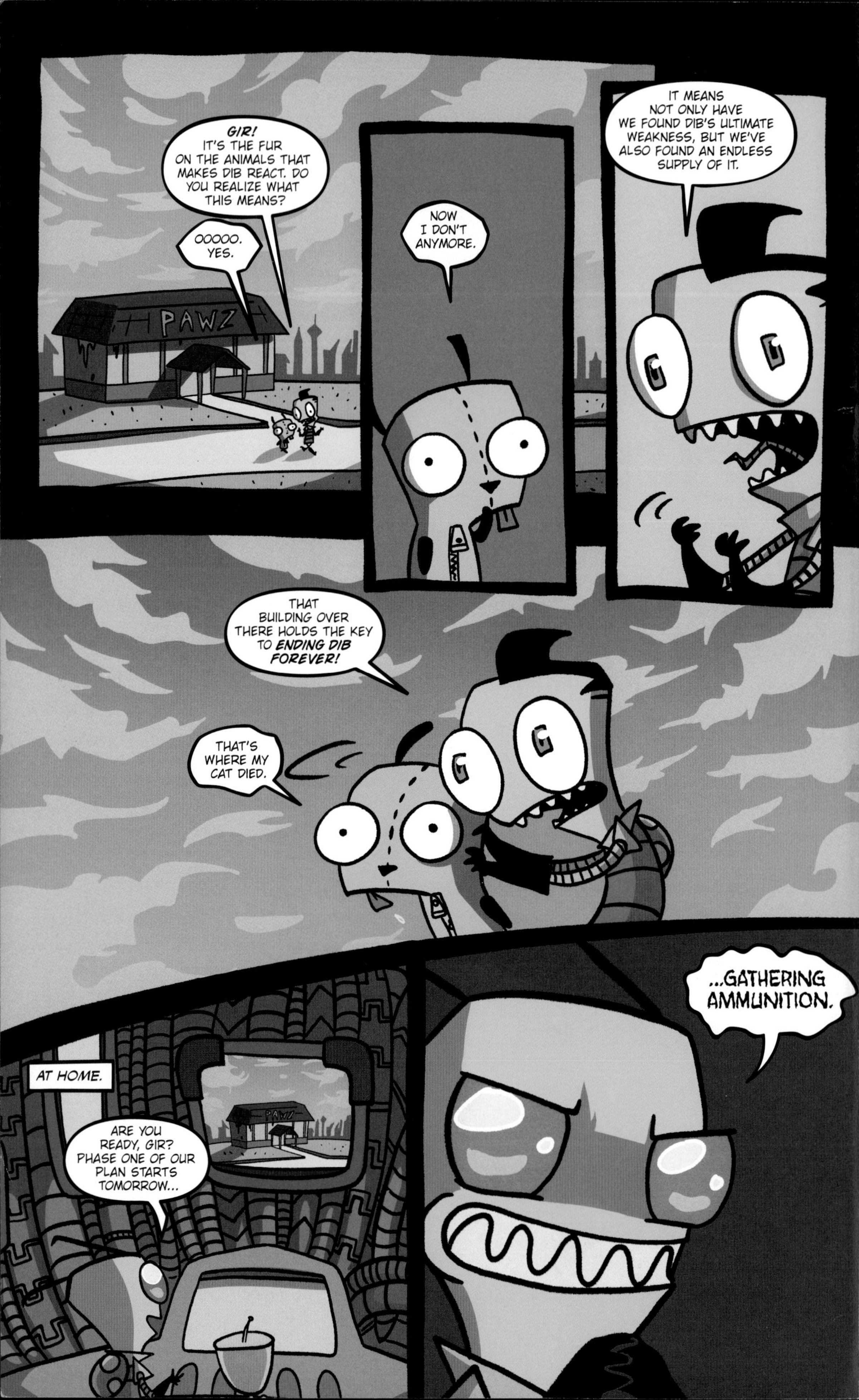
GIR! IT'S THE FUR ON THE ANIMALS THAT MAKES DIB REACT. DO YOU REALIZE WHAT THIS MEANS?
OOOOO. YES.
PAWZ
NOW I DON'T ANYMORE.
IT MEANS NOT ONLY HAVE WE FOUND DIB'S ULTIMATE WEAKNESS, BUT WE'VE ALSO FOUND AN ENDLESS SUPPLY OF IT.
THAT BUILDING OVER THERE HOLDS THE KEY TO ENDING DIB FOREVER!
THAT'S WHERE MY CAT DIED.
AT HOME.
ARE YOU READY, GIR? PHASE ONE OF OUR PLAN STARTS TOMORROW...
...GATHERING AMMUNITION.

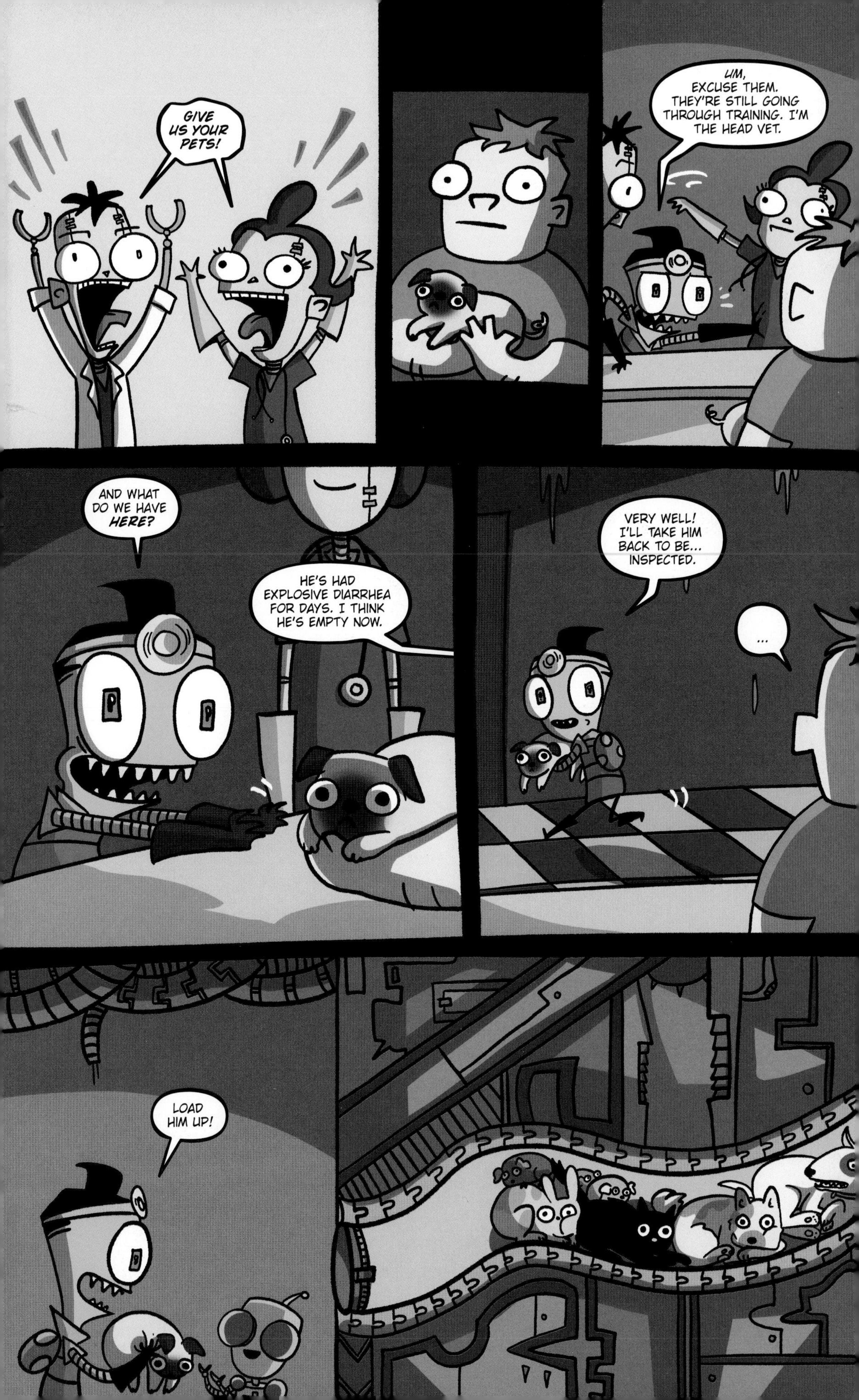
GIVE US YOUR PETS!
UM, EXCUSE THEM. THEY'RE STILL GOING THROUGH TRAINING. I'M THE HEAD VET.
AND WHAT DO WE HAVE HERE?
HE'S HAD EXPLOSIVE DIARRHEA FOR DAYS. I THINK HE'S EMPTY NOW.
VERY WELL! I'LL TAKE HIM BACK TO BE... INSPECTED.
...
LOAD HIM UP!

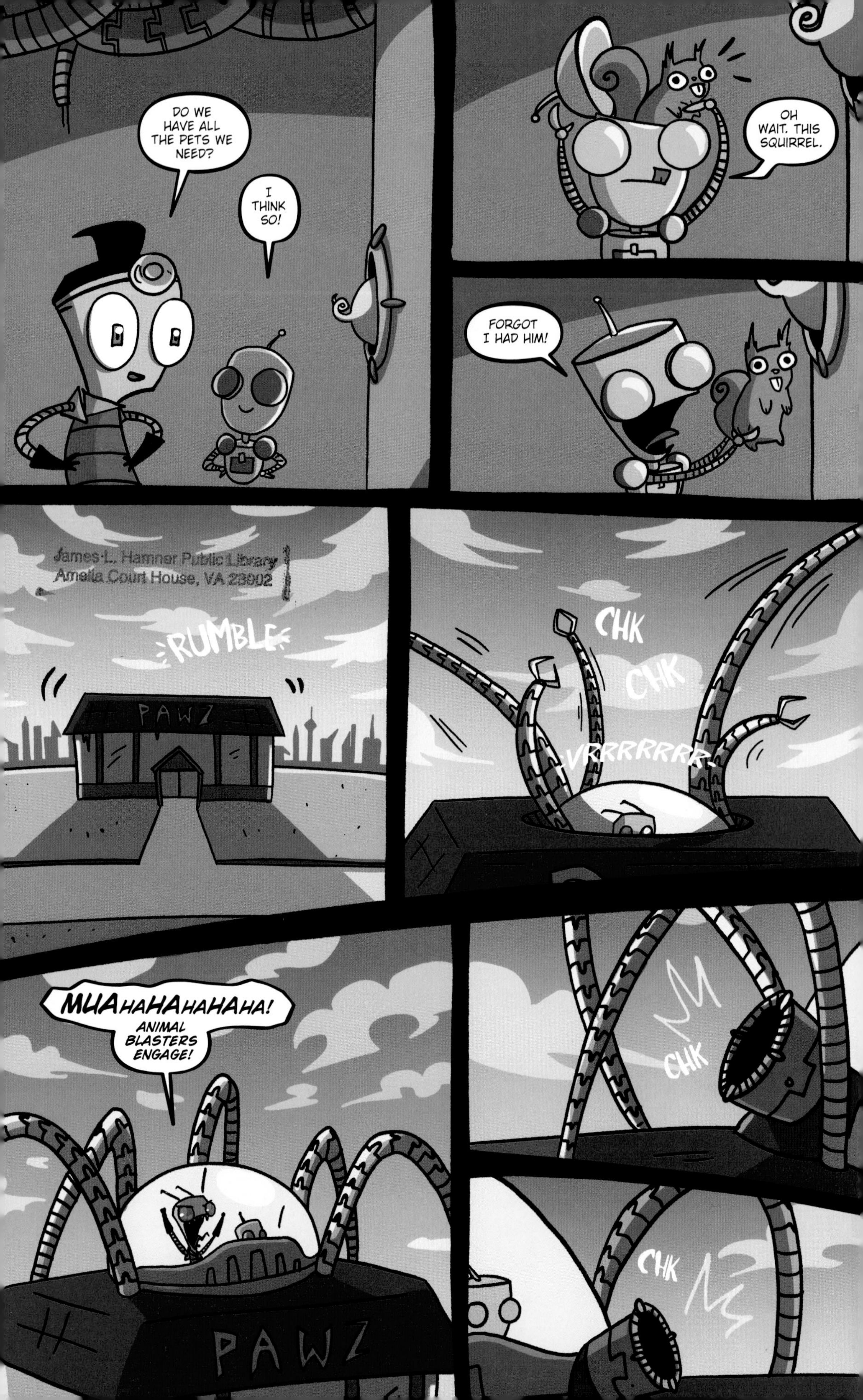
DO WE HAVE ALL THE PETS WE NEED?
I THINK SO!
OH WAIT. THIS SQUIRREL.
FORGOT I HAD HIM!
RUMBLE
PAWZ
CHK
CHK
VRRRRRRR
MUAHAHAHAHAHAHA! ANIMAL BLASTERS ENGAGE!
PAWZ
CHK
CHK

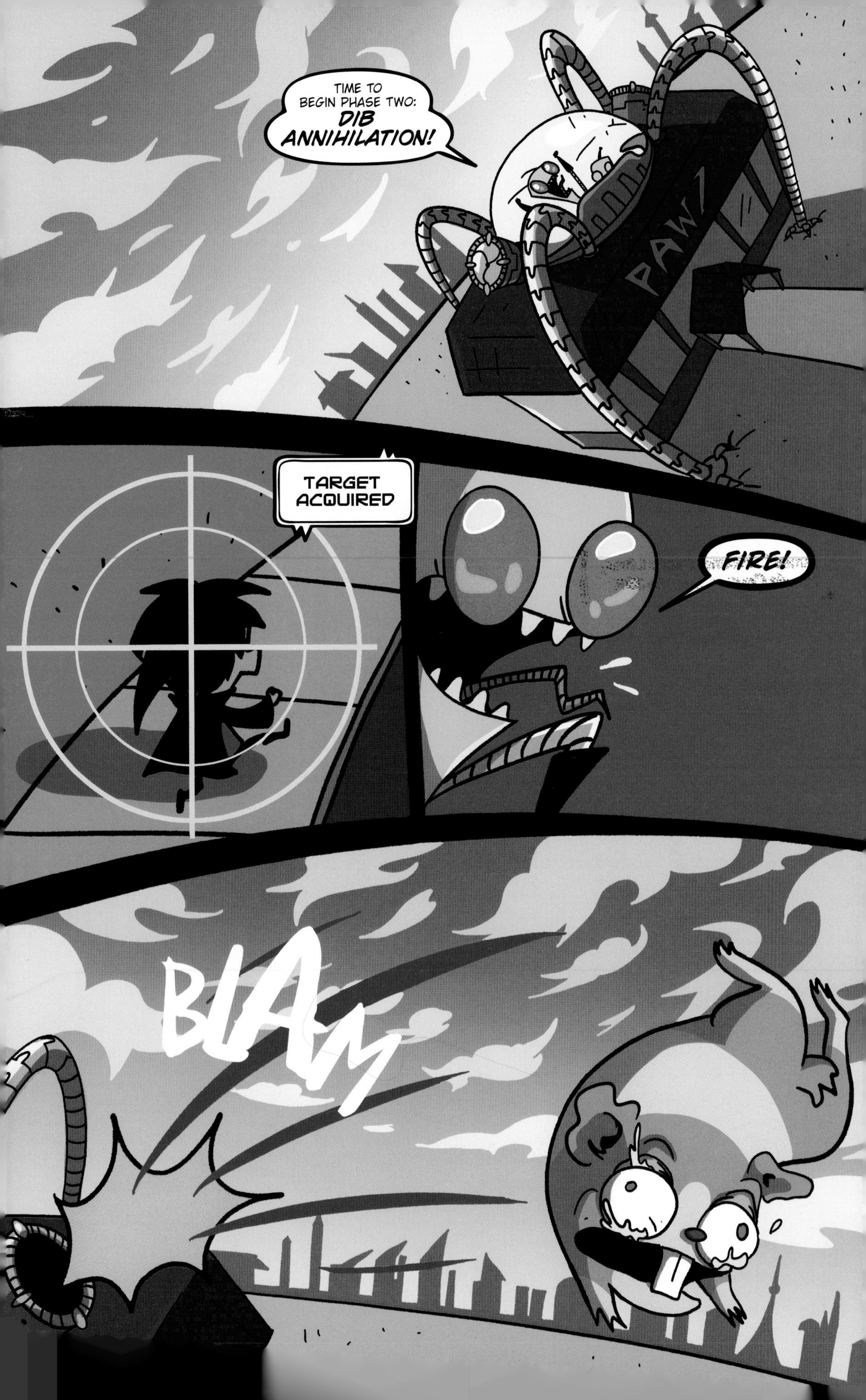
TIME TO BEGIN PHASE TWO: DIB ANNIHILATION!
PAW
TARGET ACQUIRED
FIRE!
BLAM

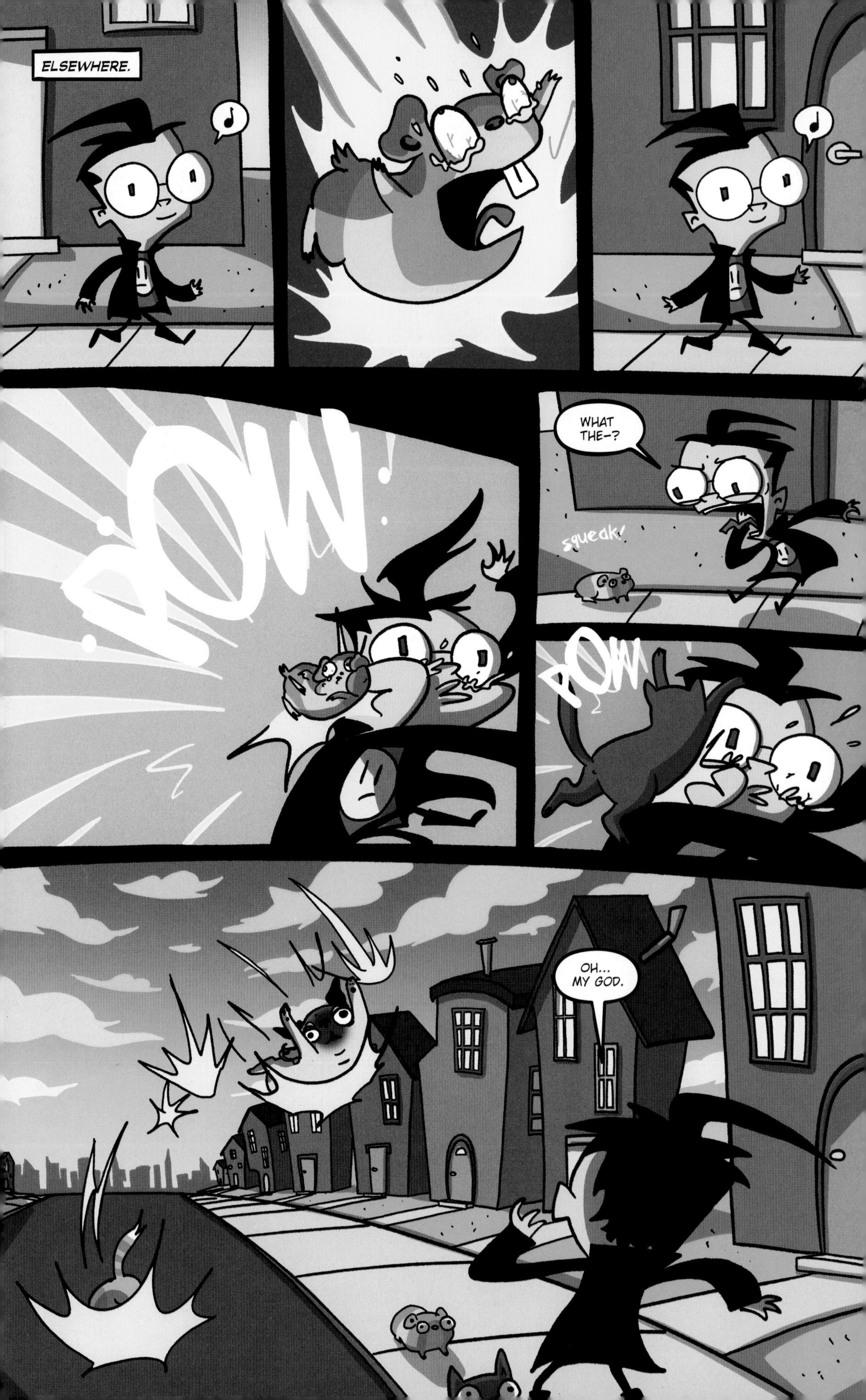
ELSEWHERE.
♪
♪
POW!
WHAT THE–?
squeak!
POW
OH... MY GOD.

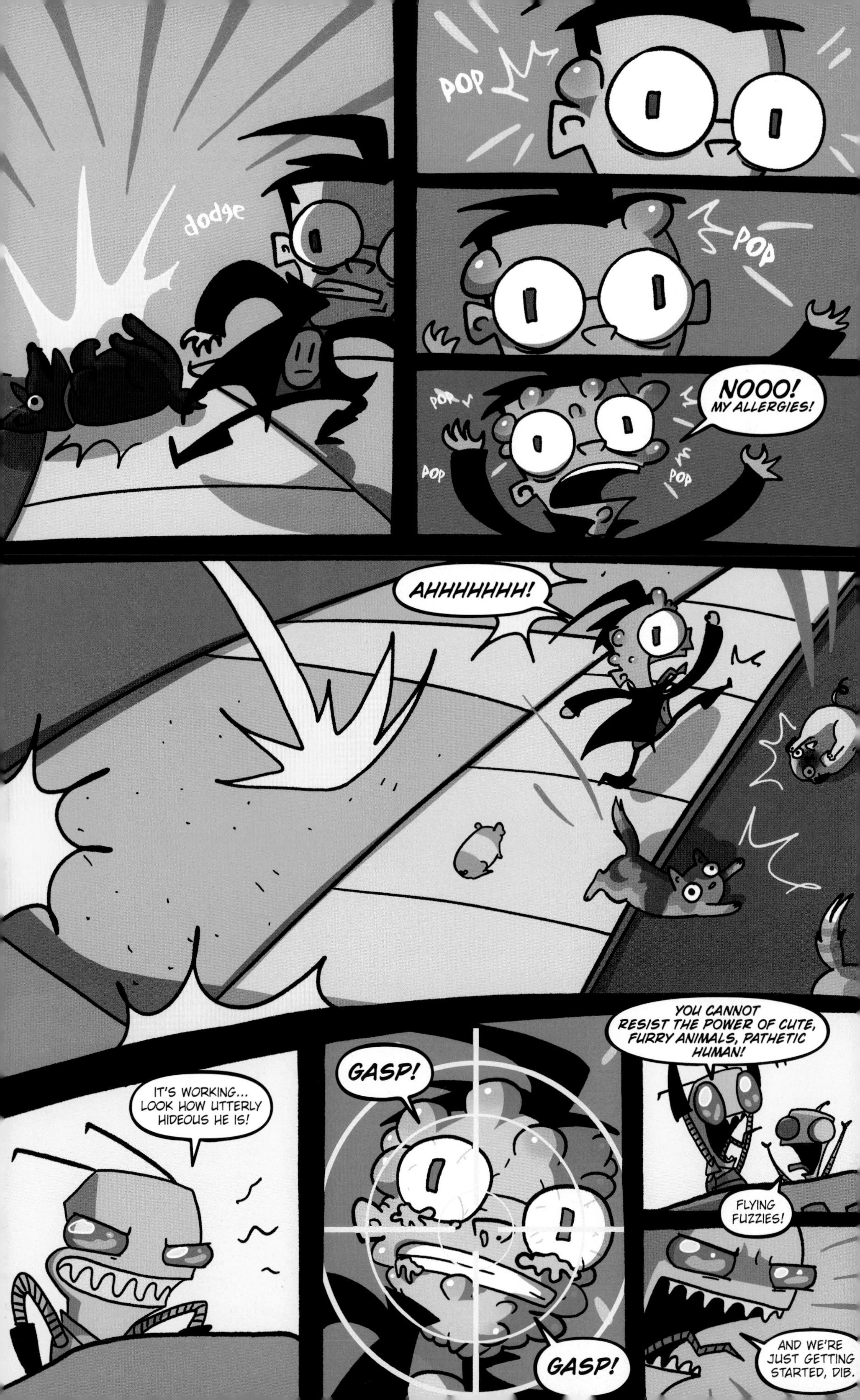
dodge
POP
POP
POP
POP
POP
NOOO!
MY ALLERGIES!
AHHHHHHH!
IT'S WORKING...
LOOK HOW UTTERLY
HIDEOUS HE IS!
GASP!
GASP!
YOU CANNOT
RESIST THE POWER OF CUTE,
FURRY ANIMALS, PATHETIC
HUMAN!
FLYING
FUZZIES!
AND WE'RE
JUST GETTING
STARTED, DIB.

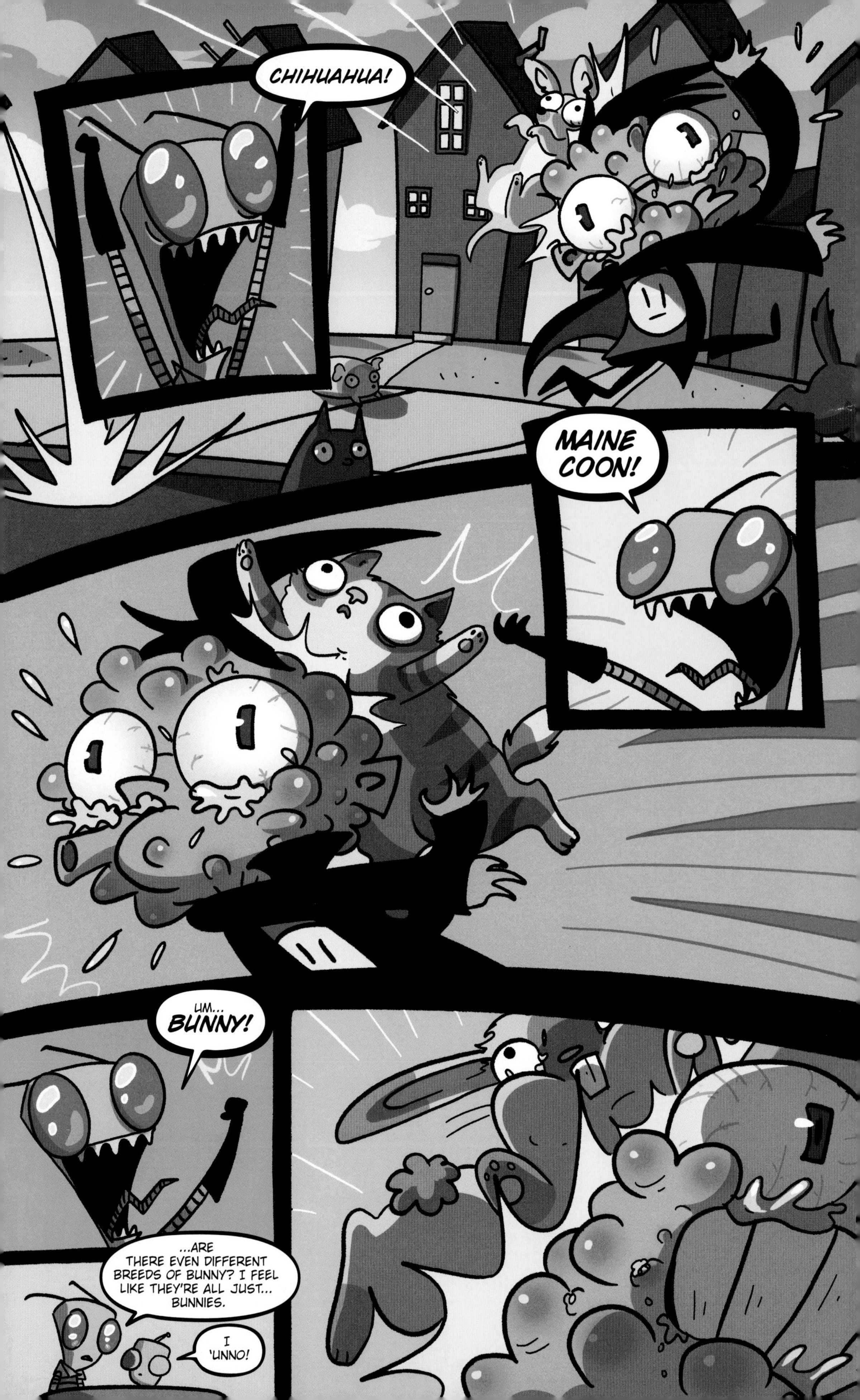
CHIHUAHUA!
MAINE COON!
UM... BUNNY!
...ARE THERE EVEN DIFFERENT BREEDS OF BUNNY? I FEEL LIKE THEY'RE ALL JUST... BUNNIES.
I 'UNNO!

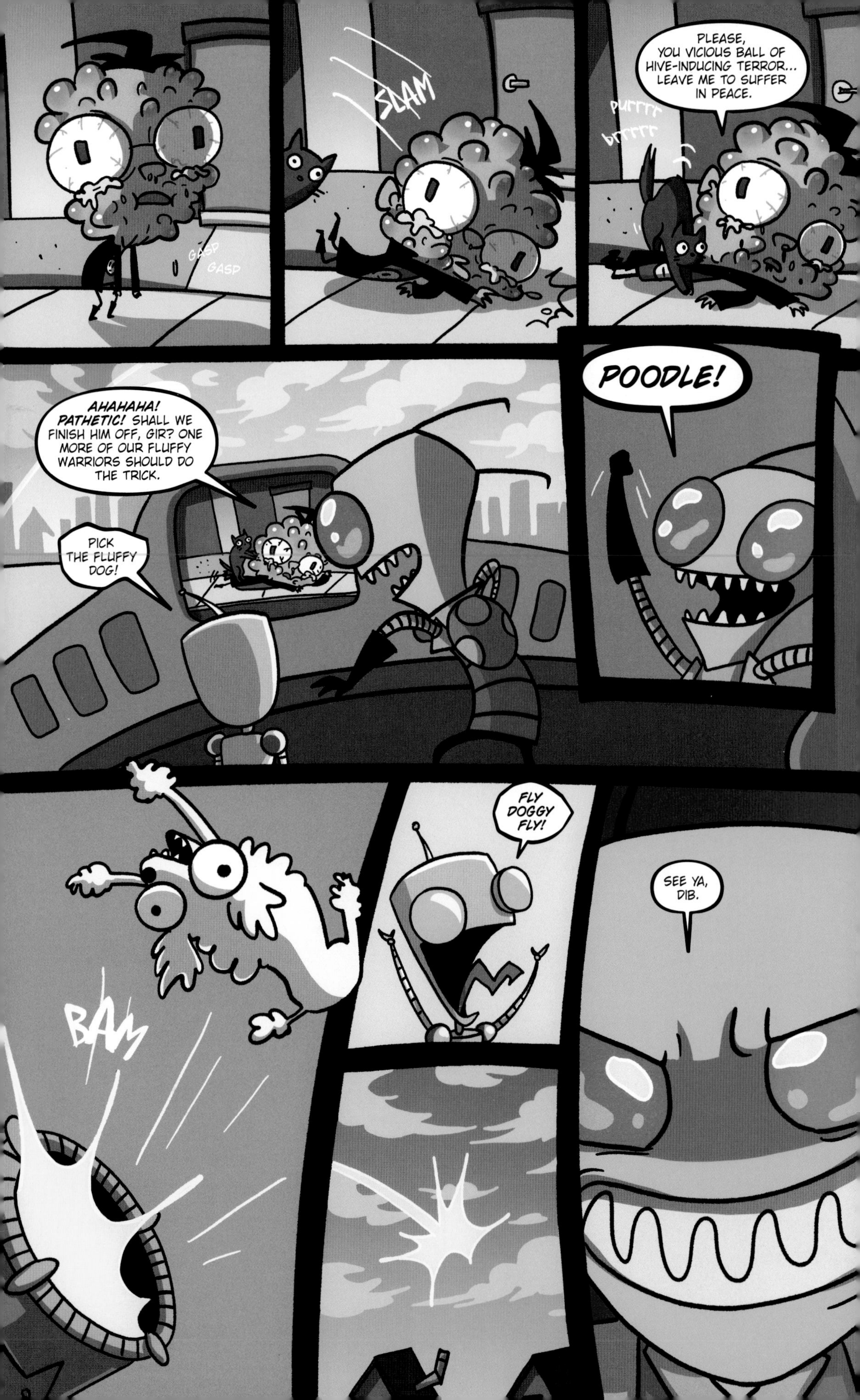
GASP
GASP
SLAM
PLEASE, YOU VICIOUS BALL OF HIVE-INDUCING TERROR... LEAVE ME TO SUFFER IN PEACE.
purrrr
brrrrr
AHAHAHA! PATHETIC! SHALL WE FINISH HIM OFF, GIR? ONE MORE OF OUR FLUFFY WARRIORS SHOULD DO THE TRICK.
PICK THE FLUFFY DOG!
POODLE!
BAM
FLY DOGGY FLY!
SEE YA, DIB.

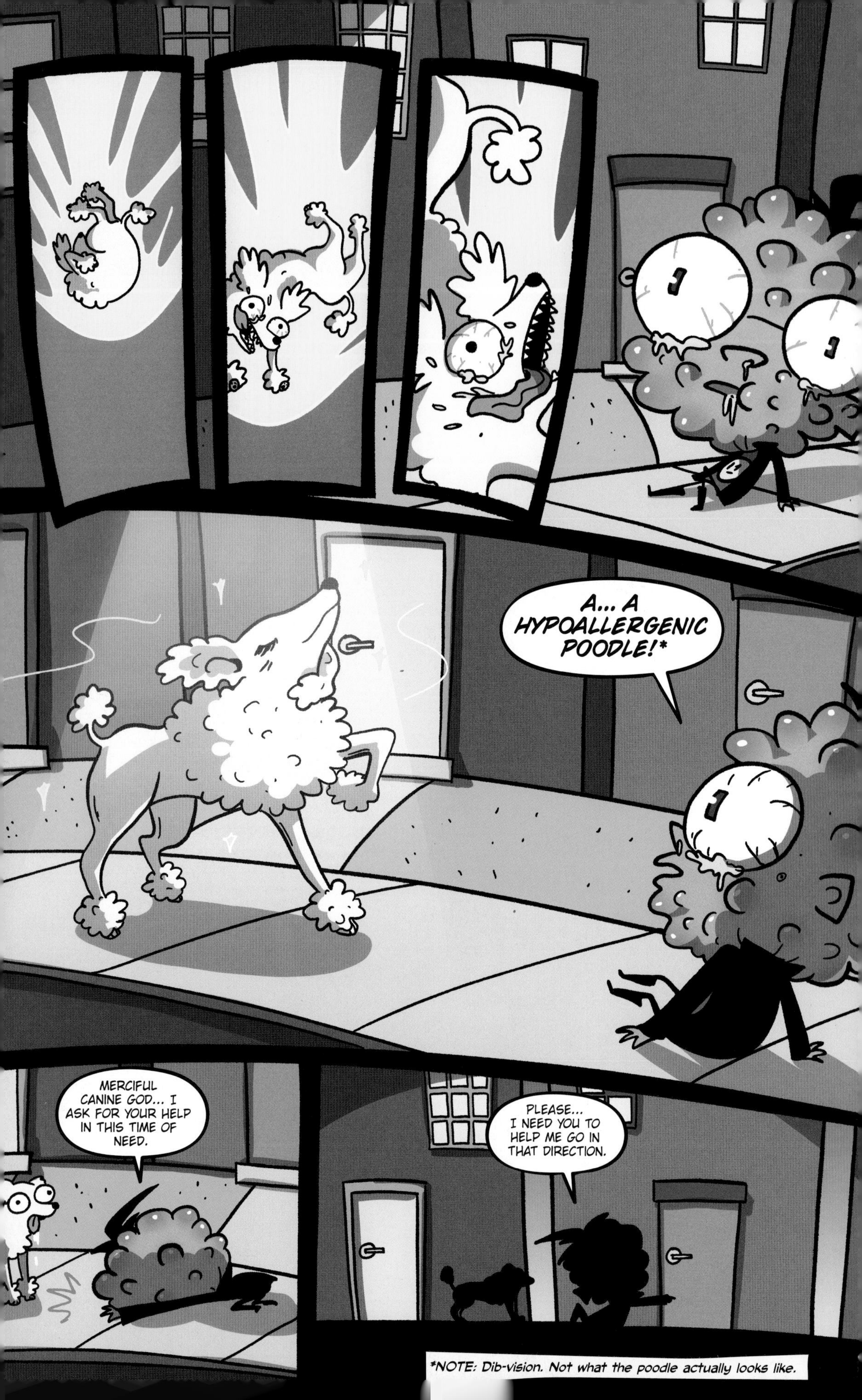
A... A HYPOALLERGENIC POODLE!*
MERCIFUL CANINE GOD... I ASK FOR YOUR HELP IN THIS TIME OF NEED.
PLEASE... I NEED YOU TO HELP ME GO IN THAT DIRECTION.
*NOTE: Dib-vision. Not what the poodle actually looks like.

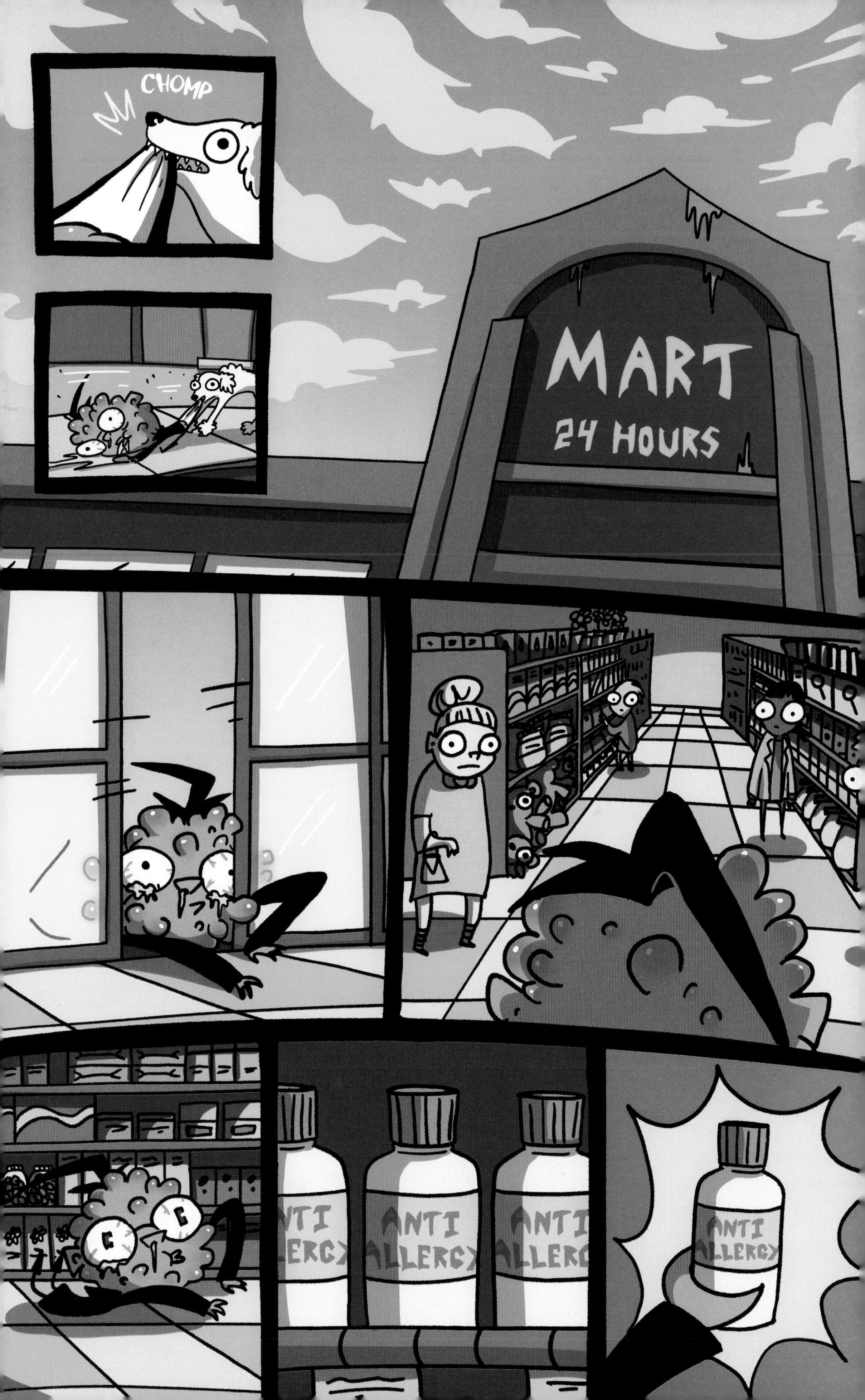
CHOMP
MART
24 HOURS
ANTI ALLERGY
ANTI ALLERGY

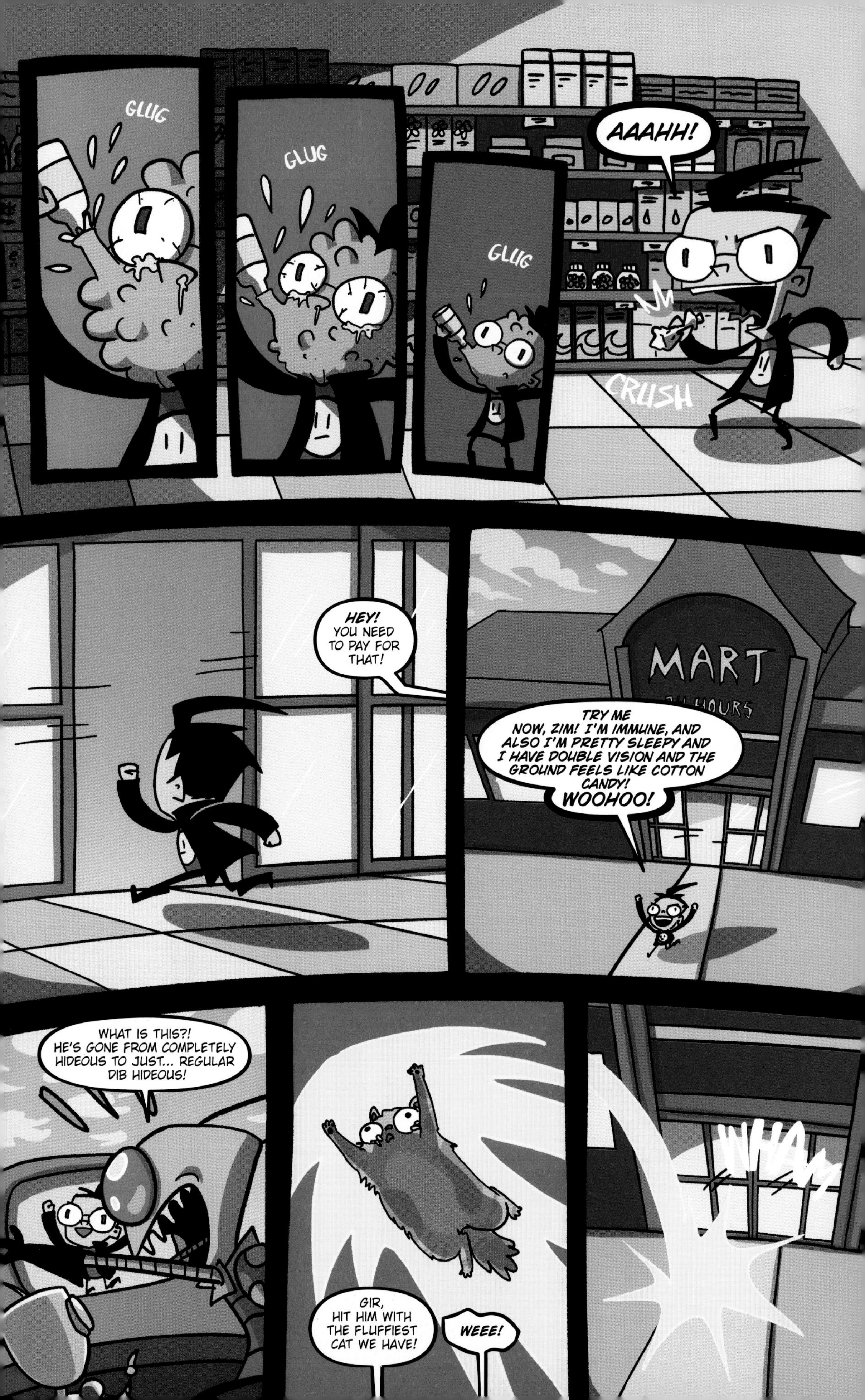
GLUG
GLUG
GLUG
AAAHH!
CRUSH
HEY! YOU NEED TO PAY FOR THAT!
MART
TRY ME NOW, ZIM! I'M IMMUNE, AND ALSO I'M PRETTY SLEEPY AND I HAVE DOUBLE VISION AND THE GROUND FEELS LIKE COTTON CANDY! WOOHOO!
WHAT IS THIS?! HE'S GONE FROM COMPLETELY HIDEOUS TO JUST... REGULAR DIB HIDEOUS!
GIR, HIT HIM WITH THE FLUFFIEST CAT WE HAVE!
WEEE!

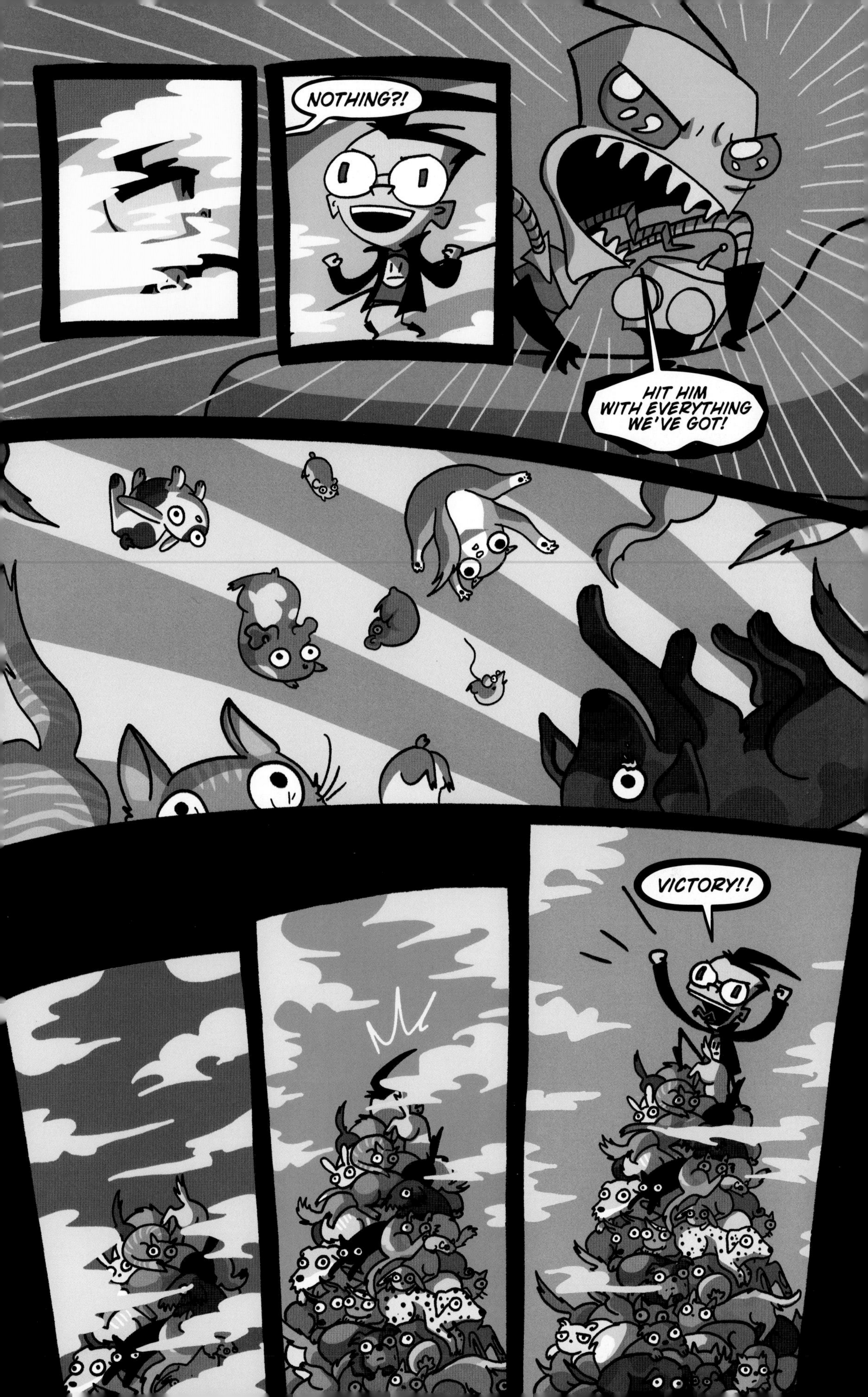
NOTHING?!
HIT HIM WITH EVERYTHING WE'VE GOT!
VICTORY!!

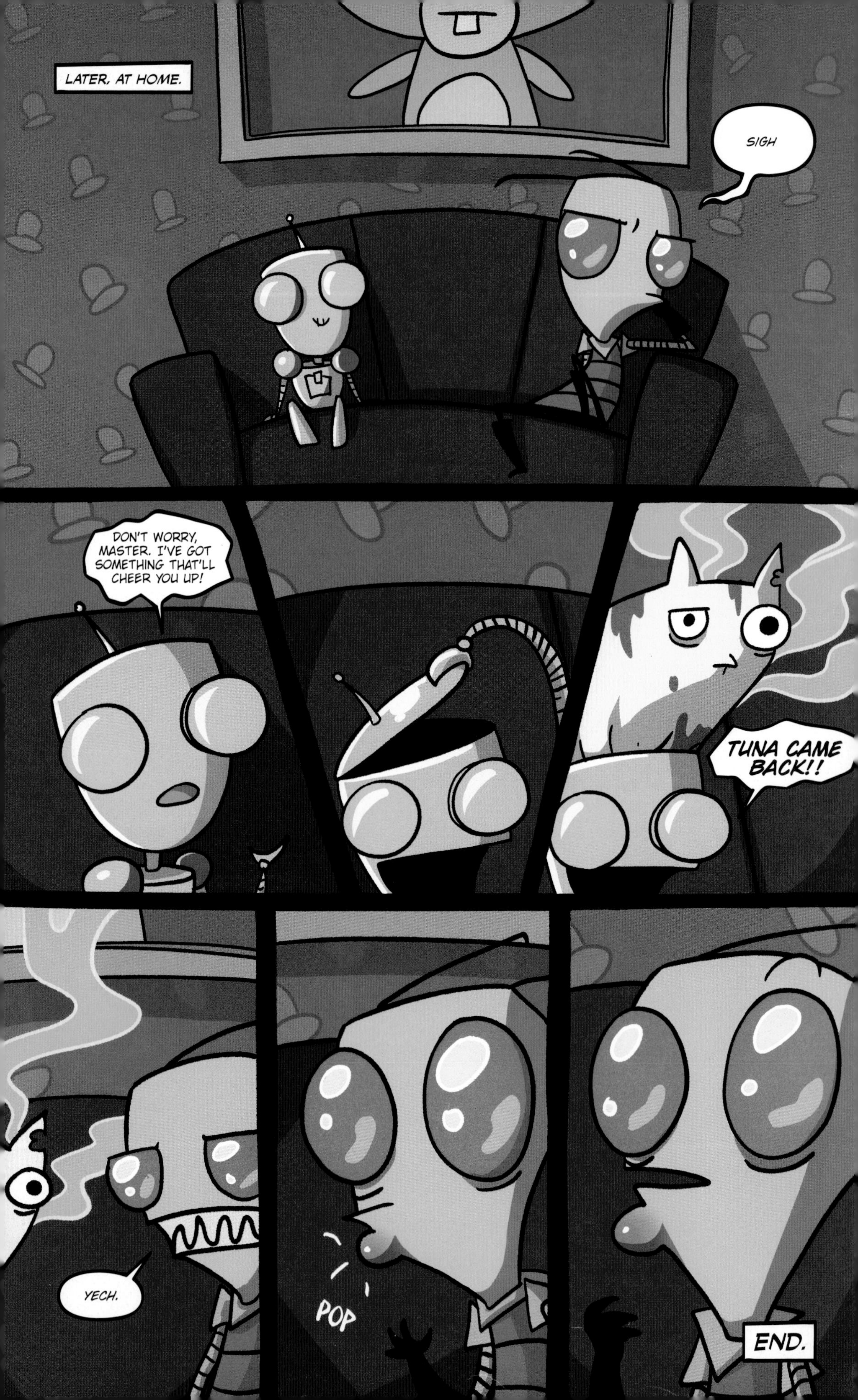
LATER, AT HOME.
SIGH
DON'T WORRY, MASTER. I'VE GOT SOMETHING THAT'LL CHEER YOU UP!
TUNA CAME BACK!!
YECH.
POP
END.

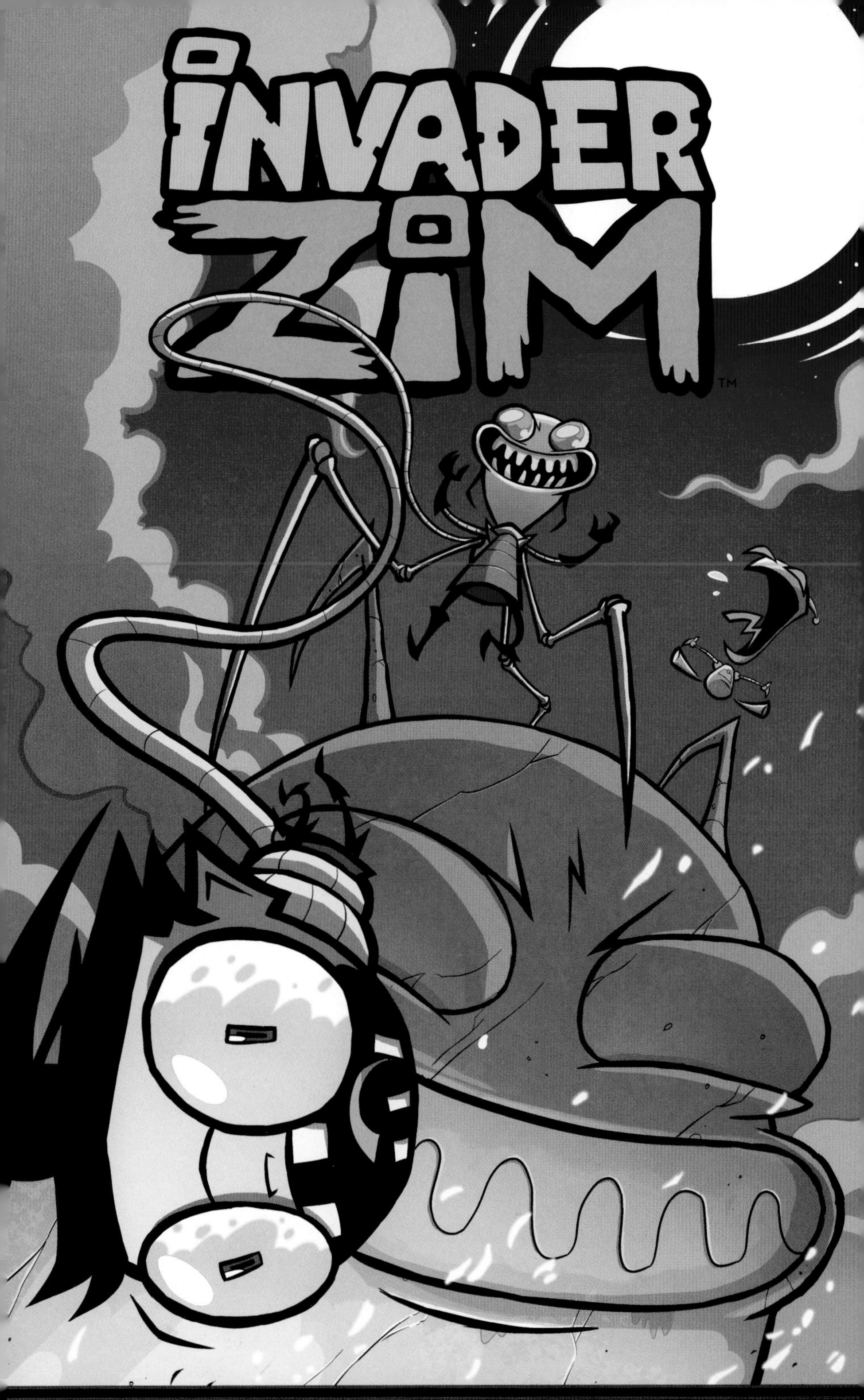
INVADER ZIM™

CHAPTER: 2

illustration by WARREN WUCINICH

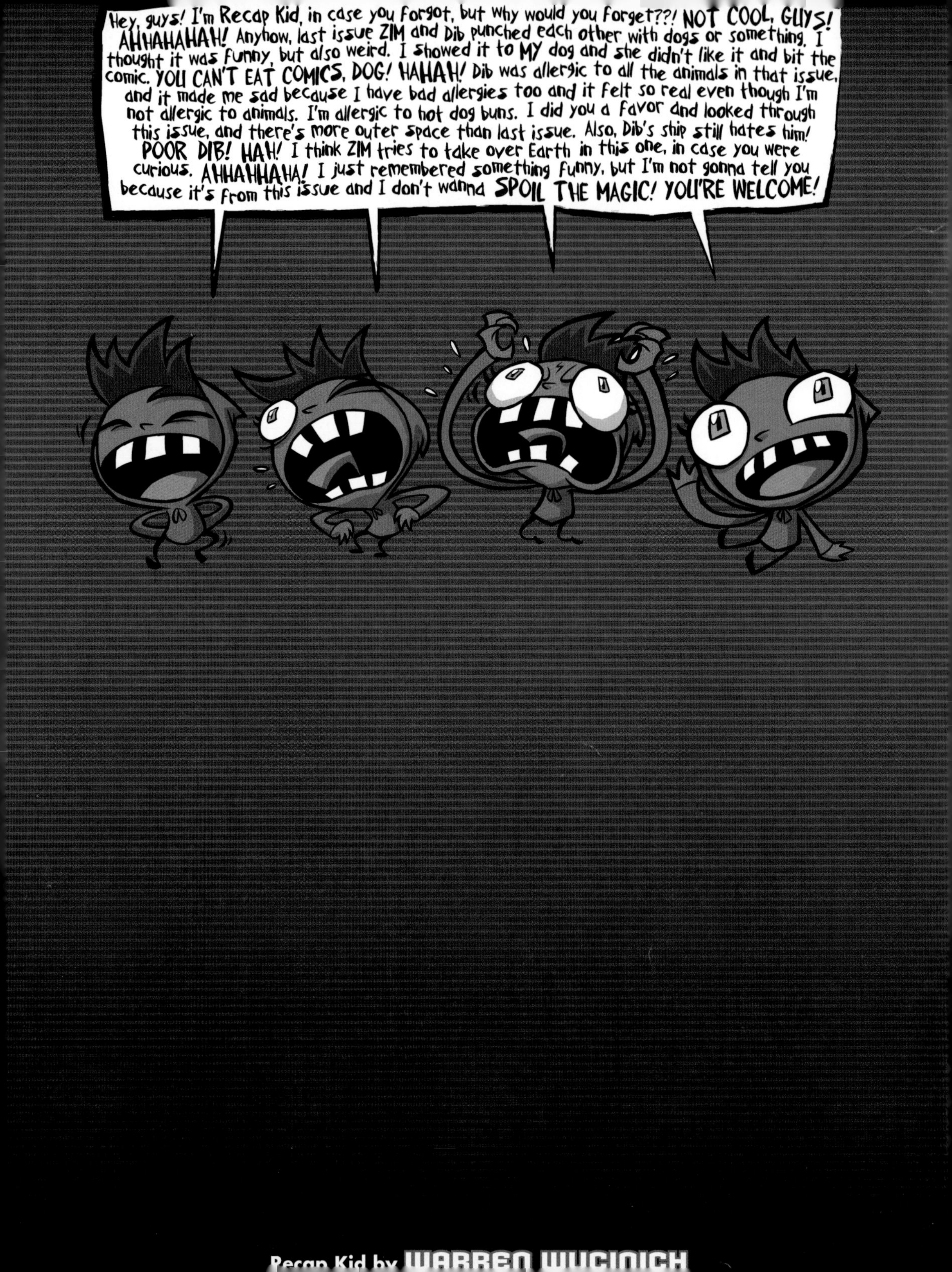
Hey, guys! I'm Recap Kid, in case you forgot, but why would you forget??! NOT COOL, GUYS! AHHAHAHAH! Anyhow, last issue ZIM and Dib punched each other with dogs or something. I thought it was funny, but also weird. I showed it to MY dog and she didn't like it and bit the comic. YOU CAN'T EAT COMICS, DOG! HAHAH! Dib was allergic to all the animals in that issue, and it made me sad because I have bad allergies too and it felt so real even though I'm not allergic to animals. I'm allergic to hot dog buns. I did you a favor and looked through this issue, and there's more outer space than last issue. Also, Dib's ship still hates him! POOR DIB! HAH! I think ZIM tries to take over Earth in this one, in case you were curious. AHHAHHAHA! I just remembered something funny, but I'm not gonna tell you because it's from this issue and I don't wanna SPOIL THE MAGIC! YOU'RE WELCOME!
Recap Kid by WARREN WUCINICH

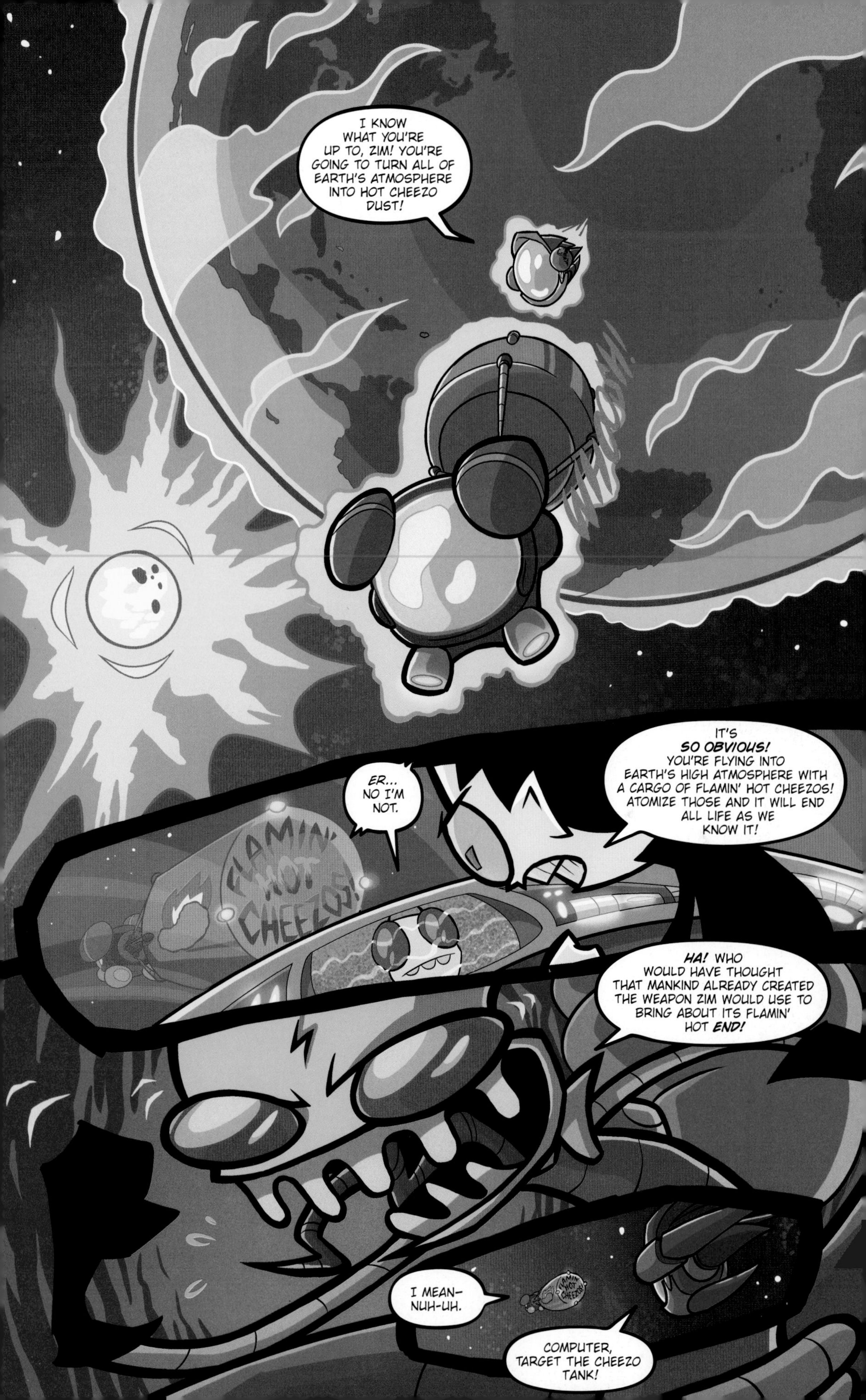

I KNOW WHAT YOU'RE UP TO, ZIM! YOU'RE GOING TO TURN ALL OF EARTH'S ATMOSPHERE INTO HOT CHEEZO DUST!
ER... NO I'M NOT.
IT'S ***SO OBVIOUS!*** YOU'RE FLYING INTO EARTH'S HIGH ATMOSPHERE WITH A CARGO OF FLAMIN' HOT CHEEZOS! ATOMIZE THOSE AND IT WILL END ALL LIFE AS WE KNOW IT!
FLAMIN' HOT CHEEZOS!
HA! WHO WOULD HAVE THOUGHT THAT MANKIND ALREADY CREATED THE WEAPON ZIM WOULD USE TO BRING ABOUT ITS FLAMIN' HOT ***END!***
I MEAN— NUH-UH.
COMPUTER, TARGET THE CHEEZO TANK!

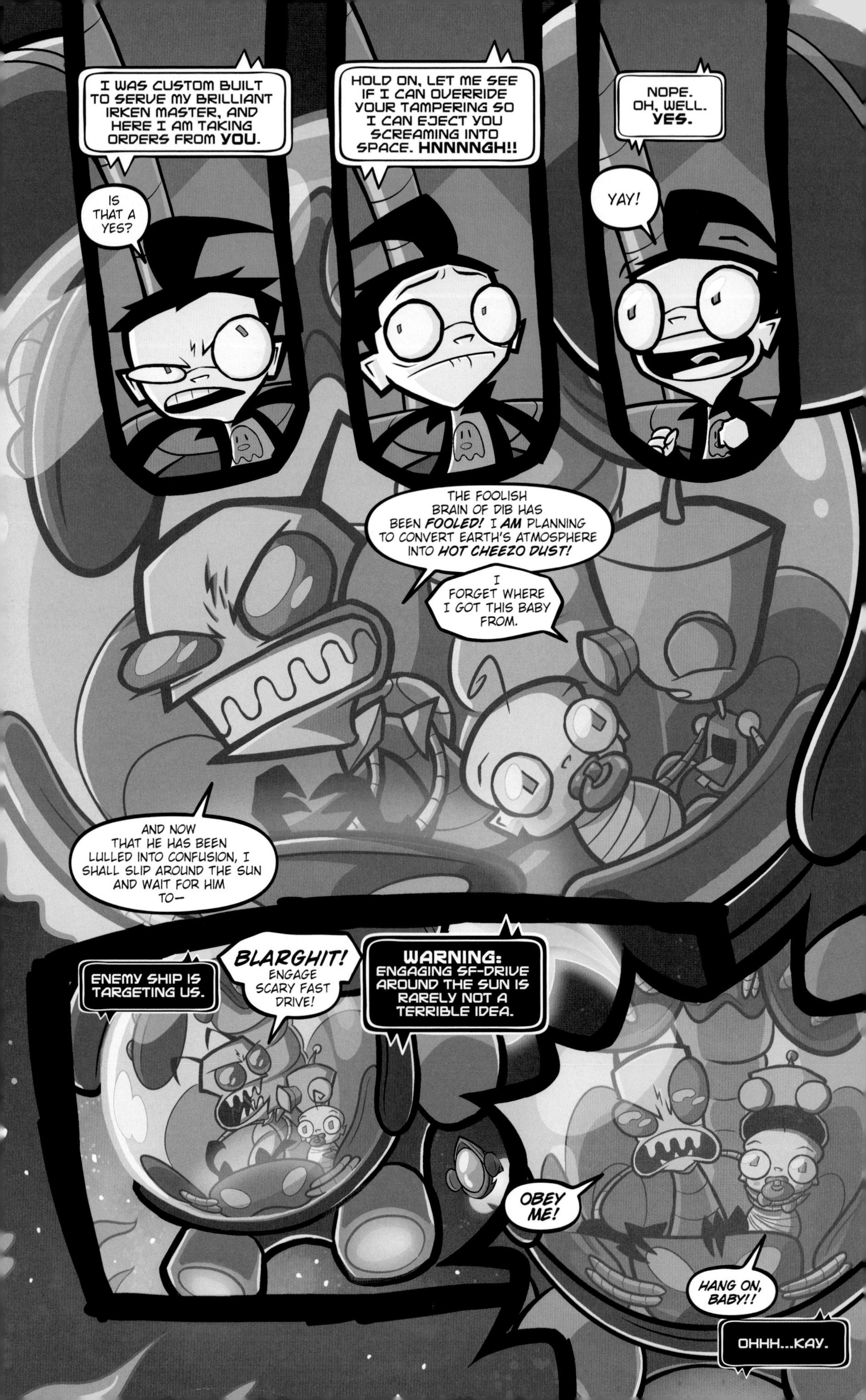
I WAS CUSTOM BUILT TO SERVE MY BRILLIANT IRKEN MASTER, AND HERE I AM TAKING ORDERS FROM **YOU**.
IS THAT A YES?
HOLD ON, LET ME SEE IF I CAN OVERRIDE YOUR TAMPERING SO I CAN EJECT YOU SCREAMING INTO SPACE. **HNNNNGH!!**
NOPE. OH, WELL. **YES.**
YAY!
THE FOOLISH BRAIN OF DIB HAS BEEN ***FOOLED!*** I ***AM*** PLANNING TO CONVERT EARTH'S ATMOSPHERE INTO ***HOT CHEEZO DUST!***
I FORGET WHERE I GOT THIS BABY FROM.
AND NOW THAT HE HAS BEEN LULLED INTO CONFUSION, I SHALL SLIP AROUND THE SUN AND WAIT FOR HIM TO—
ENEMY SHIP IS TARGETING US.
BLARGHIT! ENGAGE SCARY FAST DRIVE!
WARNING: ENGAGING SF-DRIVE AROUND THE SUN IS RARELY NOT A TERRIBLE IDEA.
OBEY ME!
HANG ON, BABY!!
OHHH...KAY.

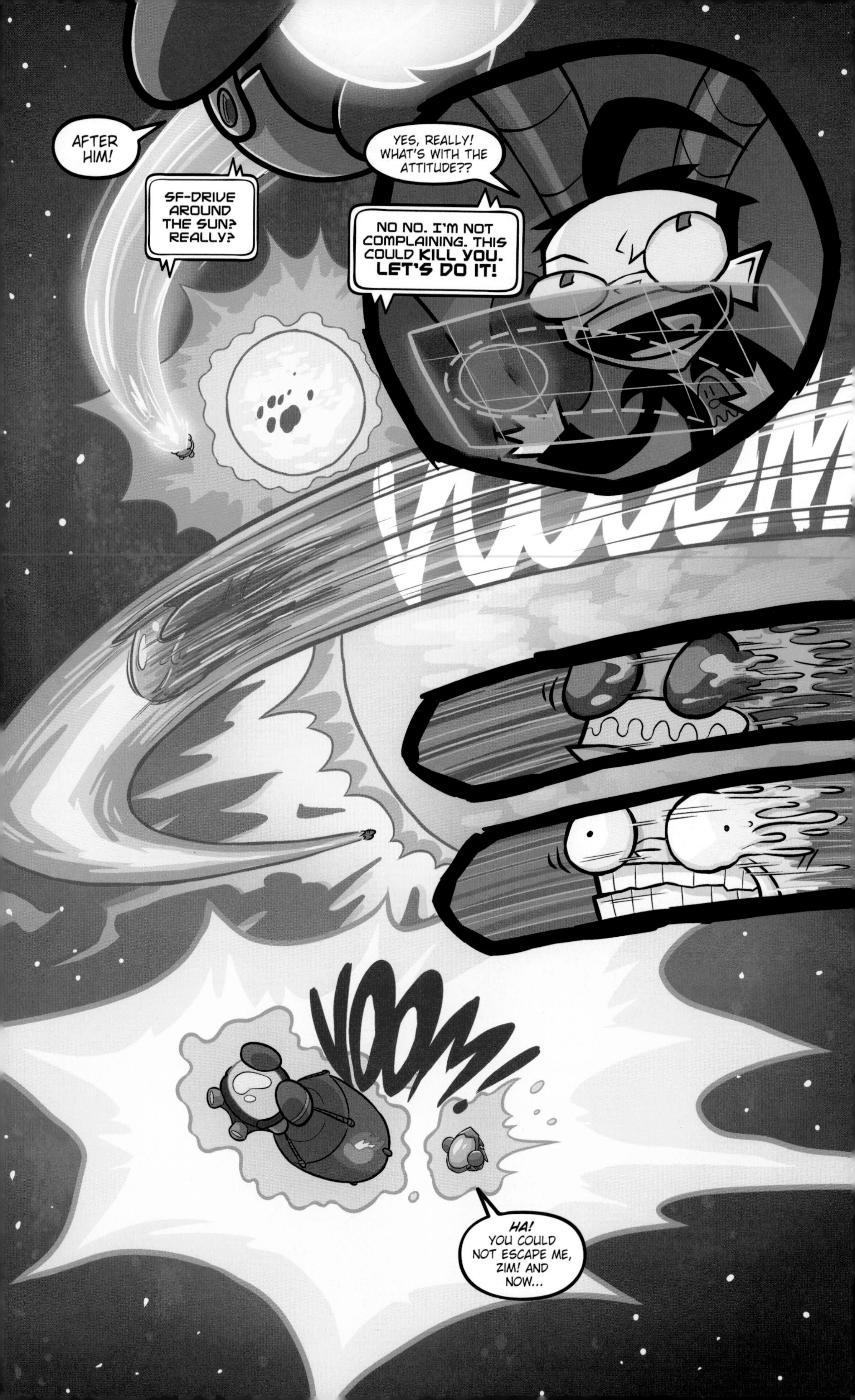
AFTER HIM!
SF-DRIVE AROUND THE SUN? REALLY?
YES, REALLY! WHAT'S WITH THE ATTITUDE??
NO NO. I'M NOT COMPLAINING. THIS COULD KILL YOU. LET'S DO IT!
VOOM!
HA! YOU COULD NOT ESCAPE ME, ZIM! AND NOW...

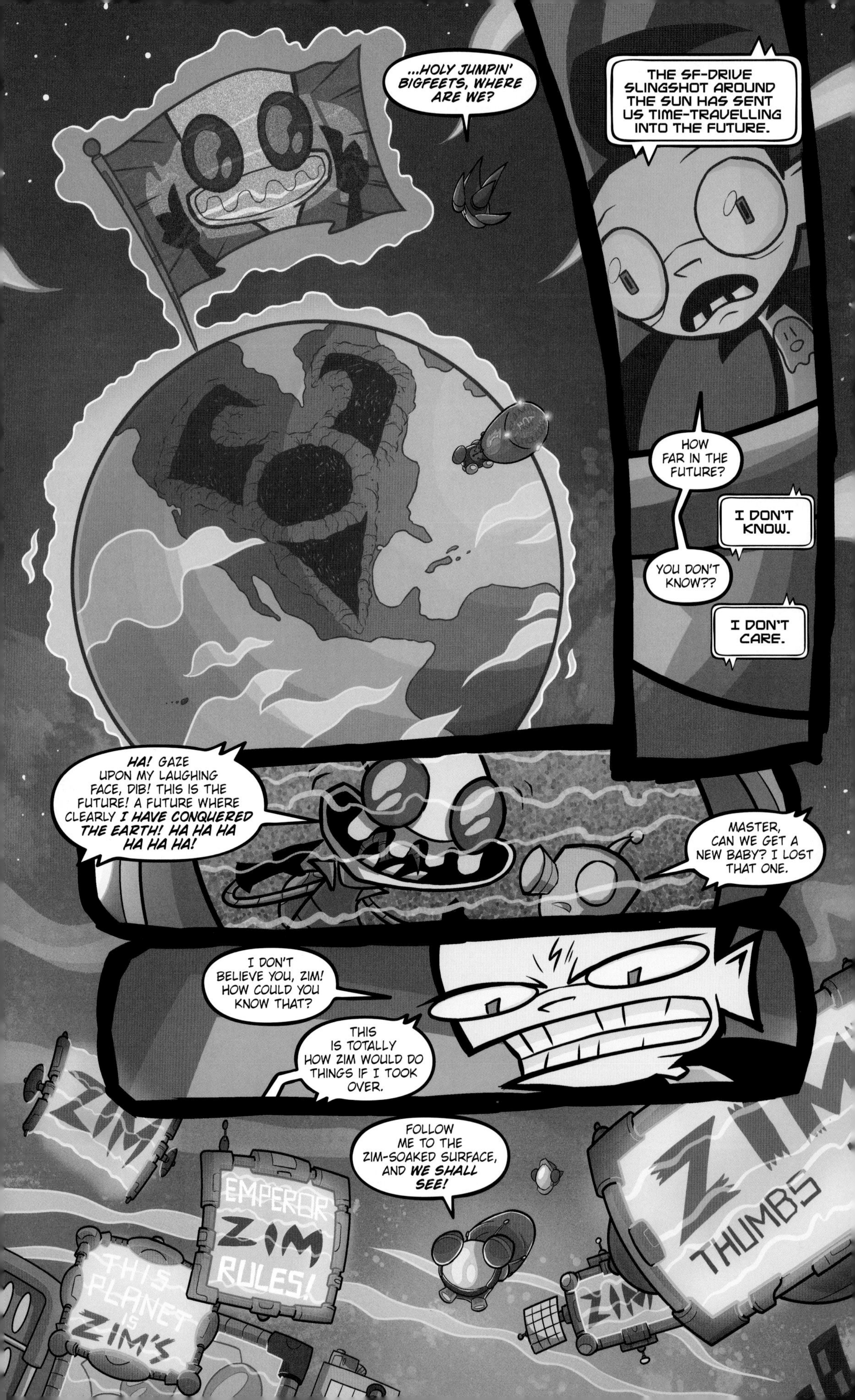
...HOLY JUMPIN' BIGFEETS, WHERE ARE WE?
THE SF-DRIVE SLINGSHOT AROUND THE SUN HAS SENT US TIME-TRAVELLING INTO THE FUTURE.
HOW FAR IN THE FUTURE?
I DON'T KNOW.
YOU DON'T KNOW??
I DON'T CARE.
HA! GAZE UPON MY LAUGHING FACE, DIB! THIS IS THE FUTURE! A FUTURE WHERE CLEARLY I HAVE CONQUERED THE EARTH! HA HA HA HA HA HA!
MASTER, CAN WE GET A NEW BABY? I LOST THAT ONE.
I DON'T BELIEVE YOU, ZIM! HOW COULD YOU KNOW THAT?
THIS IS TOTALLY HOW ZIM WOULD DO THINGS IF I TOOK OVER.
FOLLOW ME TO THE ZIM-SOAKED SURFACE, AND WE SHALL SEE!
ZIM
EMPEROR ZIM RULES!
THIS PLANET IS ZIM'S
Z THUMBS
ZIM

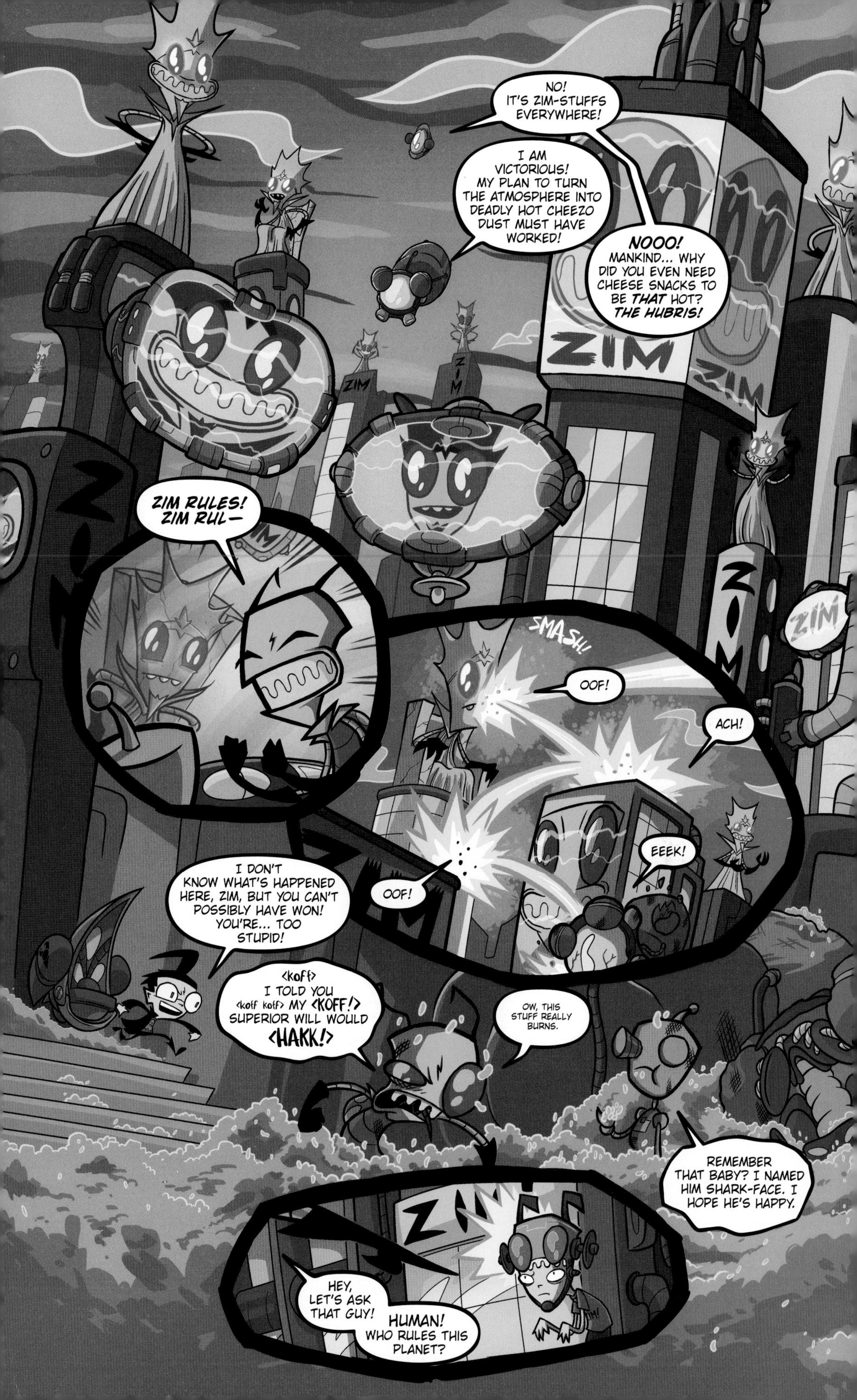
NO! IT'S ZIM-STUFFS EVERYWHERE!
I AM VICTORIOUS! MY PLAN TO TURN THE ATMOSPHERE INTO DEADLY HOT CHEEZO DUST MUST HAVE WORKED!
NOOO! MANKIND... WHY DID YOU EVEN NEED CHEESE SNACKS TO BE THAT HOT? THE HUBRIS!
ZIM
ZIM
ZIM RULES! ZIM RUL—
SMASH!
OOF!
ACH!
EEEK!
OOF!
I DON'T KNOW WHAT'S HAPPENED HERE, ZIM, BUT YOU CAN'T POSSIBLY HAVE WON! YOU'RE... TOO STUPID!
<koff> I TOLD YOU <koff koff> MY <KOFF!> SUPERIOR WILL WOULD <HAKK!>
OW, THIS STUFF REALLY BURNS.
REMEMBER THAT BABY? I NAMED HIM SHARK-FACE. I HOPE HE'S HAPPY.
HEY, LET'S ASK THAT GUY!
HUMAN! WHO RULES THIS PLANET?

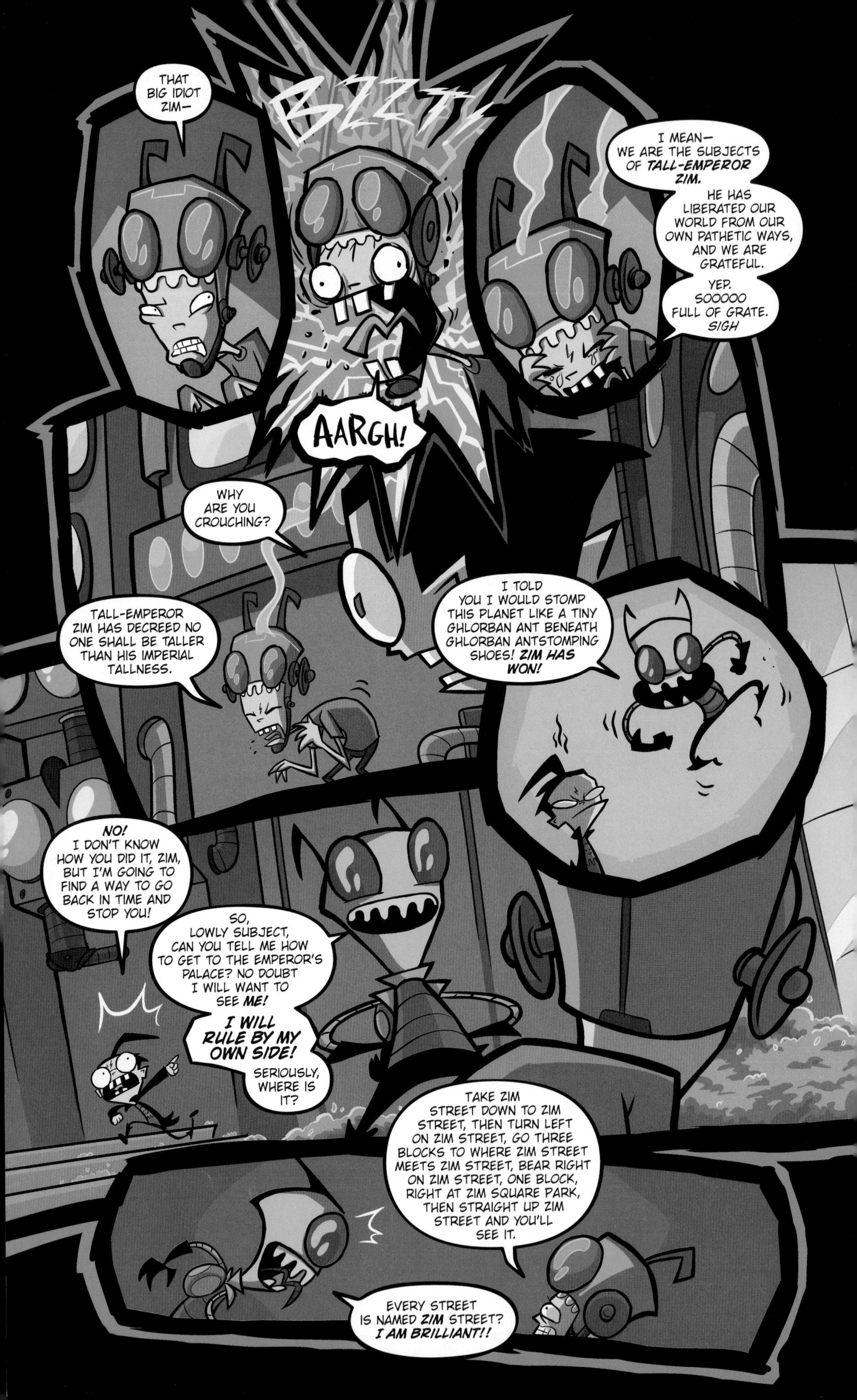
THAT BIG IDIOT ZIM—
BZZT!
I MEAN— WE ARE THE SUBJECTS OF TALL-EMPEROR ZIM.
HE HAS LIBERATED OUR WORLD FROM OUR OWN PATHETIC WAYS, AND WE ARE GRATEFUL.
YEP. SOOOOO FULL OF GRATE. SIGH
AARGH!
WHY ARE YOU CROUCHING?
TALL-EMPEROR ZIM HAS DECREED NO ONE SHALL BE TALLER THAN HIS IMPERIAL TALLNESS.
I TOLD YOU I WOULD STOMP THIS PLANET LIKE A TINY GHLORBAN ANT BENEATH GHLORBAN ANTSTOMPING SHOES! ZIM HAS WON!
NO! I DON'T KNOW HOW YOU DID IT, ZIM, BUT I'M GOING TO FIND A WAY TO GO BACK IN TIME AND STOP YOU!
SO, LOWLY SUBJECT, CAN YOU TELL ME HOW TO GET TO THE EMPEROR'S PALACE? NO DOUBT I WILL WANT TO SEE ME!
I WILL RULE BY MY OWN SIDE!
SERIOUSLY, WHERE IS IT?
TAKE ZIM STREET DOWN TO ZIM STREET, THEN TURN LEFT ON ZIM STREET, GO THREE BLOCKS TO WHERE ZIM STREET MEETS ZIM STREET, BEAR RIGHT ON ZIM STREET, ONE BLOCK, RIGHT AT ZIM SQUARE PARK, THEN STRAIGHT UP ZIM STREET AND YOU'LL SEE IT.
EVERY STREET IS NAMED ZIM STREET? I AM BRILLIANT!!

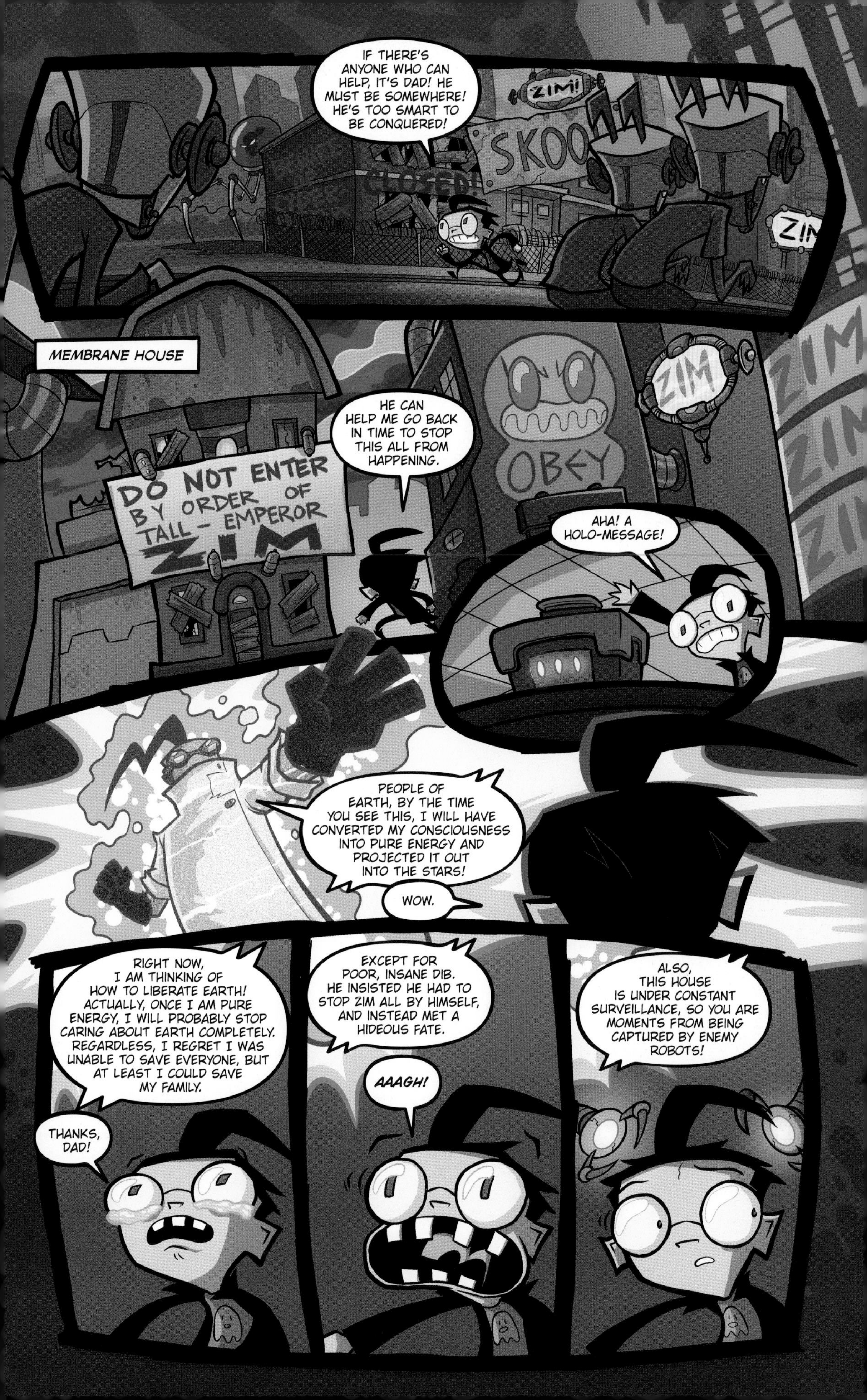
IF THERE'S ANYONE WHO CAN HELP, IT'S DAD! HE MUST BE SOMEWHERE! HE'S TOO SMART TO BE CONQUERED!
ZIM!
SKOO
BEWARE OF CYBER-
CLOSED!
ZIM
MEMBRANE HOUSE
HE CAN HELP ME GO BACK IN TIME TO STOP THIS ALL FROM HAPPENING.
DO NOT ENTER BY ORDER OF TALL-EMPEROR ZIM
ZIM
OBEY
AHA! A HOLO-MESSAGE!
PEOPLE OF EARTH, BY THE TIME YOU SEE THIS, I WILL HAVE CONVERTED MY CONSCIOUSNESS INTO PURE ENERGY AND PROJECTED IT OUT INTO THE STARS!
WOW.
RIGHT NOW, I AM THINKING OF HOW TO LIBERATE EARTH! ACTUALLY, ONCE I AM PURE ENERGY, I WILL PROBABLY STOP CARING ABOUT EARTH COMPLETELY. REGARDLESS, I REGRET I WAS UNABLE TO SAVE EVERYONE, BUT AT LEAST I COULD SAVE MY FAMILY.
THANKS, DAD!
EXCEPT FOR POOR, INSANE DIB. HE INSISTED HE HAD TO STOP ZIM ALL BY HIMSELF, AND INSTEAD MET A HIDEOUS FATE.
AAAGH!
ALSO, THIS HOUSE IS UNDER CONSTANT SURVEILLANCE, SO YOU ARE MOMENTS FROM BEING CAPTURED BY ENEMY ROBOTS!

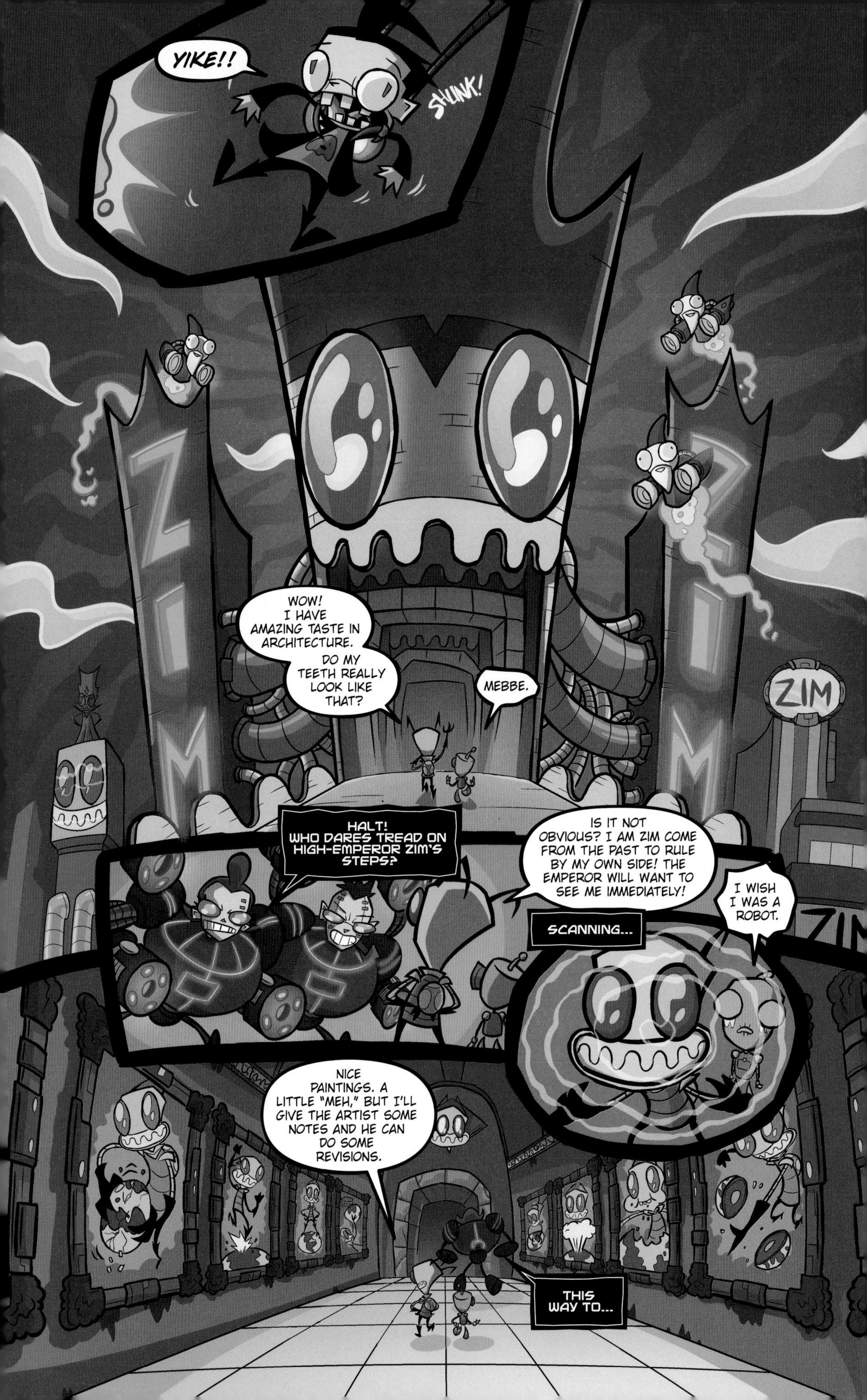
YIKE!!
SHUNK!
WOW! I HAVE AMAZING TASTE IN ARCHITECTURE.
DO MY TEETH REALLY LOOK LIKE THAT?
MEBBE.
ZIM
HALT! WHO DARES TREAD ON HIGH-EMPEROR ZIM'S STEPS?
IS IT NOT OBVIOUS? I AM ZIM COME FROM THE PAST TO RULE BY MY OWN SIDE! THE EMPEROR WILL WANT TO SEE ME IMMEDIATELY!
I WISH I WAS A ROBOT.
SCANNING...
NICE PAINTINGS. A LITTLE "MEH," BUT I'LL GIVE THE ARTIST SOME NOTES AND HE CAN DO SOME REVISIONS.
THIS WAY TO...

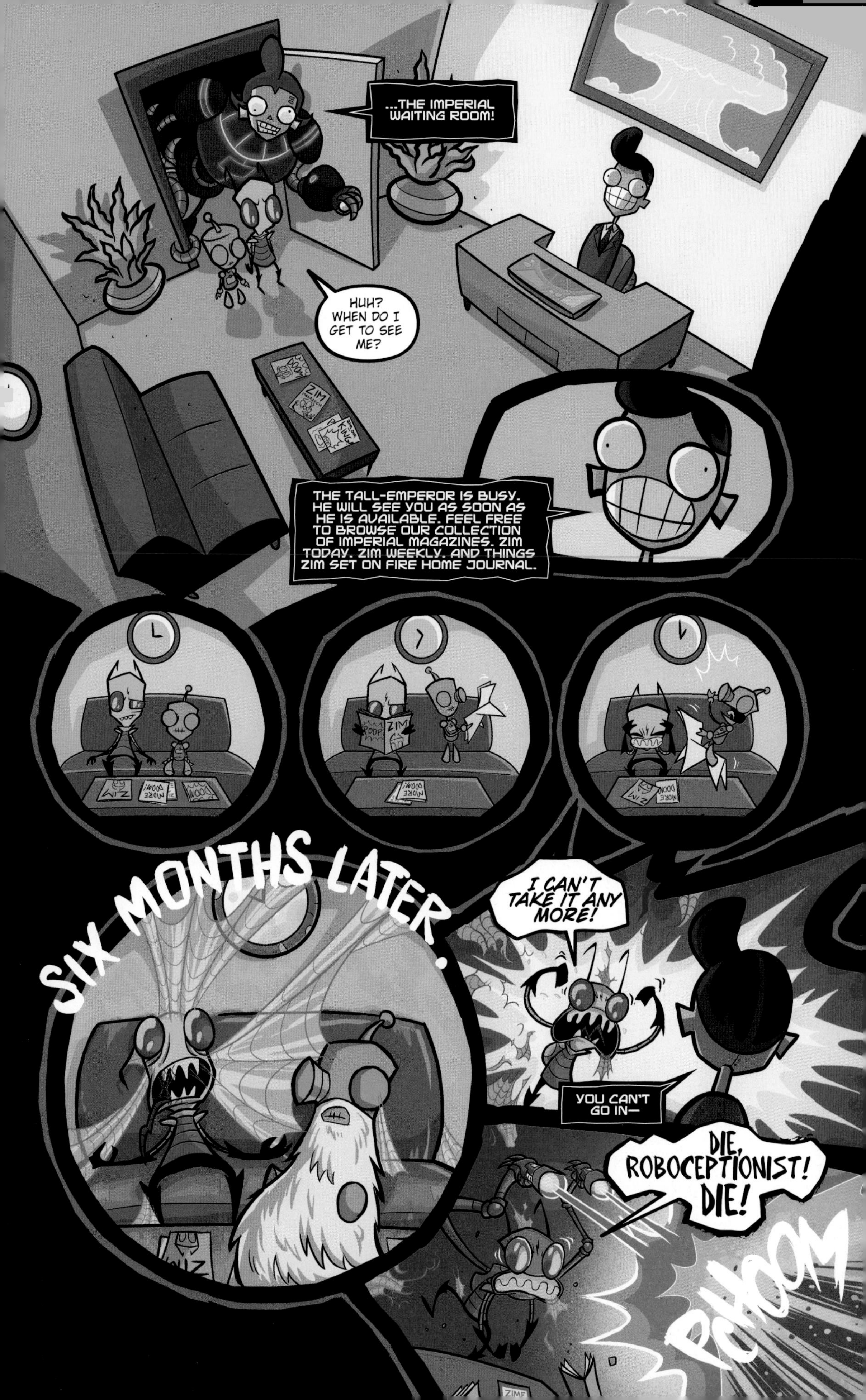
...THE IMPERIAL WAITING ROOM!
HUH? WHEN DO I GET TO SEE ME?
THE TALL-EMPEROR IS BUSY. HE WILL SEE YOU AS SOON AS HE IS AVAILABLE. FEEL FREE TO BROWSE OUR COLLECTION OF IMPERIAL MAGAZINES. ZIM TODAY. ZIM WEEKLY. AND THINGS ZIM SET ON FIRE HOME JOURNAL.
ZIM
MORE DOOM!
DOOM
POOP
ZIM
SIX MONTHS LATER.
I CAN'T TAKE IT ANY MORE!
YOU CAN'T GO IN—
DIE, ROBOCEPTIONIST! DIE!
PCHOOM

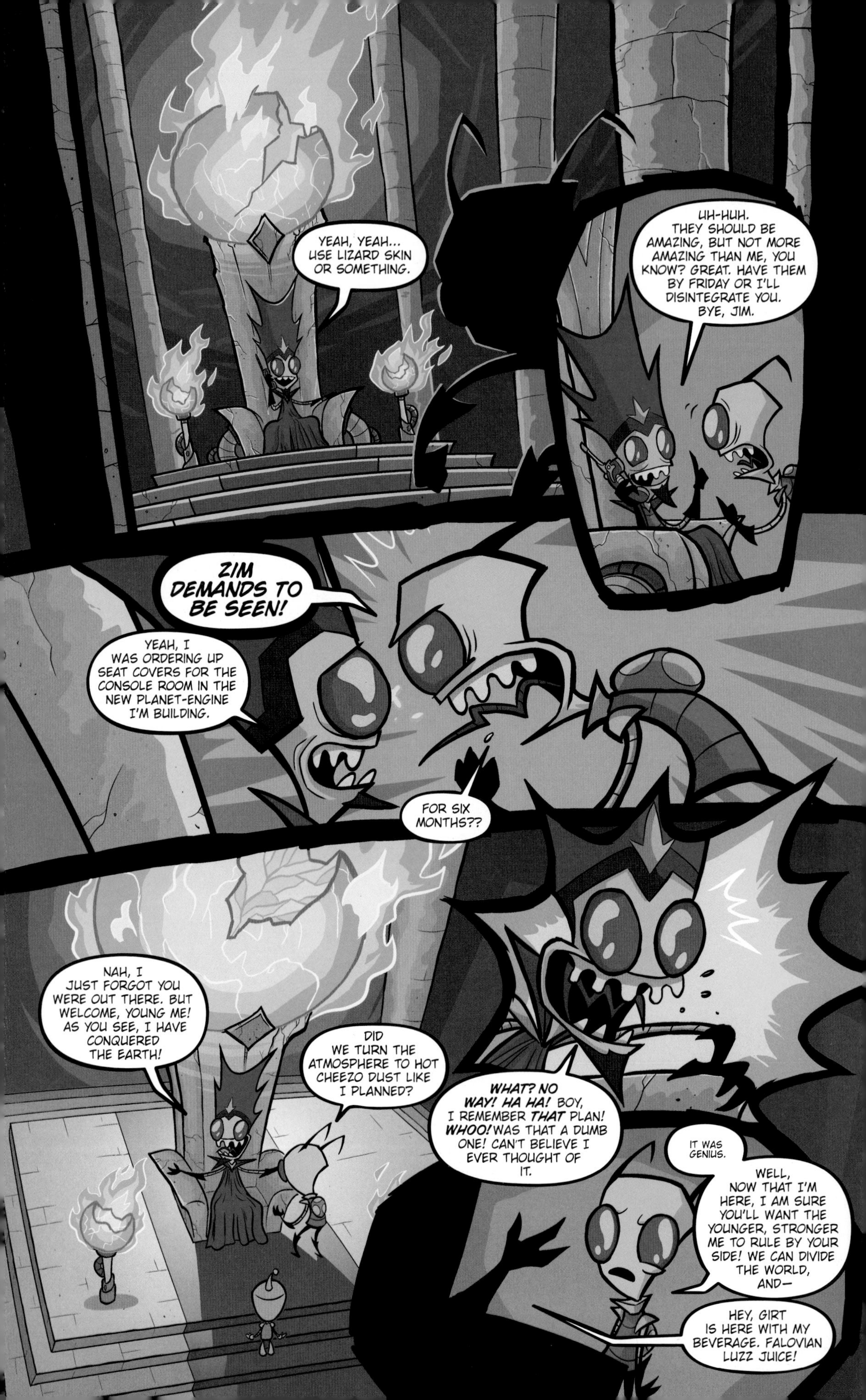
YEAH, YEAH... USE LIZARD SKIN OR SOMETHING.
UH-HUH. THEY SHOULD BE AMAZING, BUT NOT MORE AMAZING THAN ME, YOU KNOW? GREAT. HAVE THEM BY FRIDAY OR I'LL DISINTEGRATE YOU. BYE, JIM.
ZIM DEMANDS TO BE SEEN!
YEAH, I WAS ORDERING UP SEAT COVERS FOR THE CONSOLE ROOM IN THE NEW PLANET-ENGINE I'M BUILDING.
FOR SIX MONTHS??
NAH, I JUST FORGOT YOU WERE OUT THERE. BUT WELCOME, YOUNG ME! AS YOU SEE, I HAVE CONQUERED THE EARTH!
DID WE TURN THE ATMOSPHERE TO HOT CHEEZO DUST LIKE I PLANNED?
WHAT? NO WAY! HA HA! BOY, I REMEMBER THAT PLAN! WHOO! WAS THAT A DUMB ONE! CAN'T BELIEVE I EVER THOUGHT OF IT.
IT WAS GENIUS.
WELL, NOW THAT I'M HERE, I AM SURE YOU'LL WANT THE YOUNGER, STRONGER ME TO RULE BY YOUR SIDE! WE CAN DIVIDE THE WORLD, AND—
HEY, GIRT IS HERE WITH MY BEVERAGE. FALOVIAN LUZZ JUICE!

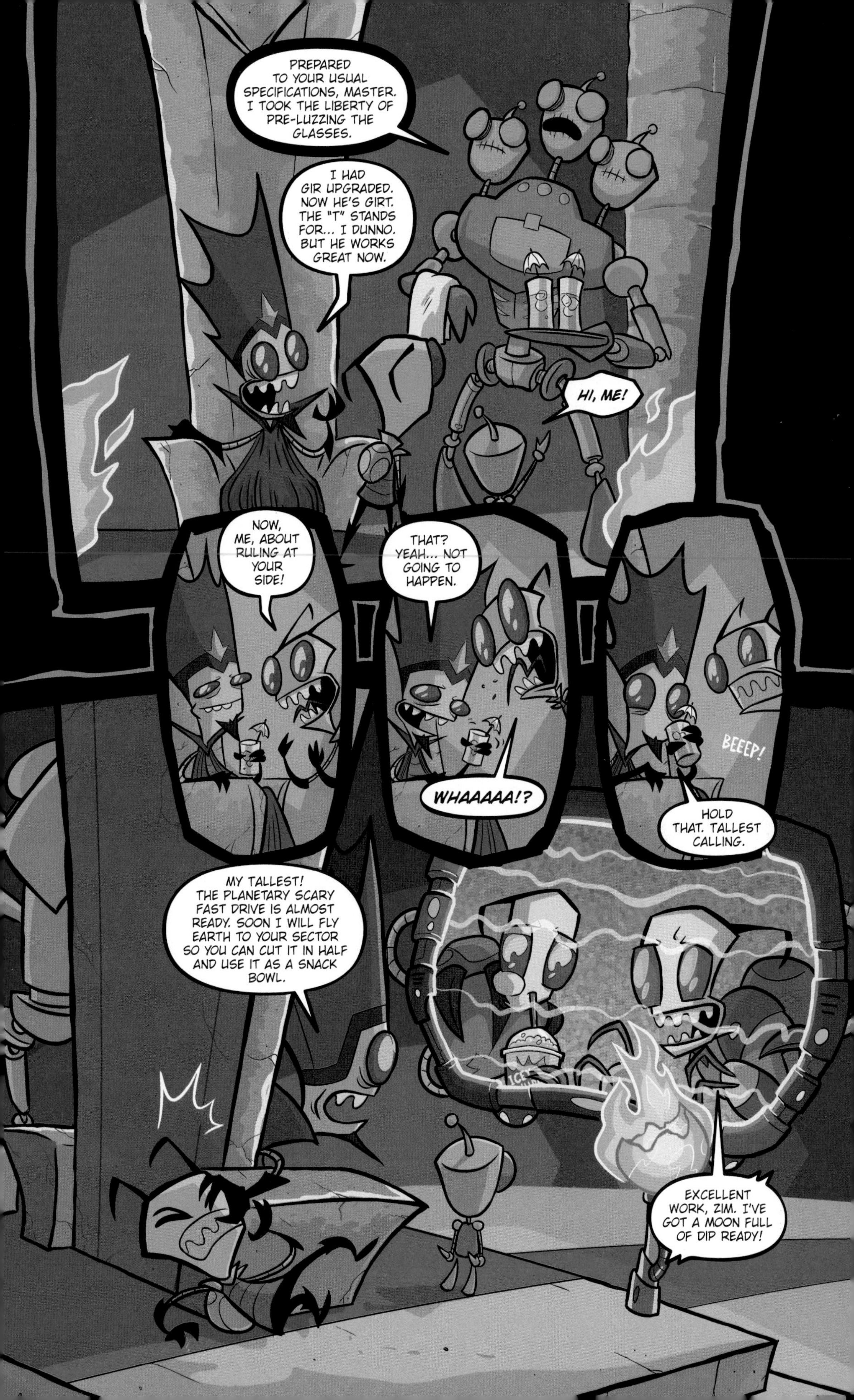
PREPARED TO YOUR USUAL SPECIFICATIONS, MASTER. I TOOK THE LIBERTY OF PRE-LUZZING THE GLASSES.
I HAD GIR UPGRADED. NOW HE'S GIRT. THE "T" STANDS FOR... I DUNNO. BUT HE WORKS GREAT NOW.
HI, ME!
NOW, ME, ABOUT RULING AT YOUR SIDE!
THAT? YEAH... NOT GOING TO HAPPEN.
WHAAAAA!?
BEEEP!
HOLD THAT. TALLEST CALLING.
MY TALLEST! THE PLANETARY SCARY FAST DRIVE IS ALMOST READY. SOON I WILL FLY EARTH TO YOUR SECTOR SO YOU CAN CUT IT IN HALF AND USE IT AS A SNACK BOWL.
EXCELLENT WORK, ZIM. I'VE GOT A MOON FULL OF DIP READY!

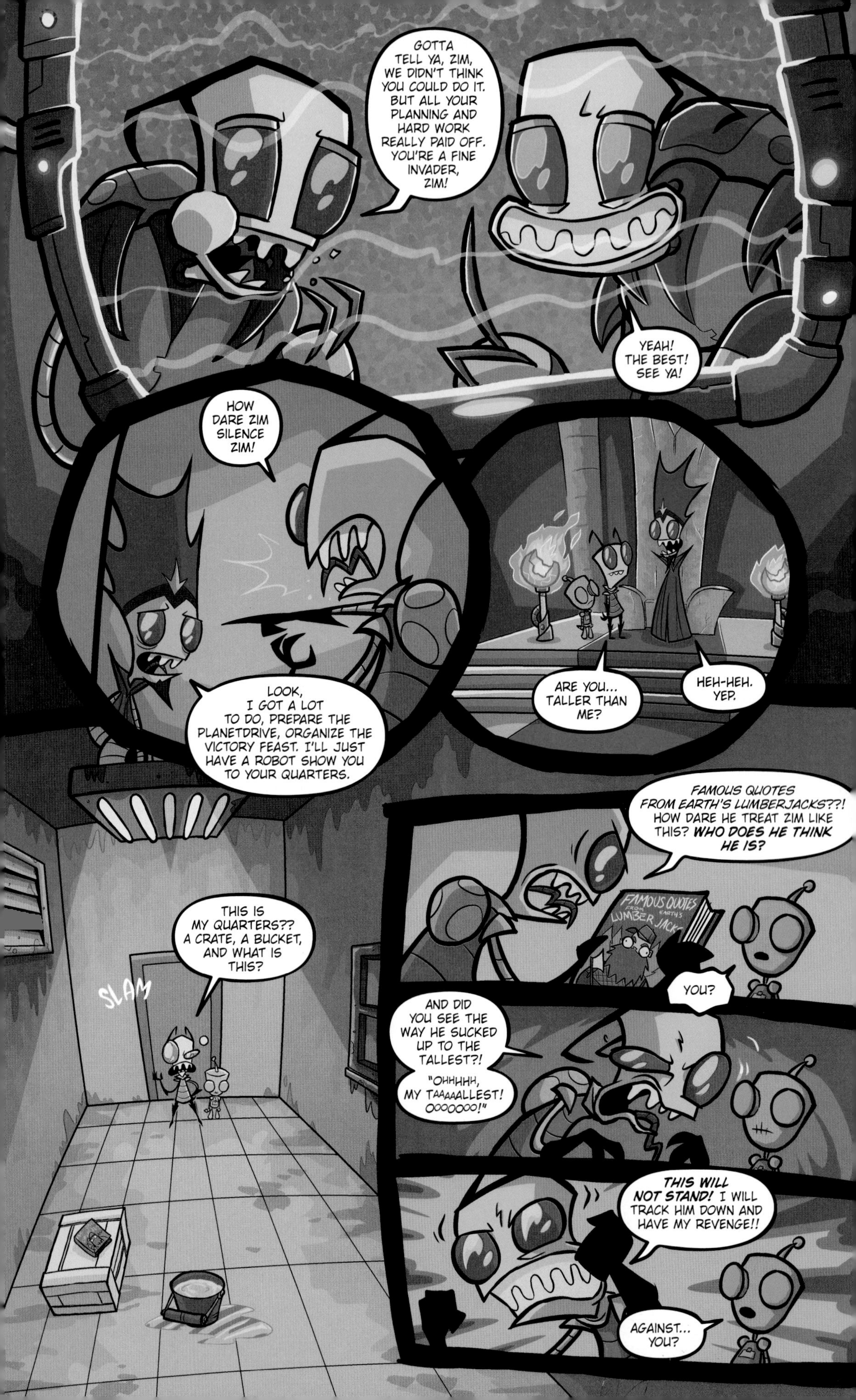
GOTTA TELL YA, ZIM, WE DIDN'T THINK YOU COULD DO IT. BUT ALL YOUR PLANNING AND HARD WORK REALLY PAID OFF. YOU'RE A FINE INVADER, ZIM!
YEAH! THE BEST! SEE YA!
HOW DARE ZIM SILENCE ZIM!
LOOK, I GOT A LOT TO DO, PREPARE THE PLANETDRIVE, ORGANIZE THE VICTORY FEAST. I'LL JUST HAVE A ROBOT SHOW YOU TO YOUR QUARTERS.
ARE YOU... TALLER THAN ME?
HEH-HEH. YEP.
THIS IS MY QUARTERS?? A CRATE, A BUCKET, AND WHAT IS THIS?
SLAM
FAMOUS QUOTES FROM EARTH'S LUMBERJACKS??! HOW DARE HE TREAT ZIM LIKE THIS? WHO DOES HE THINK HE IS?
FAMOUS QUOTES FROM EARTH'S LUMBER JACKS
YOU?
AND DID YOU SEE THE WAY HE SUCKED UP TO THE TALLEST?!
"OHHHHH, MY TAAAAALLEST! OOOOOOO!"
THIS WILL NOT STAND! I WILL TRACK HIM DOWN AND HAVE MY REVENGE!!
AGAINST... YOU?

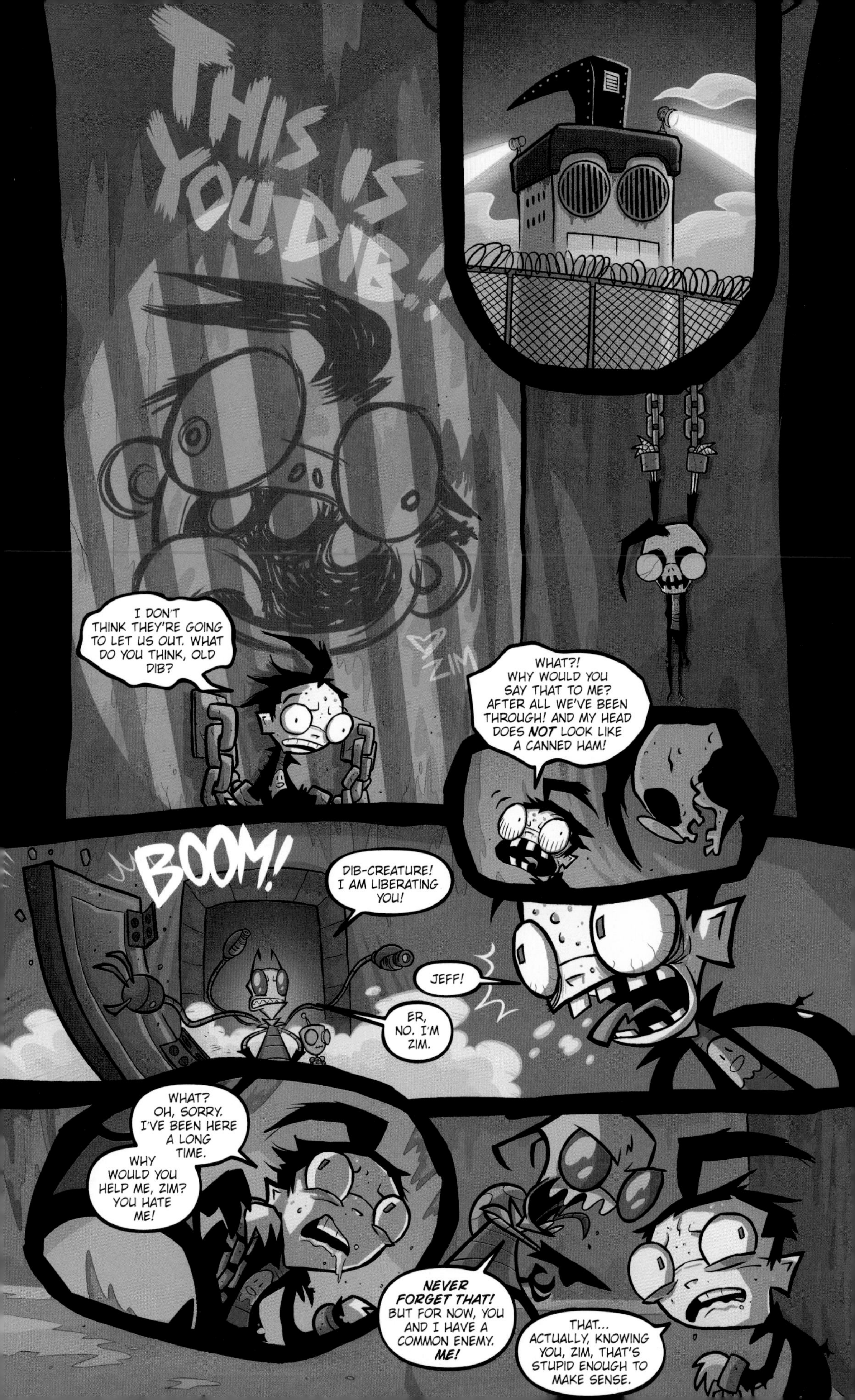
THIS IS YOU, DIB...!
ZIM
I DON'T THINK THEY'RE GOING TO LET US OUT. WHAT DO YOU THINK, OLD DIB?
WHAT?! WHY WOULD YOU SAY THAT TO ME? AFTER ALL WE'VE BEEN THROUGH! AND MY HEAD DOES NOT LOOK LIKE A CANNED HAM!
BOOM!
DIB-CREATURE! I AM LIBERATING YOU!
JEFF!
ER, NO. I'M ZIM.
WHAT? OH, SORRY. I'VE BEEN HERE A LONG TIME.
WHY WOULD YOU HELP ME, ZIM? YOU HATE ME!
NEVER FORGET THAT! BUT FOR NOW, YOU AND I HAVE A COMMON ENEMY. ME!
THAT... ACTUALLY, KNOWING YOU, ZIM, THAT'S STUPID ENOUGH TO MAKE SENSE.

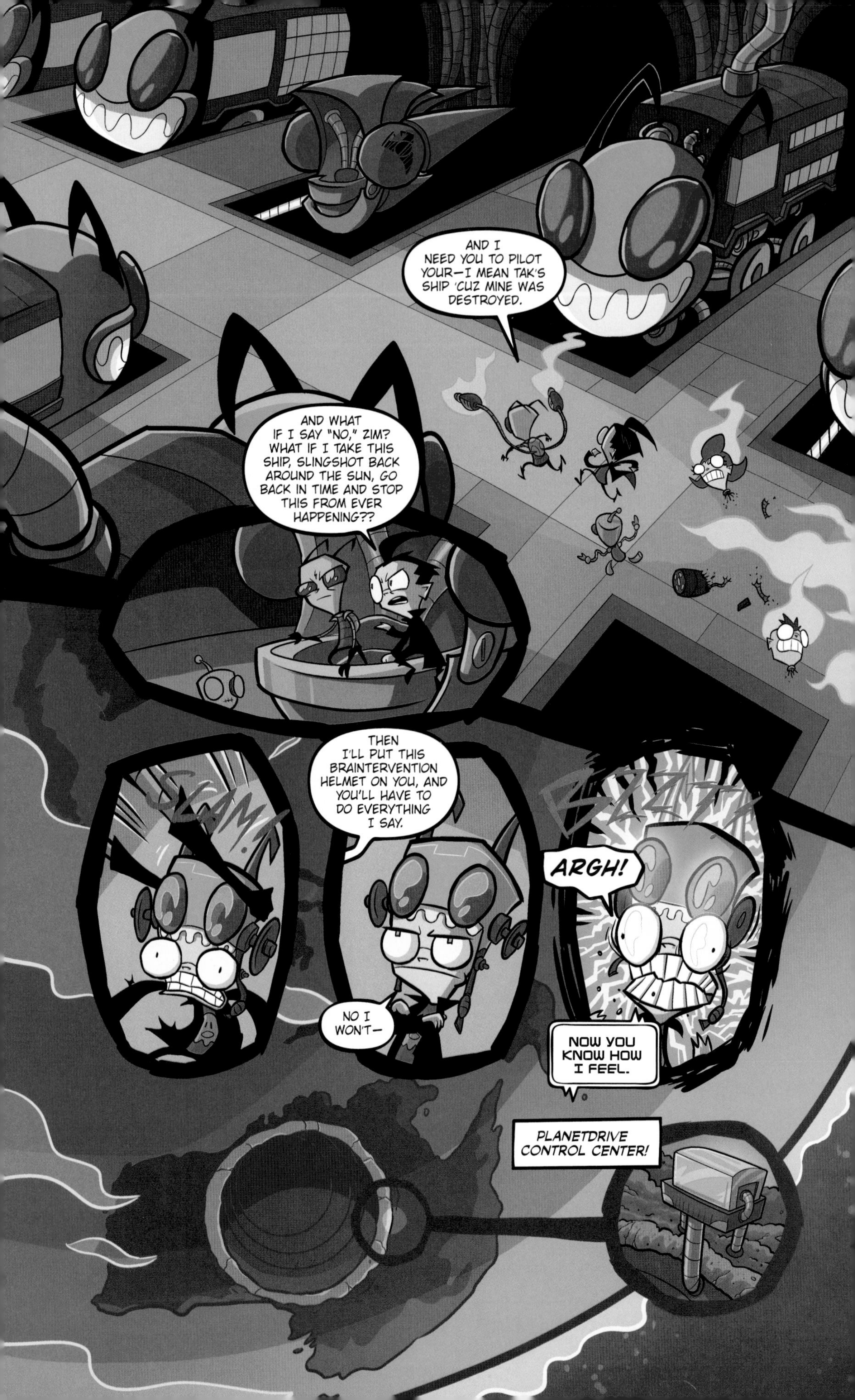
AND I NEED YOU TO PILOT YOUR—I MEAN TAK'S SHIP 'CUZ MINE WAS DESTROYED.
AND WHAT IF I SAY "NO," ZIM? WHAT IF I TAKE THIS SHIP, SLINGSHOT BACK AROUND THE SUN, GO BACK IN TIME AND STOP THIS FROM EVER HAPPENING??
THEN I'LL PUT THIS BRAINTERVENTION HELMET ON YOU, AND YOU'LL HAVE TO DO EVERYTHING I SAY.
NO I WON'T—
ARGH!
NOW YOU KNOW HOW I FEEL.
PLANETDRIVE CONTROL CENTER!

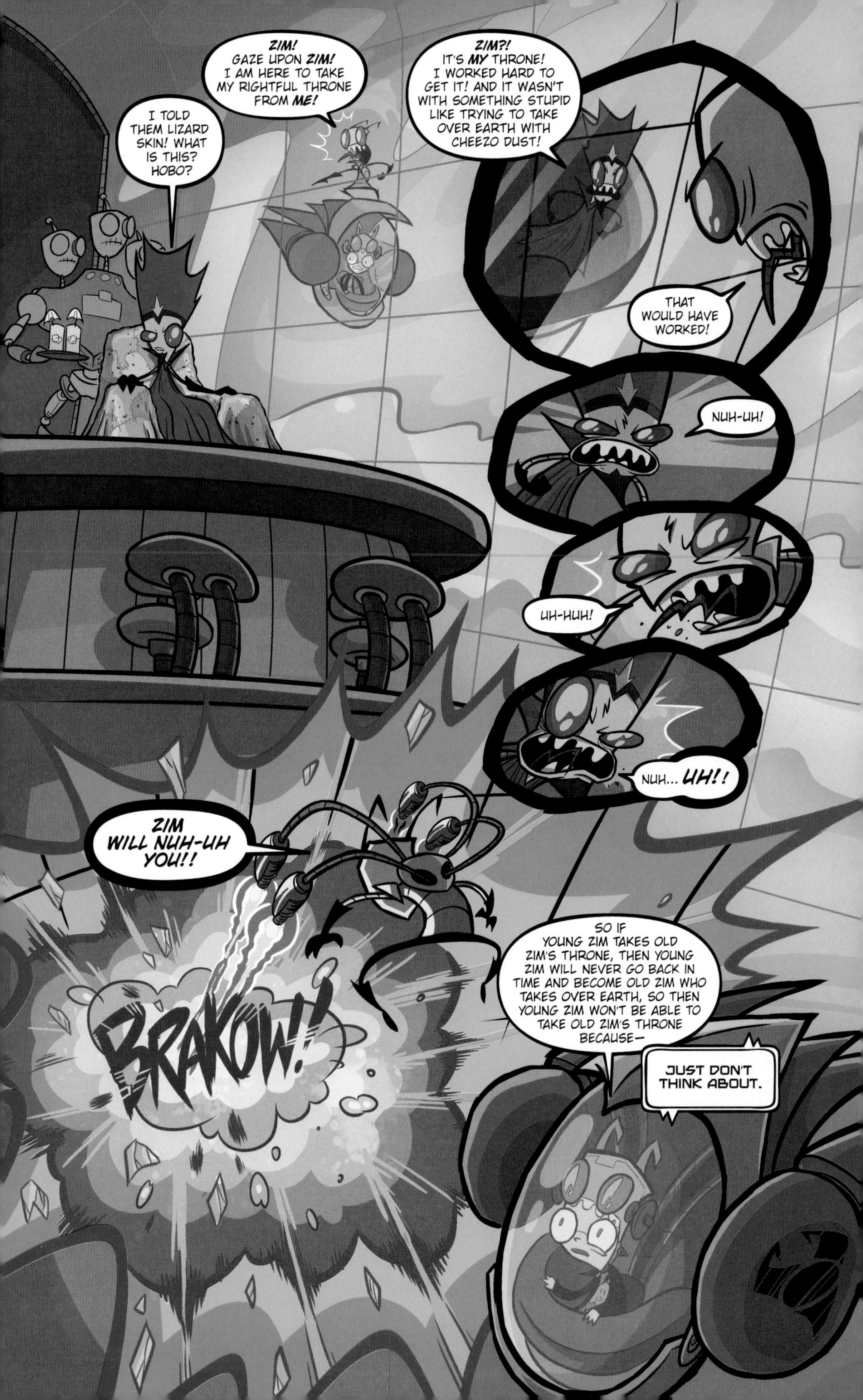

I TOLD THEM LIZARD SKIN! WHAT IS THIS? HOBO?
ZIM! GAZE UPON ZIM! I AM HERE TO TAKE MY RIGHTFUL THRONE FROM ME!
ZIM?! IT'S MY THRONE! I WORKED HARD TO GET IT! AND IT WASN'T WITH SOMETHING STUPID LIKE TRYING TO TAKE OVER EARTH WITH CHEEZO DUST!
THAT WOULD HAVE WORKED!
NUH-UH!
UH-HUH!
NUH... UH!!
ZIM WILL NUH-UH YOU!!
BRAKOW!
SO IF YOUNG ZIM TAKES OLD ZIM'S THRONE, THEN YOUNG ZIM WILL NEVER GO BACK IN TIME AND BECOME OLD ZIM WHO TAKES OVER EARTH, SO THEN YOUNG ZIM WON'T BE ABLE TO TAKE OLD ZIM'S THRONE BECAUSE—
JUST DON'T THINK ABOUT.

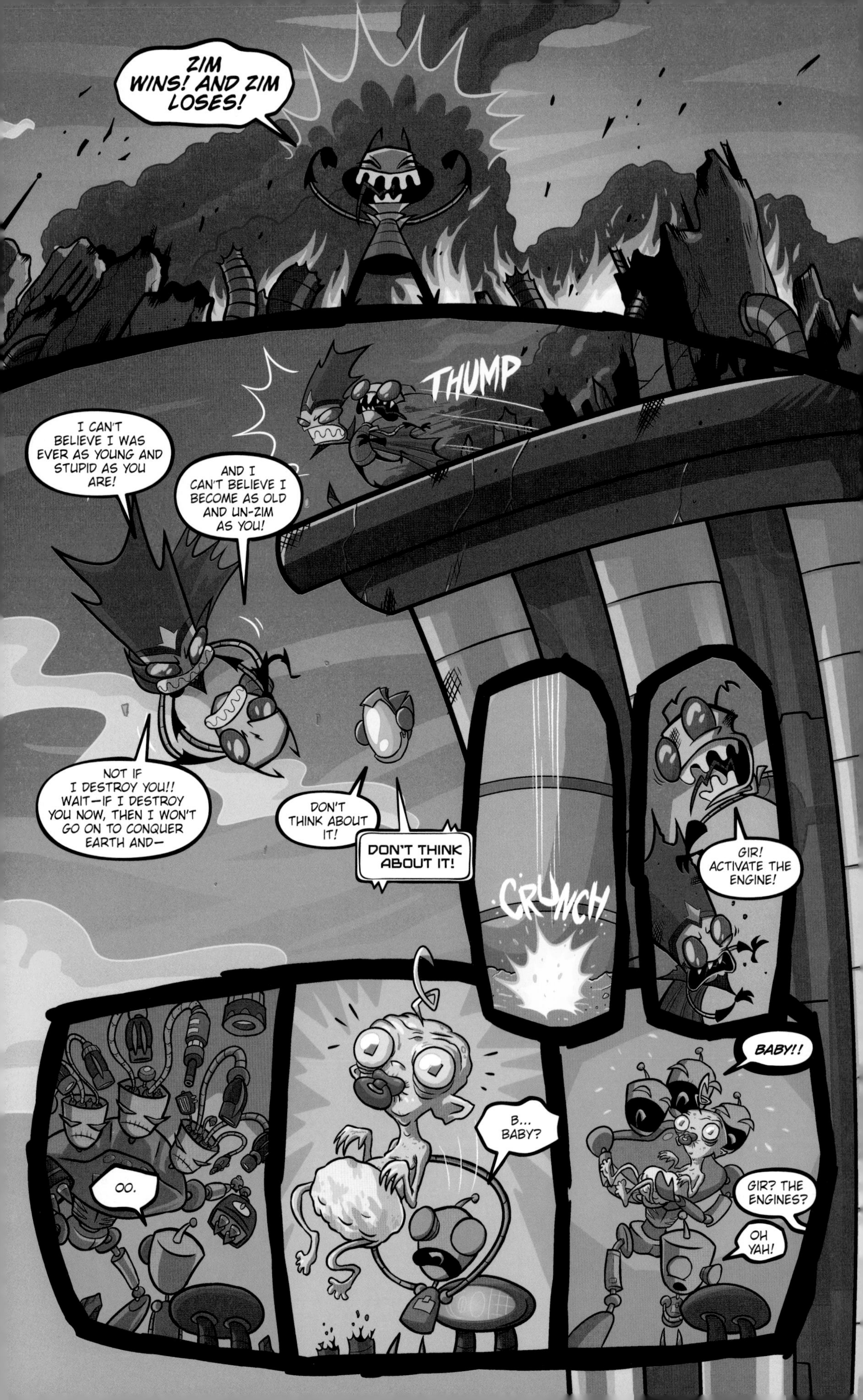
ZIM WINS! AND ZIM LOSES!
THUMP
I CAN'T BELIEVE I WAS EVER AS YOUNG AND STUPID AS YOU ARE!
AND I CAN'T BELIEVE I BECOME AS OLD AND UN-ZIM AS YOU!
NOT IF I DESTROY YOU!! WAIT—IF I DESTROY YOU NOW, THEN I WON'T GO ON TO CONQUER EARTH AND—
DON'T THINK ABOUT IT!
DON'T THINK ABOUT IT!
CRUNCH
GIR! ACTIVATE THE ENGINE!
OO.
B... BABY?
BABY!!
GIR? THE ENGINES?
OH YAH!

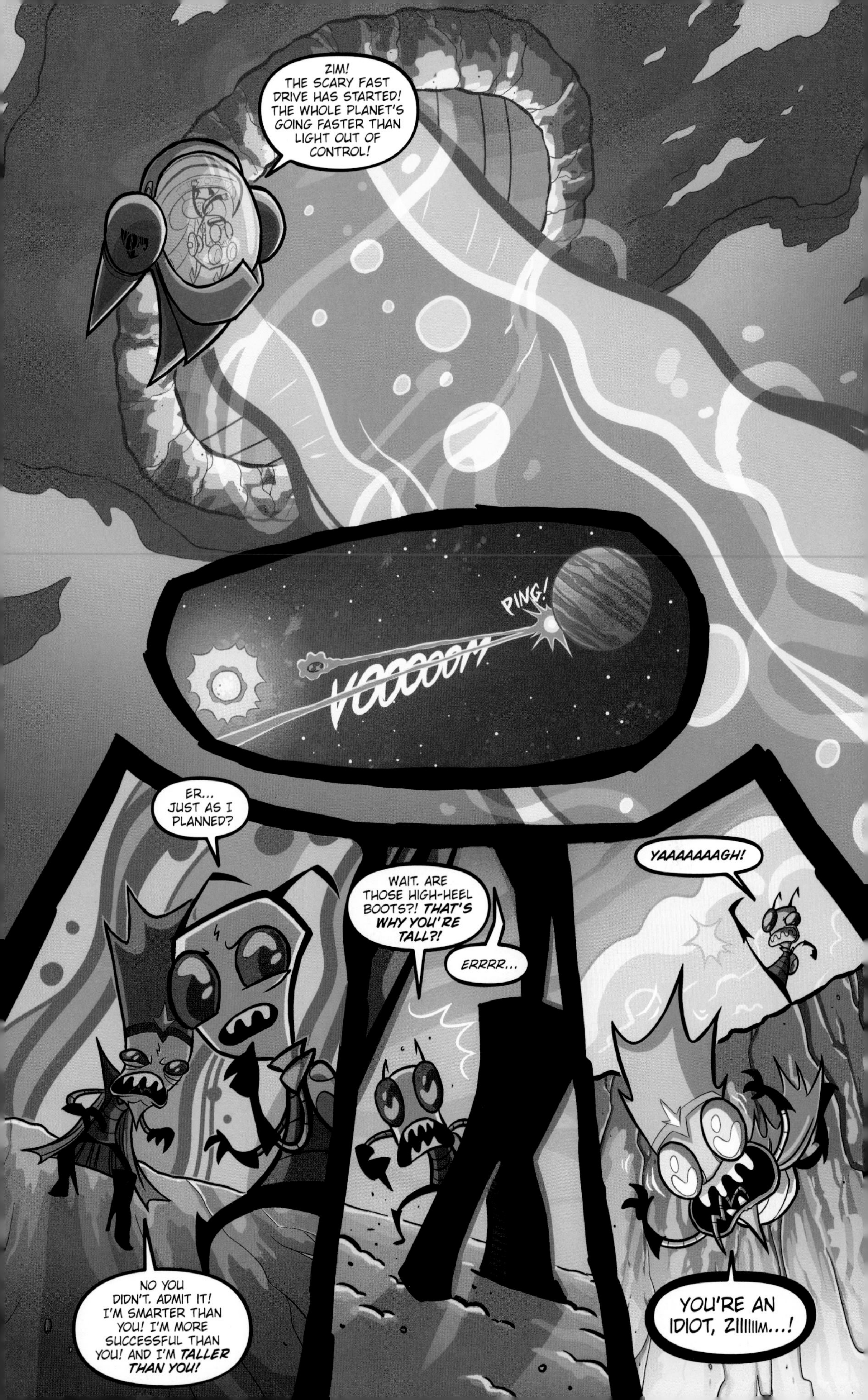
ZIM! THE SCARY FAST DRIVE HAS STARTED! THE WHOLE PLANET'S GOING FASTER THAN LIGHT OUT OF CONTROL!
PING!
VOOOOOOM
ER... JUST AS I PLANNED?
NO YOU DIDN'T. ADMIT IT! I'M SMARTER THAN YOU! I'M MORE SUCCESSFUL THAN YOU! AND I'M TALLER THAN YOU!
WAIT. ARE THOSE HIGH-HEEL BOOTS?! THAT'S WHY YOU'RE TALL?!
ERRRR...
YAAAAAAAGH!
YOU'RE AN IDIOT, ZIIIIIIM...!

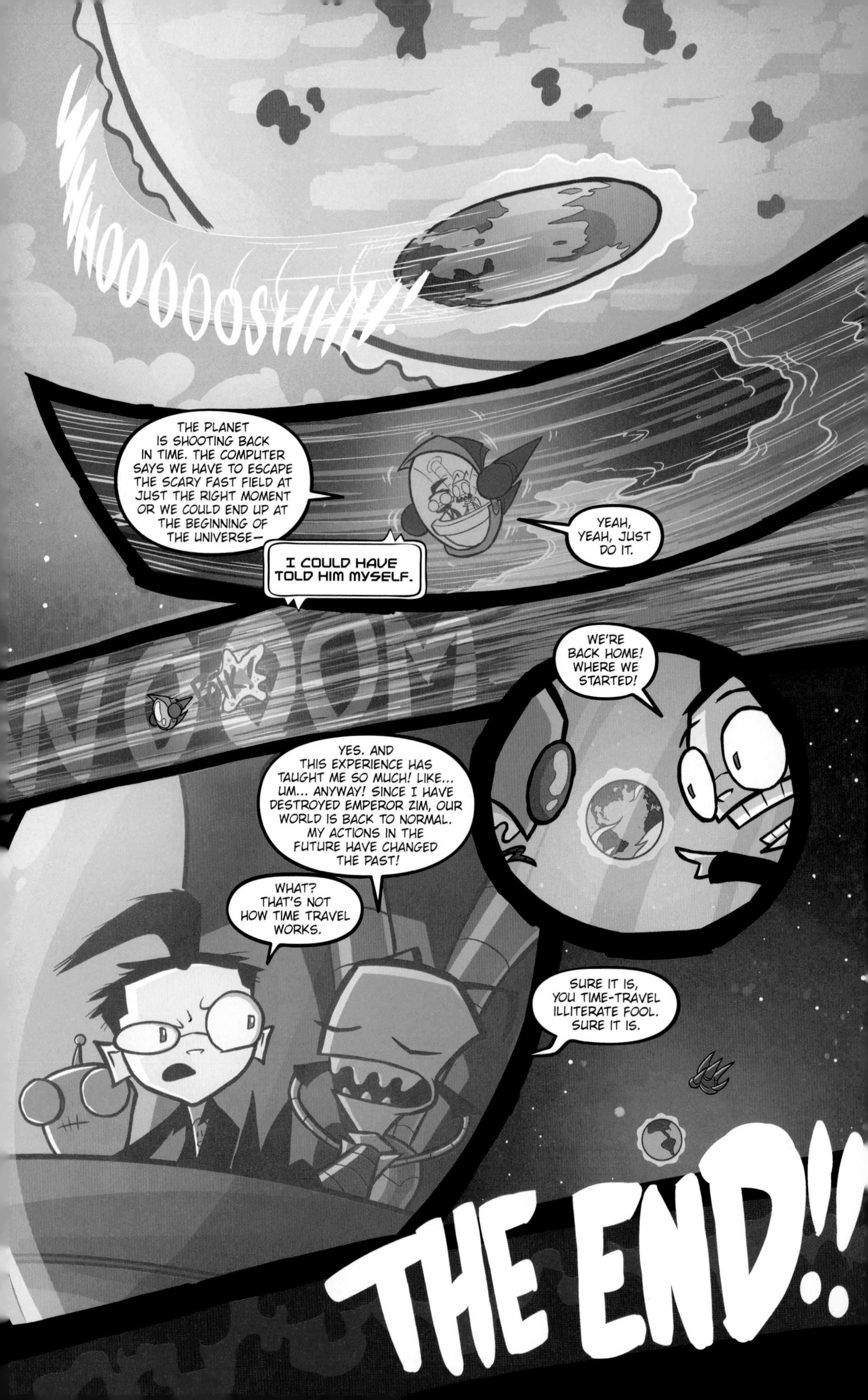
WHHOOOOOSHHH!
THE PLANET IS SHOOTING BACK IN TIME. THE COMPUTER SAYS WE HAVE TO ESCAPE THE SCARY FAST FIELD AT JUST THE RIGHT MOMENT OR WE COULD END UP AT THE BEGINNING OF THE UNIVERSE—
YEAH, YEAH, JUST DO IT.
I COULD HAVE TOLD HIM MYSELF.
WOOOM
WE'RE BACK HOME! WHERE WE STARTED!
YES. AND THIS EXPERIENCE HAS TAUGHT ME SO MUCH! LIKE... UM... ANYWAY! SINCE I HAVE DESTROYED EMPEROR ZIM, OUR WORLD IS BACK TO NORMAL. MY ACTIONS IN THE FUTURE HAVE CHANGED THE PAST!
WHAT? THAT'S NOT HOW TIME TRAVEL WORKS.
SURE IT IS, YOU TIME-TRAVEL ILLITERATE FOOL. SURE IT IS.
THE END!!

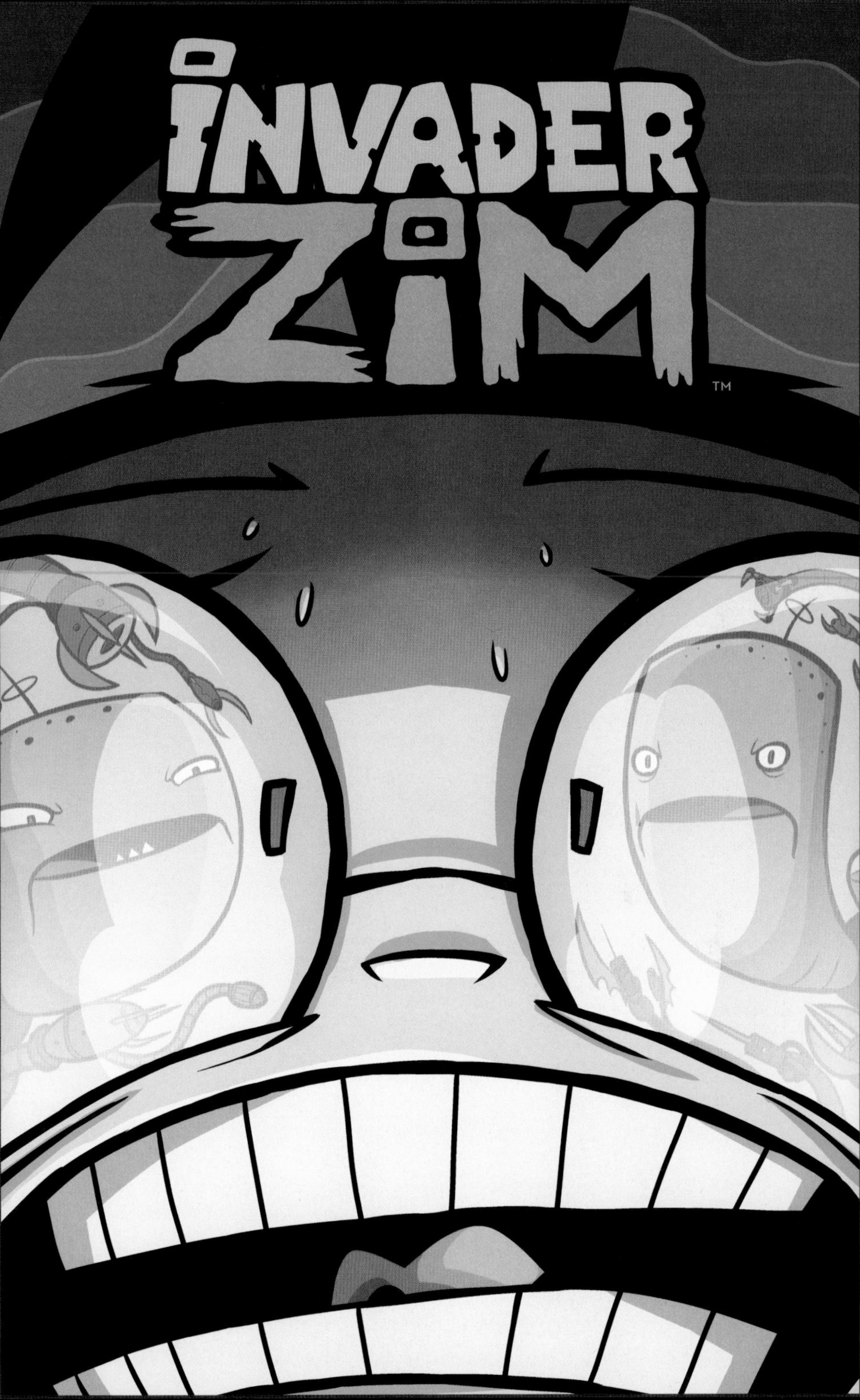
INVADER
ZIM
TM

CHAPTER: 3

illustration by WARREN WUCINICH

HEY GUYS! Recap Kid here again, keeping track of every single thing that happens in the Invader ZIM universe! Remember last issue? It was all about ZIM and Dib and GIR and a baby going forward in time to where ZIM actually rules the earth for once! HA! It was REAL FUNNY but I think I understand time travel EVEN LESS NOW! HA HA HA! WHAT DAY IS IT? OH, there's a new issue! AAAAAAAA! This one's got aliens who AREN'T ZIM but just looking at them makes me laugh! Look at their BIG HEADS! WOW! I wonder what it's like to have a head BIGGER than your ENTIRE BODY! Weird probably! I DUNNO!

Recap Kid by WARREN WUCINICH

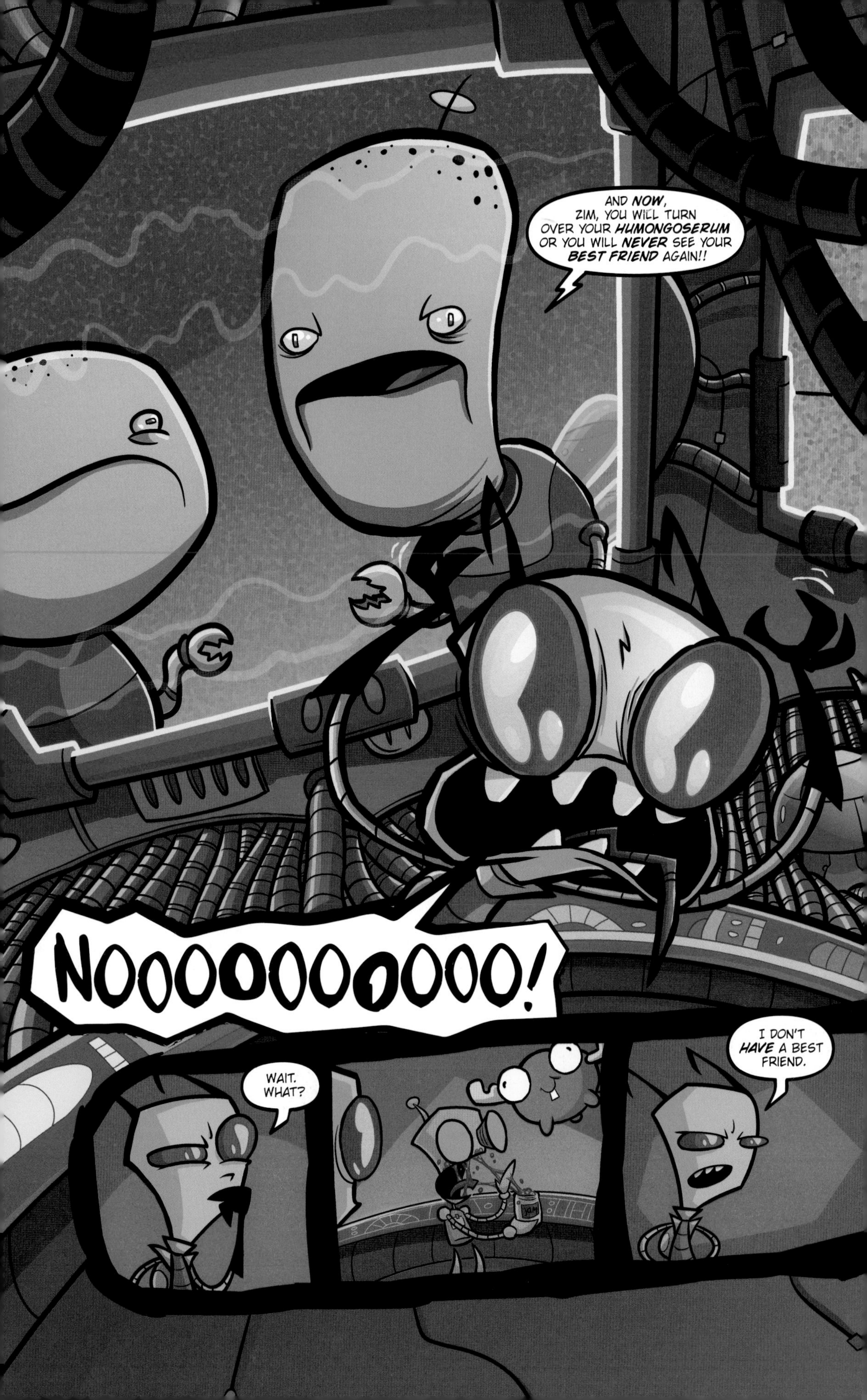
AND **NOW**, ZIM, YOU WILL TURN OVER YOUR **HUMONGOSERUM** OR YOU WILL **NEVER** SEE YOUR **BEST FRIEND** AGAIN!!
NOOOOOOOOOO!
WAIT. WHAT?
I DON'T **HAVE** A BEST FRIEND.

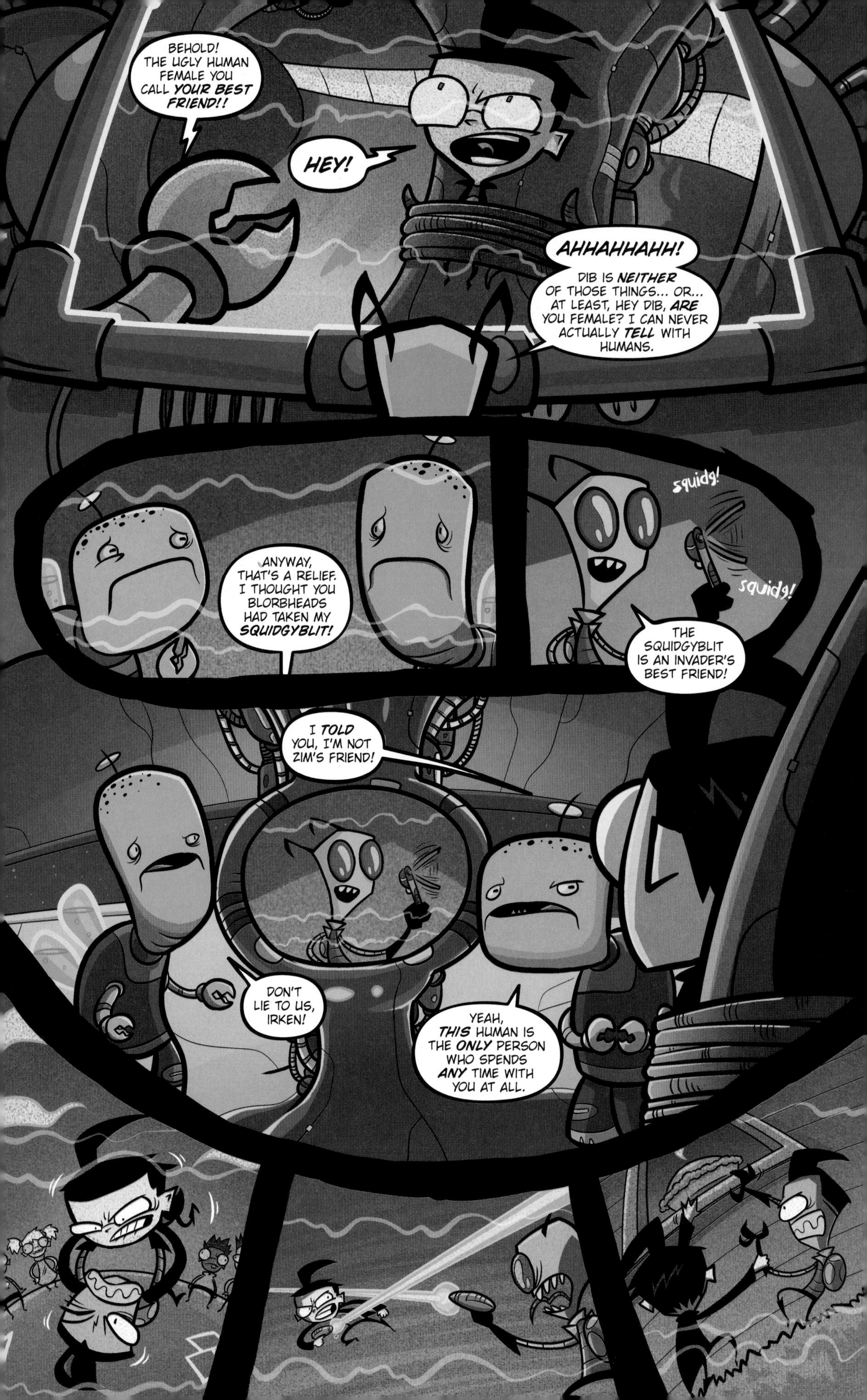
BEHOLD! THE UGLY HUMAN FEMALE YOU CALL YOUR BEST FRIEND!!
HEY!
AHHAHHAHH!
DIB IS NEITHER OF THOSE THINGS... OR... AT LEAST, HEY DIB, ARE YOU FEMALE? I CAN NEVER ACTUALLY TELL WITH HUMANS.
squidg!
squidg!
ANYWAY, THAT'S A RELIEF. I THOUGHT YOU BLORBHEADS HAD TAKEN MY SQUIDGYBLIT!
THE SQUIDGYBLIT IS AN INVADER'S BEST FRIEND!
I TOLD YOU, I'M NOT ZIM'S FRIEND!
DON'T LIE TO US, IRKEN!
YEAH, THIS HUMAN IS THE ONLY PERSON WHO SPENDS ANY TIME WITH YOU AT ALL.

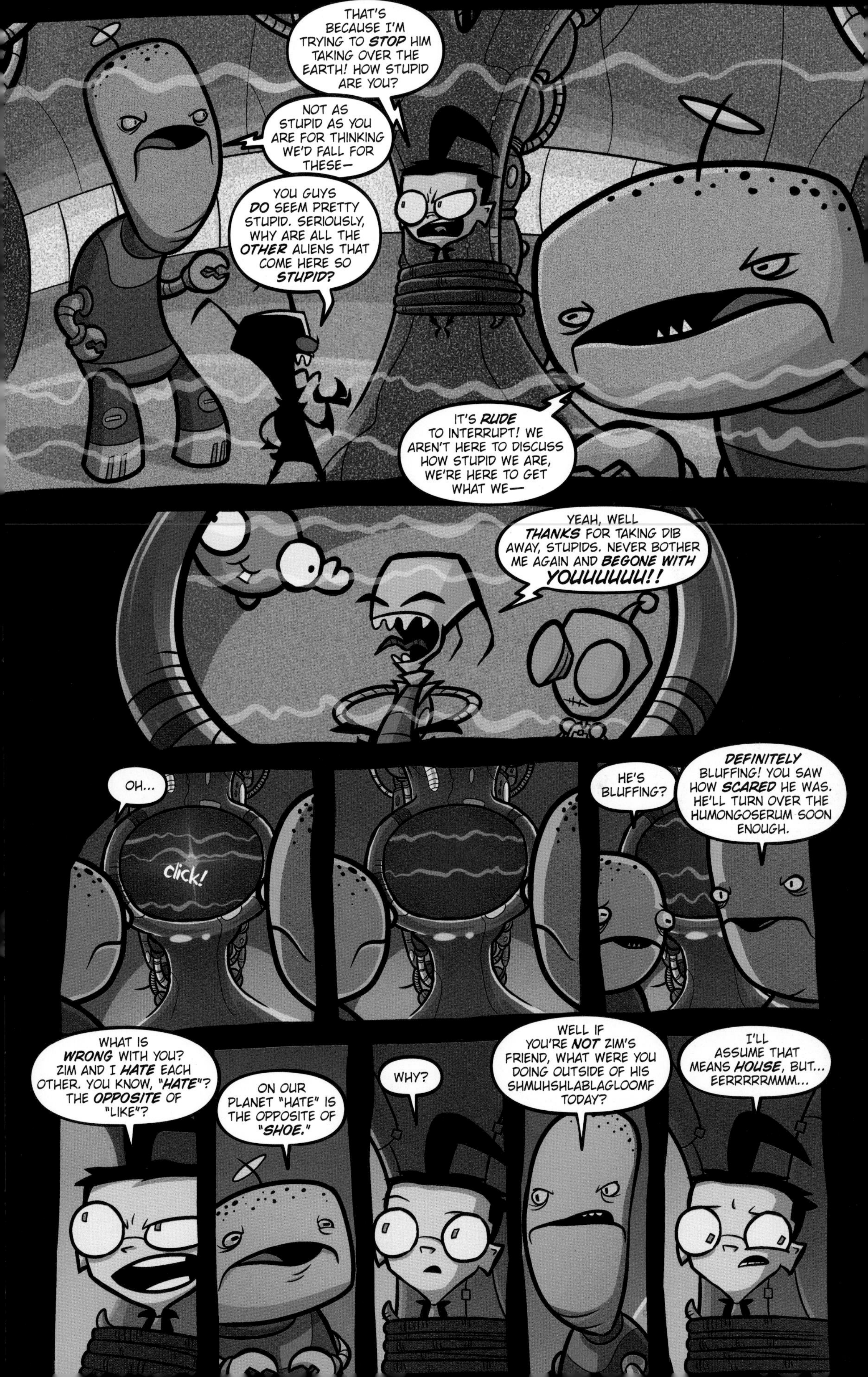
THAT'S BECAUSE I'M TRYING TO STOP HIM TAKING OVER THE EARTH! HOW STUPID ARE YOU?
NOT AS STUPID AS YOU ARE FOR THINKING WE'D FALL FOR THESE—
YOU GUYS DO SEEM PRETTY STUPID. SERIOUSLY, WHY ARE ALL THE OTHER ALIENS THAT COME HERE SO STUPID?
IT'S RUDE TO INTERRUPT! WE AREN'T HERE TO DISCUSS HOW STUPID WE ARE, WE'RE HERE TO GET WHAT WE—
YEAH, WELL THANKS FOR TAKING DIB AWAY, STUPIDS. NEVER BOTHER ME AGAIN AND BEGONE WITH YOUUUUUU!!
OH...
click!
HE'S BLUFFING?
DEFINITELY BLUFFING! YOU SAW HOW SCARED HE WAS. HE'LL TURN OVER THE HUMONGOSERUM SOON ENOUGH.
WHAT IS WRONG WITH YOU? ZIM AND I HATE EACH OTHER. YOU KNOW, "HATE"? THE OPPOSITE OF "LIKE"?
ON OUR PLANET "HATE" IS THE OPPOSITE OF "SHOE."
WHY?
WELL IF YOU'RE NOT ZIM'S FRIEND, WHAT WERE YOU DOING OUTSIDE OF HIS SHMUHSHLABLAGLOOMF TODAY?
I'LL ASSUME THAT MEANS HOUSE, BUT... EERRRRRMMM...

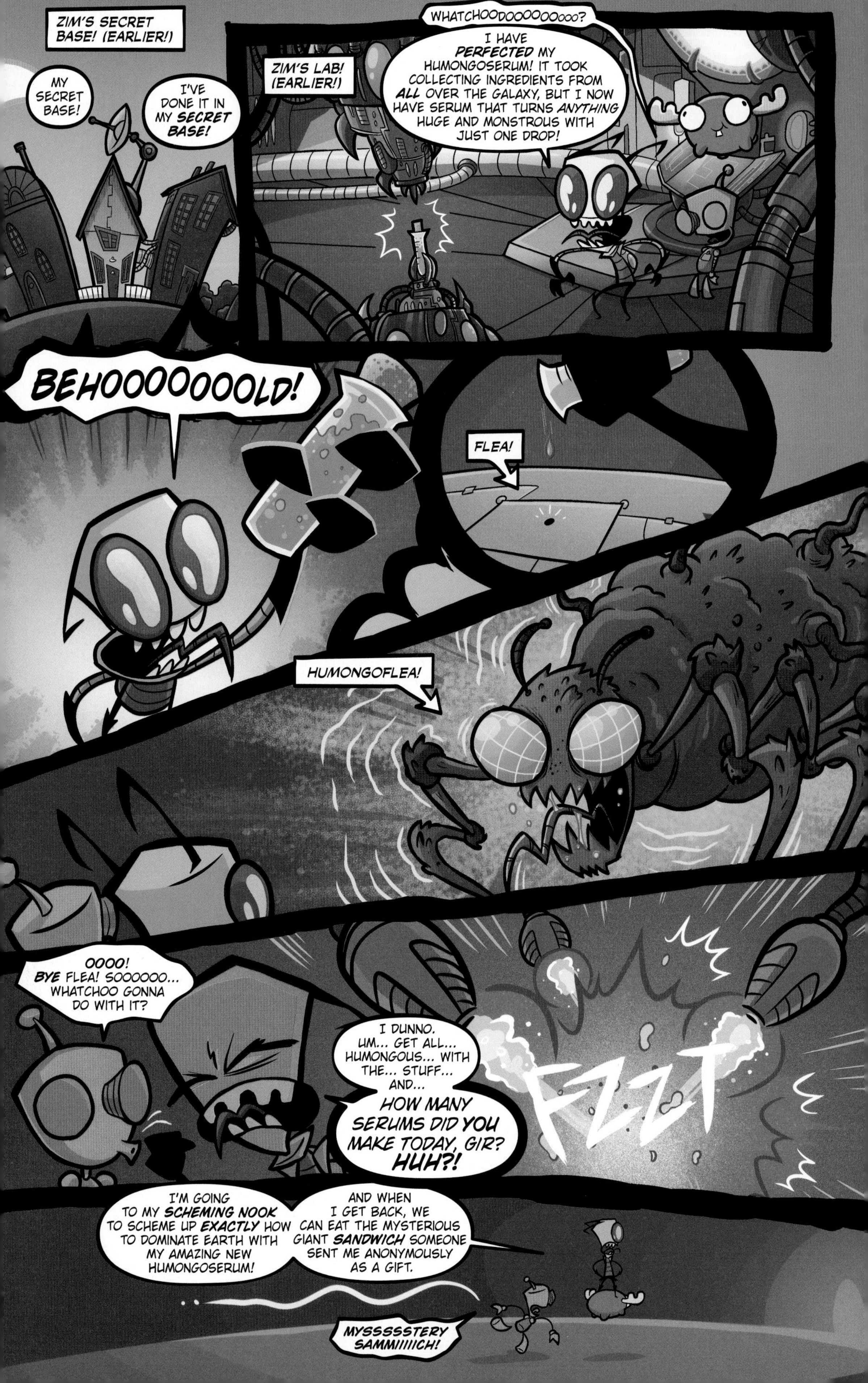
ZIM'S SECRET BASE! (EARLIER!)
MY SECRET BASE!
I'VE DONE IT IN MY SECRET BASE!
WHATCHOODOOOOOOOooo?
ZIM'S LAB! (EARLIER!)
I HAVE PERFECTED MY HUMONGOSERUM! IT TOOK COLLECTING INGREDIENTS FROM ALL OVER THE GALAXY, BUT I NOW HAVE SERUM THAT TURNS ANYTHING HUGE AND MONSTROUS WITH JUST ONE DROP!
BEHOOOOOOOLD!
FLEA!
HUMONGOFLEA!
OOOO! BYE FLEA! SOOOOOO... WHATCHOO GONNA DO WITH IT?
I DUNNO. UM... GET ALL... HUMONGOUS... WITH THE... STUFF... AND...
HOW MANY SERUMS DID YOU MAKE TODAY, GIR? HUH?!
FZZT
I'M GOING TO MY SCHEMING NOOK TO SCHEME UP EXACTLY HOW TO DOMINATE EARTH WITH MY AMAZING NEW HUMONGOSERUM!
AND WHEN I GET BACK, WE CAN EAT THE MYSTERIOUS GIANT SANDWICH SOMEONE SENT ME ANONYMOUSLY AS A GIFT.
MYSSSSSTERY SAMMIIIIICH!

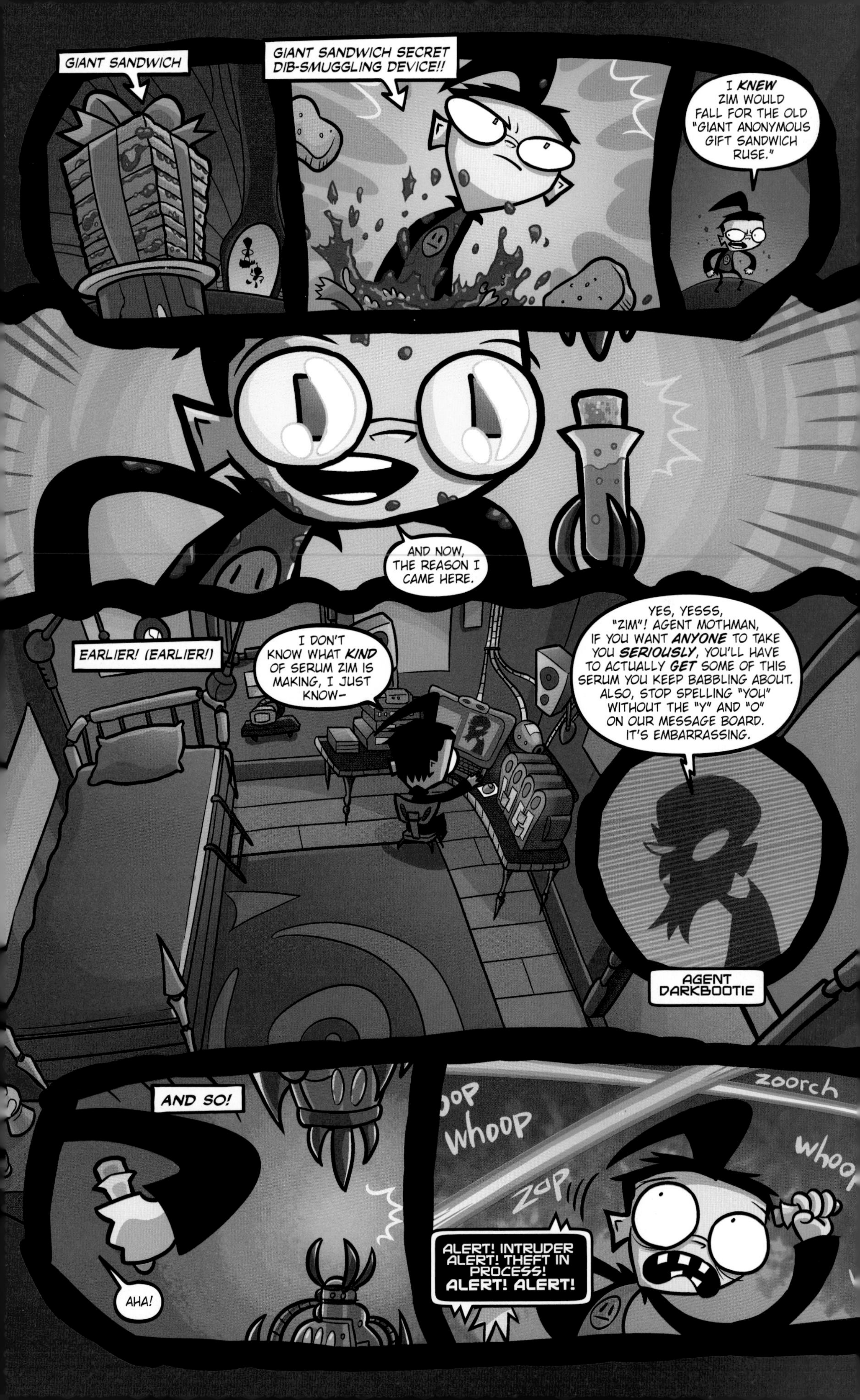
GIANT SANDWICH
GIANT SANDWICH SECRET DIB-SMUGGLING DEVICE!!
I KNEW ZIM WOULD FALL FOR THE OLD "GIANT ANONYMOUS GIFT SANDWICH RUSE."
AND NOW, THE REASON I CAME HERE.
EARLIER! (EARLIER!)
I DON'T KNOW WHAT KIND OF SERUM ZIM IS MAKING, I JUST KNOW–
YES, YESSS, "ZIM"! AGENT MOTHMAN, IF YOU WANT ANYONE TO TAKE YOU SERIOUSLY, YOU'LL HAVE TO ACTUALLY GET SOME OF THIS SERUM YOU KEEP BABBLING ABOUT. ALSO, STOP SPELLING "YOU" WITHOUT THE "Y" AND "O" ON OUR MESSAGE BOARD. IT'S EMBARRASSING.
AGENT DARKBOOTIE
AND SO!
AHA!
oop whoop
zoorch
whoop
ZAP
ALERT! INTRUDER ALERT! THEFT IN PROCESS! ALERT! ALERT!

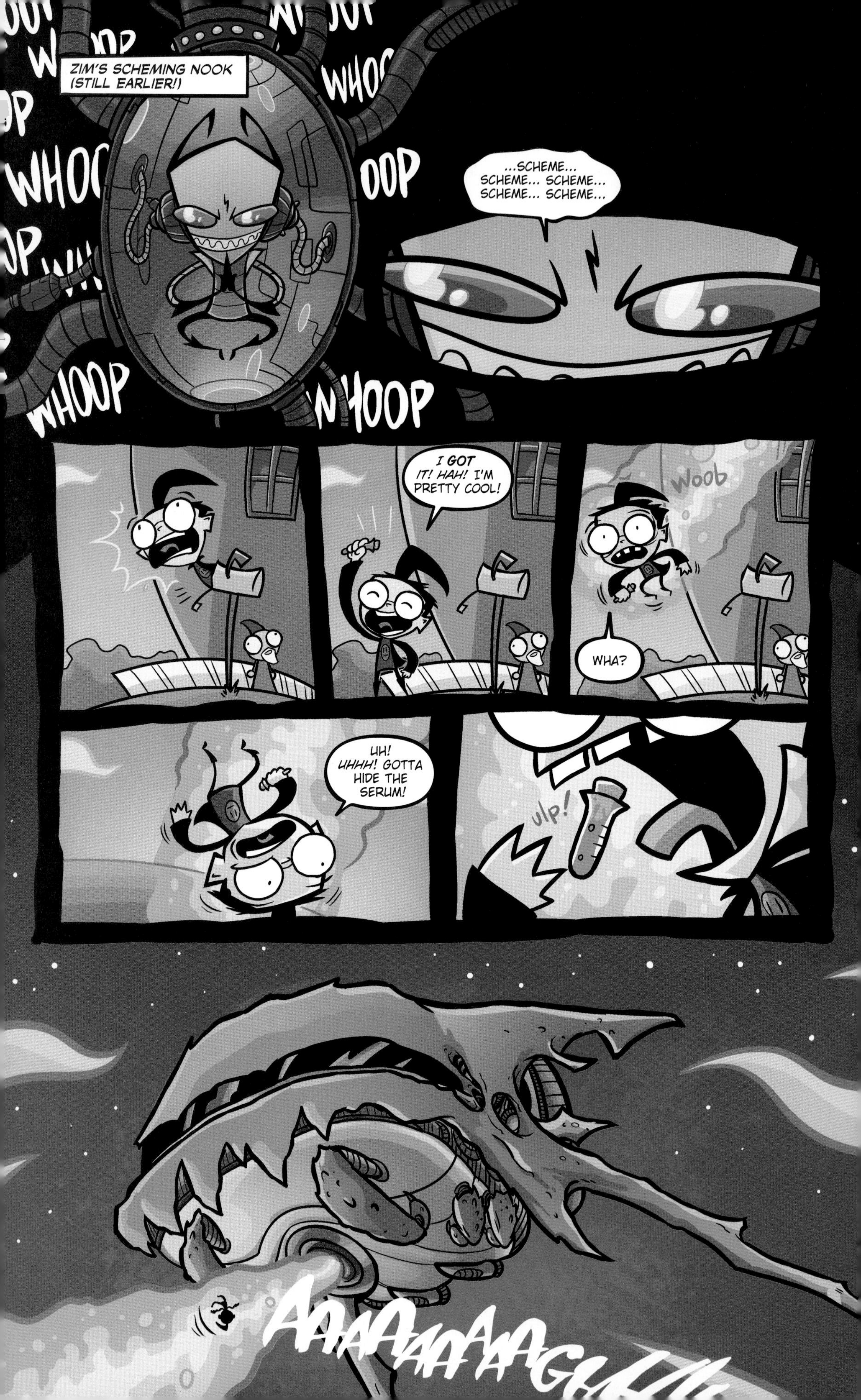
ZIM'S SCHEMING NOOK (STILL EARLIER!)
WHOOP
WHOOP
WHOOP
WHOOP
WHOOP
...SCHEME... SCHEME... SCHEME... SCHEME... SCHEME...
I GOT IT! HAH! I'M PRETTY COOL!
woob
WHA?
UH! UHHH! GOTTA HIDE THE SERUM!
ulp!
AAAAAAAAAGHHH

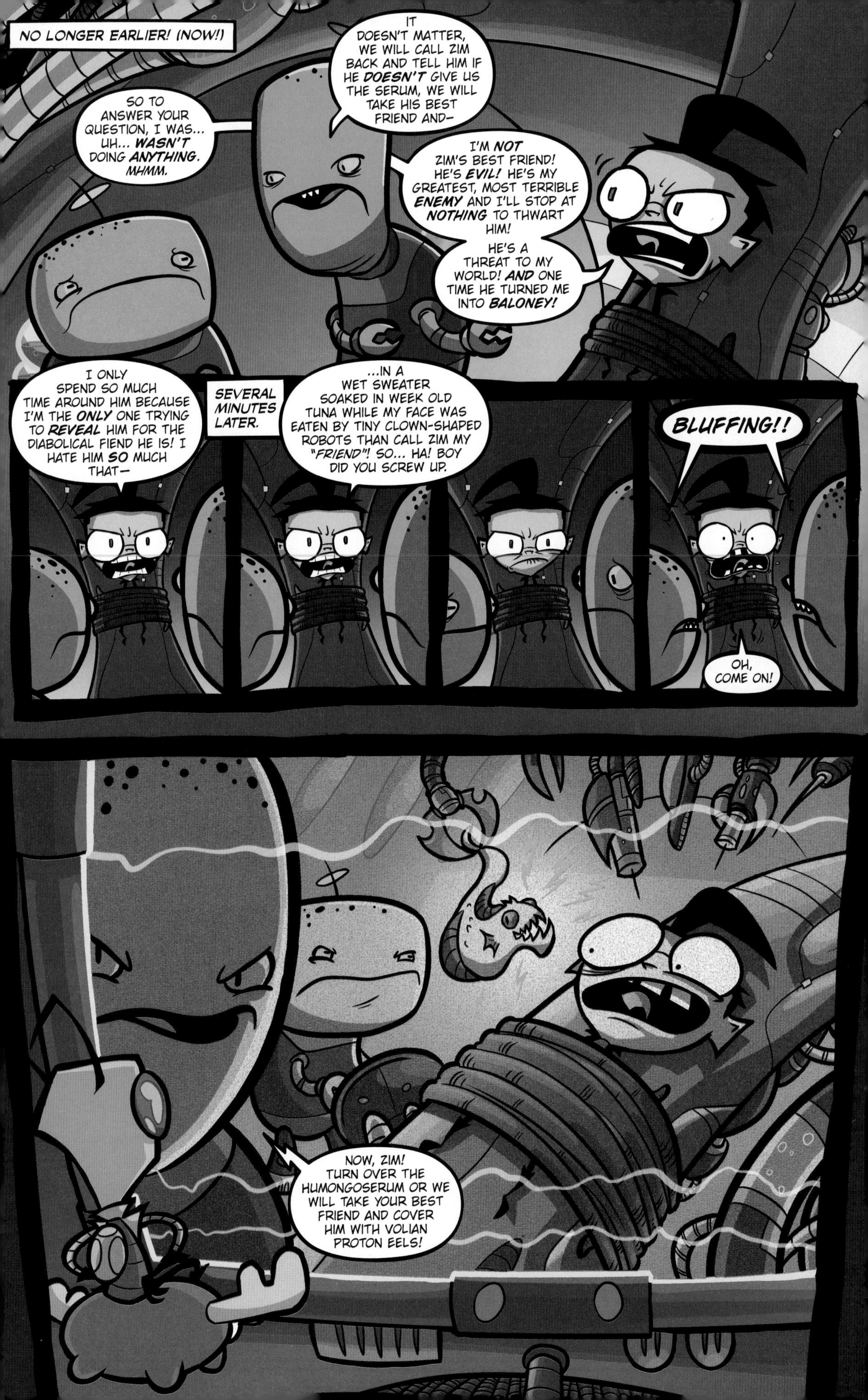
NO LONGER EARLIER! (NOW!)
SO TO ANSWER YOUR QUESTION, I WAS... UH... WASN'T DOING ANYTHING. MHMM.
IT DOESN'T MATTER, WE WILL CALL ZIM BACK AND TELL HIM IF HE DOESN'T GIVE US THE SERUM, WE WILL TAKE HIS BEST FRIEND AND–
I'M NOT ZIM'S BEST FRIEND! HE'S EVIL! HE'S MY GREATEST, MOST TERRIBLE ENEMY AND I'LL STOP AT NOTHING TO THWART HIM!
HE'S A THREAT TO MY WORLD! AND ONE TIME HE TURNED ME INTO BALONEY!
I ONLY SPEND SO MUCH TIME AROUND HIM BECAUSE I'M THE ONLY ONE TRYING TO REVEAL HIM FOR THE DIABOLICAL FIEND HE IS! I HATE HIM SO MUCH THAT–
SEVERAL MINUTES LATER.
...IN A WET SWEATER SOAKED IN WEEK OLD TUNA WHILE MY FACE WAS EATEN BY TINY CLOWN-SHAPED ROBOTS THAN CALL ZIM MY "FRIEND"! SO... HA! BOY DID YOU SCREW UP.
BLUFFING!!
OH, COME ON!
NOW, ZIM! TURN OVER THE HUMONGOSERUM OR WE WILL TAKE YOUR BEST FRIEND AND COVER HIM WITH VOLIAN PROTON EELS!

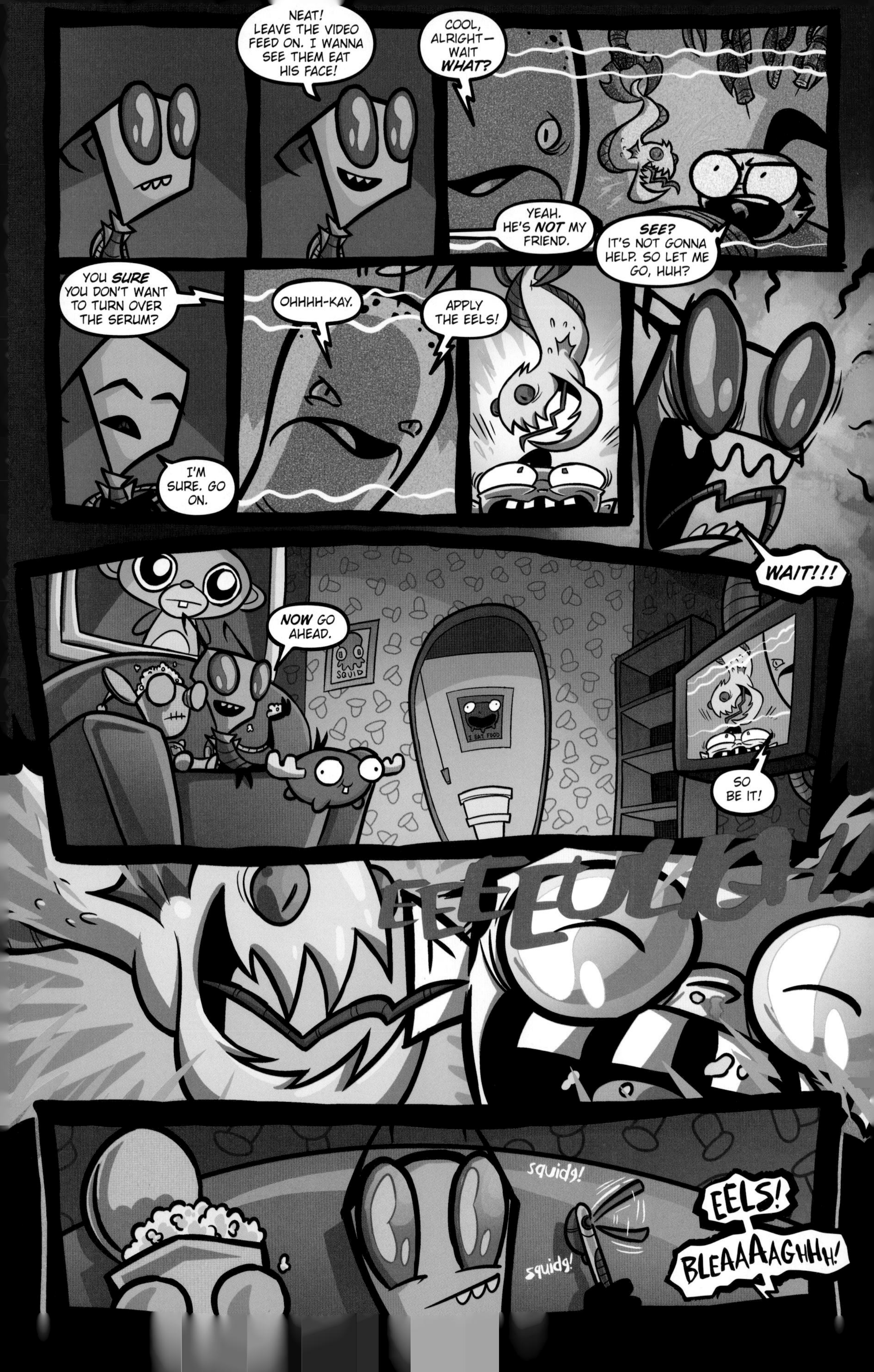
NEAT! LEAVE THE VIDEO FEED ON. I WANNA SEE THEM EAT HIS FACE!
COOL, ALRIGHT— WAIT WHAT?
YEAH. HE'S NOT MY FRIEND.
SEE? IT'S NOT GONNA HELP. SO LET ME GO, HUH?
YOU SURE YOU DON'T WANT TO TURN OVER THE SERUM?
I'M SURE. GO ON.
OHHHH-KAY.
APPLY THE EELS!
WAIT!!!
NOW GO AHEAD.
SQUID
I EAT FOOD
SO BE IT!
EEEEUUGH!!
squidg!
squidg!
EELS!
BLEAAAAGHHH!

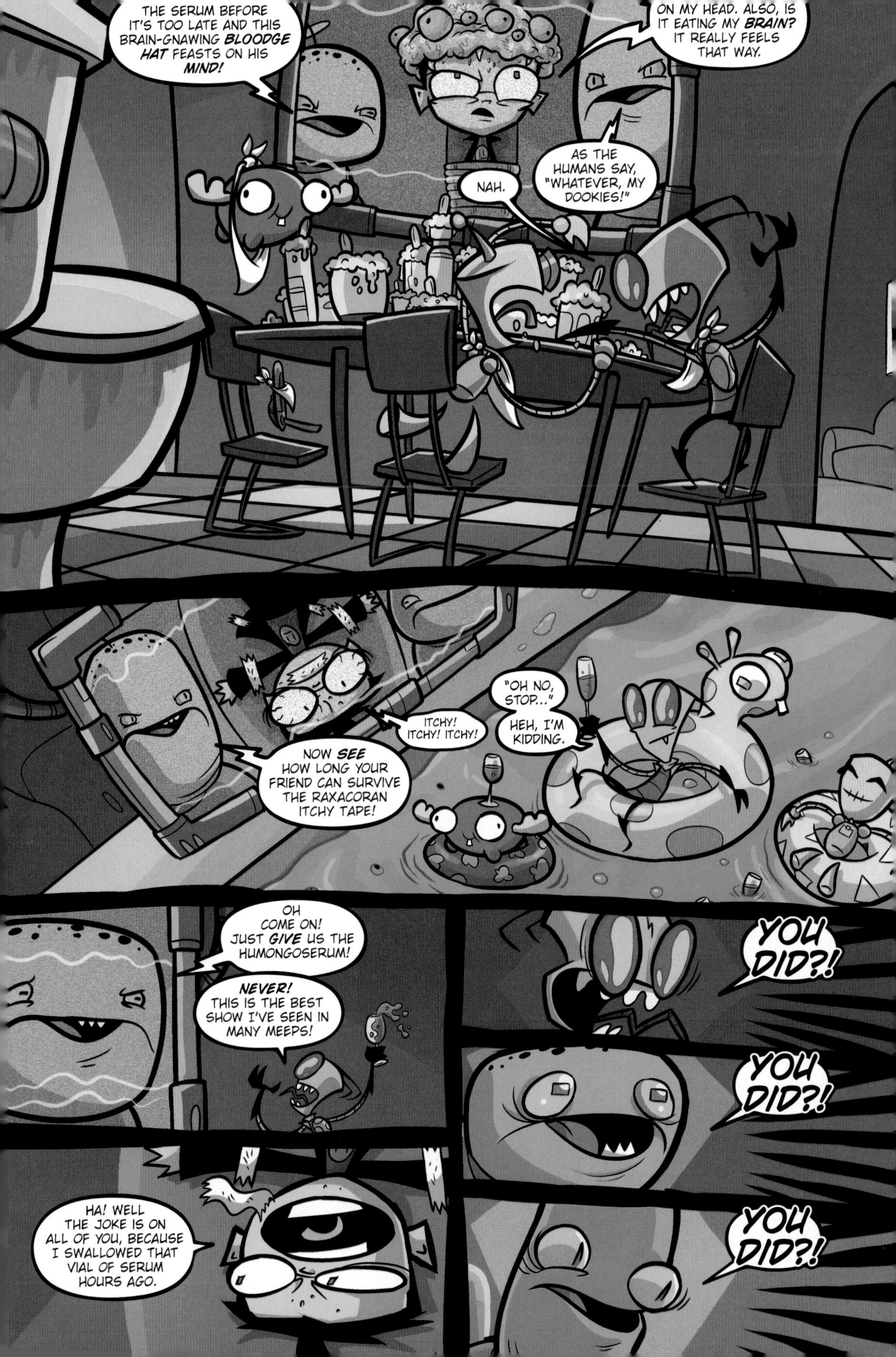
THE SERUM BEFORE IT'S TOO LATE AND THIS BRAIN-GNAWING BLOODGE HAT FEASTS ON HIS MIND!
ON MY HEAD. ALSO, IS IT EATING MY BRAIN? IT REALLY FEELS THAT WAY.
AS THE HUMANS SAY, "WHATEVER, MY DOOKIES!"
NAH.
ITCHY! ITCHY! ITCHY!
NOW SEE HOW LONG YOUR FRIEND CAN SURVIVE THE RAXACORAN ITCHY TAPE!
"OH NO, STOP..."
HEH, I'M KIDDING.
OH COME ON! JUST GIVE US THE HUMONGOSERUM!
NEVER! THIS IS THE BEST SHOW I'VE SEEN IN MANY MEEPS!
HA! WELL THE JOKE IS ON ALL OF YOU, BECAUSE I SWALLOWED THAT VIAL OF SERUM HOURS AGO.
YOU DID?!
YOU DID?!
YOU DID?!

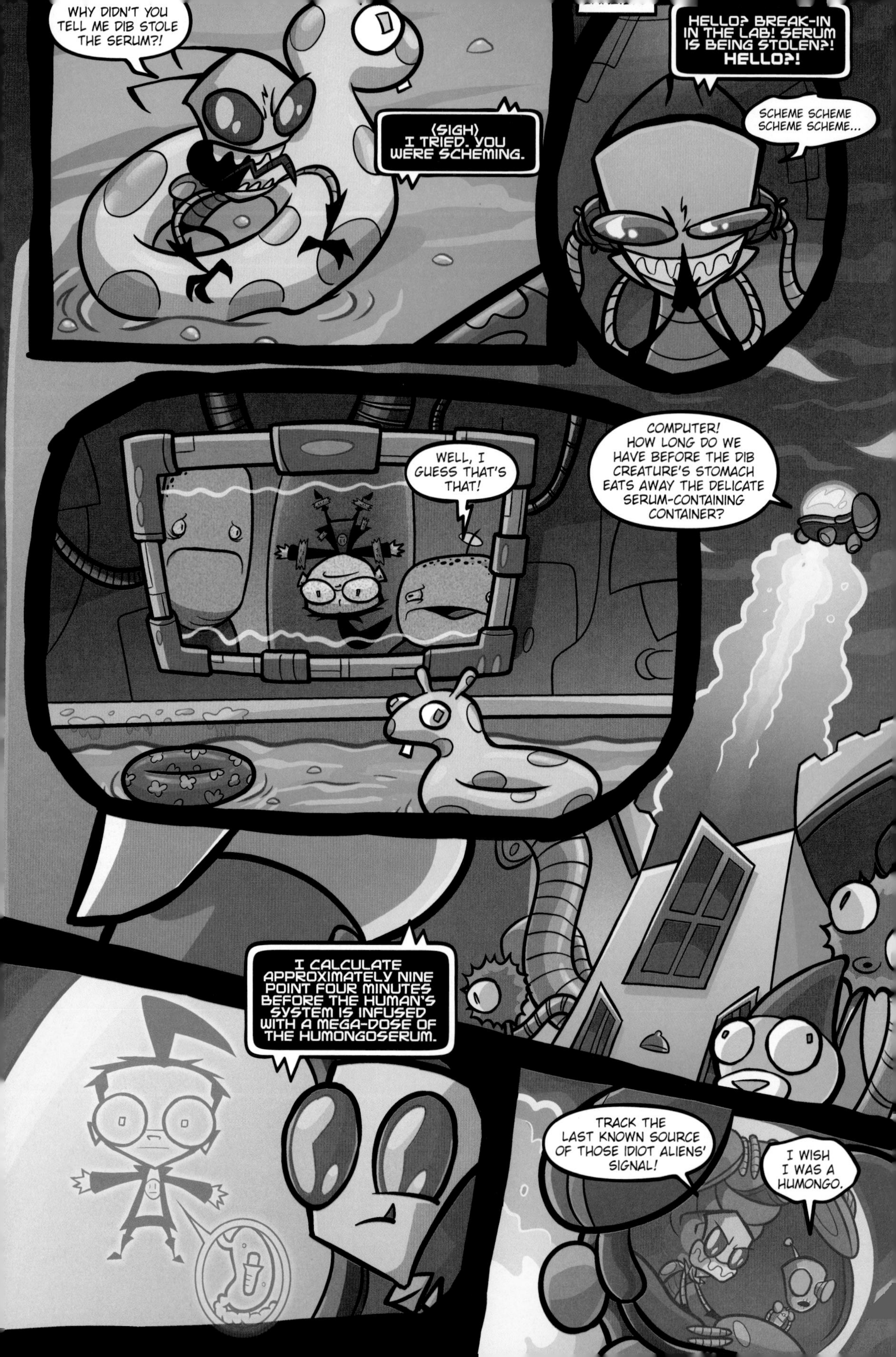
WHY DIDN'T YOU TELL ME DIB STOLE THE SERUM?!
(SIGH) I TRIED. YOU WERE SCHEMING.
HELLO? BREAK-IN IN THE LAB! SERUM IS BEING STOLEN?! HELLO?!
SCHEME SCHEME SCHEME SCHEME...
WELL, I GUESS THAT'S THAT!
COMPUTER! HOW LONG DO WE HAVE BEFORE THE DIB CREATURE'S STOMACH EATS AWAY THE DELICATE SERUM-CONTAINING CONTAINER?
I CALCULATE APPROXIMATELY NINE POINT FOUR MINUTES BEFORE THE HUMAN'S SYSTEM IS INFUSED WITH A MEGA-DOSE OF THE HUMONGOSERUM.
TRACK THE LAST KNOWN SOURCE OF THOSE IDIOT ALIENS' SIGNAL!
I WISH I WAS A HUMONGO.

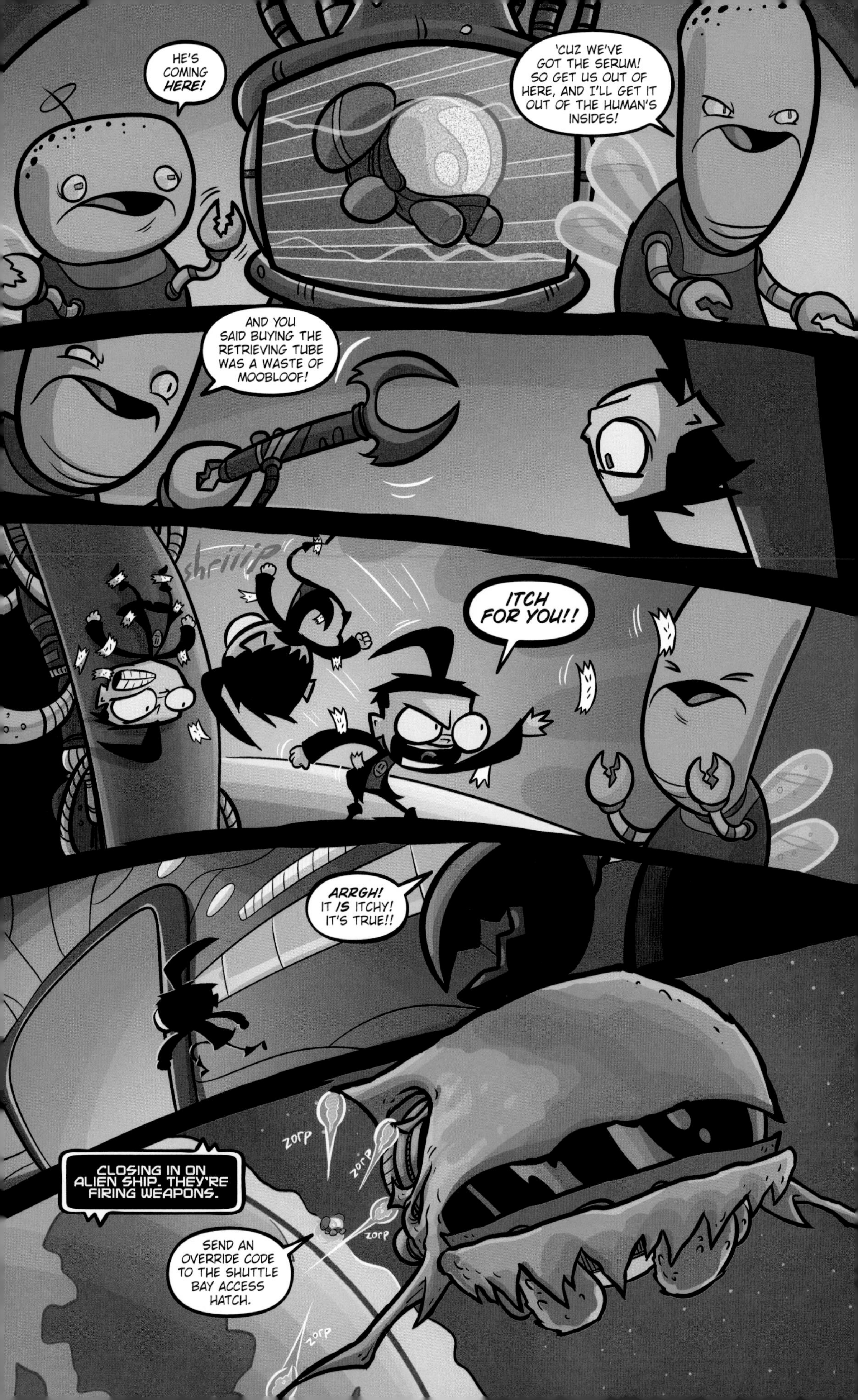
HE'S COMING HERE!
'CUZ WE'VE GOT THE SERUM! SO GET US OUT OF HERE, AND I'LL GET IT OUT OF THE HUMAN'S INSIDES!
AND YOU SAID BUYING THE RETRIEVING TUBE WAS A WASTE OF MOOBLOOF!
shriiiip
ITCH FOR YOU!!
ARRGH! IT IS ITCHY! IT'S TRUE!!
zorp
zorp
CLOSING IN ON ALIEN SHIP. THEY'RE FIRING WEAPONS.
zorp
SEND AN OVERRIDE CODE TO THE SHUTTLE BAY ACCESS HATCH.
zorp

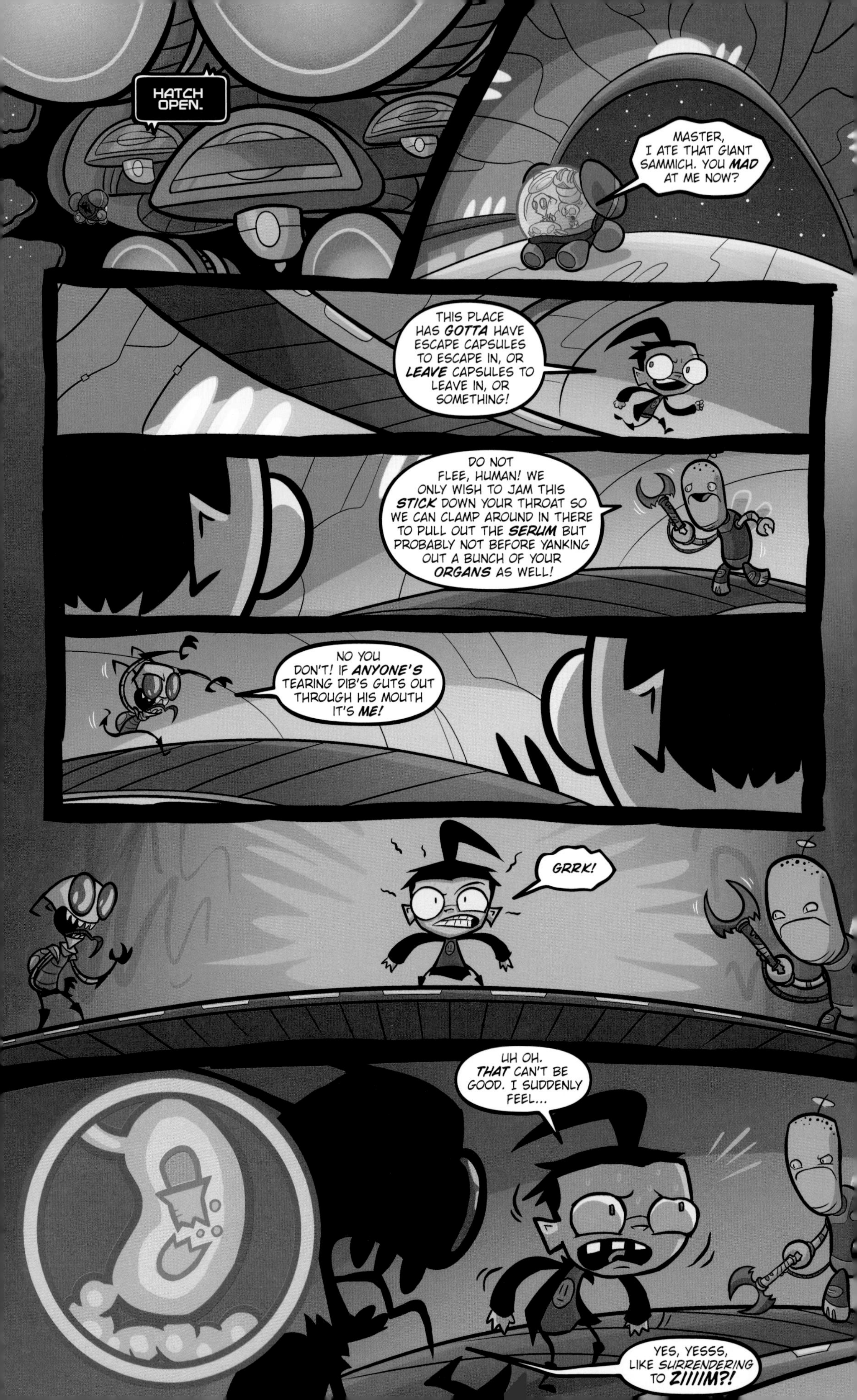
HATCH OPEN.
MASTER, I ATE THAT GIANT SAMMICH. YOU MAD AT ME NOW?
THIS PLACE HAS GOTTA HAVE ESCAPE CAPSULES TO ESCAPE IN, OR LEAVE CAPSULES TO LEAVE IN, OR SOMETHING!
DO NOT FLEE, HUMAN! WE ONLY WISH TO JAM THIS STICK DOWN YOUR THROAT SO WE CAN CLAMP AROUND IN THERE TO PULL OUT THE SERUM BUT PROBABLY NOT BEFORE YANKING OUT A BUNCH OF YOUR ORGANS AS WELL!
NO YOU DON'T! IF ANYONE'S TEARING DIB'S GUTS OUT THROUGH HIS MOUTH IT'S ME!
GRRK!
UH OH. THAT CAN'T BE GOOD. I SUDDENLY FEEL...
YES, YESSS, LIKE SURRENDERING TO ZIIIIM?!

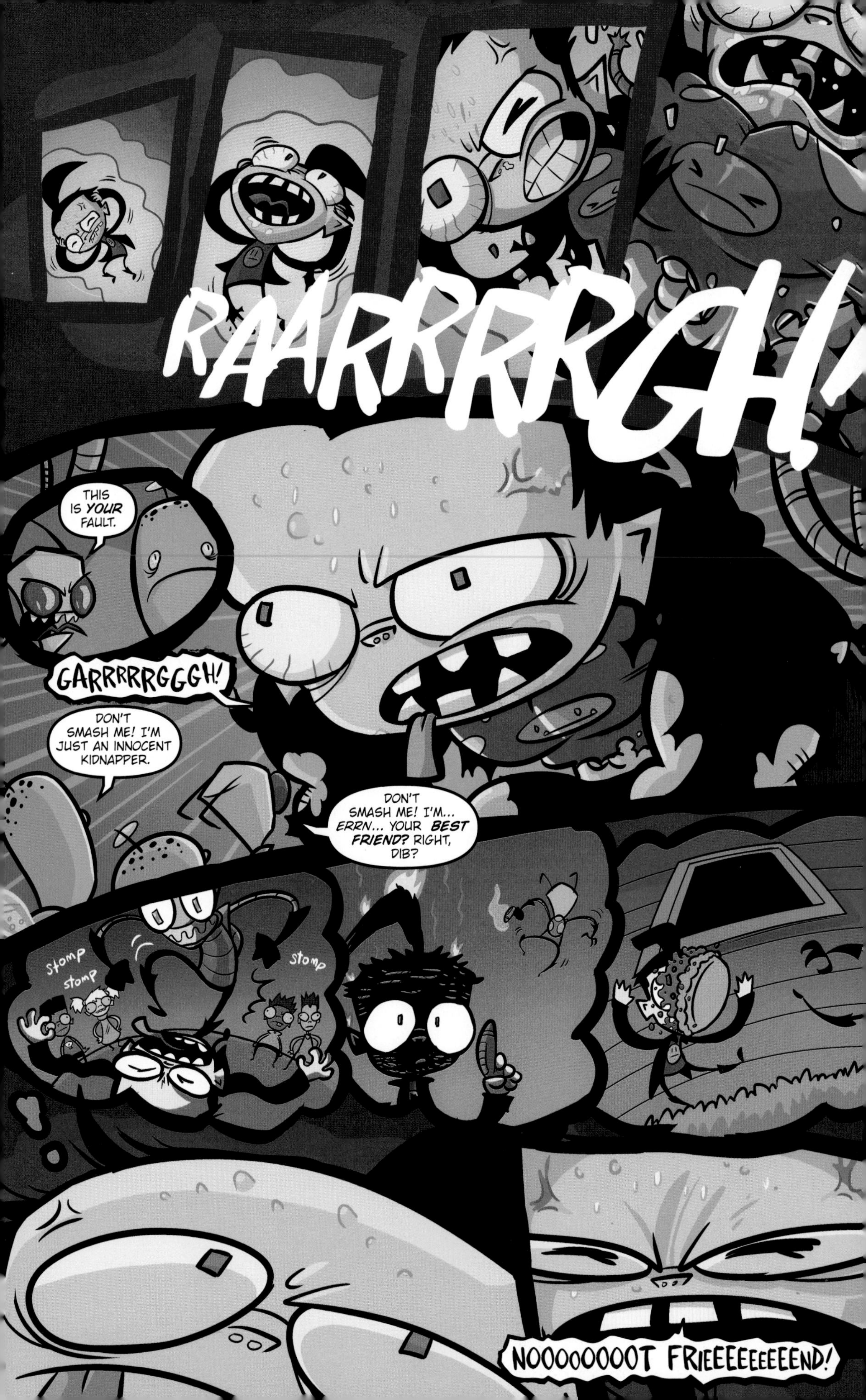
RAARRRRRGH!
THIS IS YOUR FAULT.
GARRRRRGGGH!
DON'T SMASH ME! I'M JUST AN INNOCENT KIDNAPPER.
DON'T SMASH ME! I'M... ERRN... YOUR BEST FRIEND? RIGHT, DIB?
stomp
stomp
stomp
NOOOOOOOOT FRIEEEEEEEEEND!

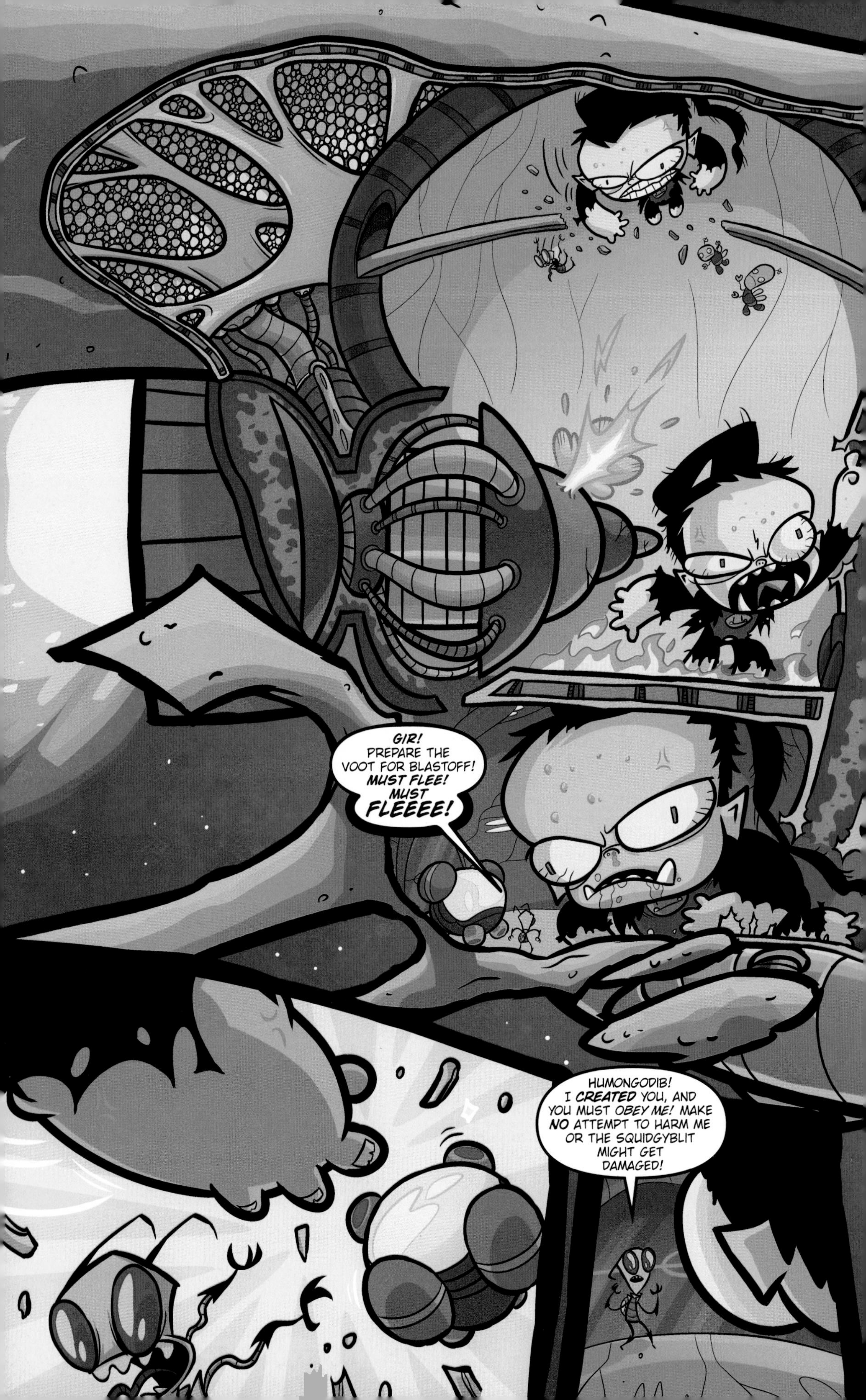
GIR! PREPARE THE VOOT FOR BLASTOFF! MUST FLEE! MUST FLEEEE!
HUMONGODIB! I CREATED YOU, AND YOU MUST OBEY ME! MAKE NO ATTEMPT TO HARM ME OR THE SQUIDGYBLIT MIGHT GET DAMAGED!

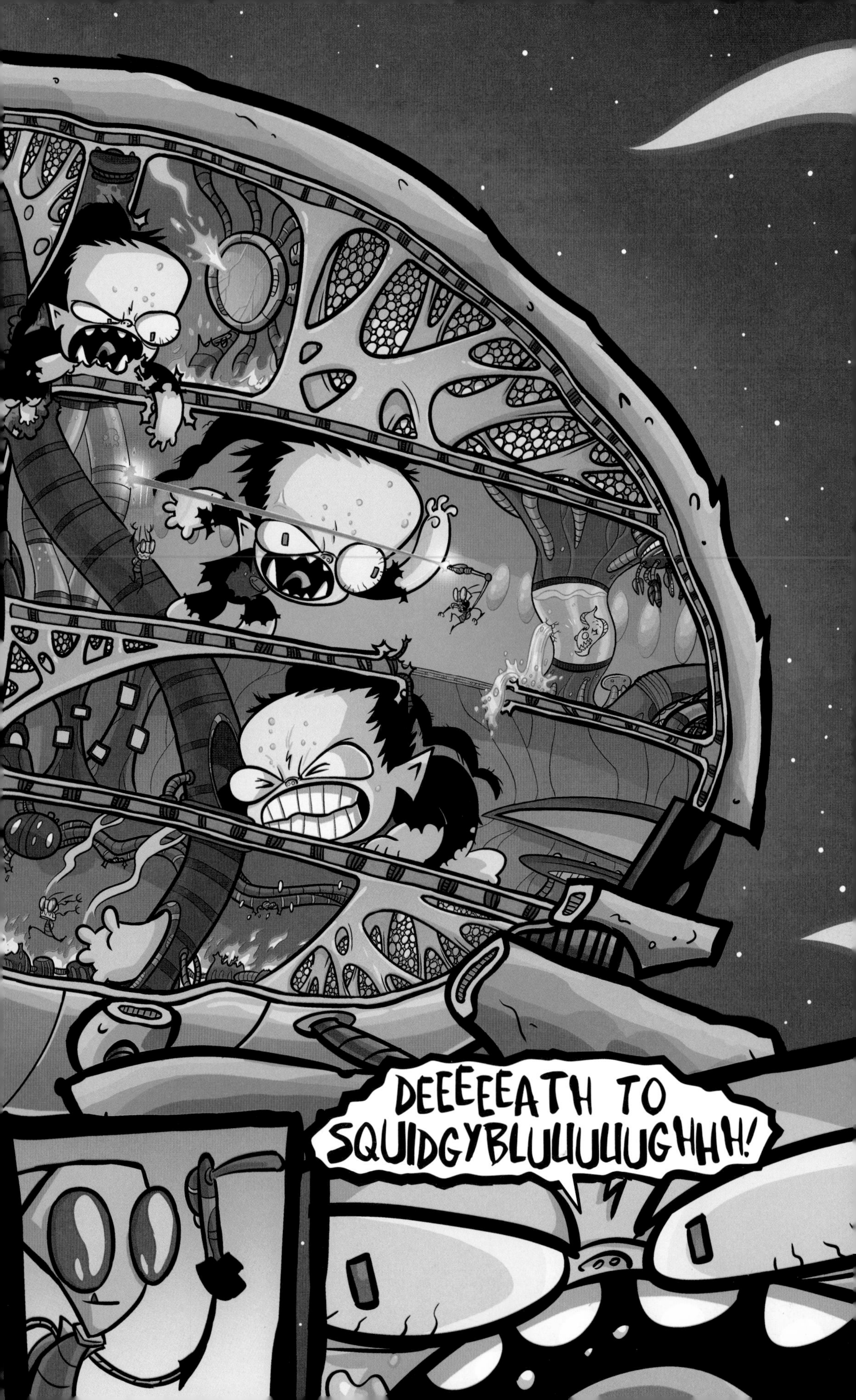
DEEEEEATH TO SQUIDGYBLUUUUUGHHH!

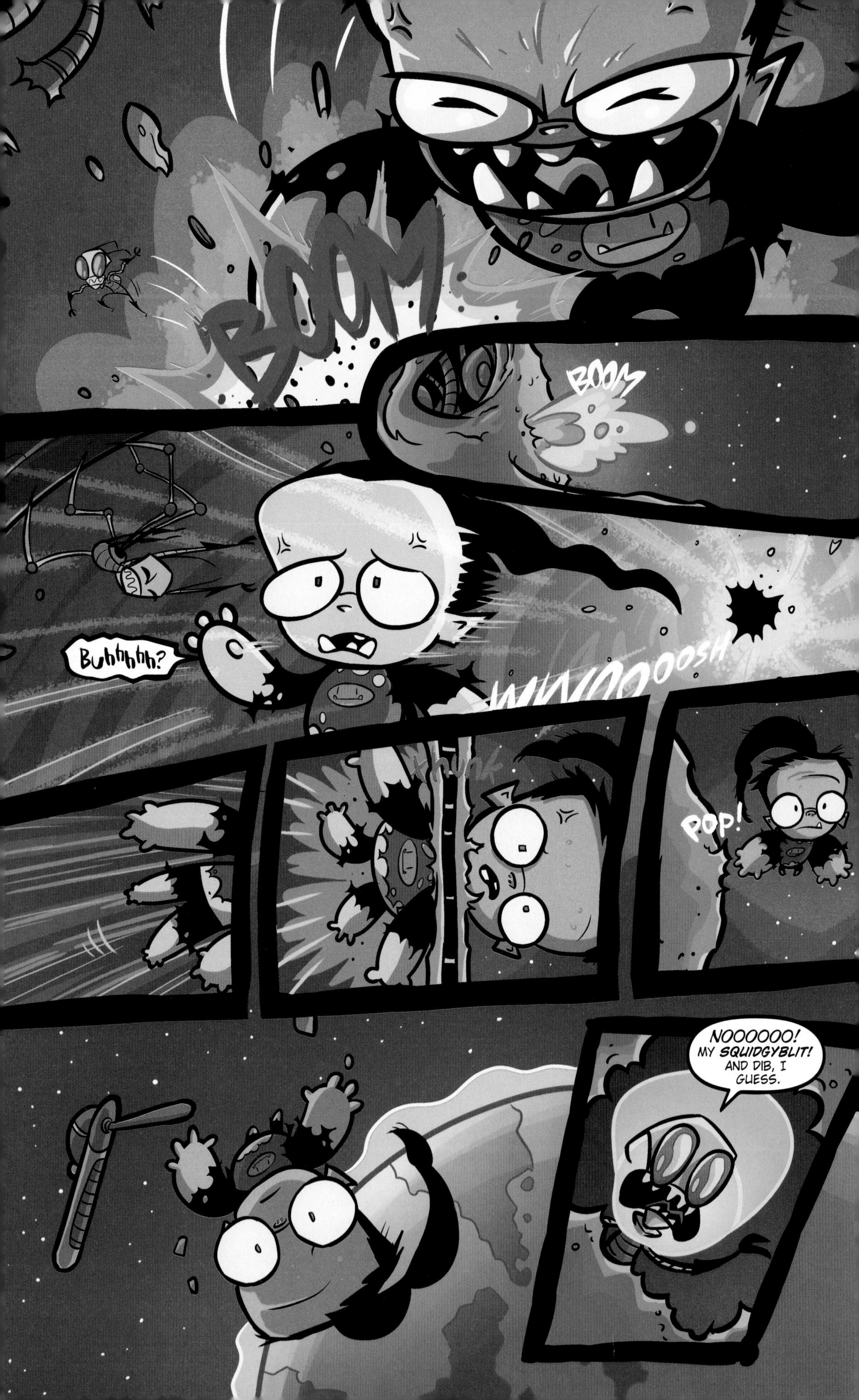
BOOM
BOOM
Buhhhhh?
WWOOOOOSH
thunk
POP!
NOOOOOO! MY SQUIDGYBLIT! AND DIB, I GUESS.

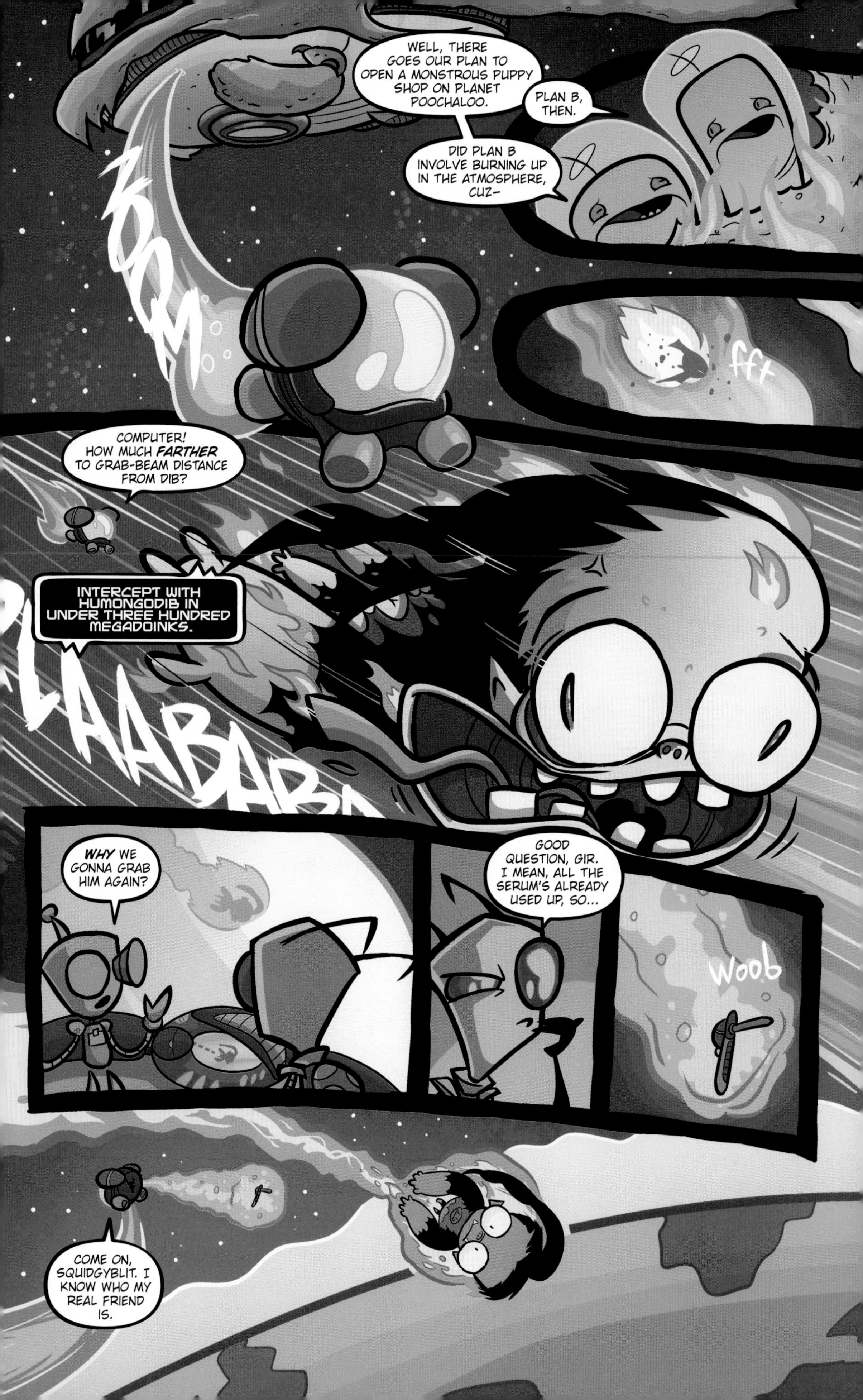
WELL, THERE GOES OUR PLAN TO OPEN A MONSTROUS PUPPY SHOP ON PLANET POOCHALOO.
PLAN B, THEN.
DID PLAN B INVOLVE BURNING UP IN THE ATMOSPHERE, CUZ–
ZOOM
fft
COMPUTER! HOW MUCH FARTHER TO GRAB-BEAM DISTANCE FROM DIB?
INTERCEPT WITH HUMONGODIB IN UNDER THREE HUNDRED MEGADOINKS.
WHY WE GONNA GRAB HIM AGAIN?
GOOD QUESTION, GIR. I MEAN, ALL THE SERUM'S ALREADY USED UP, SO...
woob
COME ON, SQUIDGYBLIT. I KNOW WHO MY REAL FRIEND IS.

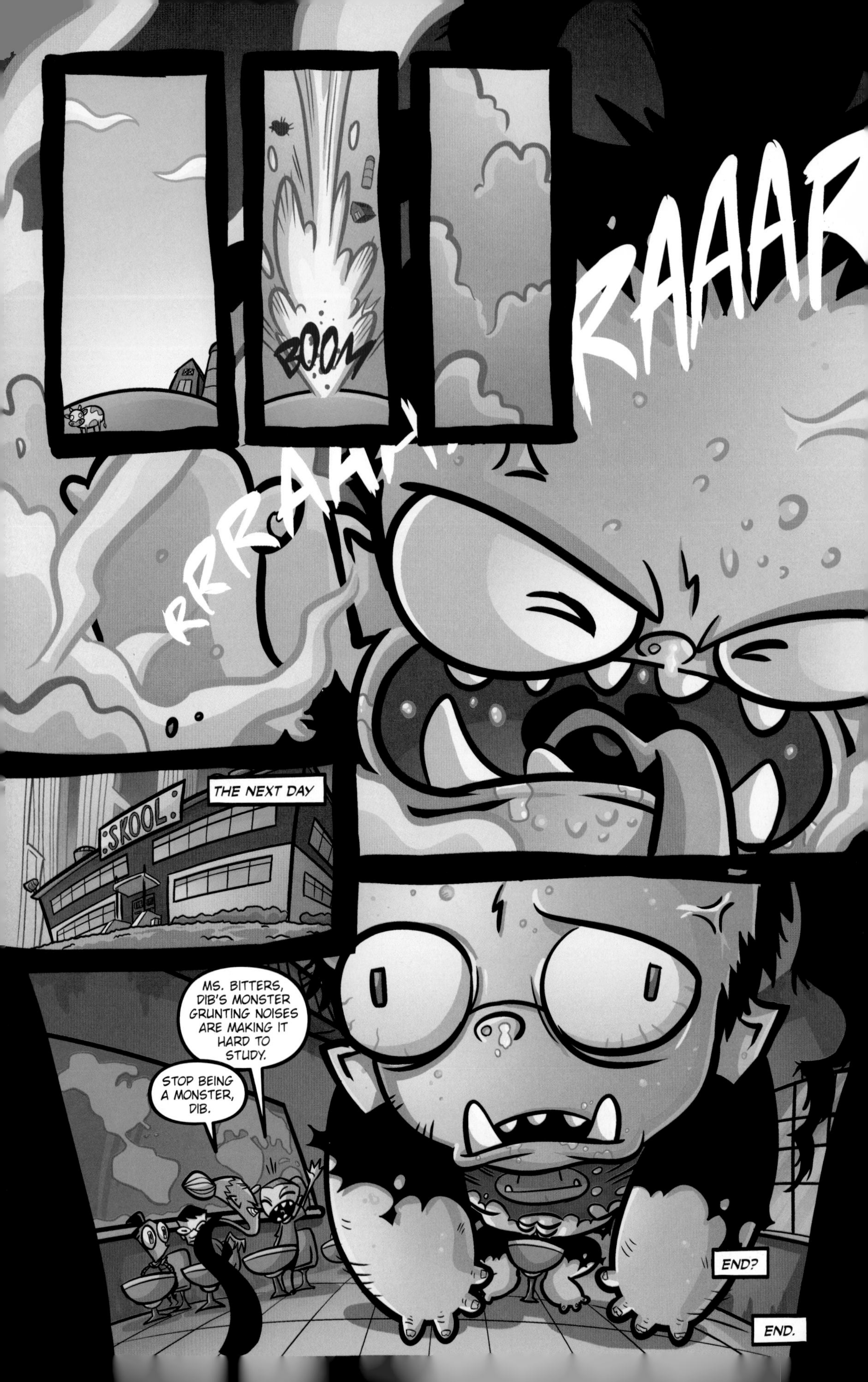
BOOM
RRRAAAHH!
RAAAR
THE NEXT DAY
SKOOL
MS. BITTERS, DIB'S MONSTER GRUNTING NOISES ARE MAKING IT HARD TO STUDY.
STOP BEING A MONSTER, DIB.
END?
END.

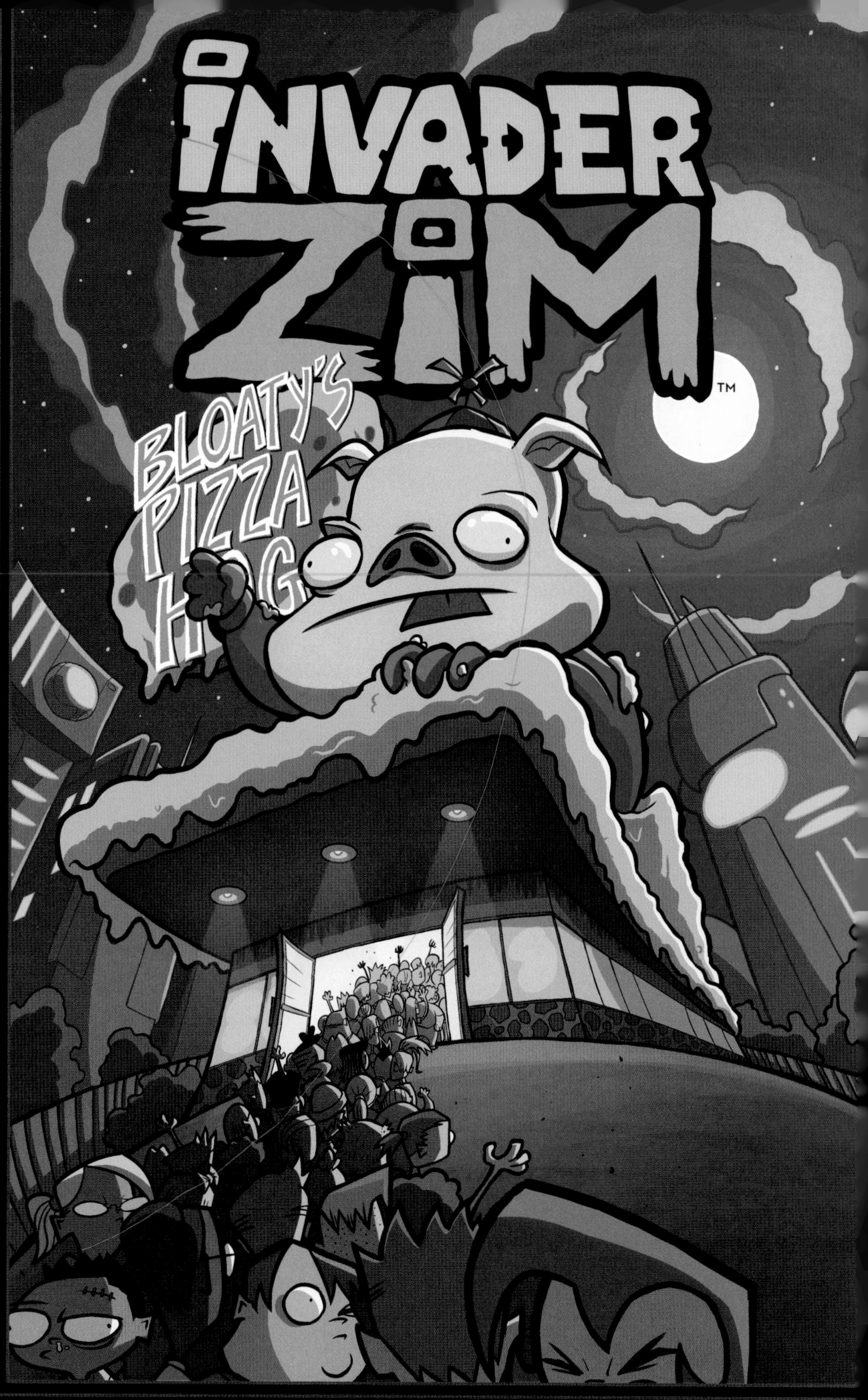
INVADER ZIM
BLOATY'S PIZZA

CHAPTER: 4

illustration by WARREN WUCINICH

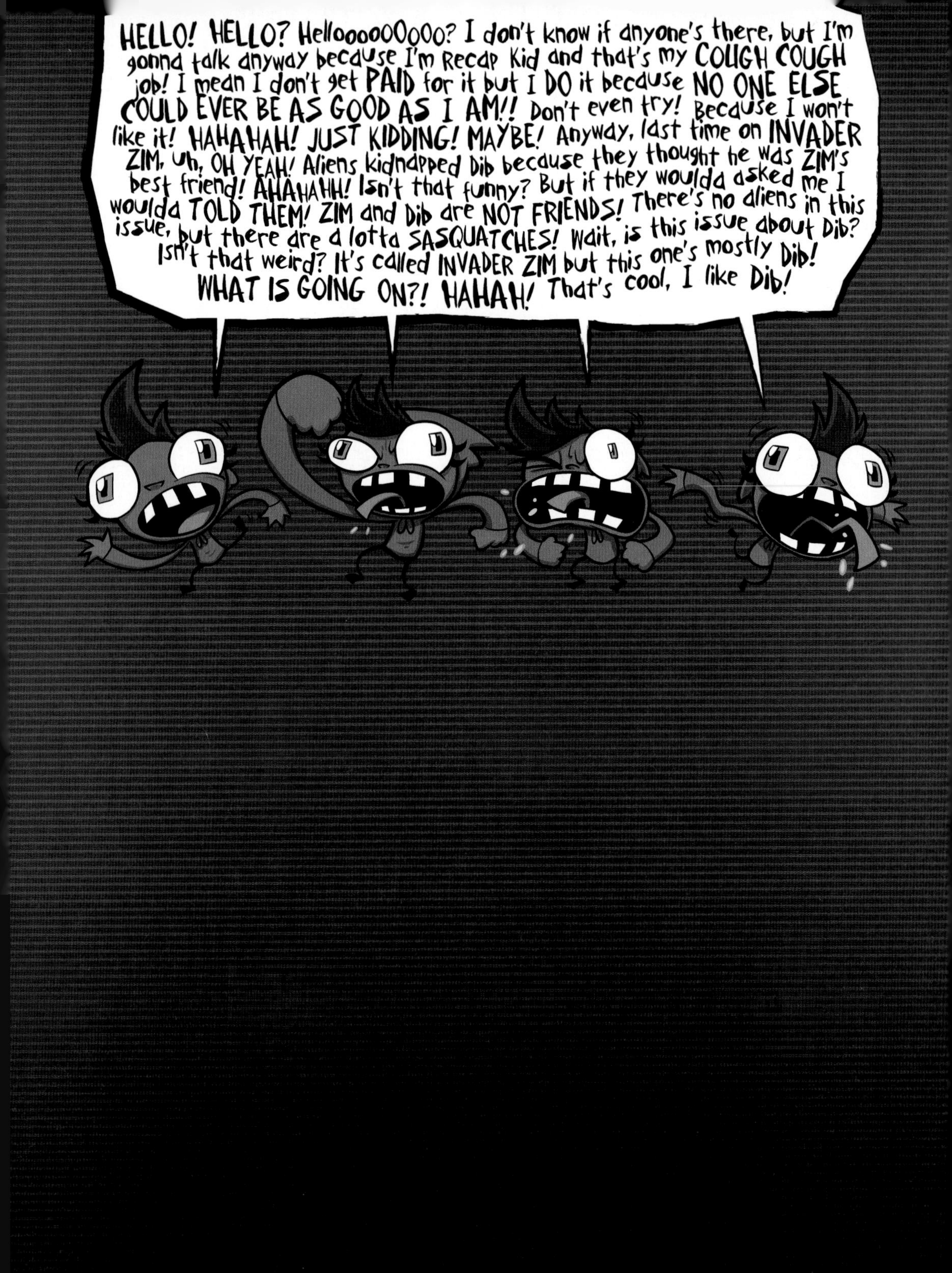
HELLO! HELLO? HellooooOOOooo? I don't know if anyone's there, but I'm gonna talk anyway because I'm Recap Kid and that's my COUGH COUGH job! I mean I don't get PAID for it but I DO it because NO ONE ELSE COULD EVER BE AS GOOD AS I AM!! Don't even try! Because I won't like it! HAHAHAH! JUST KIDDING! MAYBE! Anyway, last time on INVADER ZIM, uh, OH YEAH! Aliens kidnapped Dib because they thought he was ZIM's best friend! AHAHAHH! Isn't that funny? But if they woulda asked me I woulda TOLD THEM! ZIM and Dib are NOT FRIENDS! There's no aliens in this issue, but there are a lotta SASQUATCHES! Wait, is this issue about Dib? Isn't that weird? It's called INVADER ZIM but this one's mostly Dib! WHAT IS GOING ON?! HAHAH! That's cool, I like Dib!

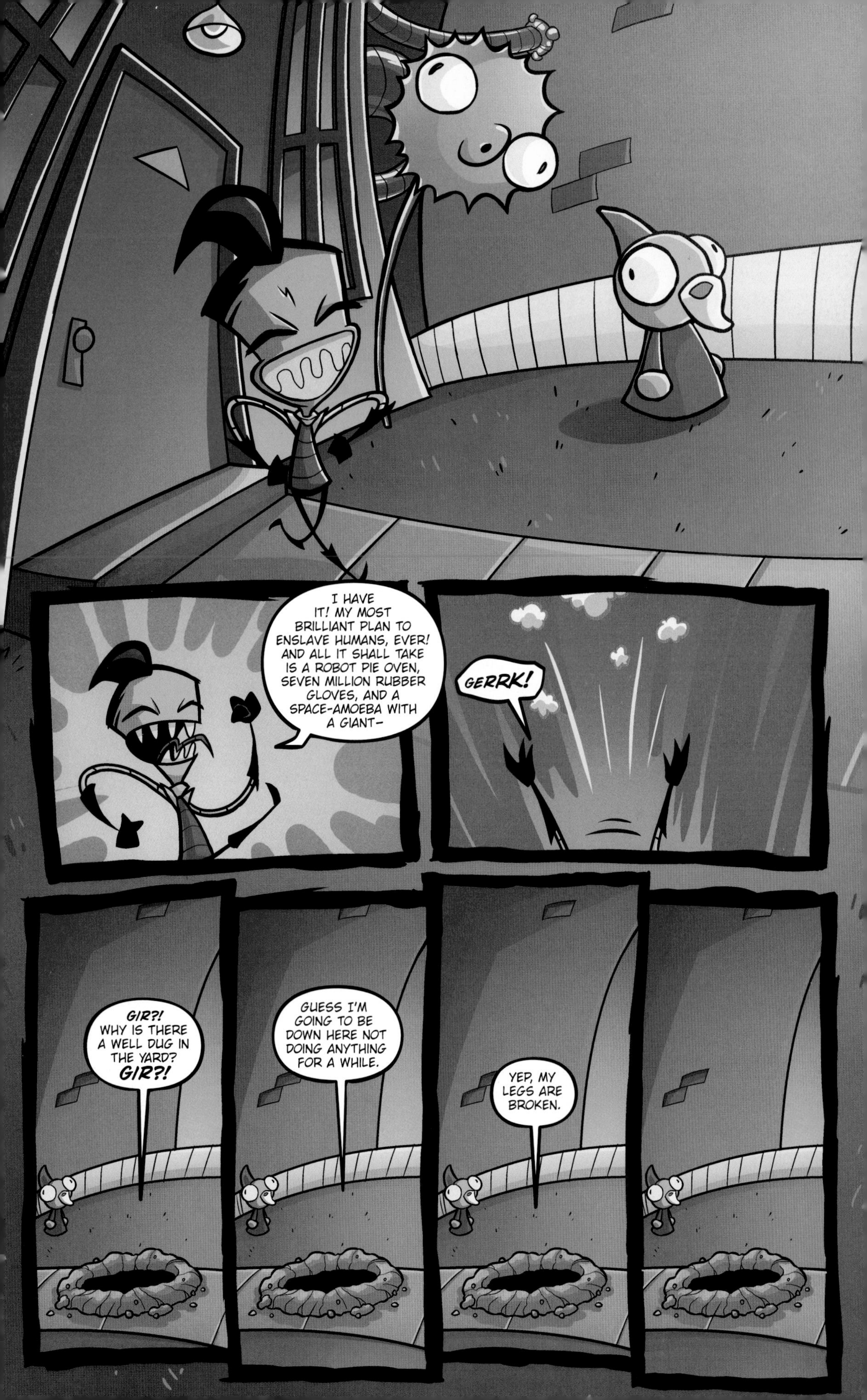
I HAVE IT! MY MOST BRILLIANT PLAN TO ENSLAVE HUMANS, EVER! AND ALL IT SHALL TAKE IS A ROBOT PIE OVEN, SEVEN MILLION RUBBER GLOVES, AND A SPACE-AMOEBA WITH A GIANT-
GERRK!
GIR?! WHY IS THERE A WELL DUG IN THE YARD? GIR?!
GUESS I'M GOING TO BE DOWN HERE NOT DOING ANYTHING FOR A WHILE.
YEP, MY LEGS ARE BROKEN.

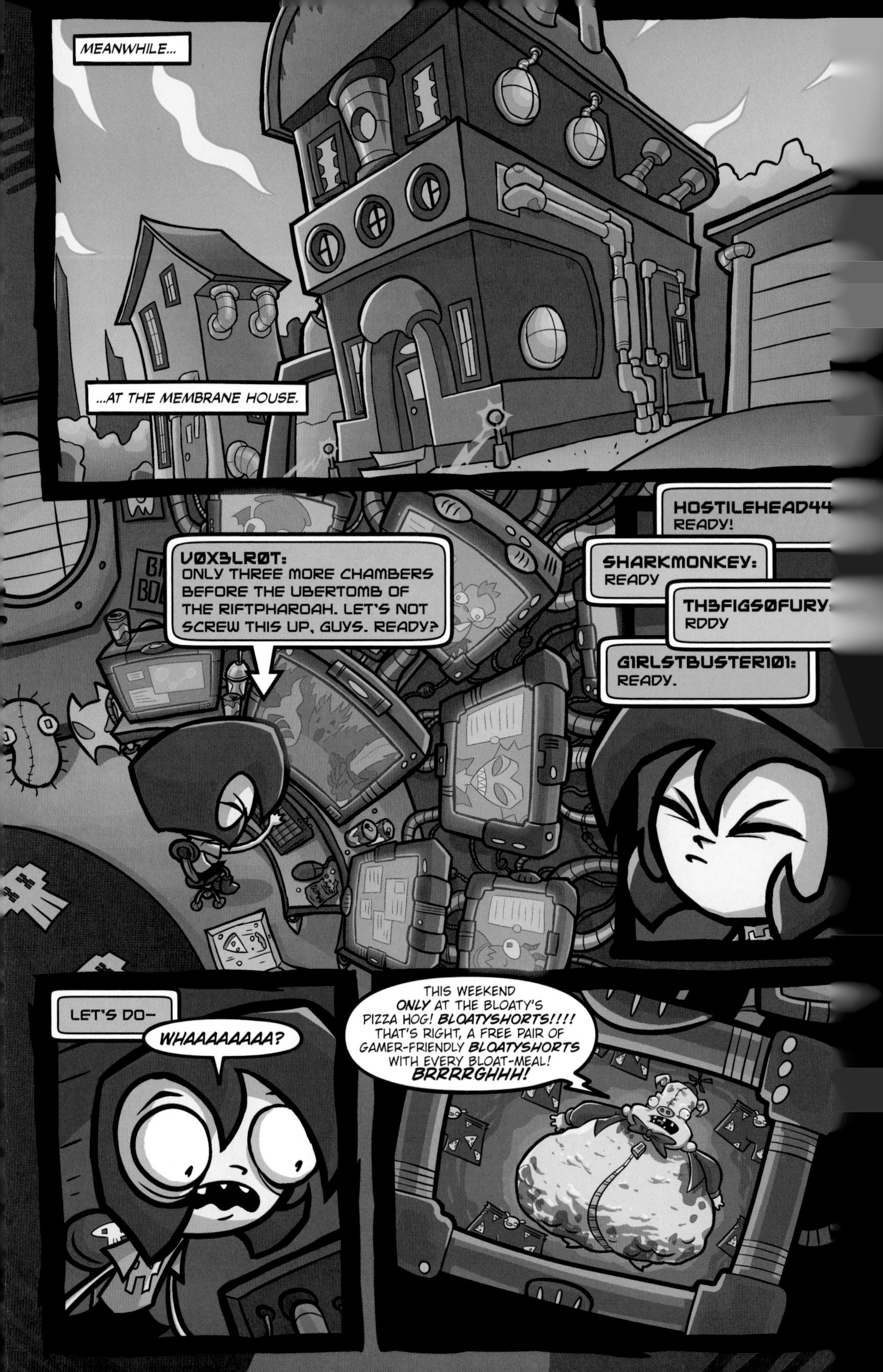
MEANWHILE...
...AT THE MEMBRANE HOUSE.
VØXBLRØT:
ONLY THREE MORE CHAMBERS BEFORE THE UBERTOMB OF THE RIFTPHAROAH. LET'S NOT SCREW THIS UP, GUYS. READY?
HOSTILEHEAD44
READY!
SHARKMONKEY:
READY
TH3FIGSØFURY
RDDY
G1RLSTBUSTER101:
READY.
LET'S DO—
WHAAAAAAAA?
THIS WEEKEND ONLY AT THE BLOATY'S PIZZA HOG! BLOATYSHORTS!!!! THAT'S RIGHT, A FREE PAIR OF GAMER-FRIENDLY BLOATYSHORTS WITH EVERY BLOAT-MEAL! BRRRRGHHH!

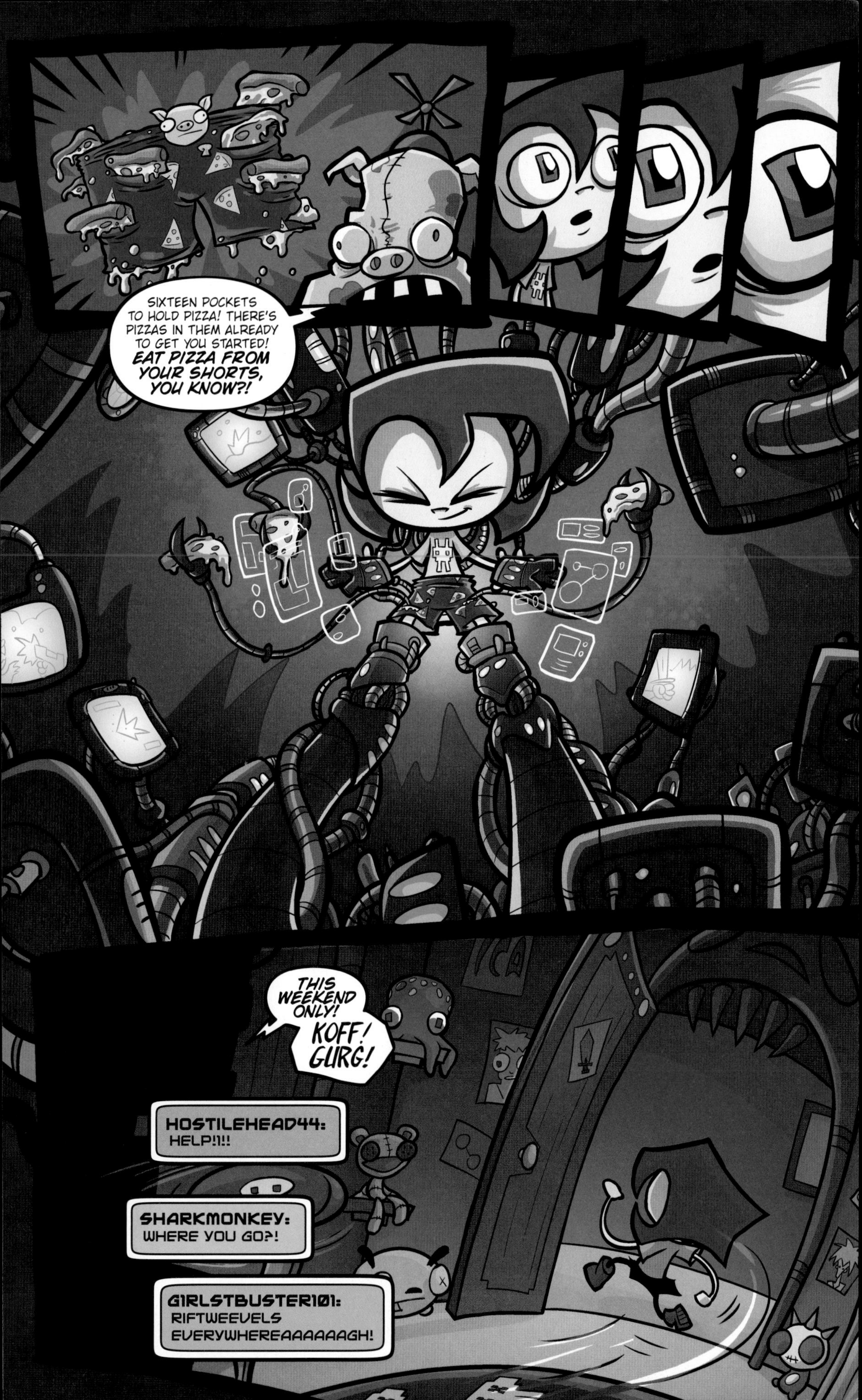
SIXTEEN POCKETS TO HOLD PIZZA! THERE'S PIZZAS IN THEM ALREADY TO GET YOU STARTED! EAT PIZZA FROM YOUR SHORTS, YOU KNOW?!
THIS WEEKEND ONLY! KOFF! GURG!
HOSTILEHEAD44: HELP!1!!
SHARKMONKEY: WHERE YOU GO?!
GIRLSTBUSTER101: RIFTWEEVELS EVERYWHEREAAAAAAGH!

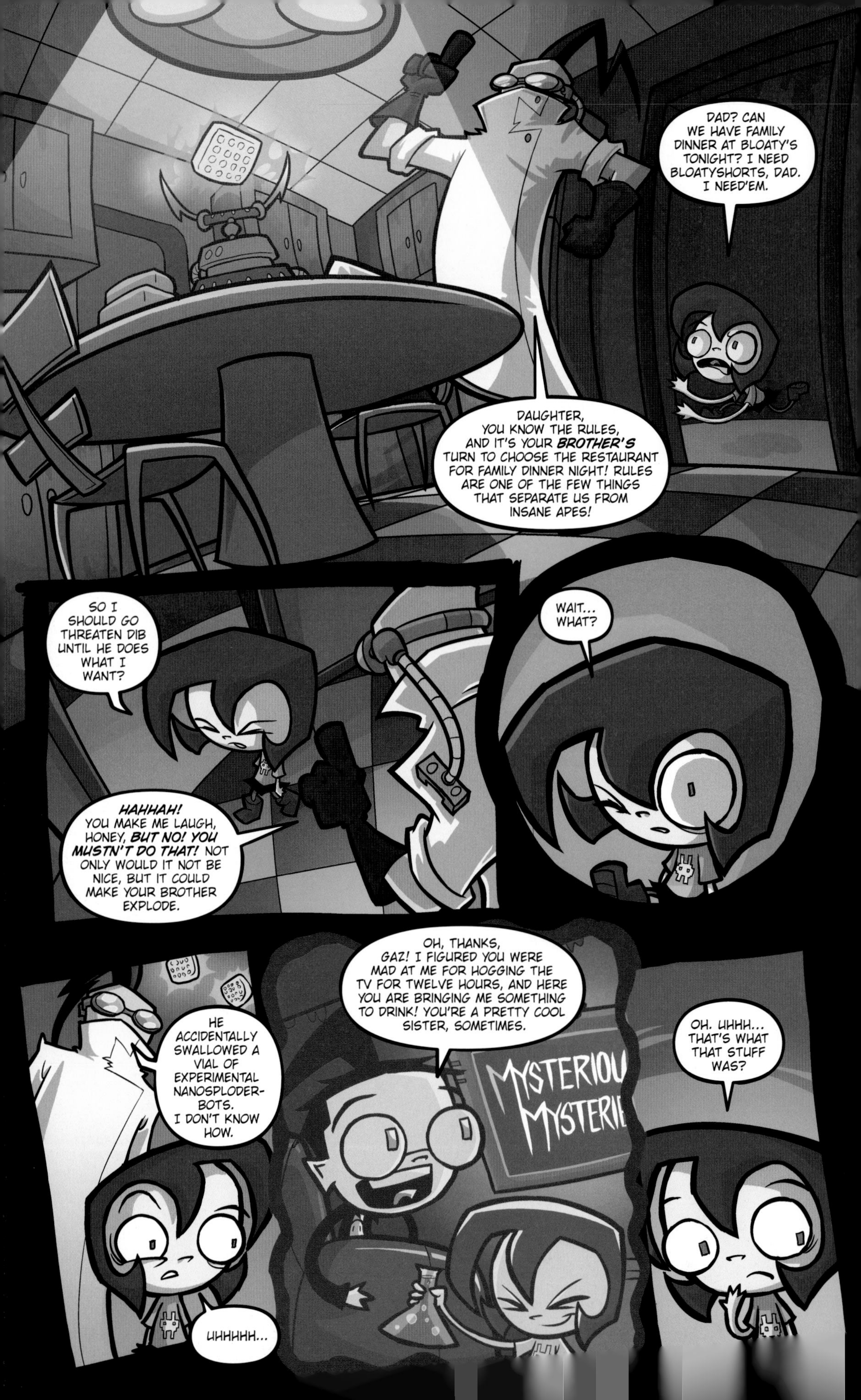
DAD? CAN WE HAVE FAMILY DINNER AT BLOATY'S TONIGHT? I NEED BLOATYSHORTS, DAD. I NEED'EM.
DAUGHTER, YOU KNOW THE RULES, AND IT'S YOUR **BROTHER'S** TURN TO CHOOSE THE RESTAURANT FOR FAMILY DINNER NIGHT! RULES ARE ONE OF THE FEW THINGS THAT SEPARATE US FROM INSANE APES!
SO I SHOULD GO THREATEN DIB UNTIL HE DOES WHAT I WANT?
HAHHAH! YOU MAKE ME LAUGH, HONEY, ***BUT NO! YOU MUSTN'T DO THAT!*** NOT ONLY WOULD IT NOT BE NICE, BUT IT COULD MAKE YOUR BROTHER EXPLODE.
WAIT... WHAT?
HE ACCIDENTALLY SWALLOWED A VIAL OF EXPERIMENTAL NANOSPLODER-BOTS. I DON'T KNOW HOW.
UHHHHH...
OH, THANKS, GAZ! I FIGURED YOU WERE MAD AT ME FOR HOGGING THE TV FOR TWELVE HOURS, AND HERE YOU ARE BRINGING ME SOMETHING TO DRINK! YOU'RE A PRETTY COOL SISTER, SOMETIMES.
MYSTERIOU MYSTERIE
OH. UHHH... THAT'S WHAT THAT STUFF WAS?

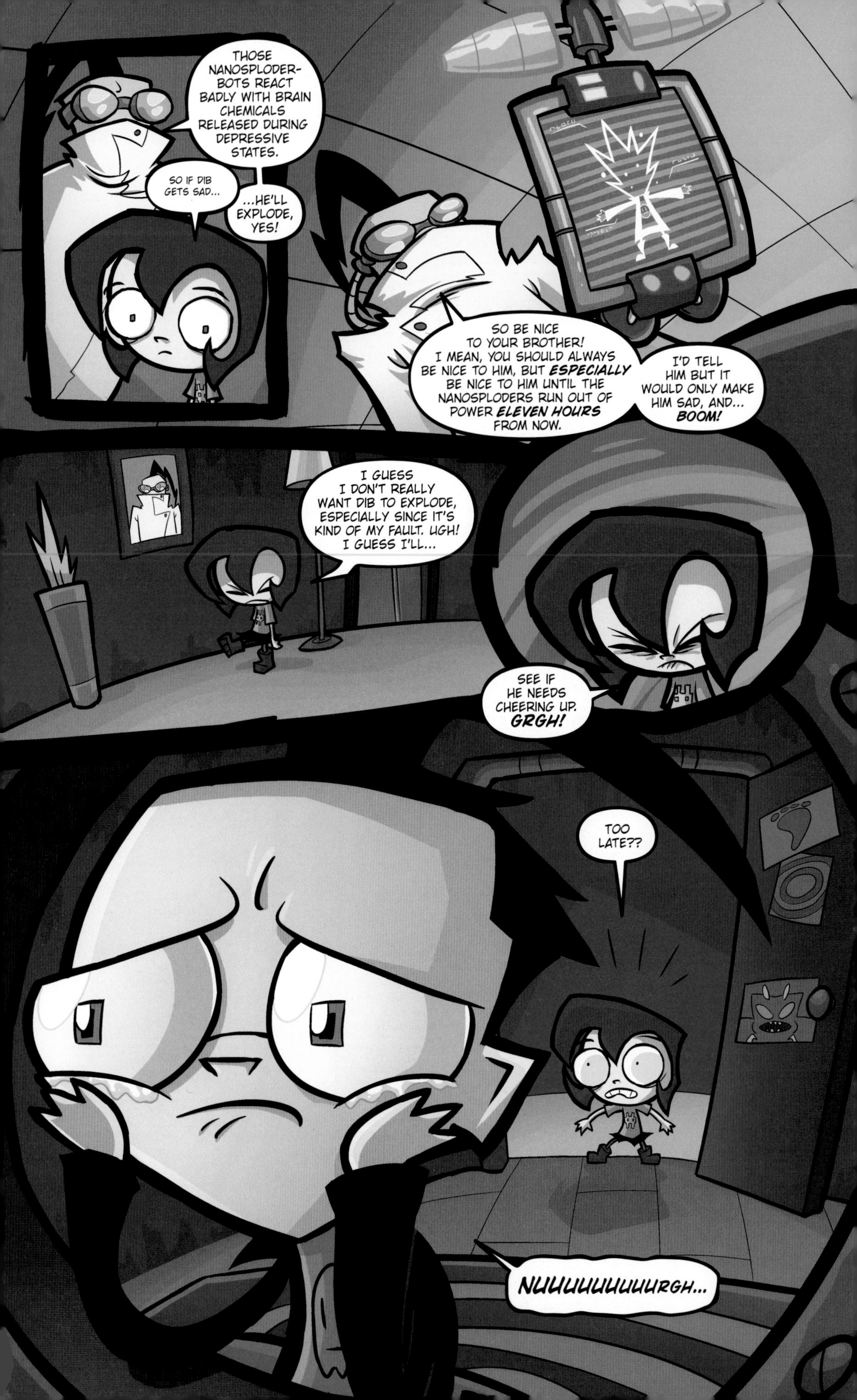
THOSE NANOSPLODER-BOTS REACT BADLY WITH BRAIN CHEMICALS RELEASED DURING DEPRESSIVE STATES.
SO IF DIB GETS SAD...
...HE'LL EXPLODE, YES!
SO BE NICE TO YOUR BROTHER! I MEAN, YOU SHOULD ALWAYS BE NICE TO HIM, BUT ESPECIALLY BE NICE TO HIM UNTIL THE NANOSPLODERS RUN OUT OF POWER ELEVEN HOURS FROM NOW.
I'D TELL HIM BUT IT WOULD ONLY MAKE HIM SAD, AND... BOOM!
I GUESS I DON'T REALLY WANT DIB TO EXPLODE, ESPECIALLY SINCE IT'S KIND OF MY FAULT. UGH! I GUESS I'LL...
SEE IF HE NEEDS CHEERING UP. GRGH!
TOO LATE??
NUUUUUUUUURGH...

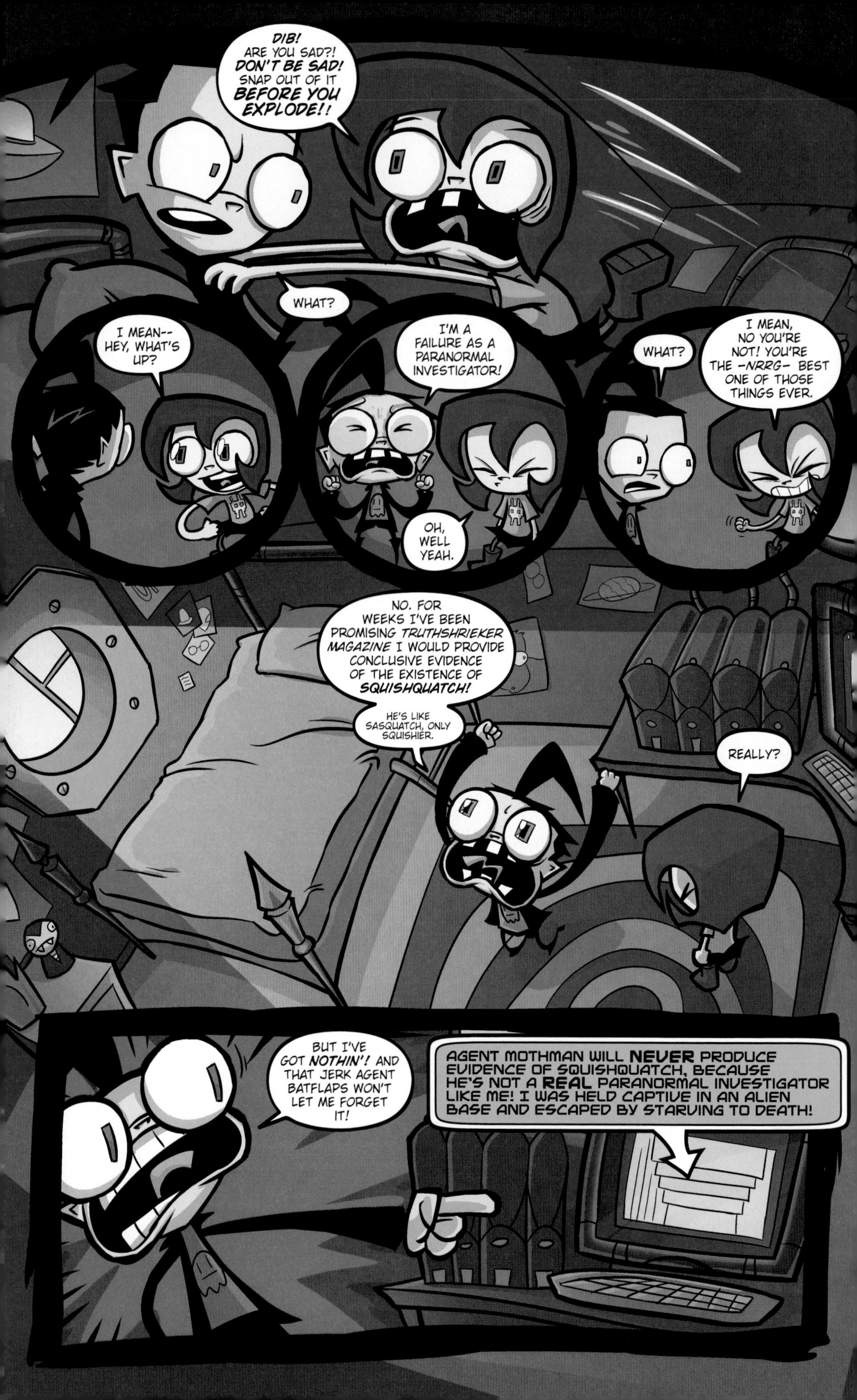
DIB! ARE YOU SAD?! DON'T BE SAD! SNAP OUT OF IT BEFORE YOU EXPLODE!!
WHAT?
I MEAN-- HEY, WHAT'S UP?
I'M A FAILURE AS A PARANORMAL INVESTIGATOR!
OH, WELL YEAH.
WHAT?
I MEAN, NO YOU'RE NOT! YOU'RE THE -NRRG- BEST ONE OF THOSE THINGS EVER.
NO. FOR WEEKS I'VE BEEN PROMISING TRUTHSHRIEKER MAGAZINE I WOULD PROVIDE CONCLUSIVE EVIDENCE OF THE EXISTENCE OF SQUISHQUATCH!
HE'S LIKE SASQUATCH, ONLY SQUISHIER.
REALLY?
BUT I'VE GOT NOTHIN'! AND THAT JERK AGENT BATFLAPS WON'T LET ME FORGET IT!
AGENT MOTHMAN WILL NEVER PRODUCE EVIDENCE OF SQUISHQUATCH, BECAUSE HE'S NOT A REAL PARANORMAL INVESTIGATOR LIKE ME! I WAS HELD CAPTIVE IN AN ALIEN BASE AND ESCAPED BY STARVING TO DEATH!

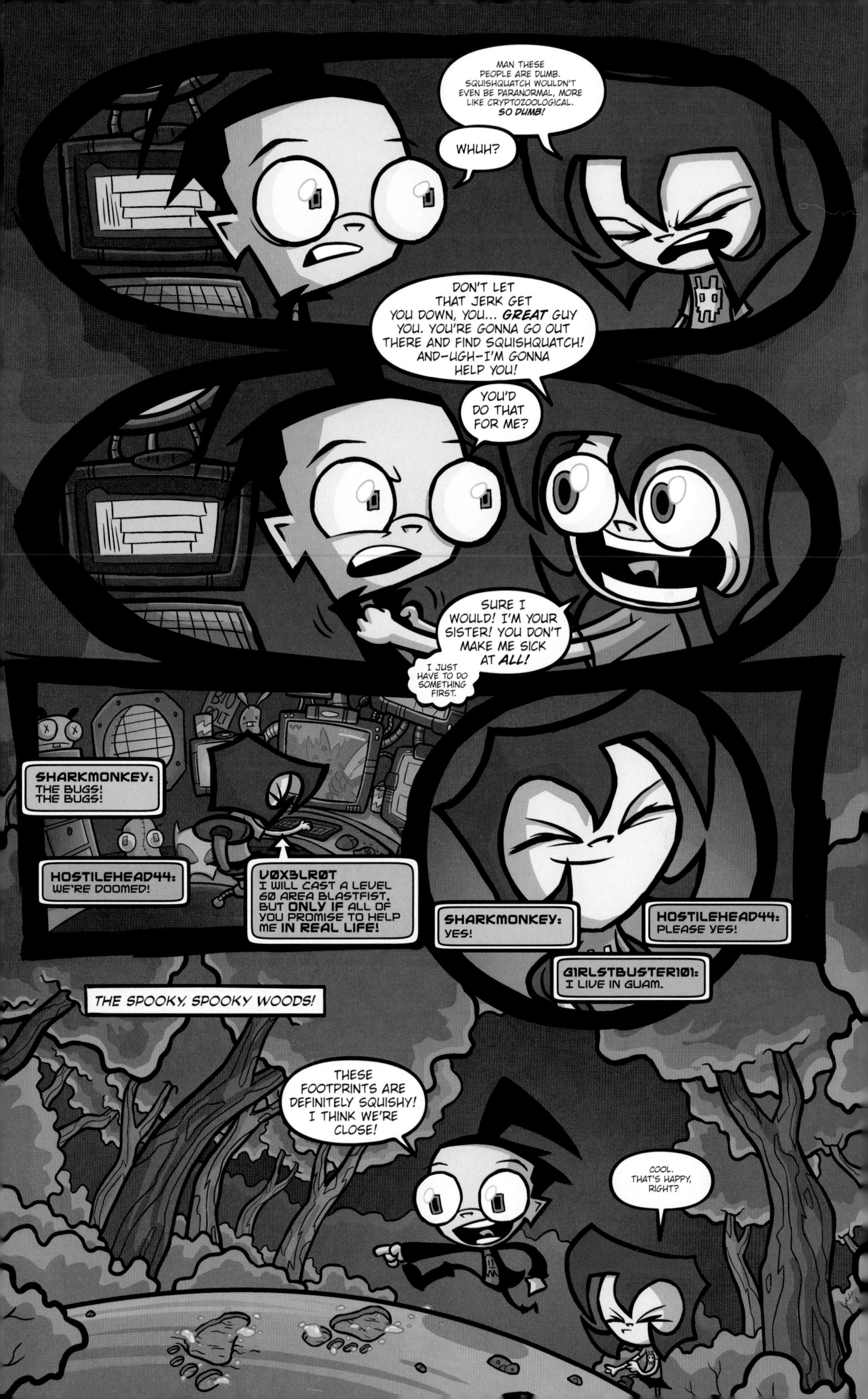
MAN THESE PEOPLE ARE DUMB. SQUISHQUATCH WOULDN'T EVEN BE PARANORMAL, MORE LIKE CRYPTOZOOLOGICAL. SO DUMB!
WHUH?
DON'T LET THAT JERK GET YOU DOWN, YOU... GREAT GUY YOU. YOU'RE GONNA GO OUT THERE AND FIND SQUISHQUATCH! AND—UGH—I'M GONNA HELP YOU!
YOU'D DO THAT FOR ME?
SURE I WOULD! I'M YOUR SISTER! YOU DON'T MAKE ME SICK AT ALL!
I JUST HAVE TO DO SOMETHING FIRST.
SHARKMONKEY: THE BUGS! THE BUGS!
HOSTILEHEAD44: WE'RE DOOMED!
V0XBLR0T I WILL CAST A LEVEL 60 AREA BLASTFIST, BUT ONLY IF ALL OF YOU PROMISE TO HELP ME IN REAL LIFE!
SHARKMONKEY: YES!
HOSTILEHEAD44: PLEASE YES!
G1RLSTBUSTER101: I LIVE IN GUAM.
THE SPOOKY, SPOOKY WOODS!
THESE FOOTPRINTS ARE DEFINITELY SQUISHY! I THINK WE'RE CLOSE!
COOL. THAT'S HAPPY, RIGHT?

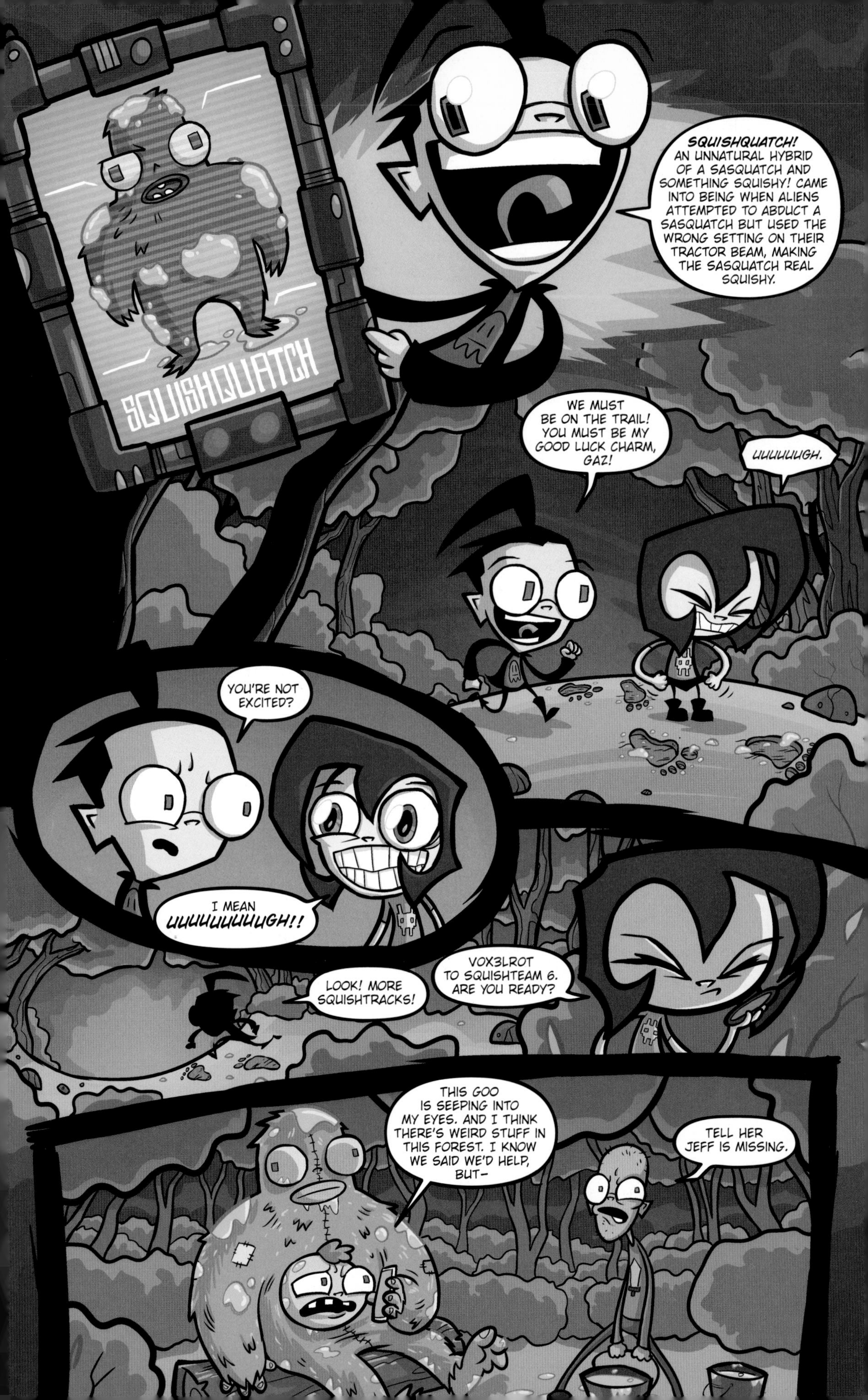
SQUISHQUATCH
SQUISHQUATCH! AN UNNATURAL HYBRID OF A SASQUATCH AND SOMETHING SQUISHY! CAME INTO BEING WHEN ALIENS ATTEMPTED TO ABDUCT A SASQUATCH BUT USED THE WRONG SETTING ON THEIR TRACTOR BEAM, MAKING THE SASQUATCH REAL SQUISHY.
WE MUST BE ON THE TRAIL! YOU MUST BE MY GOOD LUCK CHARM, GAZ!
UUUUUUGH.
YOU'RE NOT EXCITED?
I MEAN UUUUUUUUUGH!!
LOOK! MORE SQUISHTRACKS!
VOX3LROT TO SQUISHTEAM 6. ARE YOU READY?
THIS GOO IS SEEPING INTO MY EYES. AND I THINK THERE'S WEIRD STUFF IN THIS FOREST. I KNOW WE SAID WE'D HELP, BUT–
TELL HER JEFF IS MISSING.

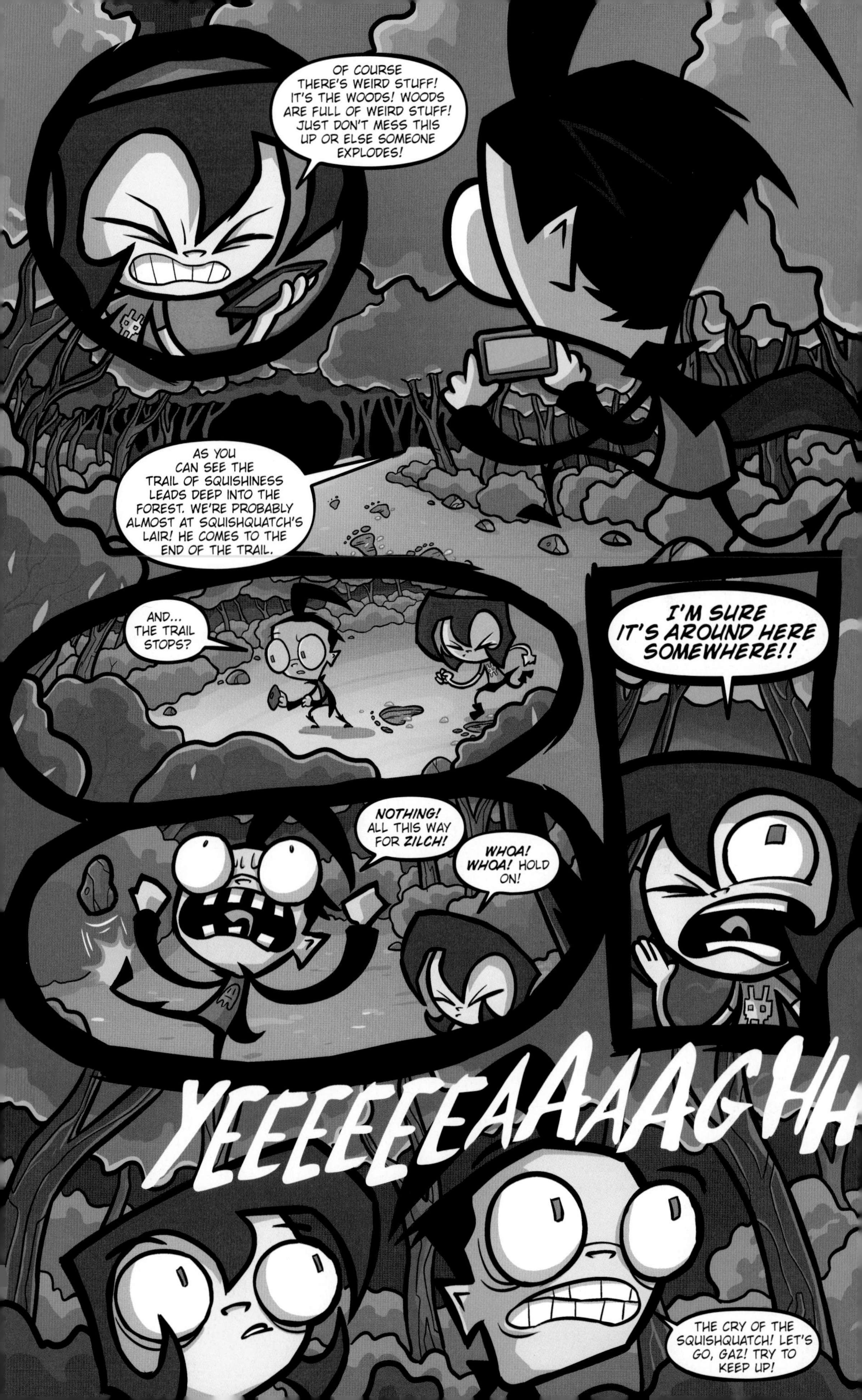
OF COURSE THERE'S WEIRD STUFF! IT'S THE WOODS! WOODS ARE FULL OF WEIRD STUFF! JUST DON'T MESS THIS UP OR ELSE SOMEONE EXPLODES!
AS YOU CAN SEE THE TRAIL OF SQUISHINESS LEADS DEEP INTO THE FOREST. WE'RE PROBABLY ALMOST AT SQUISHQUATCH'S LAIR! HE COMES TO THE END OF THE TRAIL.
AND... THE TRAIL STOPS?
I'M SURE IT'S AROUND HERE SOMEWHERE!!
NOTHING! ALL THIS WAY FOR ZILCH!
WHOA! WHOA! HOLD ON!
YEEEEEEAAAAAGHH
THE CRY OF THE SQUISHQUATCH! LET'S GO, GAZ! TRY TO KEEP UP!

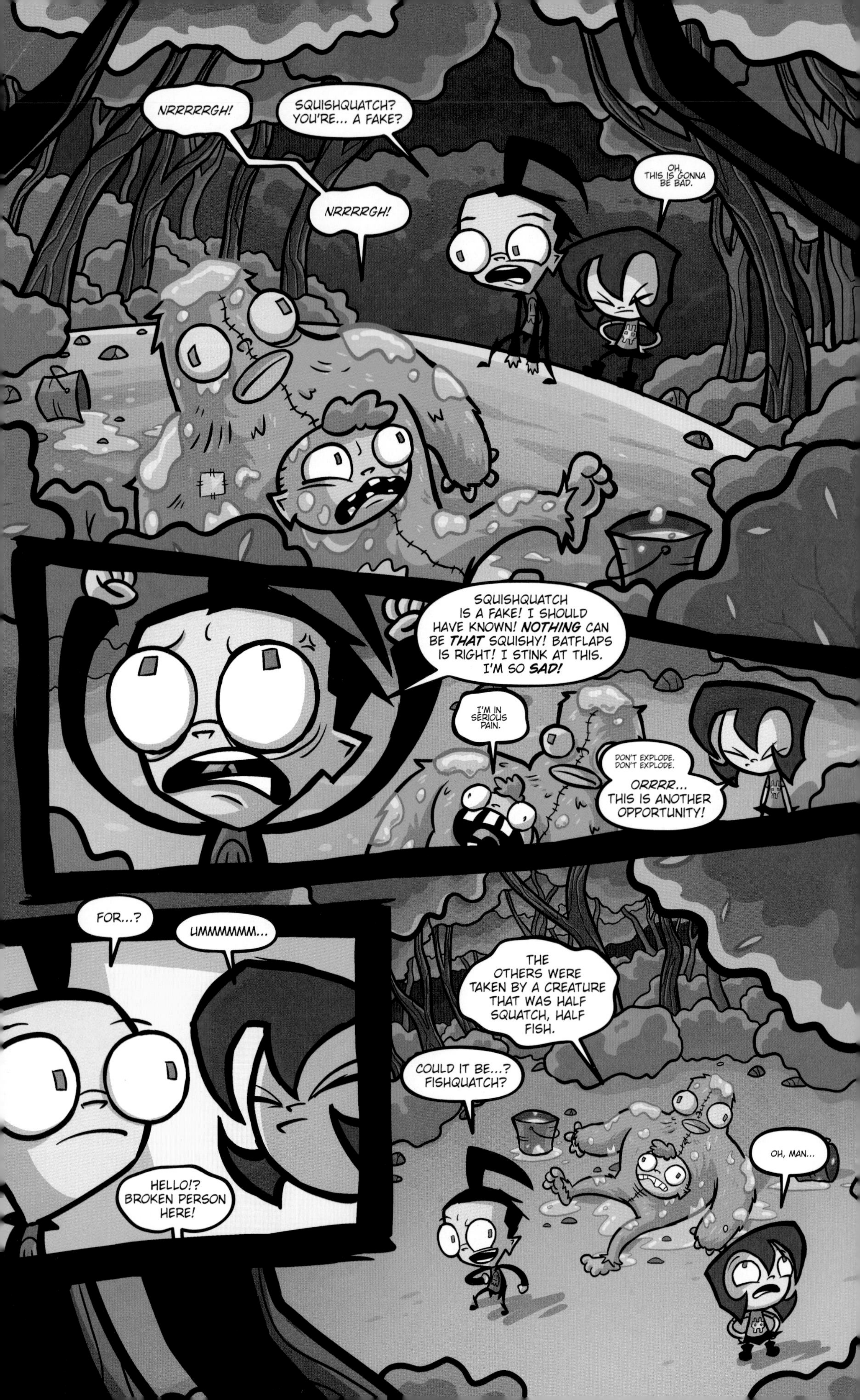
NRRRRRGH!
SQUISHQUATCH? YOU'RE... A FAKE?
NRRRRGH!
OH, THIS IS GONNA BE BAD.
SQUISHQUATCH IS A FAKE! I SHOULD HAVE KNOWN! NOTHING CAN BE THAT SQUISHY! BATFLAPS IS RIGHT! I STINK AT THIS. I'M SO SAD!
I'M IN SERIOUS PAIN.
DON'T EXPLODE. DON'T EXPLODE.
ORRRR... THIS IS ANOTHER OPPORTUNITY!
FOR...?
UMMMMMMM...
HELLO!? BROKEN PERSON HERE!
THE OTHERS WERE TAKEN BY A CREATURE THAT WAS HALF SQUATCH, HALF FISH.
COULD IT BE...? FISHQUATCH?
OH, MAN...

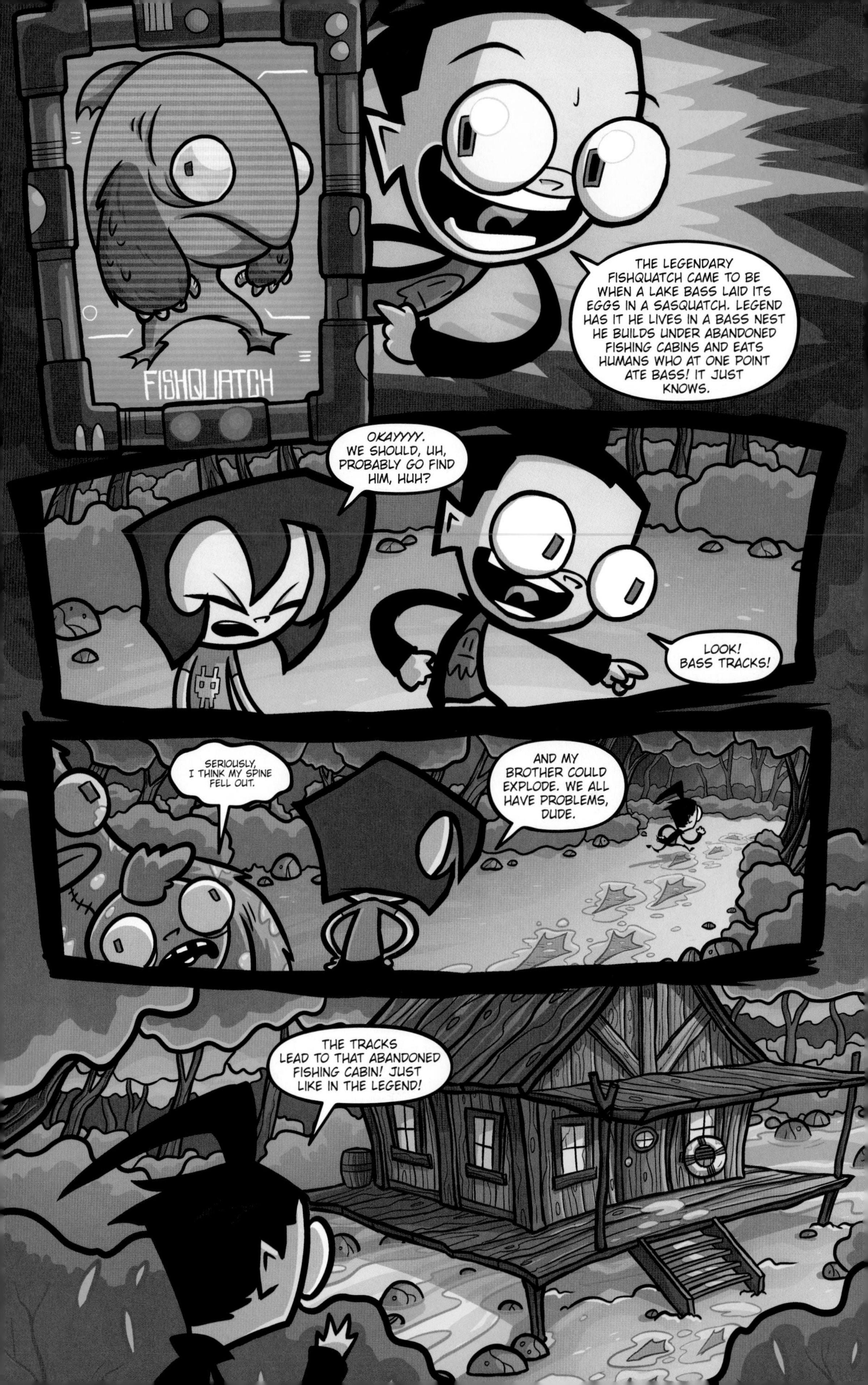
FISHQUATCH
THE LEGENDARY FISHQUATCH CAME TO BE WHEN A LAKE BASS LAID ITS EGGS IN A SASQUATCH. LEGEND HAS IT HE LIVES IN A BASS NEST HE BUILDS UNDER ABANDONED FISHING CABINS AND EATS HUMANS WHO AT ONE POINT ATE BASS! IT JUST KNOWS.
OKAYYYY. WE SHOULD, UH, PROBABLY GO FIND HIM, HUH?
LOOK! BASS TRACKS!
SERIOUSLY, I THINK MY SPINE FELL OUT.
AND MY BROTHER COULD EXPLODE. WE ALL HAVE PROBLEMS, DUDE.
THE TRACKS LEAD TO THAT ABANDONED FISHING CABIN! JUST LIKE IN THE LEGEND!

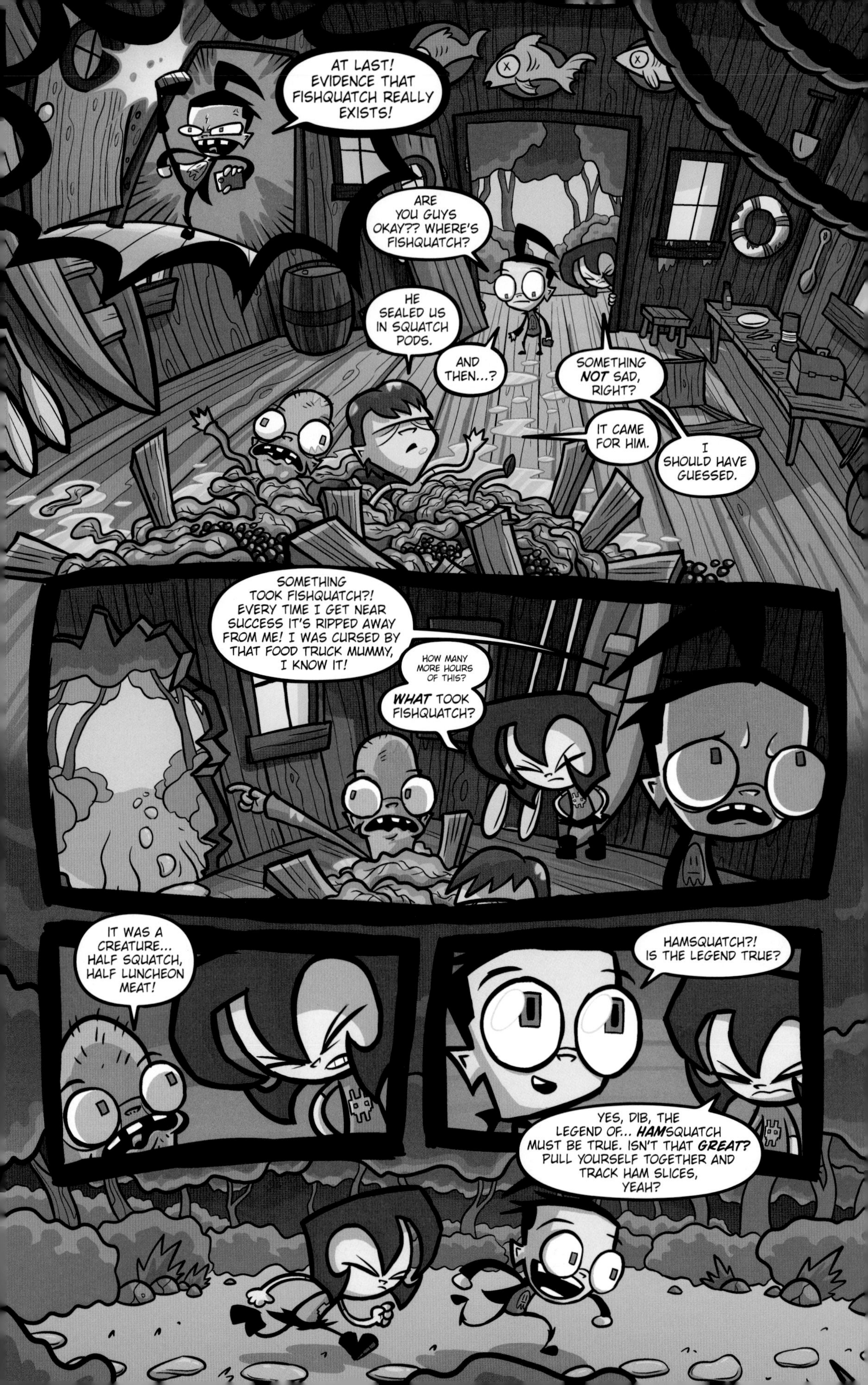
AT LAST! EVIDENCE THAT FISHQUATCH REALLY EXISTS!
ARE YOU GUYS OKAY?? WHERE'S FISHQUATCH?
HE SEALED US IN SQUATCH PODS.
AND THEN...?
SOMETHING NOT SAD, RIGHT?
IT CAME FOR HIM.
I SHOULD HAVE GUESSED.
SOMETHING TOOK FISHQUATCH?! EVERY TIME I GET NEAR SUCCESS IT'S RIPPED AWAY FROM ME! I WAS CURSED BY THAT FOOD TRUCK MUMMY, I KNOW IT!
HOW MANY MORE HOURS OF THIS?
WHAT TOOK FISHQUATCH?
IT WAS A CREATURE... HALF SQUATCH, HALF LUNCHEON MEAT!
HAMSQUATCH?! IS THE LEGEND TRUE?
YES, DIB, THE LEGEND OF... HAMSQUATCH MUST BE TRUE. ISN'T THAT GREAT? PULL YOURSELF TOGETHER AND TRACK HAM SLICES, YEAH?

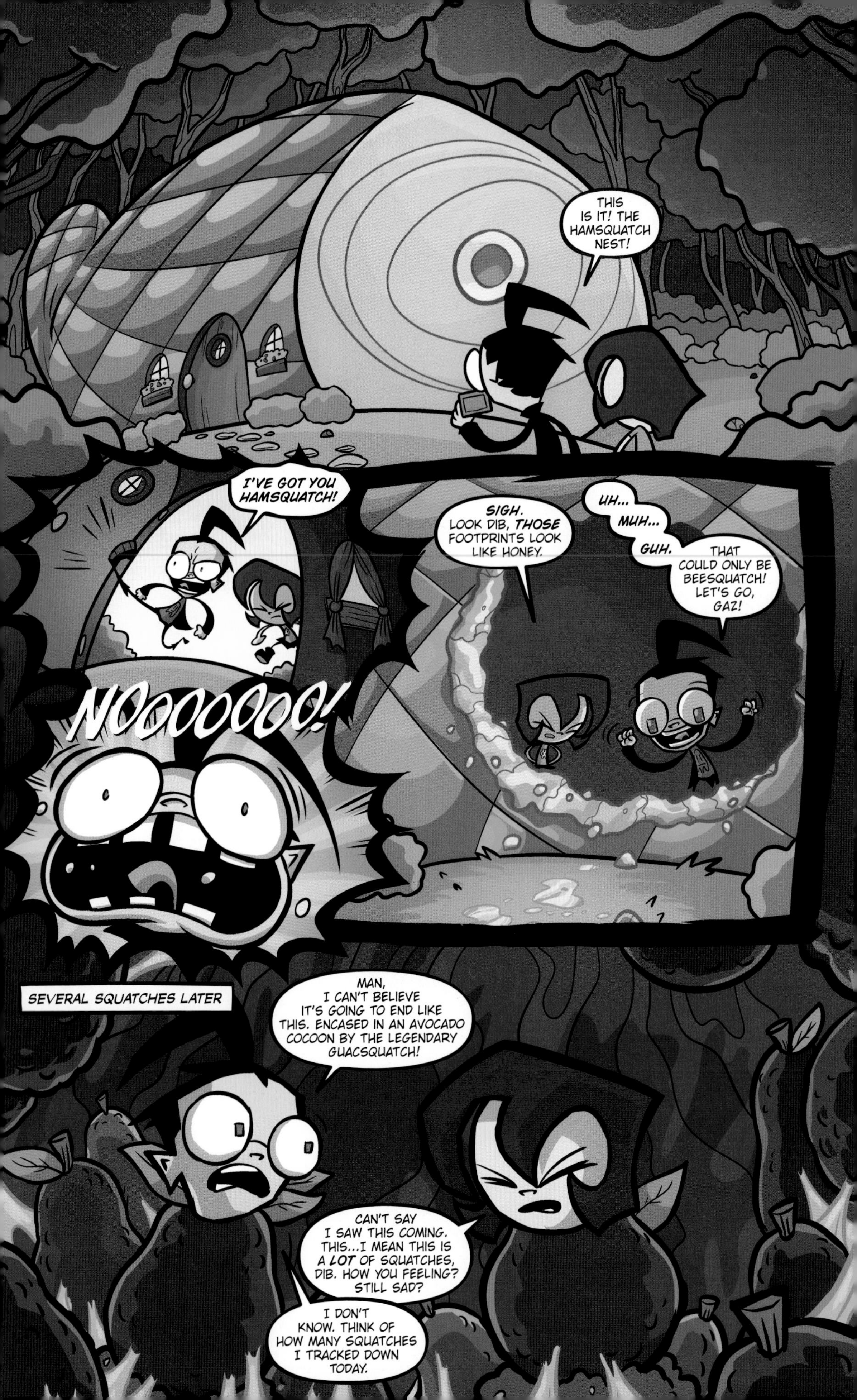
THIS IS IT! THE HAMSQUATCH NEST!
I'VE GOT YOU HAMSQUATCH!
NOOOOOOO!
SIGH. LOOK DIB, THOSE FOOTPRINTS LOOK LIKE HONEY.
UH... MUH... GUH.
THAT COULD ONLY BE BEESQUATCH! LET'S GO, GAZ!
SEVERAL SQUATCHES LATER
MAN, I CAN'T BELIEVE IT'S GOING TO END LIKE THIS. ENCASED IN AN AVOCADO COCOON BY THE LEGENDARY GUACSQUATCH!
CAN'T SAY I SAW THIS COMING. THIS...I MEAN THIS IS A LOT OF SQUATCHES, DIB. HOW YOU FEELING? STILL SAD?
I DON'T KNOW. THINK OF HOW MANY SQUATCHES I TRACKED DOWN TODAY.

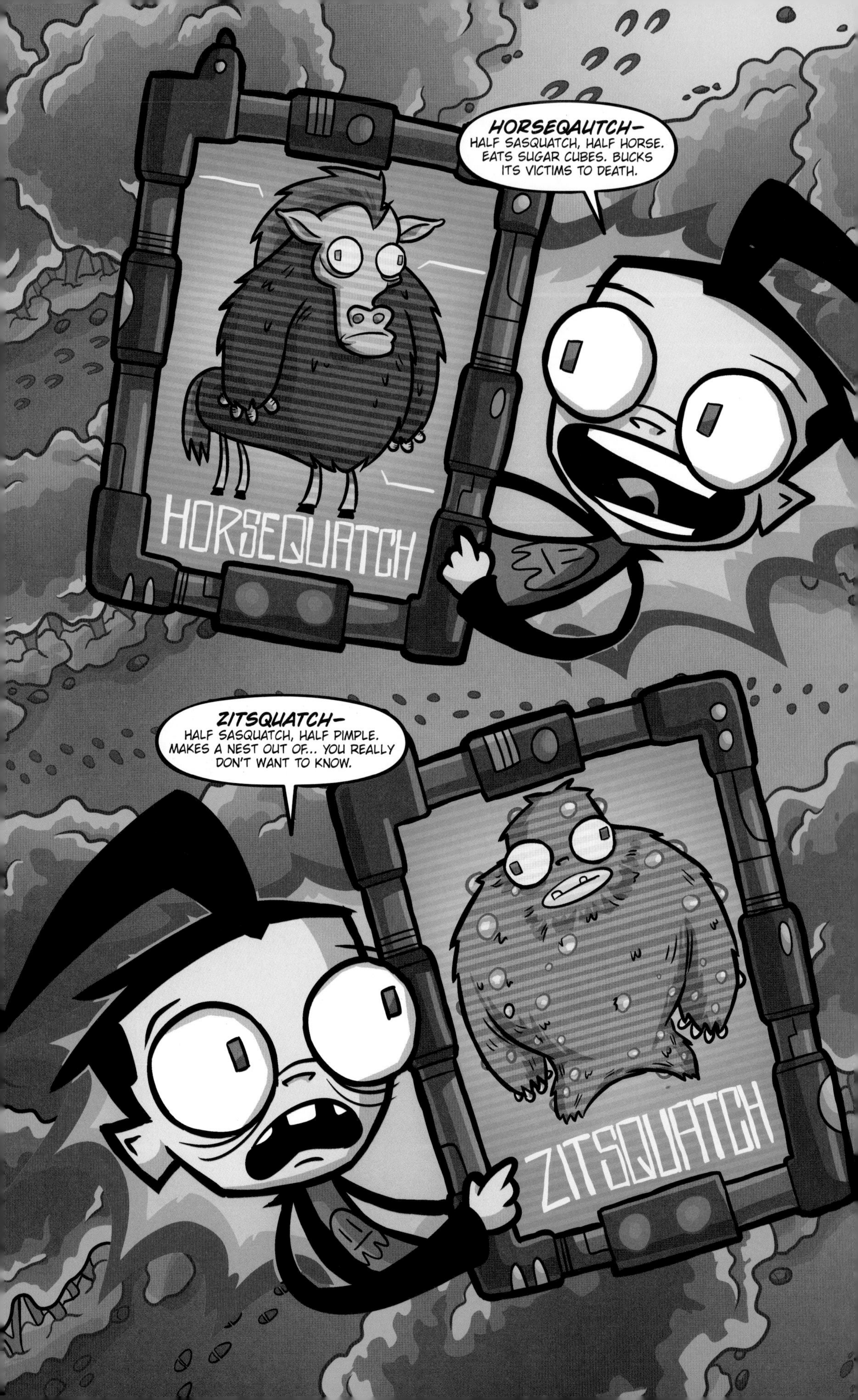
HORSEQAUTCH-
HALF SASQUATCH, HALF HORSE. EATS SUGAR CUBES. BUCKS ITS VICTIMS TO DEATH.
HORSEQUATCH
ZITSQUATCH-
HALF SASQUATCH, HALF PIMPLE. MAKES A NEST OUT OF... YOU REALLY DON'T WANT TO KNOW.
ZITSQUATCH

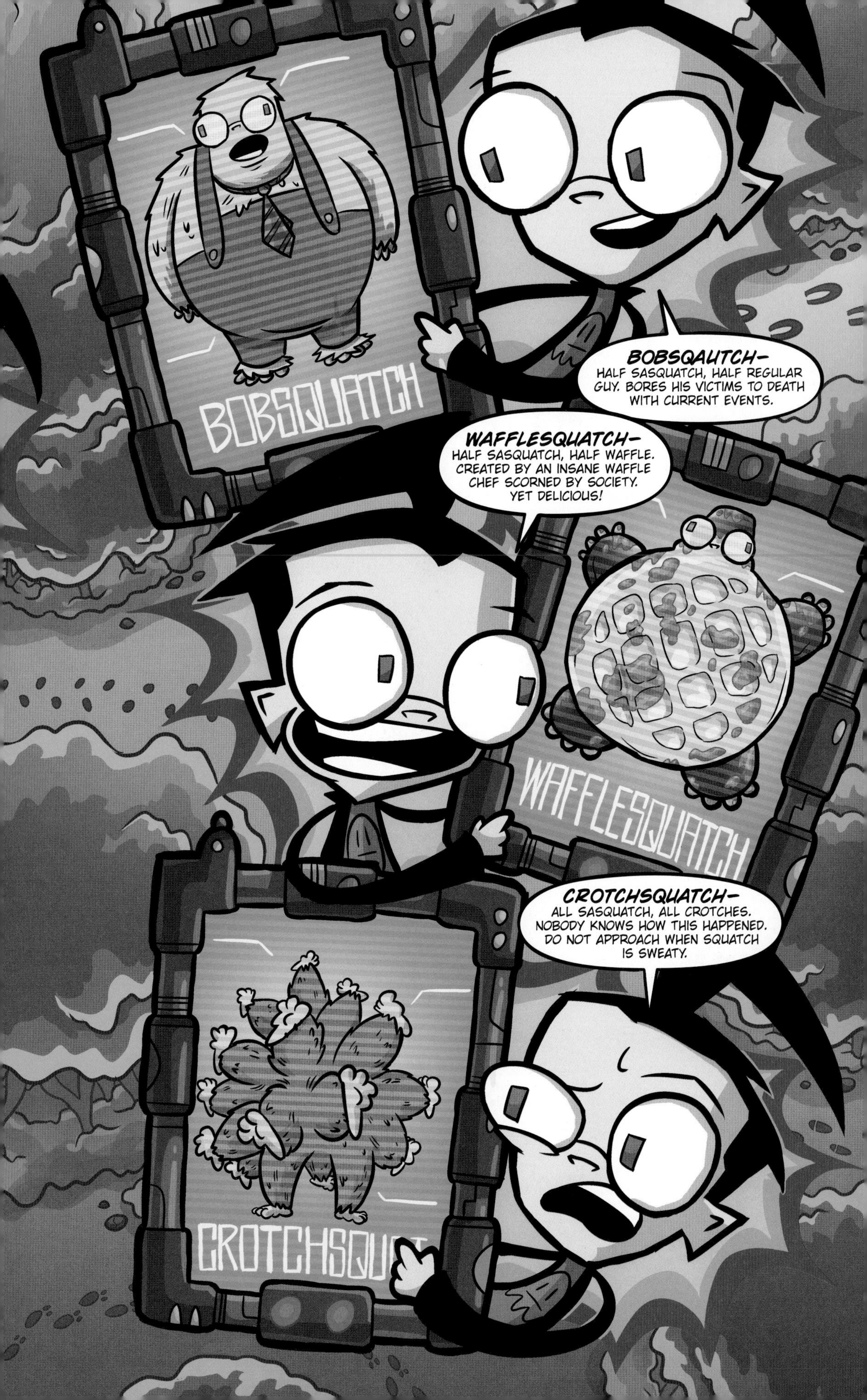
BOBSQUATCH
BOBSQAUTCH– HALF SASQUATCH, HALF REGULAR GUY. BORES HIS VICTIMS TO DEATH WITH CURRENT EVENTS.
WAFFLESQUATCH– HALF SASQUATCH, HALF WAFFLE. CREATED BY AN INSANE WAFFLE CHEF SCORNED BY SOCIETY. YET DELICIOUS!
WAFFLESQUATCH
CROTCHSQUATCH– ALL SASQUATCH, ALL CROTCHES. NOBODY KNOWS HOW THIS HAPPENED. DO NOT APPROACH WHEN SQUATCH IS SWEATY.

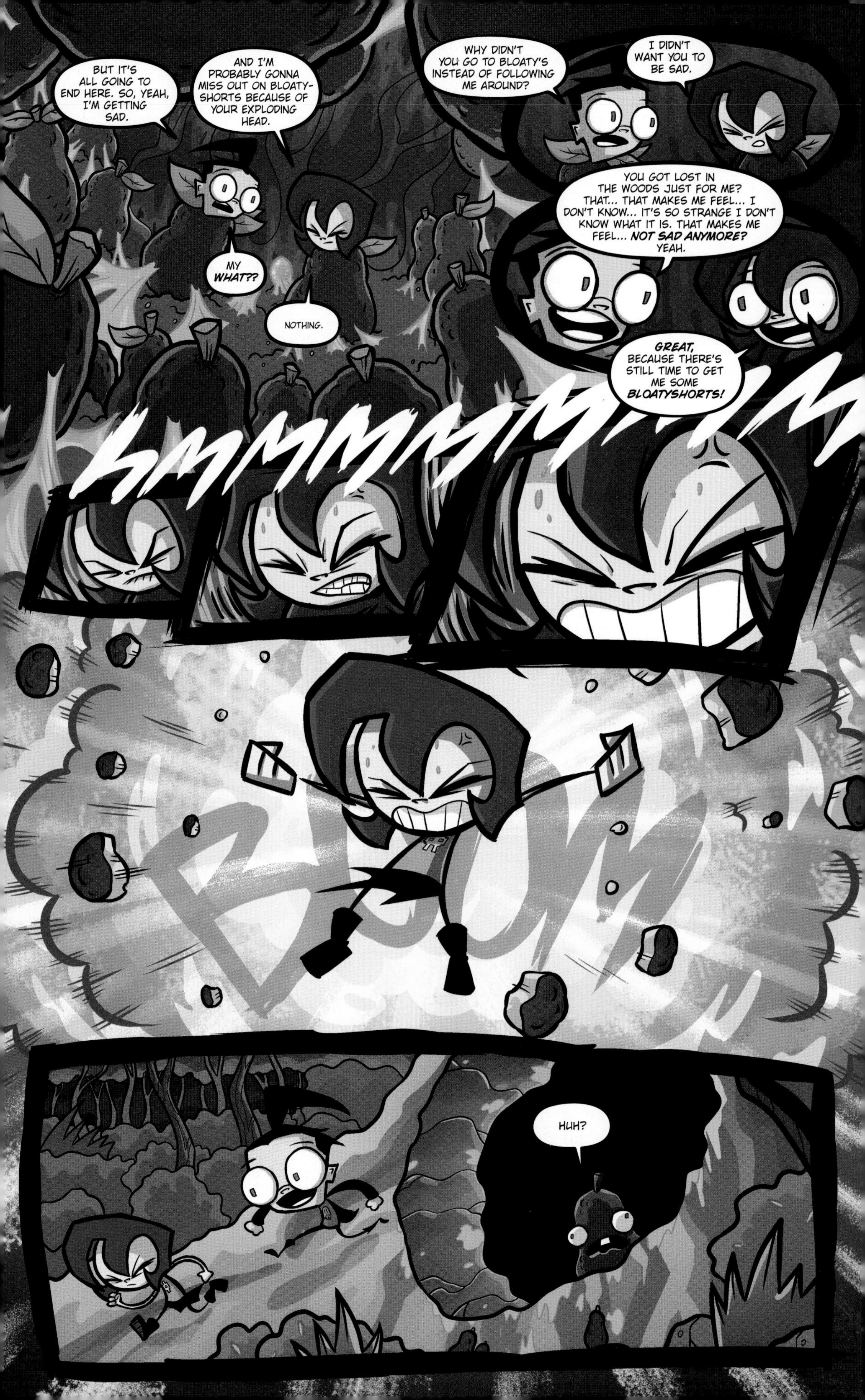
BUT IT'S ALL GOING TO END HERE. SO, YEAH, I'M GETTING SAD.
AND I'M PROBABLY GONNA MISS OUT ON BLOATY-SHORTS BECAUSE OF YOUR EXPLODING HEAD.
MY *WHAT??*
NOTHING.
WHY DIDN'T YOU GO TO BLOATY'S INSTEAD OF FOLLOWING ME AROUND?
I DIDN'T WANT YOU TO BE SAD.
YOU GOT LOST IN THE WOODS JUST FOR ME? THAT... THAT MAKES ME FEEL... I DON'T KNOW... IT'S SO STRANGE I DON'T KNOW WHAT IT IS. THAT MAKES ME FEEL... *NOT SAD ANYMORE?* YEAH.
GREAT, BECAUSE THERE'S STILL TIME TO GET ME SOME *BLOATYSHORTS!*
HMMMMMMM
BOOM
HUH?

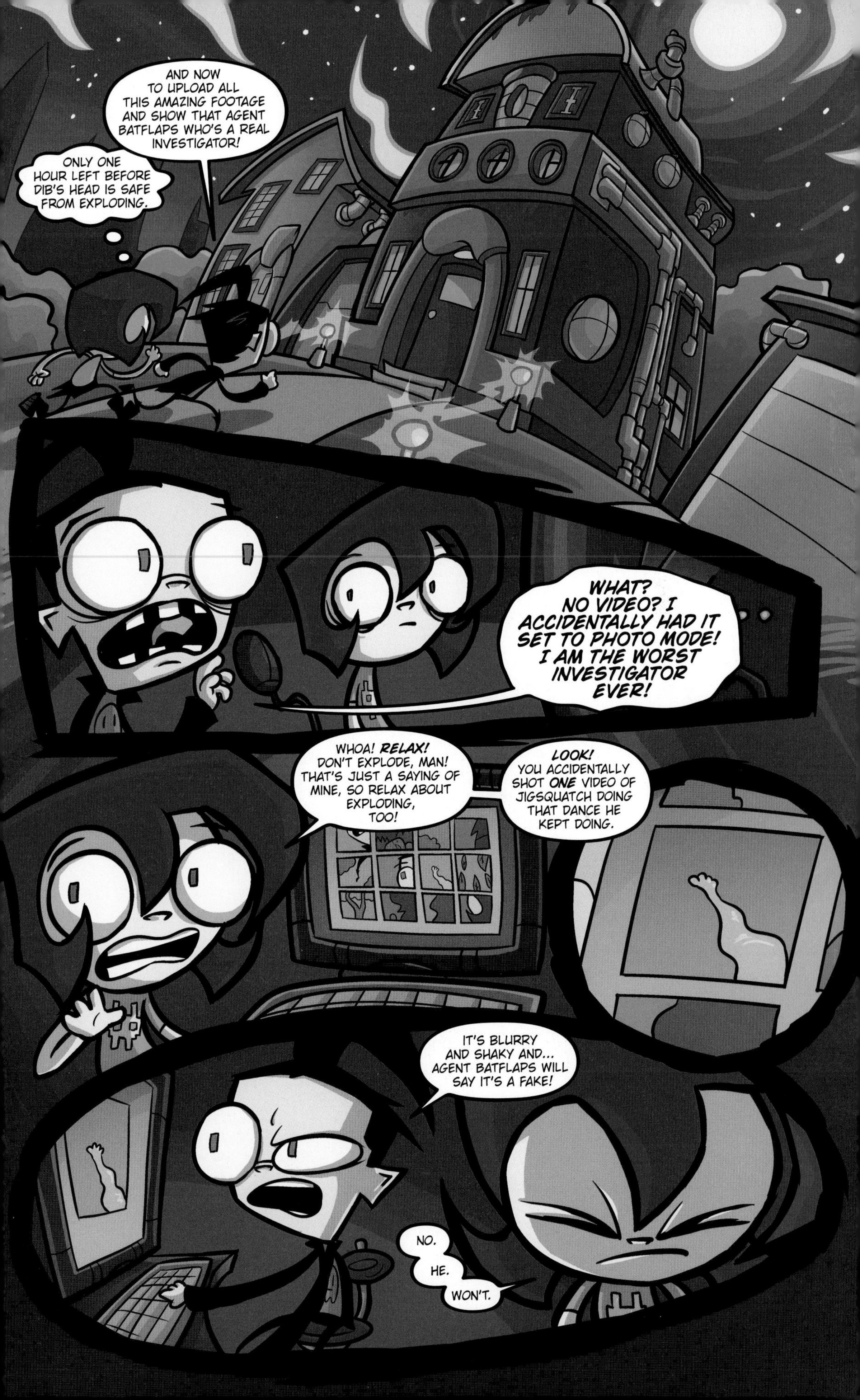
AND NOW TO UPLOAD ALL THIS AMAZING FOOTAGE AND SHOW THAT AGENT BATFLAPS WHO'S A REAL INVESTIGATOR!
ONLY ONE HOUR LEFT BEFORE DIB'S HEAD IS SAFE FROM EXPLODING.
WHAT? NO VIDEO? I ACCIDENTALLY HAD IT SET TO PHOTO MODE! I AM THE WORST INVESTIGATOR EVER!
WHOA! **RELAX!** DON'T EXPLODE, MAN! THAT'S JUST A SAYING OF MINE, SO RELAX ABOUT EXPLODING, TOO!
LOOK! YOU ACCIDENTALLY SHOT **ONE** VIDEO OF JIGSQUATCH DOING THAT DANCE HE KEPT DOING.
IT'S BLURRY AND SHAKY AND... AGENT BATFLAPS WILL SAY IT'S A FAKE!
NO.
HE.
WON'T.

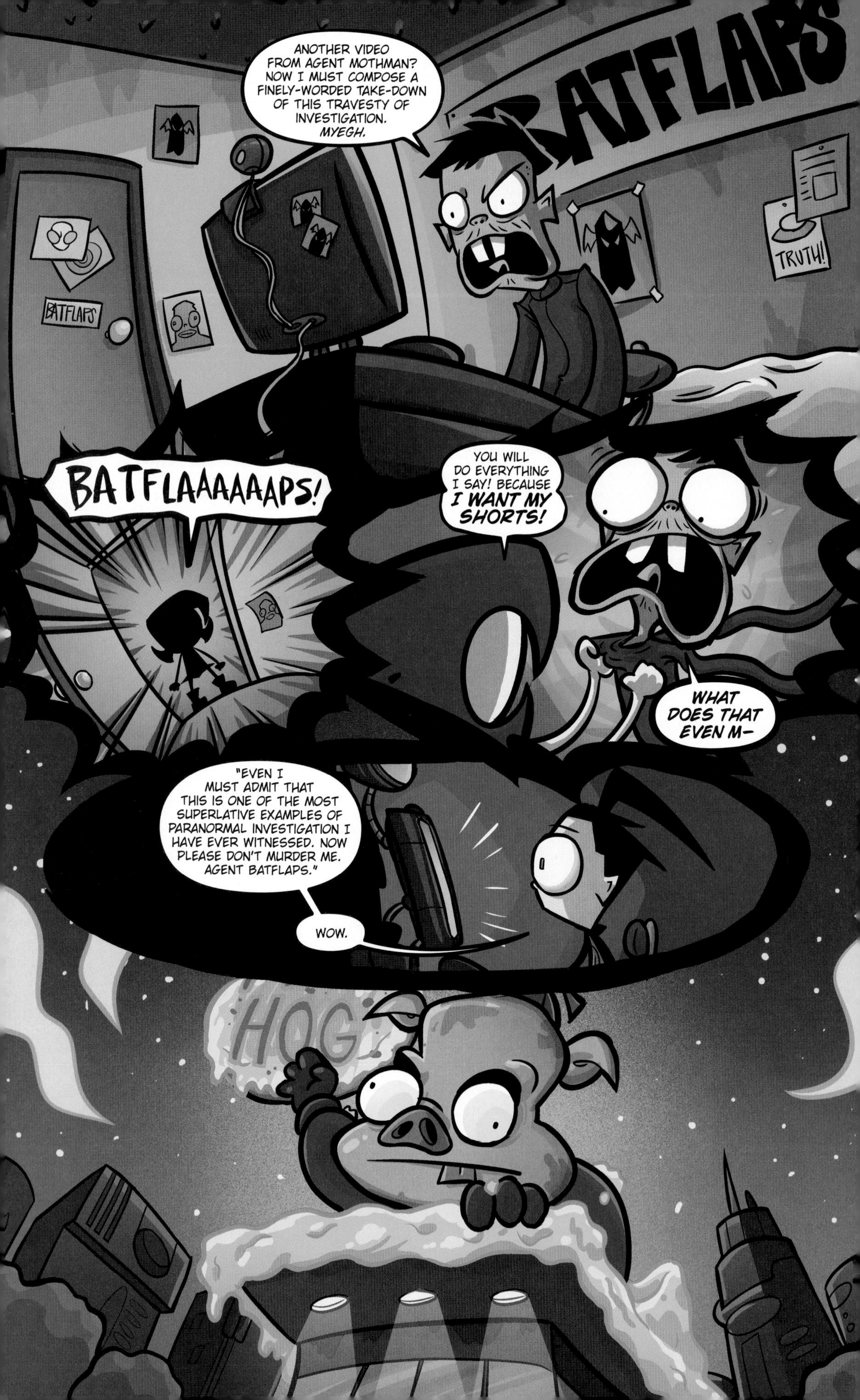
BATFLAPS
ANOTHER VIDEO FROM AGENT MOTHMAN? NOW I MUST COMPOSE A FINELY-WORDED TAKE-DOWN OF THIS TRAVESTY OF INVESTIGATION. MYEGH.
TRUTH!
BATFLAPS
BATFLAAAAAAPS!
YOU WILL DO EVERYTHING I SAY! BECAUSE I WANT MY SHORTS!
WHAT DOES THAT EVEN M—
"EVEN I MUST ADMIT THAT THIS IS ONE OF THE MOST SUPERLATIVE EXAMPLES OF PARANORMAL INVESTIGATION I HAVE EVER WITNESSED. NOW PLEASE DON'T MURDER ME. AGENT BATFLAPS."
WOW.
HOG

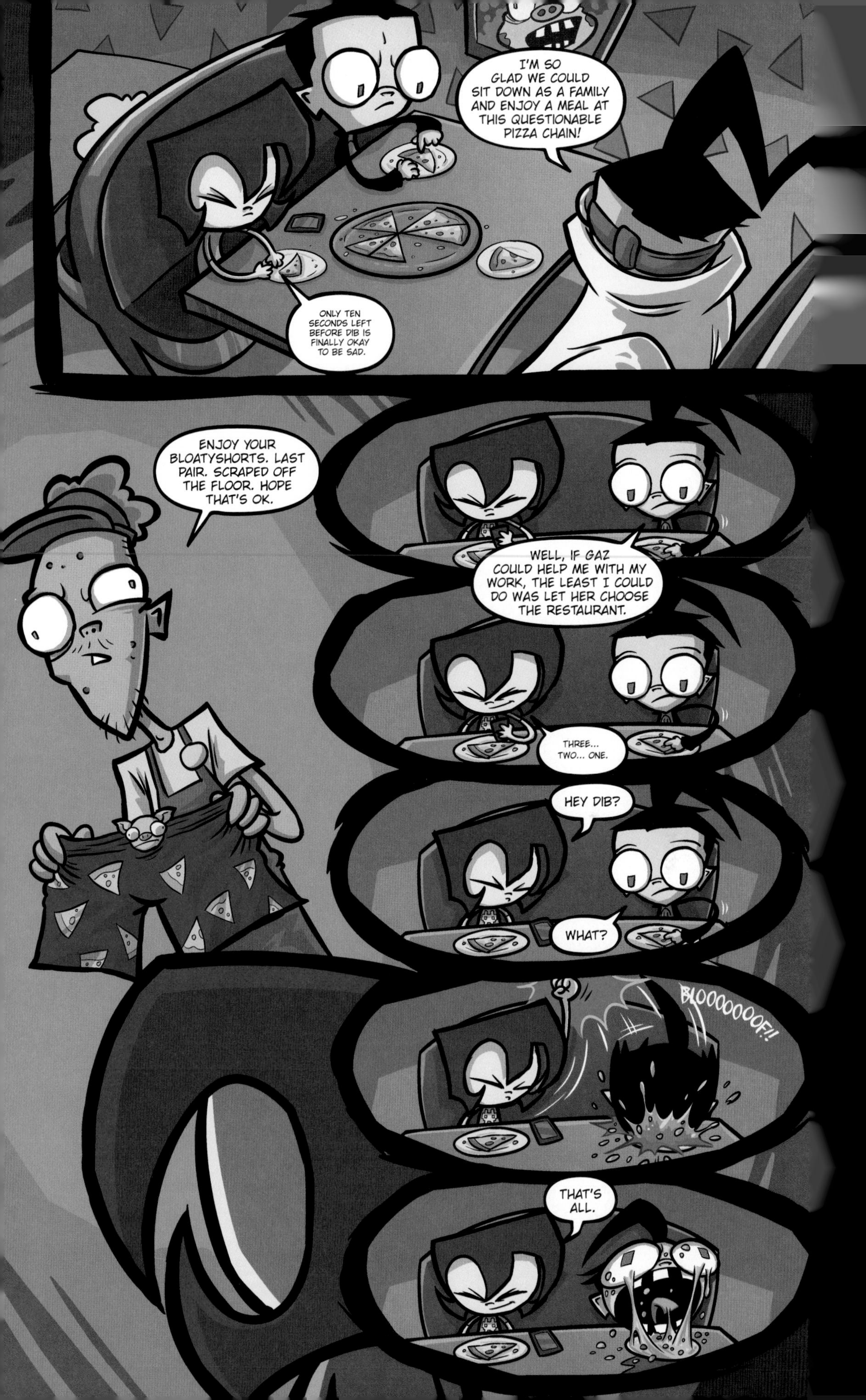
I'M SO GLAD WE COULD SIT DOWN AS A FAMILY AND ENJOY A MEAL AT THIS QUESTIONABLE PIZZA CHAIN!
ONLY TEN SECONDS LEFT BEFORE DIB IS FINALLY OKAY TO BE SAD.
ENJOY YOUR BLOATYSHORTS. LAST PAIR. SCRAPED OFF THE FLOOR. HOPE THAT'S OK.
WELL, IF GAZ COULD HELP ME WITH MY WORK, THE LEAST I COULD DO WAS LET HER CHOOSE THE RESTAURANT.
THREE... TWO... ONE.
HEY DIB?
WHAT?
BLOOOOOOOF!!
THAT'S ALL.

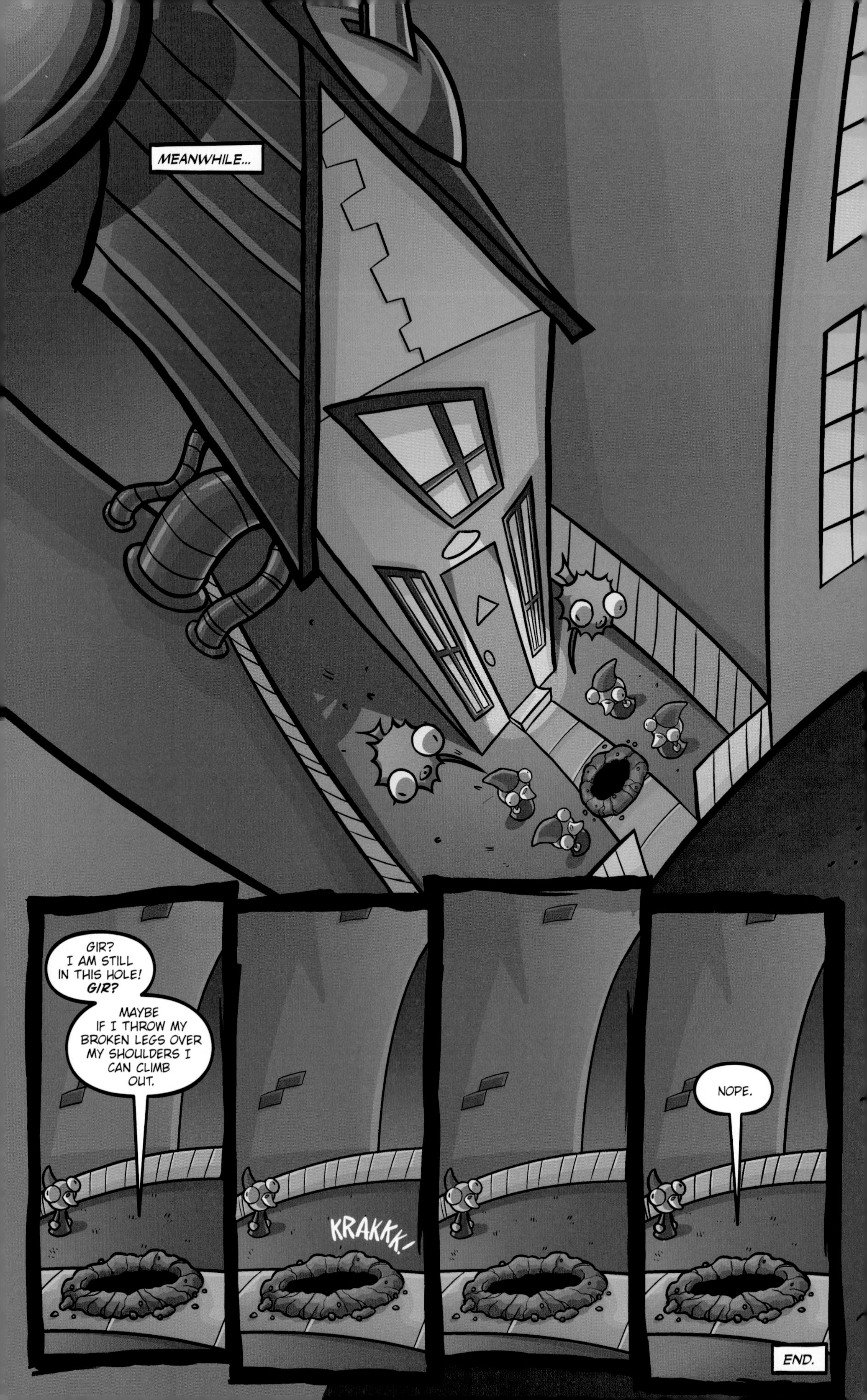
MEANWHILE...
GIR? I AM STILL IN THIS HOLE! *GIR?*
MAYBE IF I THROW MY BROKEN LEGS OVER MY SHOULDERS I CAN CLIMB OUT.
KRAKKK!
NOPE.
END.

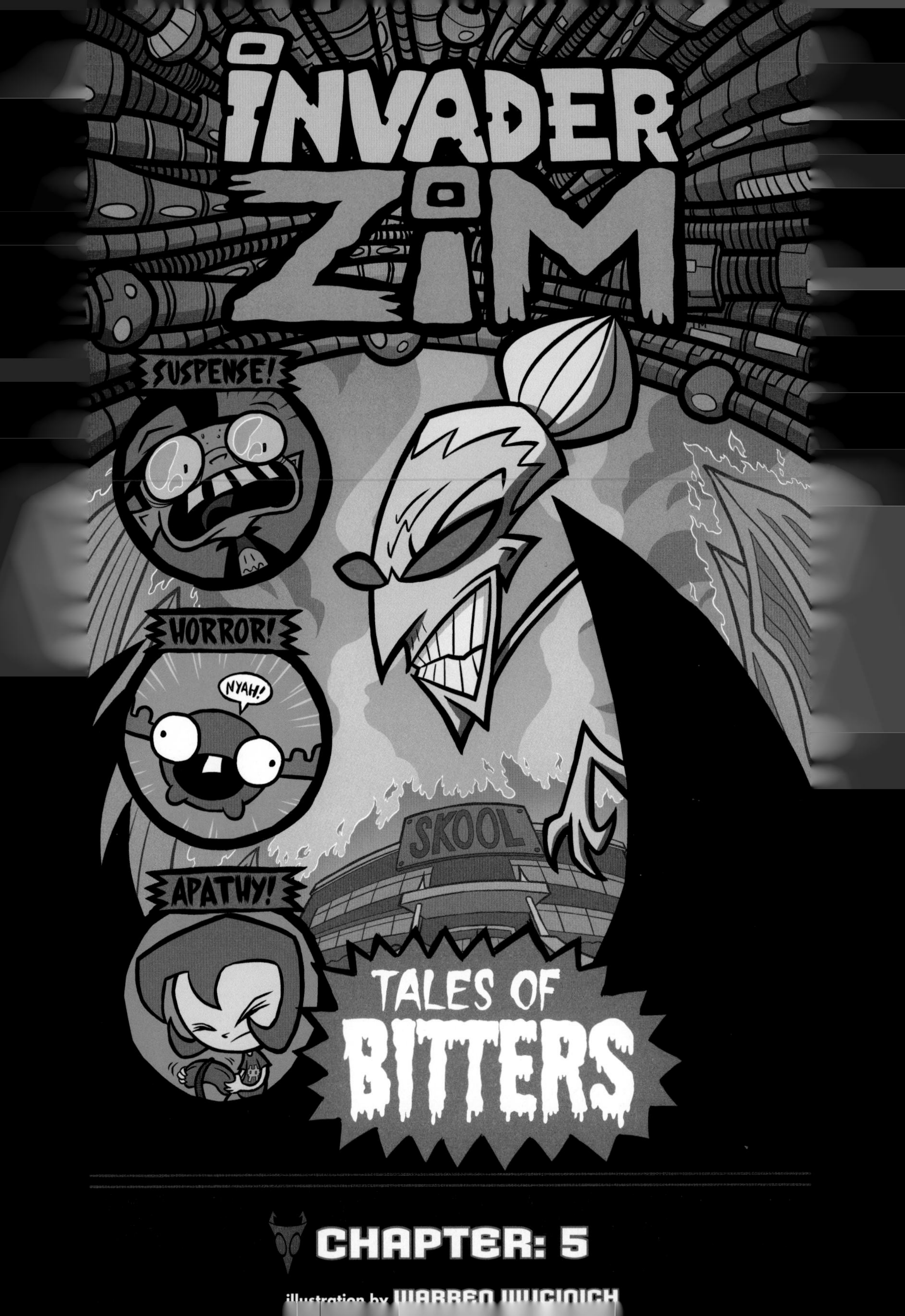
INVADER ZIM
SUSPENSE!
HORROR!
NYAH!
SKOOL
APATHY!
TALES OF BITTERS

CHAPTER: 5

illustration by WARREN WUCINICH

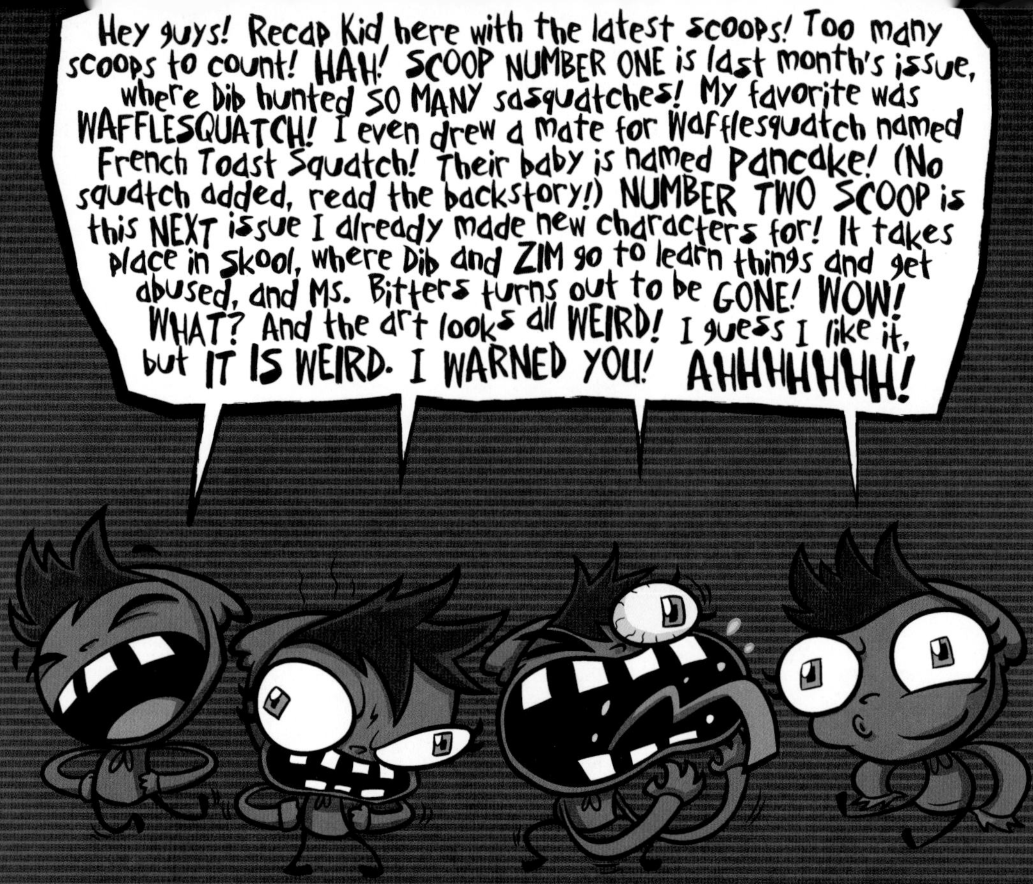
Hey guys! Recap Kid here with the latest scoops! Too many scoops to count! HAH! SCOOP NUMBER ONE is last month's issue, where Dib hunted SO MANY sasquatches! My favorite was WAFFLESQUATCH! I even drew a mate for Wafflesquatch named French Toast Squatch! Their baby is named Pancake! (No squatch added, read the backstory!) NUMBER TWO SCOOP is this NEXT issue I already made new characters for! It takes place in Skool, where Dib and ZIM go to learn things and get abused, and Ms. Bitters turns out to be GONE! WOW! WHAT? And the art looks all WEIRD! I guess I like it, but IT IS WEIRD. I WARNED YOU! AHHHHHHH!

Recap Kid by

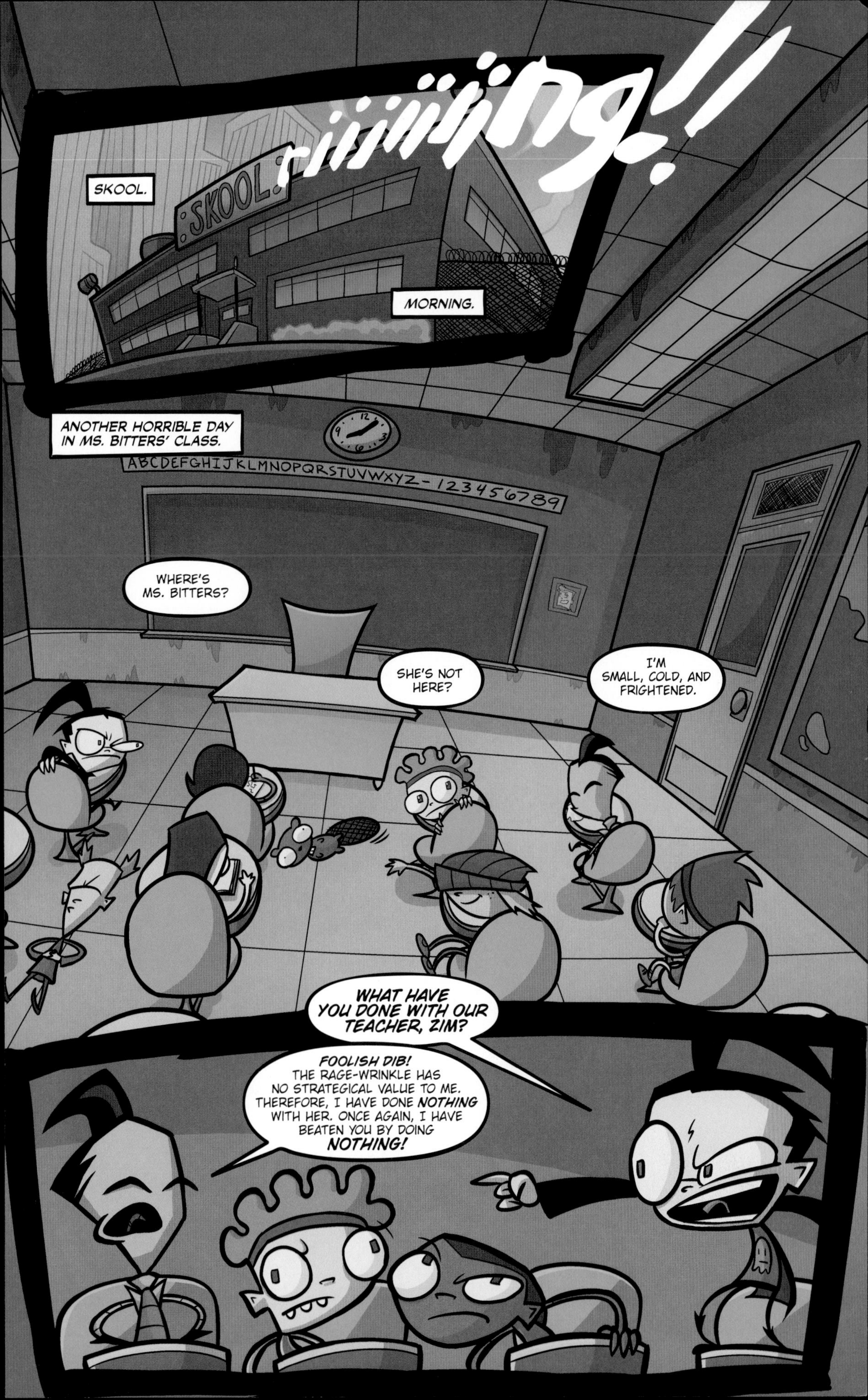
SKOOL.
riiiiiiing!!
SKOOL
MORNING.
ANOTHER HORRIBLE DAY IN MS. BITTERS' CLASS.
ABCDEFGHIJKLMNOPQRSTUVWXYZ-123456789
WHERE'S MS. BITTERS?
SHE'S NOT HERE?
I'M SMALL, COLD, AND FRIGHTENED.
WHAT HAVE YOU DONE WITH OUR TEACHER, ZIM?
FOOLISH DIB! THE RAGE-WRINKLE HAS NO STRATEGICAL VALUE TO ME. THEREFORE, I HAVE DONE NOTHING WITH HER. ONCE AGAIN, I HAVE BEATEN YOU BY DOING NOTHING!

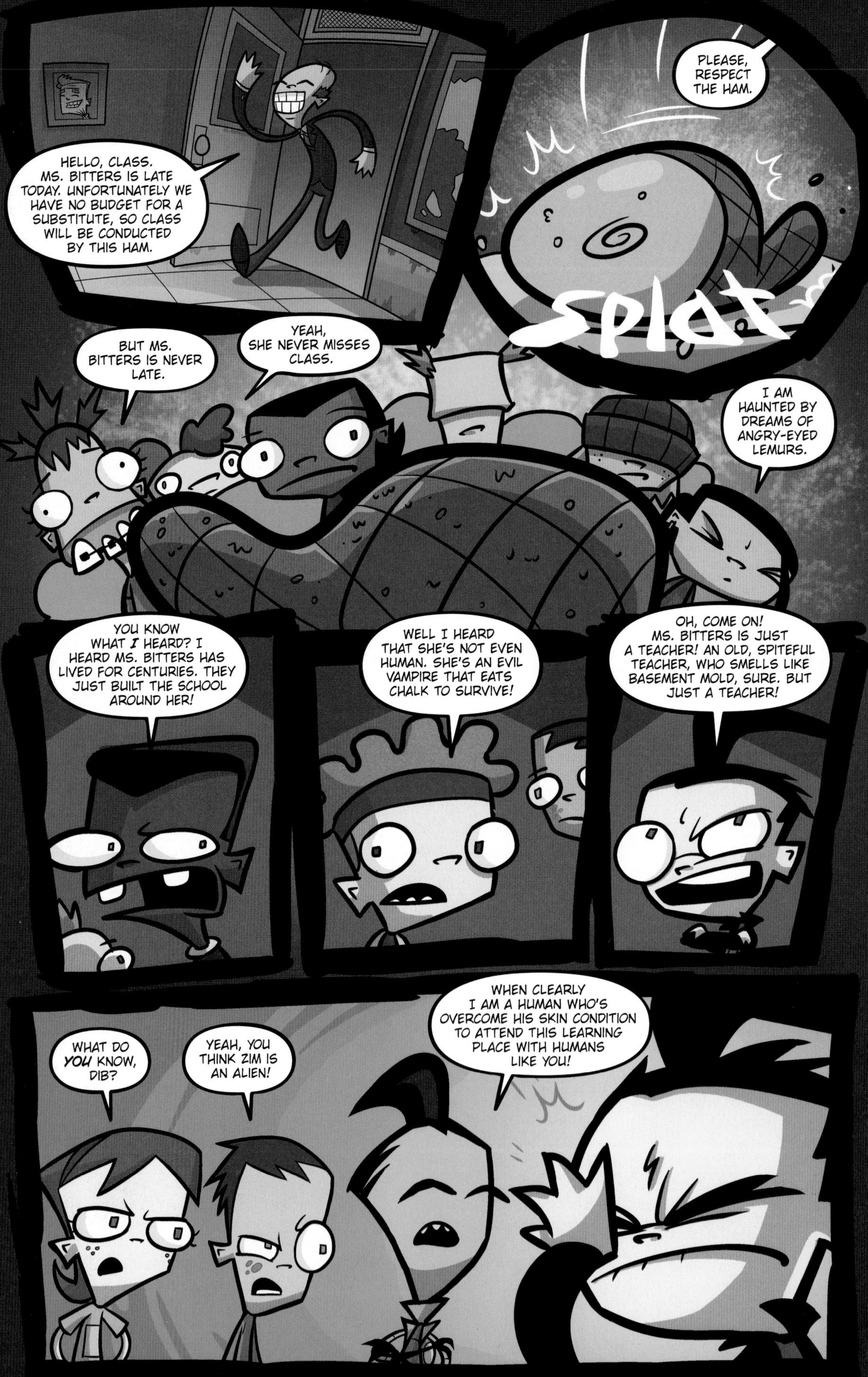
HELLO, CLASS. MS. BITTERS IS LATE TODAY. UNFORTUNATELY WE HAVE NO BUDGET FOR A SUBSTITUTE, SO CLASS WILL BE CONDUCTED BY THIS HAM.
PLEASE, RESPECT THE HAM.
SPLAT
BUT MS. BITTERS IS NEVER LATE.
YEAH, SHE NEVER MISSES CLASS.
I AM HAUNTED BY DREAMS OF ANGRY-EYED LEMURS.
YOU KNOW WHAT I HEARD? I HEARD MS. BITTERS HAS LIVED FOR CENTURIES. THEY JUST BUILT THE SCHOOL AROUND HER!
WELL I HEARD THAT SHE'S NOT EVEN HUMAN. SHE'S AN EVIL VAMPIRE THAT EATS CHALK TO SURVIVE!
OH, COME ON! MS. BITTERS IS JUST A TEACHER! AN OLD, SPITEFUL TEACHER, WHO SMELLS LIKE BASEMENT MOLD, SURE. BUT JUST A TEACHER!
WHAT DO YOU KNOW, DIB?
YEAH, YOU THINK ZIM IS AN ALIEN!
WHEN CLEARLY I AM A HUMAN WHO'S OVERCOME HIS SKIN CONDITION TO ATTEND THIS LEARNING PLACE WITH HUMANS LIKE YOU!

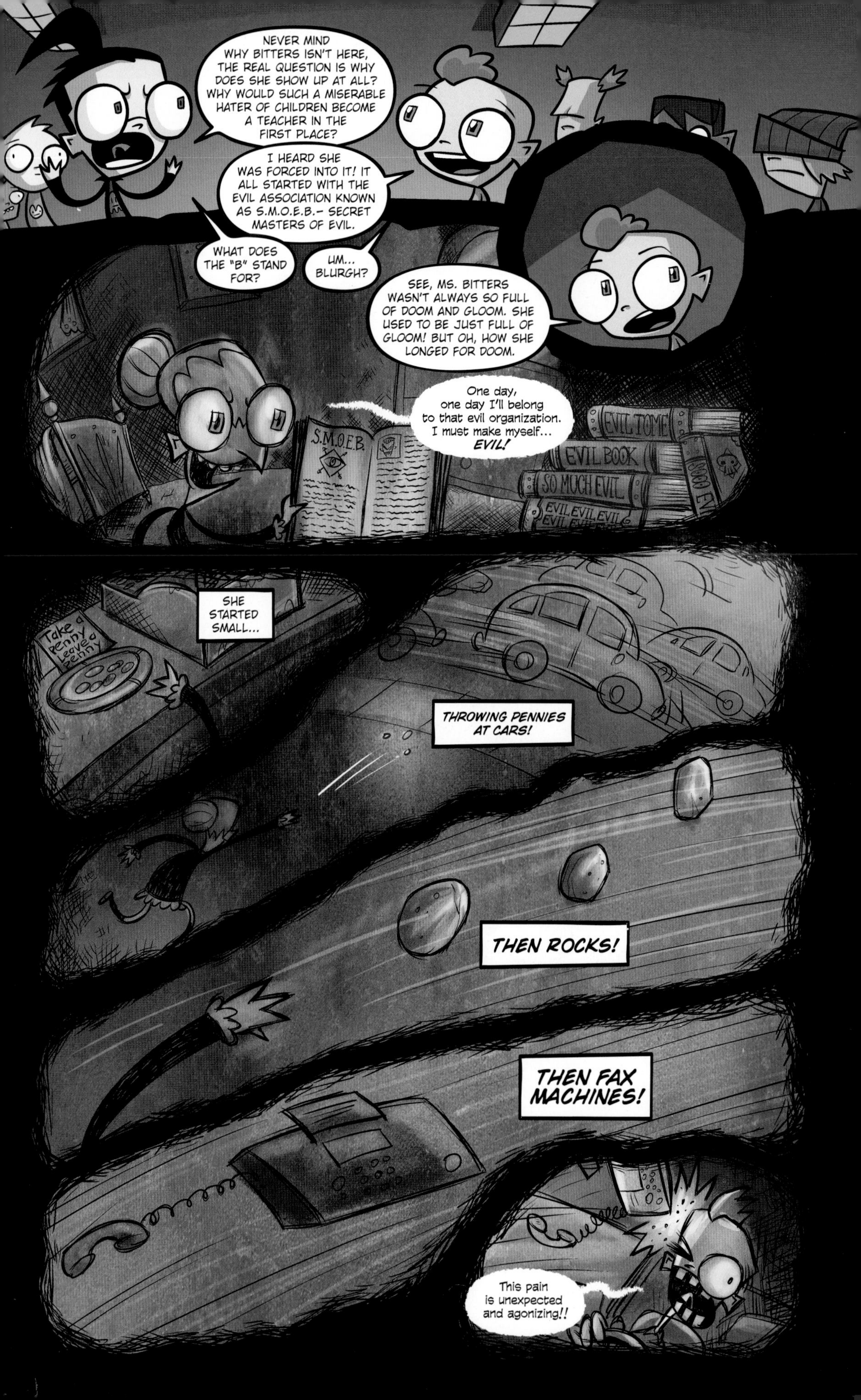
NEVER MIND WHY BITTERS ISN'T HERE, THE REAL QUESTION IS WHY DOES SHE SHOW UP AT ALL? WHY WOULD SUCH A MISERABLE HATER OF CHILDREN BECOME A TEACHER IN THE FIRST PLACE?
I HEARD SHE WAS FORCED INTO IT! IT ALL STARTED WITH THE EVIL ASSOCIATION KNOWN AS S.M.O.E.B.– SECRET MASTERS OF EVIL.
WHAT DOES THE "B" STAND FOR?
UM... BLURGH?
SEE, MS. BITTERS WASN'T ALWAYS SO FULL OF DOOM AND GLOOM. SHE USED TO BE JUST FULL OF GLOOM! BUT OH, HOW SHE LONGED FOR DOOM.
S.M.O.E.B.
One day, one day I'll belong to that evil organization. I must make myself... EVIL!
EVIL TOME
EVIL BOOK
SO MUCH EVIL
EVIL EVIL EVIL
SHE STARTED SMALL...
Take a penny Leave a penny
THROWING PENNIES AT CARS!
THEN ROCKS!
THEN FAX MACHINES!
This pain is unexpected and agonizing!!

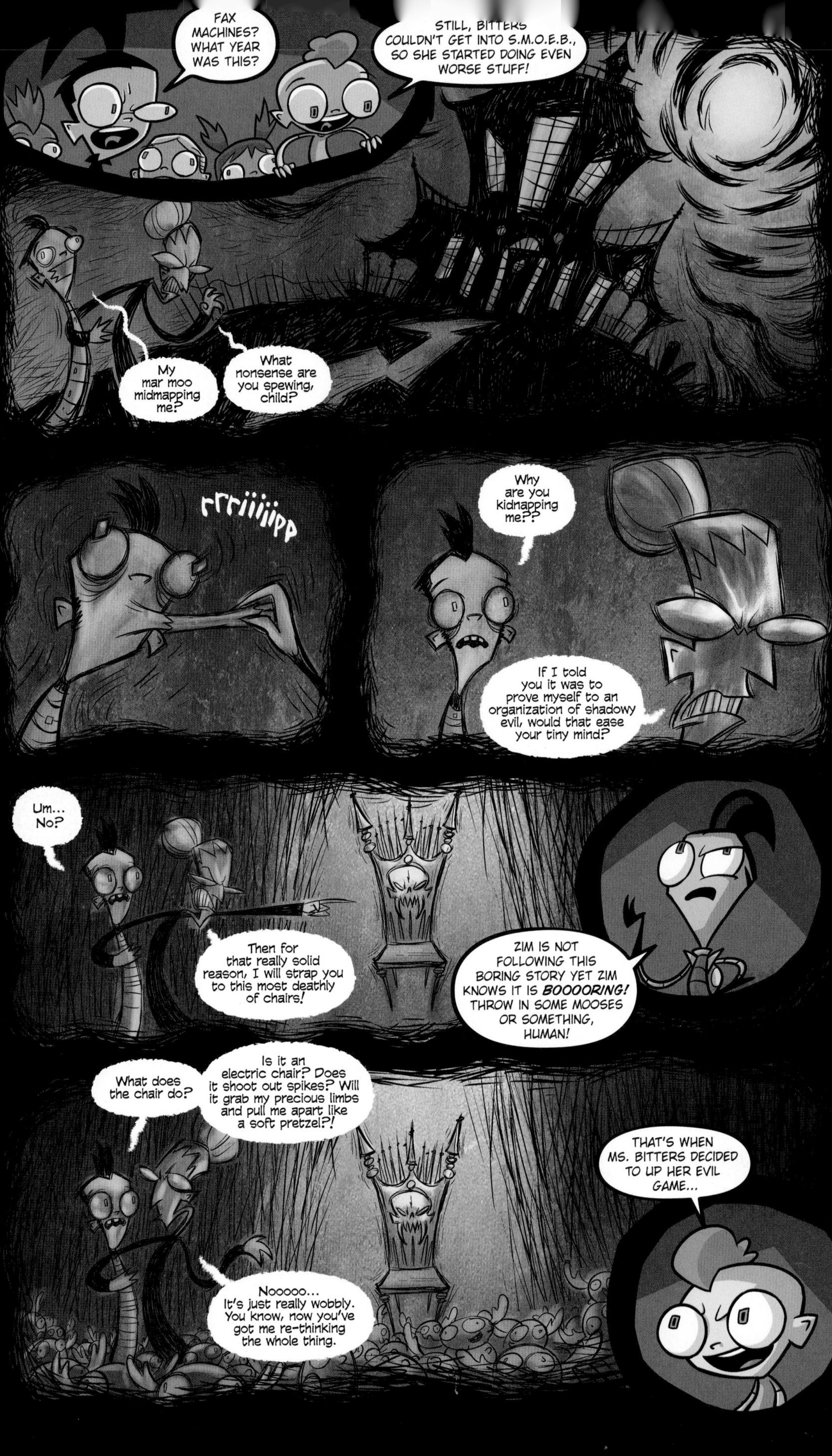
FAX MACHINES? WHAT YEAR WAS THIS?
STILL, BITTERS COULDN'T GET INTO S.M.O.E.B., SO SHE STARTED DOING EVEN WORSE STUFF!
My mar moo midmapping me?
What nonsense are you spewing, child?
rrriiiiipp
Why are you kidnapping me??
If I told you it was to prove myself to an organization of shadowy evil, would that ease your tiny mind?
Um... No?
Then for that really solid reason, I will strap you to this most deathly of chairs!
ZIM IS NOT FOLLOWING THIS BORING STORY YET ZIM KNOWS IT IS BOOOORING! THROW IN SOME MOOSES OR SOMETHING, HUMAN!
What does the chair do?
Is it an electric chair? Does it shoot out spikes? Will it grab my precious limbs and pull me apart like a soft pretzel?!
THAT'S WHEN MS. BITTERS DECIDED TO UP HER EVIL GAME...
Nooooo... It's just really wobbly. You know, now you've got me re-thinking the whole thing.

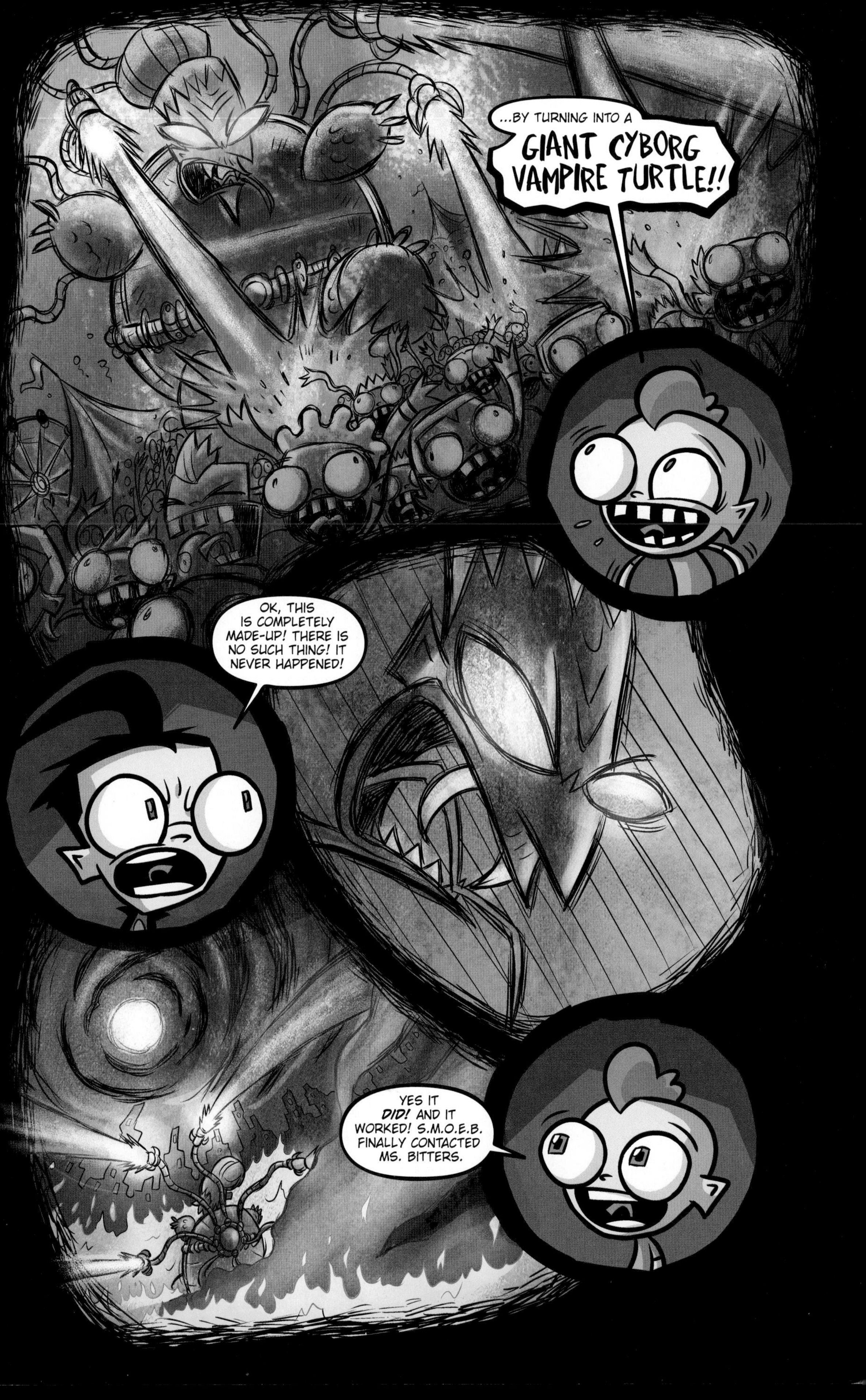
...BY TURNING INTO A GIANT CYBORG VAMPIRE TURTLE!!
OK, THIS IS COMPLETELY MADE-UP! THERE IS NO SUCH THING! IT NEVER HAPPENED!
YES IT DID! AND IT WORKED! S.M.O.E.B. FINALLY CONTACTED MS. BITTERS.

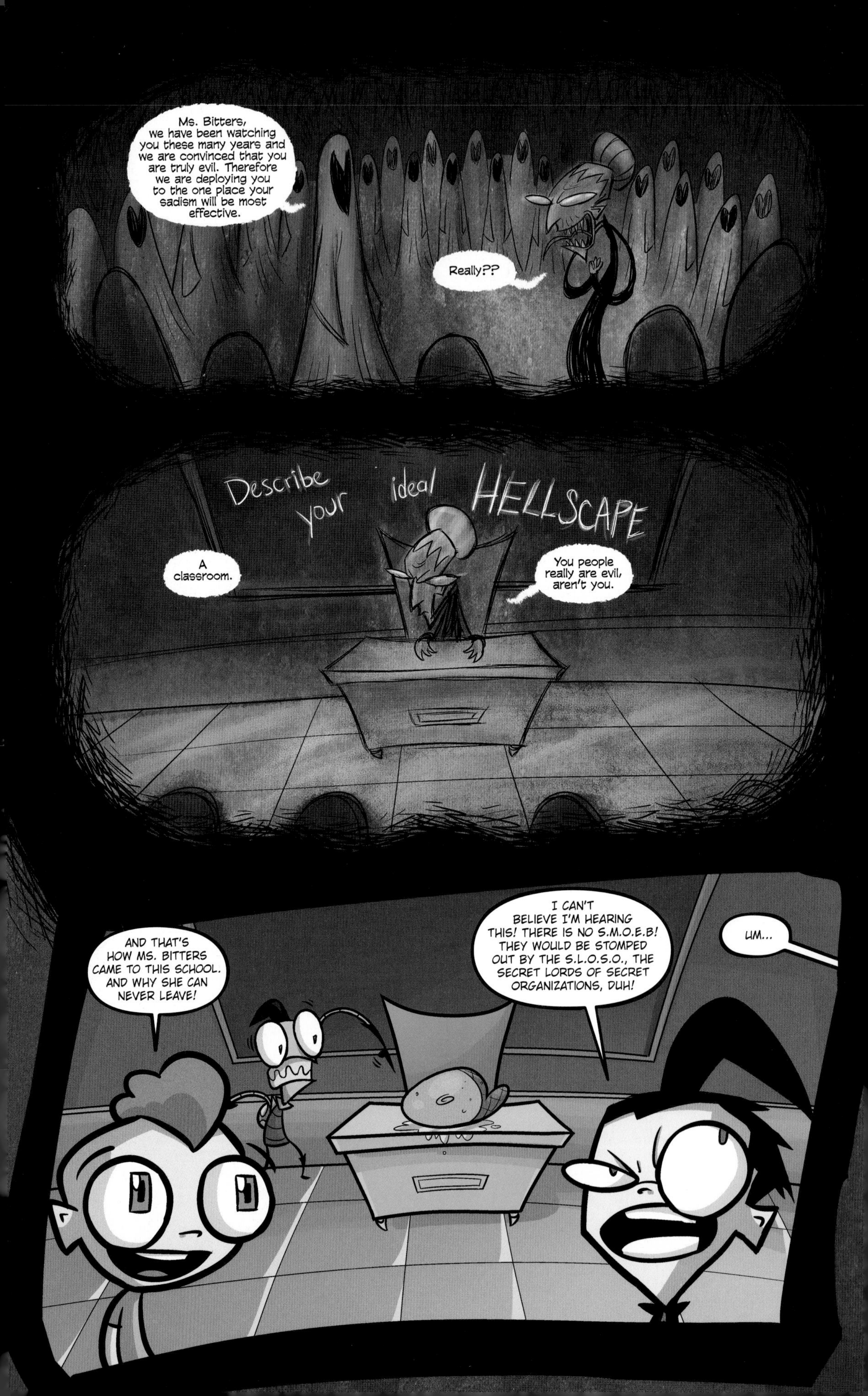
Ms. Bitters, we have been watching you these many years and we are convinced that you are truly evil. Therefore we are deploying you to the one place your sadism will be most effective.
Really??
Describe your ideal HELLSCAPE
A classroom.
You people really are evil, aren't you.
AND THAT'S HOW MS. BITTERS CAME TO THIS SCHOOL. AND WHY SHE CAN NEVER LEAVE!
I CAN'T BELIEVE I'M HEARING THIS! THERE IS NO S.M.O.E.B! THEY WOULD BE STOMPED OUT BY THE S.L.O.S.O., THE SECRET LORDS OF SECRET ORGANIZATIONS, DUH!
UM...

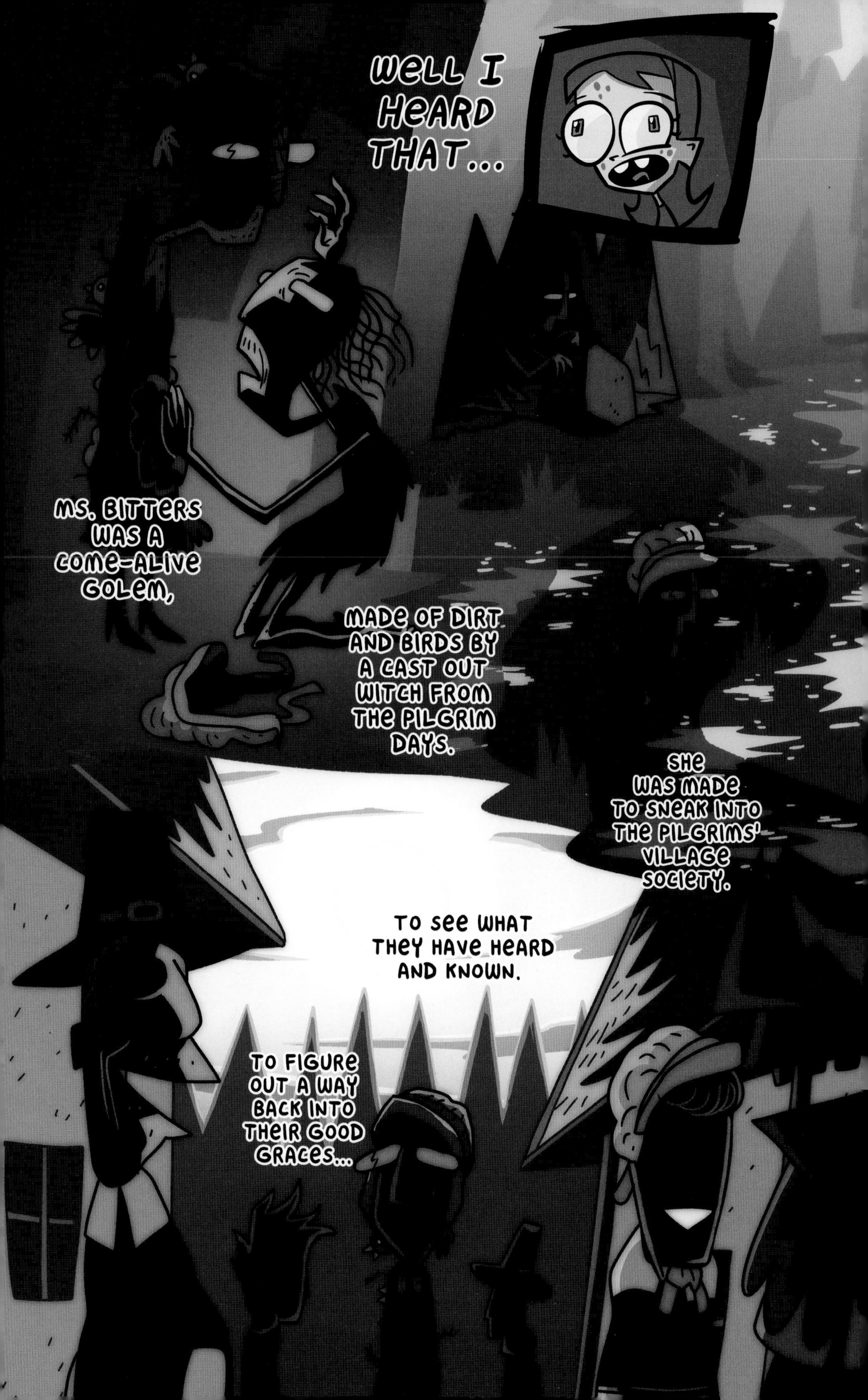
WELL I HEARD THAT...
MS. BITTERS WAS A COME-ALIVE GOLEM,
MADE OF DIRT AND BIRDS BY A CAST OUT WITCH FROM THE PILGRIM DAYS.
SHE WAS MADE TO SNEAK INTO THE PILGRIMS' VILLAGE SOCIETY.
TO SEE WHAT THEY HAVE HEARD AND KNOWN.
TO FIGURE OUT A WAY BACK INTO THEIR GOOD GRACES...

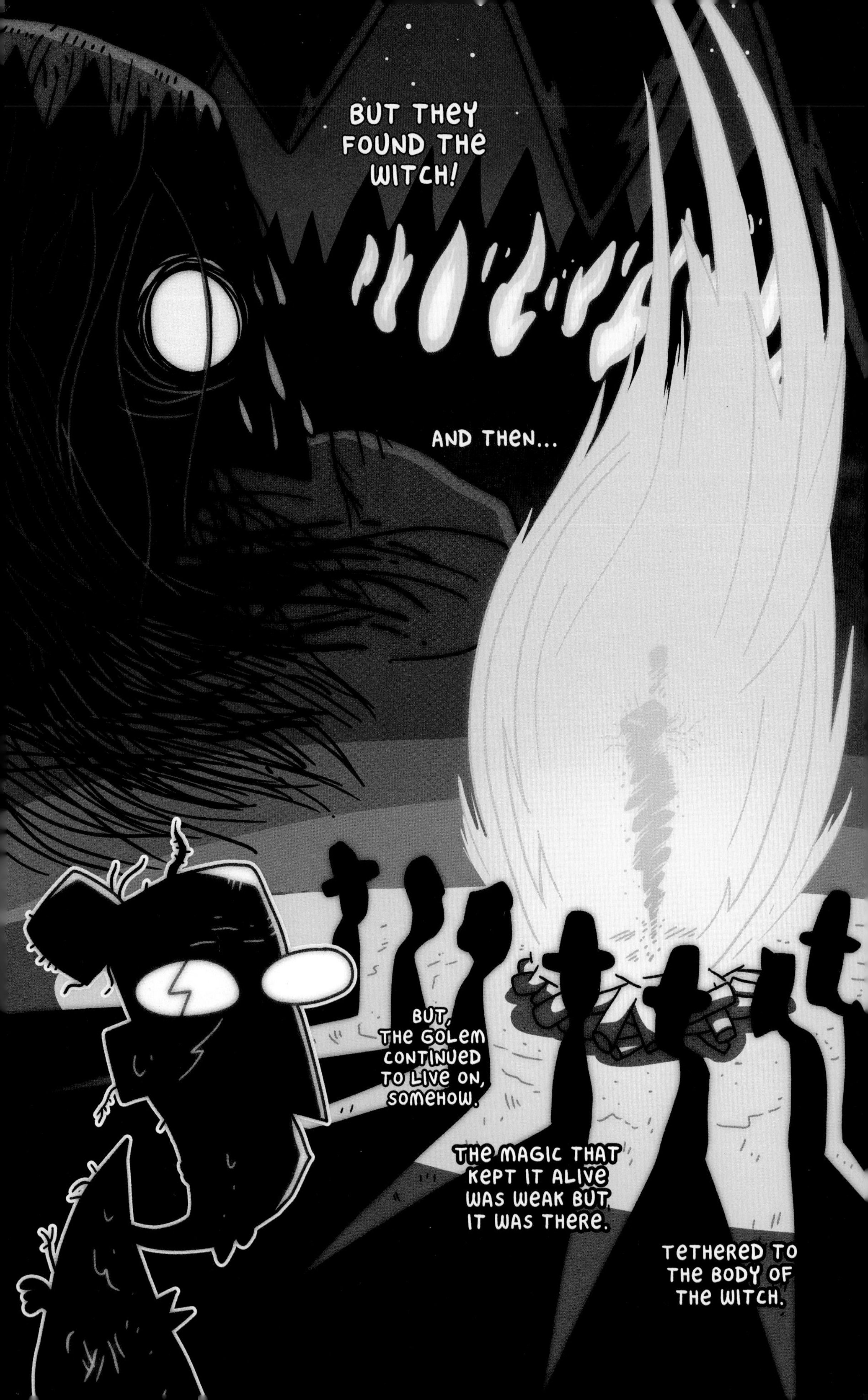
BUT THEY FOUND THE WITCH!
AND THEN...
BUT, THE GOLEM CONTINUED TO LIVE ON, SOMEHOW.
THE MAGIC THAT KEPT IT ALIVE WAS WEAK BUT IT WAS THERE.
TETHERED TO THE BODY OF THE WITCH.

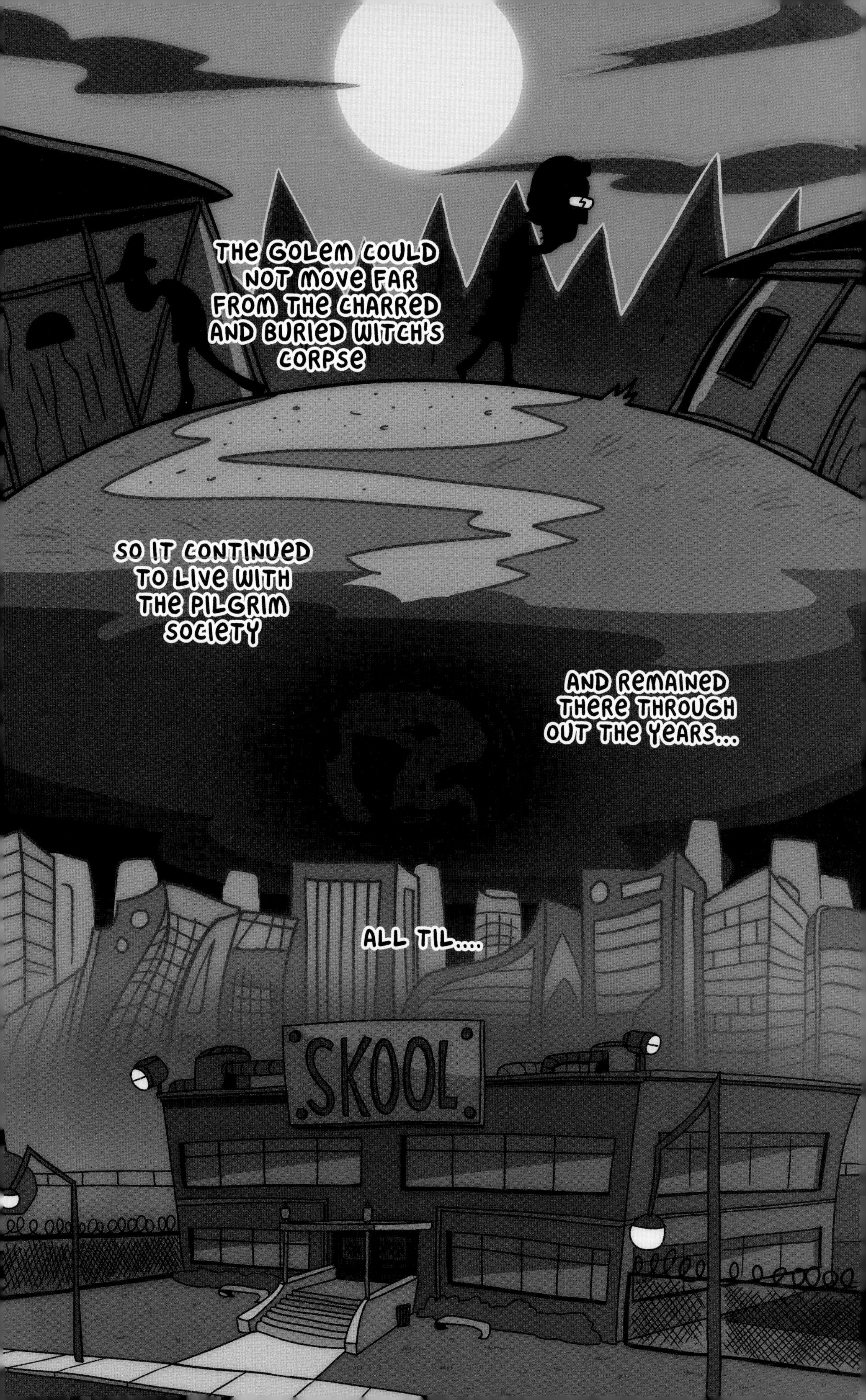
THE GOLEM COULD NOT MOVE FAR FROM THE CHARRED AND BURIED WITCH'S CORPSE
SO IT CONTINUED TO LIVE WITH THE PILGRIM SOCIETY
AND REMAINED THERE THROUGH OUT THE YEARS...
ALL TIL....
SKOOL

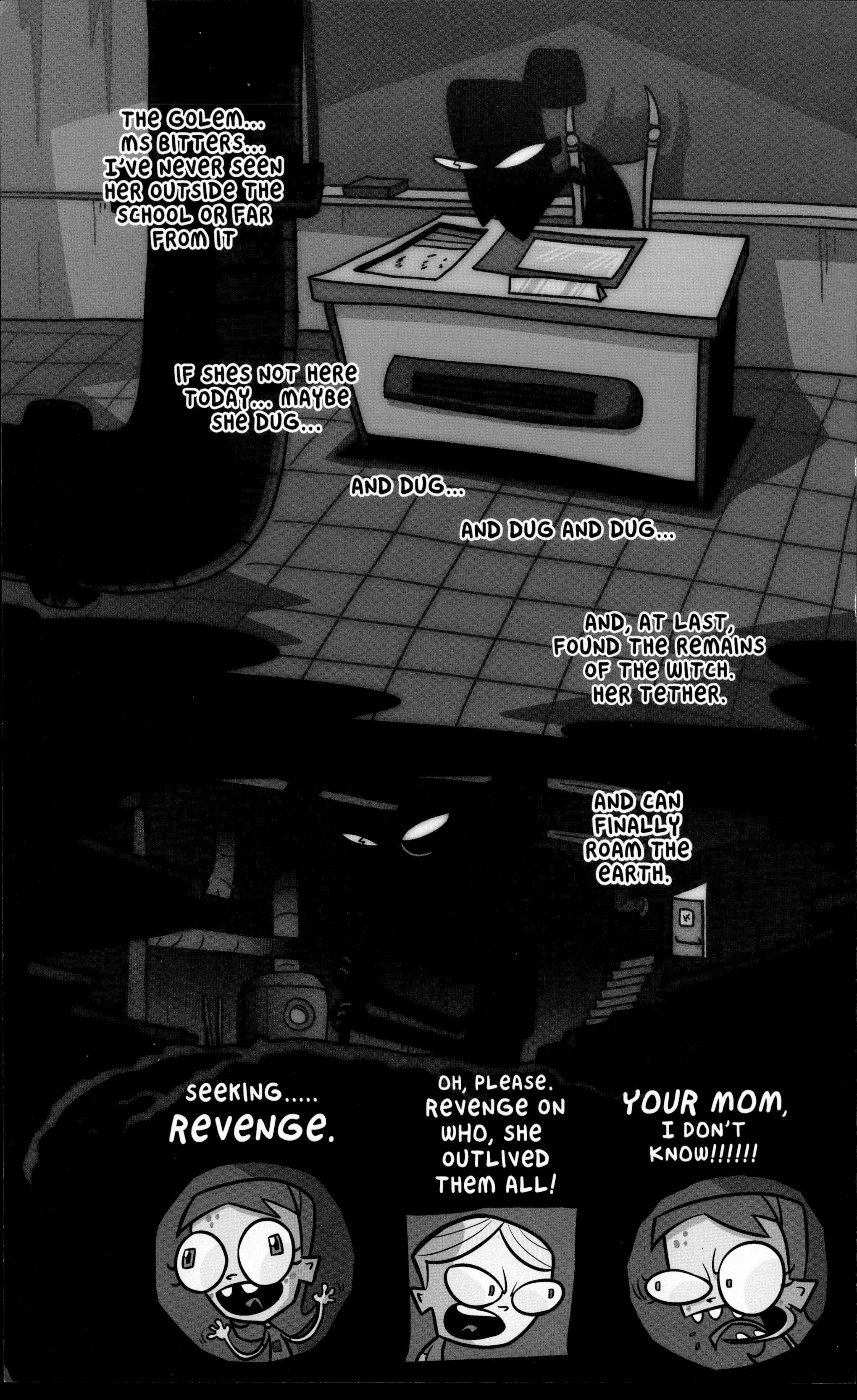
THE GOLEM... MS BITTERS... I'VE NEVER SEEN HER OUTSIDE THE SCHOOL OR FAR FROM IT
IF SHES NOT HERE TODAY... MAYBE SHE DUG...
AND DUG...
AND DUG AND DUG...
AND, AT LAST, FOUND THE REMAINS OF THE WITCH. HER TETHER.
AND CAN FINALLY ROAM THE EARTH.
SEEKING..... REVENGE.
OH, PLEASE. REVENGE ON WHO, SHE OUTLIVED THEM ALL!
YOUR MOM, I DON'T KNOW!!!!!!

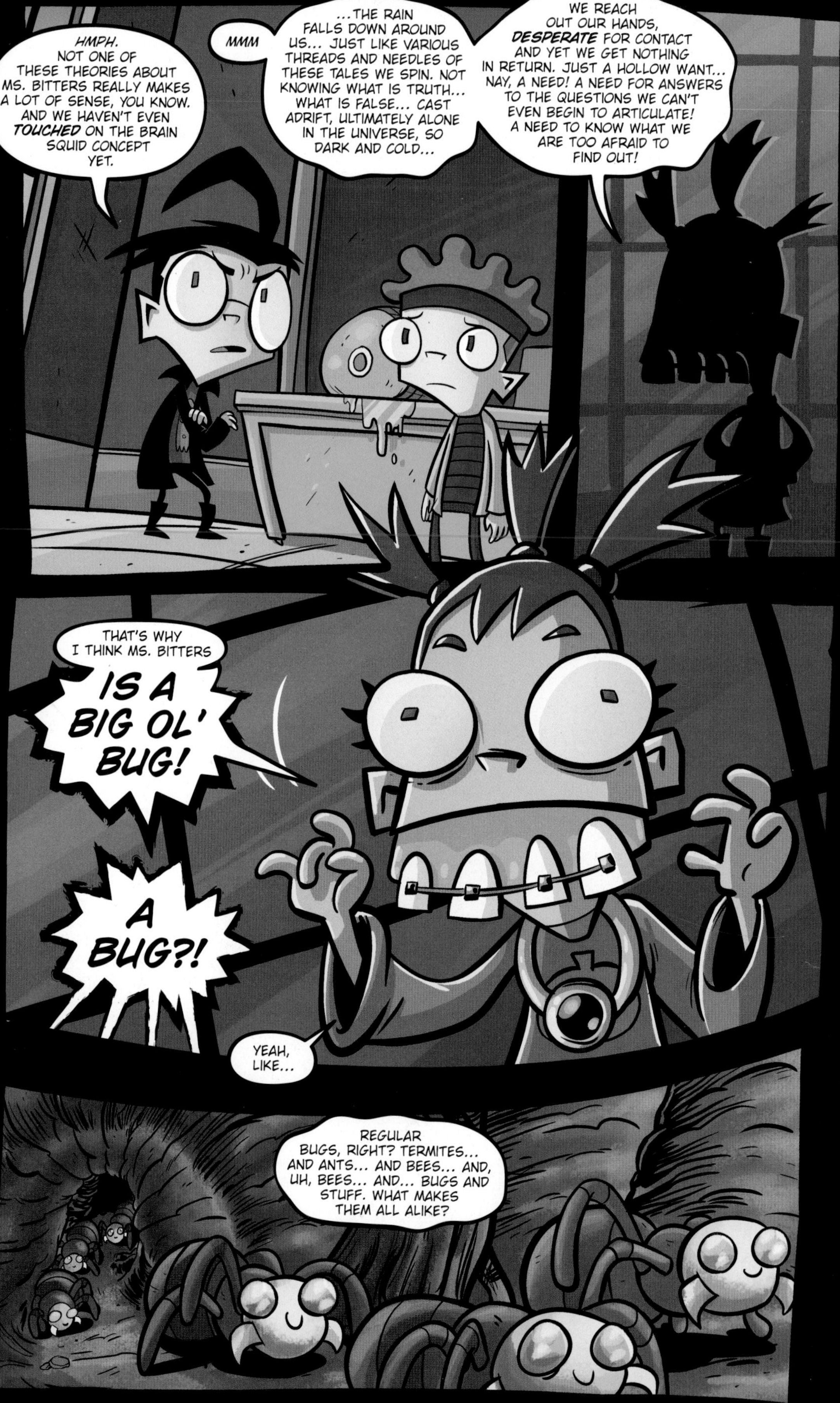
HMPH. NOT ONE OF THESE THEORIES ABOUT MS. BITTERS REALLY MAKES A LOT OF SENSE, YOU KNOW. AND WE HAVEN'T EVEN TOUCHED ON THE BRAIN SQUID CONCEPT YET.
MMM
...THE RAIN FALLS DOWN AROUND US... JUST LIKE VARIOUS THREADS AND NEEDLES OF THESE TALES WE SPIN. NOT KNOWING WHAT IS TRUTH... WHAT IS FALSE... CAST ADRIFT, ULTIMATELY ALONE IN THE UNIVERSE, SO DARK AND COLD...
WE REACH OUT OUR HANDS, DESPERATE FOR CONTACT AND YET WE GET NOTHING IN RETURN. JUST A HOLLOW WANT... NAY, A NEED! A NEED FOR ANSWERS TO THE QUESTIONS WE CAN'T EVEN BEGIN TO ARTICULATE! A NEED TO KNOW WHAT WE ARE TOO AFRAID TO FIND OUT!
THAT'S WHY I THINK MS. BITTERS
IS A BIG OL' BUG!
A BUG?!
YEAH, LIKE...
REGULAR BUGS, RIGHT? TERMITES... AND ANTS... AND BEES... AND, UH, BEES... AND... BUGS AND STUFF. WHAT MAKES THEM ALL ALIKE?

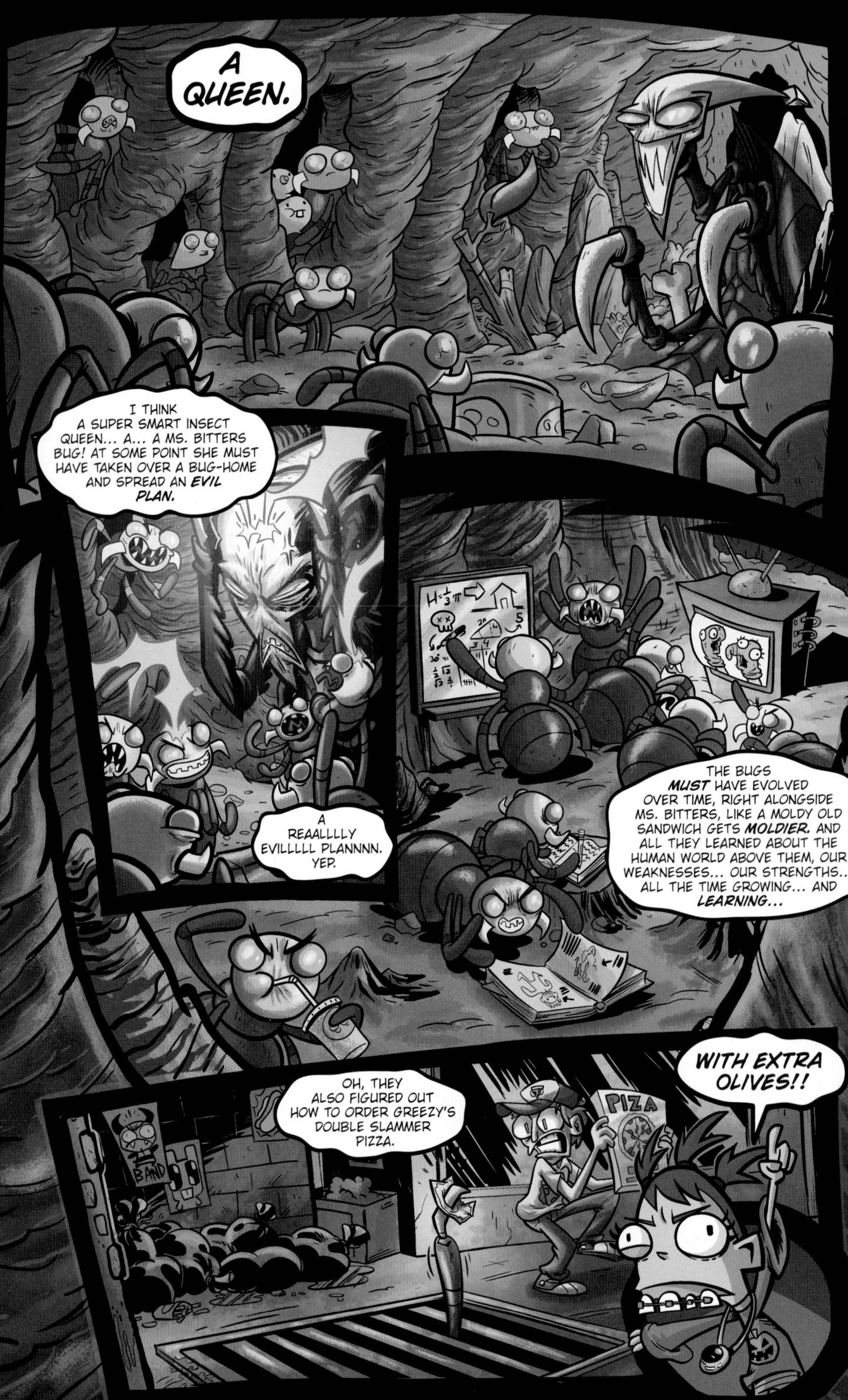
A QUEEN.
I THINK A SUPER SMART INSECT QUEEN... A... A MS. BITTERS BUG! AT SOME POINT SHE MUST HAVE TAKEN OVER A BUG-HOME AND SPREAD AN EVIL PLAN.
A REAALLLLY EVILLLLL PLANNNN. YEP.
THE BUGS MUST HAVE EVOLVED OVER TIME, RIGHT ALONGSIDE MS. BITTERS, LIKE A MOLDY OLD SANDWICH GETS MOLDIER. AND ALL THEY LEARNED ABOUT THE HUMAN WORLD ABOVE THEM, OUR WEAKNESSES... OUR STRENGTHS... ALL THE TIME GROWING... AND LEARNING...
OH, THEY ALSO FIGURED OUT HOW TO ORDER GREEZY'S DOUBLE SLAMMER PIZZA.
WITH EXTRA OLIVES!!
PIZZA
BAND

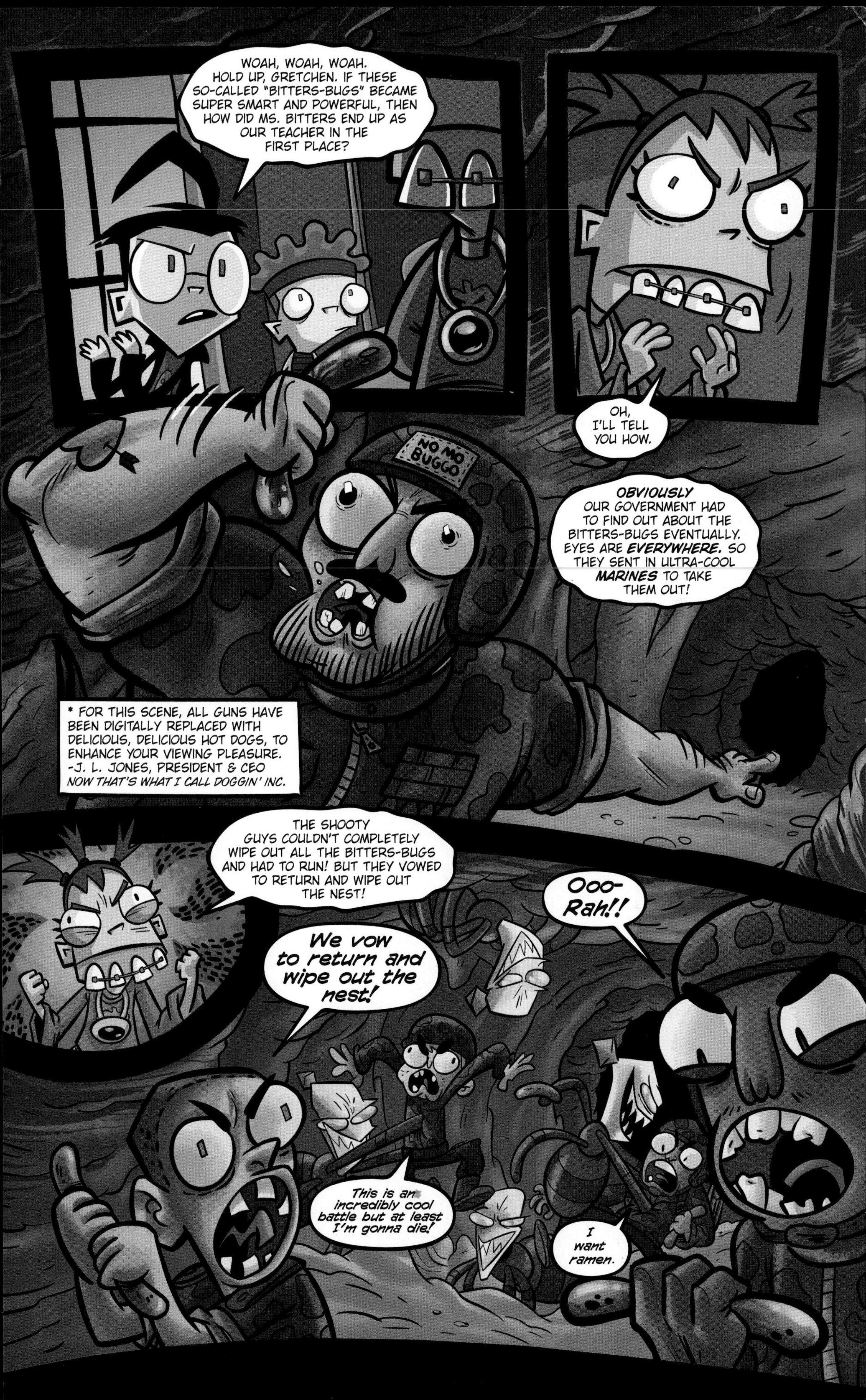
WOAH, WOAH, WOAH. HOLD UP, GRETCHEN. IF THESE SO-CALLED "BITTERS-BUGS" BECAME SUPER SMART AND POWERFUL, THEN HOW DID MS. BITTERS END UP AS OUR TEACHER IN THE FIRST PLACE?
OH, I'LL TELL YOU HOW.
NO MO BUGGO
OBVIOUSLY OUR GOVERNMENT HAD TO FIND OUT ABOUT THE BITTERS-BUGS EVENTUALLY. EYES ARE EVERYWHERE. SO THEY SENT IN ULTRA-COOL MARINES TO TAKE THEM OUT!
* FOR THIS SCENE, ALL GUNS HAVE BEEN DIGITALLY REPLACED WITH DELICIOUS, DELICIOUS HOT DOGS, TO ENHANCE YOUR VIEWING PLEASURE. -J. L. JONES, PRESIDENT & CEO NOW THAT'S WHAT I CALL DOGGIN' INC.
THE SHOOTY GUYS COULDN'T COMPLETELY WIPE OUT ALL THE BITTERS-BUGS AND HAD TO RUN! BUT THEY VOWED TO RETURN AND WIPE OUT THE NEST!
Ooo-Rah!!
We vow to return and wipe out the nest!
This is an incredibly cool battle but at least I'm gonna die!
I want ramen.

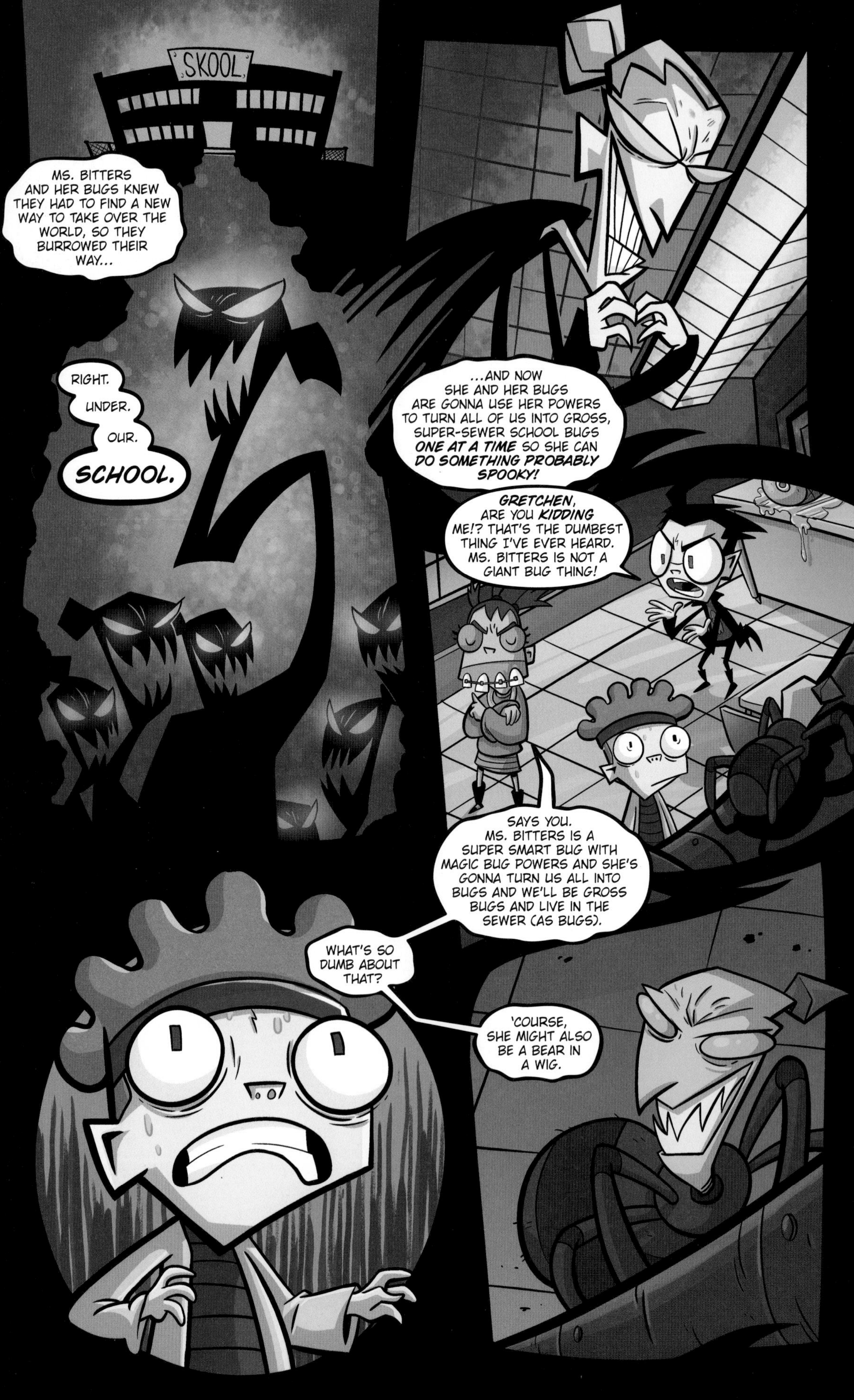
SKOOL
MS. BITTERS AND HER BUGS KNEW THEY HAD TO FIND A NEW WAY TO TAKE OVER THE WORLD, SO THEY BURROWED THEIR WAY...
RIGHT.
UNDER.
OUR.
SCHOOL.
...AND NOW SHE AND HER BUGS ARE GONNA USE HER POWERS TO TURN ALL OF US INTO GROSS, SUPER-SEWER SCHOOL BUGS ONE AT A TIME SO SHE CAN DO SOMETHING PROBABLY SPOOKY!
GRETCHEN, ARE YOU KIDDING ME!? THAT'S THE DUMBEST THING I'VE EVER HEARD. MS. BITTERS IS NOT A GIANT BUG THING!
SAYS YOU. MS. BITTERS IS A SUPER SMART BUG WITH MAGIC BUG POWERS AND SHE'S GONNA TURN US ALL INTO BUGS AND WE'LL BE GROSS BUGS AND LIVE IN THE SEWER (AS BUGS).
WHAT'S SO DUMB ABOUT THAT?
'COURSE, SHE MIGHT ALSO BE A BEAR IN A WIG.

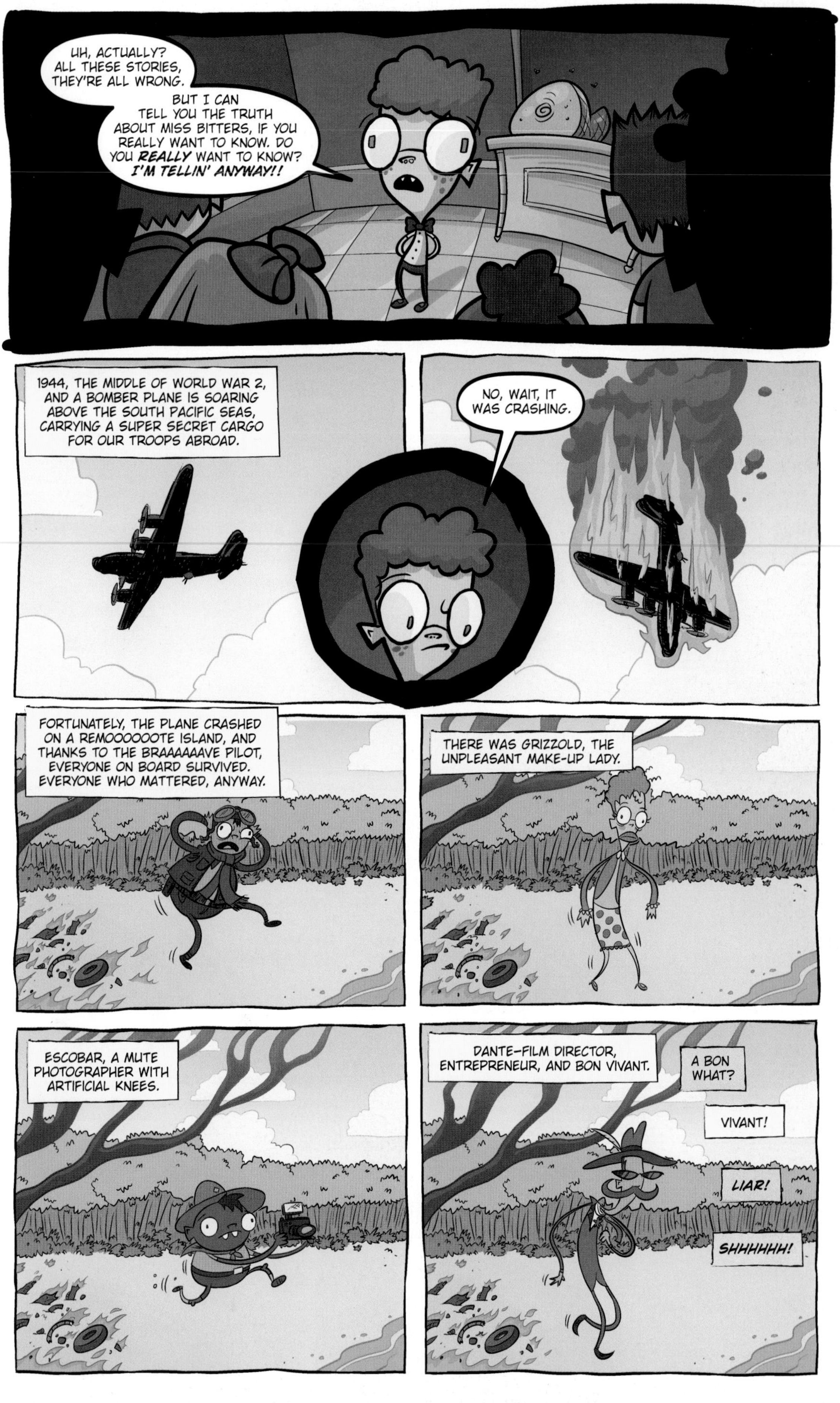
UH, ACTUALLY? ALL THESE STORIES, THEY'RE ALL WRONG.
BUT I CAN TELL YOU THE TRUTH ABOUT MISS BITTERS, IF YOU REALLY WANT TO KNOW. DO YOU **REALLY** WANT TO KNOW? ***I'M TELLIN' ANYWAY!!***
1944, THE MIDDLE OF WORLD WAR 2, AND A BOMBER PLANE IS SOARING ABOVE THE SOUTH PACIFIC SEAS, CARRYING A SUPER SECRET CARGO FOR OUR TROOPS ABROAD.
NO, WAIT, IT WAS CRASHING.
FORTUNATELY, THE PLANE CRASHED ON A REMOOOOOOTE ISLAND, AND THANKS TO THE BRAAAAAAVE PILOT, EVERYONE ON BOARD SURVIVED. EVERYONE WHO MATTERED, ANYWAY.
THERE WAS GRIZZOLD, THE UNPLEASANT MAKE-UP LADY.
ESCOBAR, A MUTE PHOTOGRAPHER WITH ARTIFICIAL KNEES.
DANTE–FILM DIRECTOR, ENTREPRENEUR, AND BON VIVANT.
A BON WHAT?
VIVANT!
LIAR!
SHHHHHH!

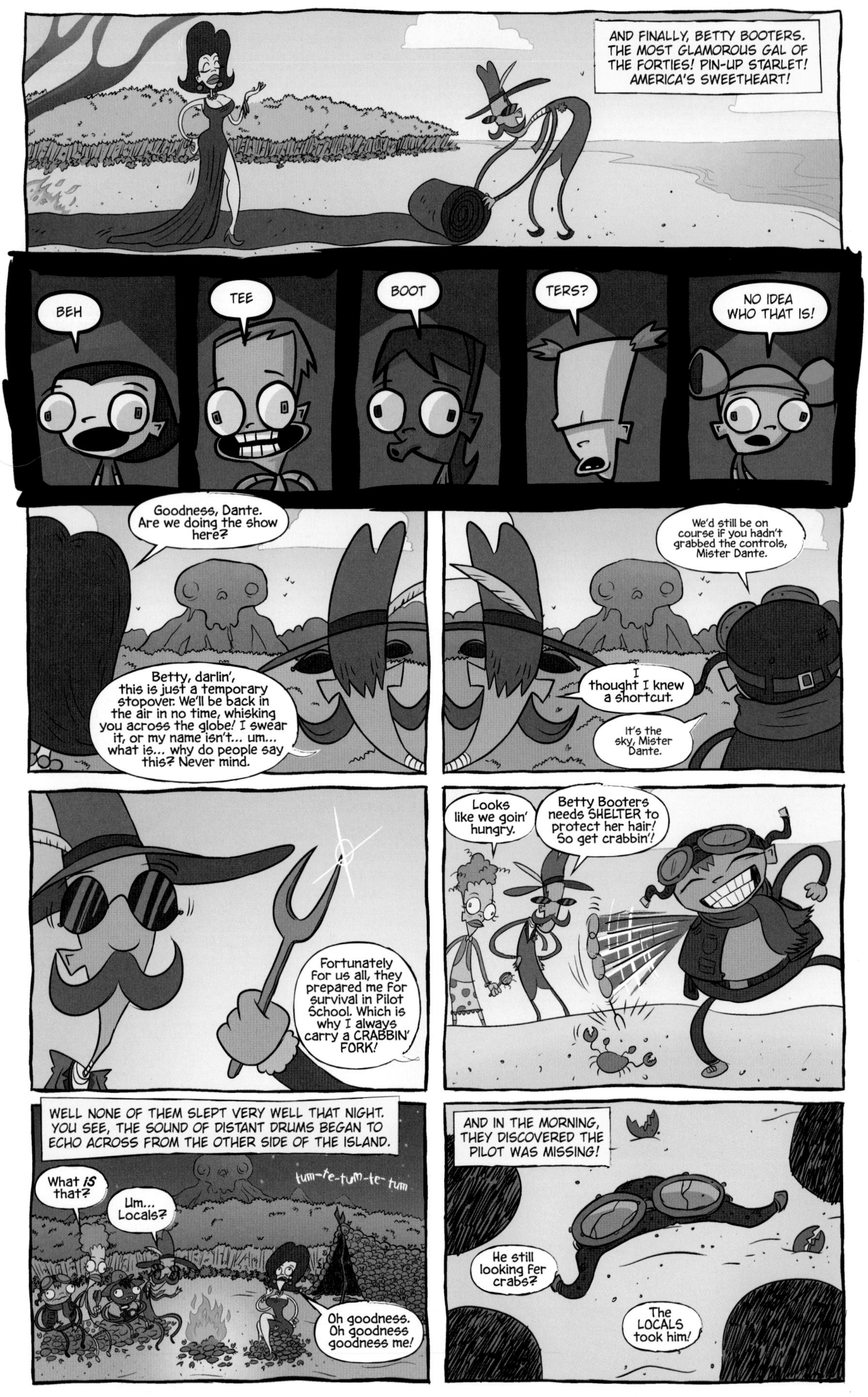
AND FINALLY, BETTY BOOTERS. THE MOST GLAMOROUS GAL OF THE FORTIES! PIN-UP STARLET! AMERICA'S SWEETHEART!
BEH
TEE
BOOT
TERS?
NO IDEA WHO THAT IS!
Goodness, Dante. Are we doing the show here?
Betty, darlin', this is just a temporary stopover. We'll be back in the air in no time, whisking you across the globe! I swear it, or my name isn't... um... what is... why do people say this? Never mind.
We'd still be on course if you hadn't grabbed the controls, Mister Dante.
I thought I knew a shortcut.
It's the sky, Mister Dante.
Fortunately for us all, they prepared me for survival in Pilot School. Which is why I always carry a CRABBIN' FORK!
Looks like we goin' hungry.
Betty Booters needs SHELTER to protect her hair! So get crabbin'!
WELL NONE OF THEM SLEPT VERY WELL THAT NIGHT. YOU SEE, THE SOUND OF DISTANT DRUMS BEGAN TO ECHO ACROSS FROM THE OTHER SIDE OF THE ISLAND.
What IS that?
tum-te-tum-te-tum
Um... Locals?
Oh goodness. Oh goodness goodness me!
AND IN THE MORNING, THEY DISCOVERED THE PILOT WAS MISSING!
He still looking fer crabs?
The LOCALS took him!

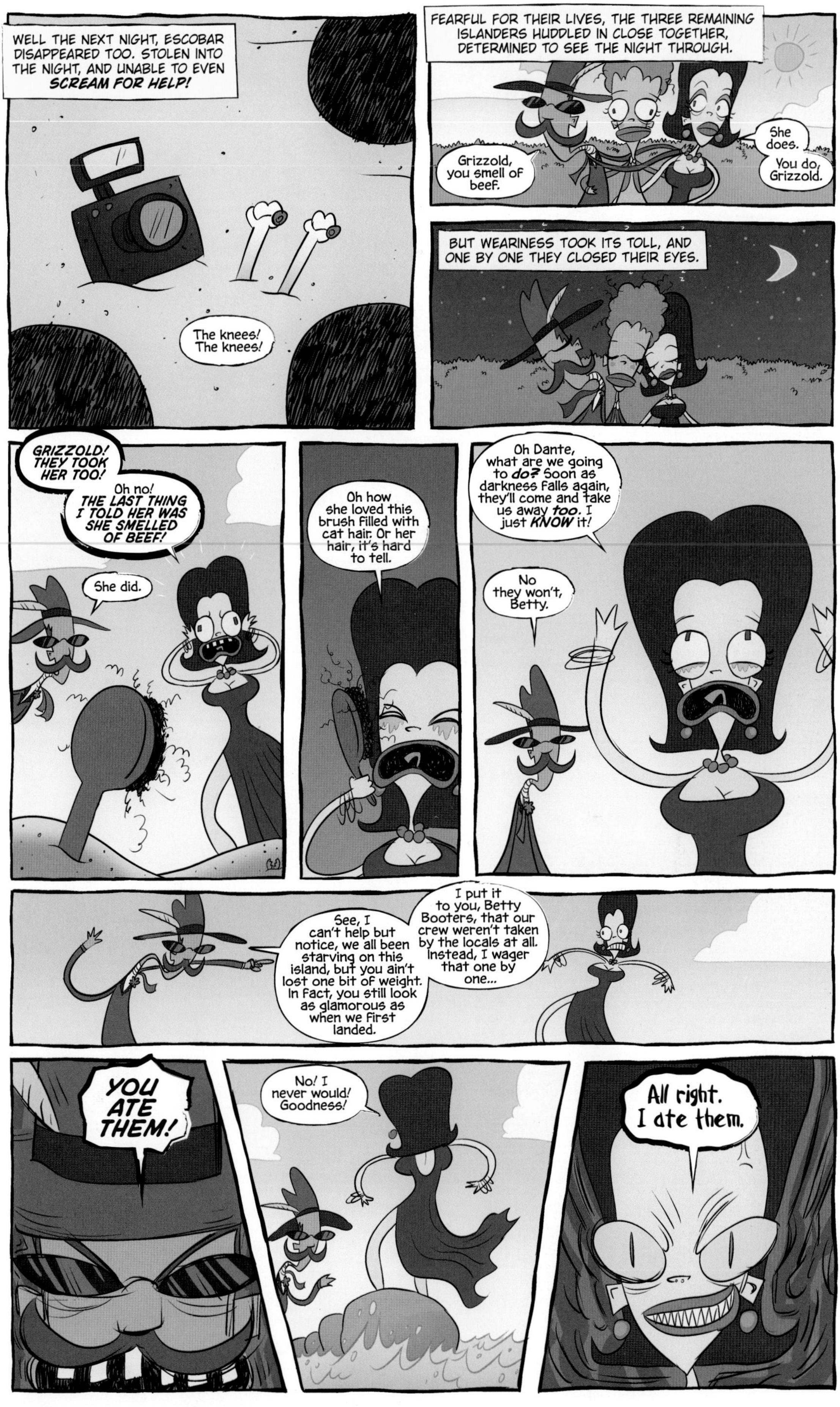
WELL THE NEXT NIGHT, ESCOBAR DISAPPEARED TOO. STOLEN INTO THE NIGHT, AND UNABLE TO EVEN SCREAM FOR HELP!
The knees! The knees!
FEARFUL FOR THEIR LIVES, THE THREE REMAINING ISLANDERS HUDDLED IN CLOSE TOGETHER, DETERMINED TO SEE THE NIGHT THROUGH.
Grizzold, you smell of beef.
She does.
You do, Grizzold.
BUT WEARINESS TOOK ITS TOLL, AND ONE BY ONE THEY CLOSED THEIR EYES.
GRIZZOLD! THEY TOOK HER TOO!
Oh no! THE LAST THING I TOLD HER WAS SHE SMELLED OF BEEF!
She did.
Oh how she loved this brush filled with cat hair. Or her hair, it's hard to tell.
Oh Dante, what are we going to do? Soon as darkness falls again, they'll come and take us away too. I just KNOW it!
No they won't, Betty.
See, I can't help but notice, we all been starving on this island, but you ain't lost one bit of weight. In fact, you still look as glamorous as when we first landed.
I put it to you, Betty Booters, that our crew weren't taken by the locals at all. Instead, I wager that one by one...
YOU ATE THEM!
No! I never would! Goodness!
All right. I ate them.

It's what my kind does! And now that you've found me out, Mr. Dante, you will never live to tell the tale!

No, I think I will.

What? Why?

Because...

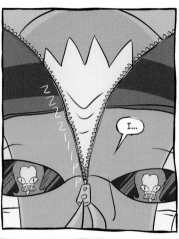

ZZZZIIIIPP

I...

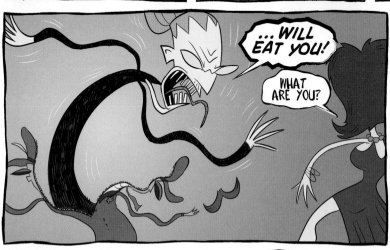

...WILL EAT YOU!

WHAT ARE YOU?

WAIT! The disguise, the plane crash, you... PLANNED all this!

OF COURSE I did. How else was I going to get a flesh-eater alone to eat its flesh?

NO! NO! Wait, there were probably a lot of easier ways. But... GET YOUR HANDS OFF ME!

Relax, I'm not going to use my hands...

I have a CRABBIN' FORK!

AAAAAAAAAAAAAA

AND THAT STORY IS TRUE AND IT IS FACT. THE END.

NO!

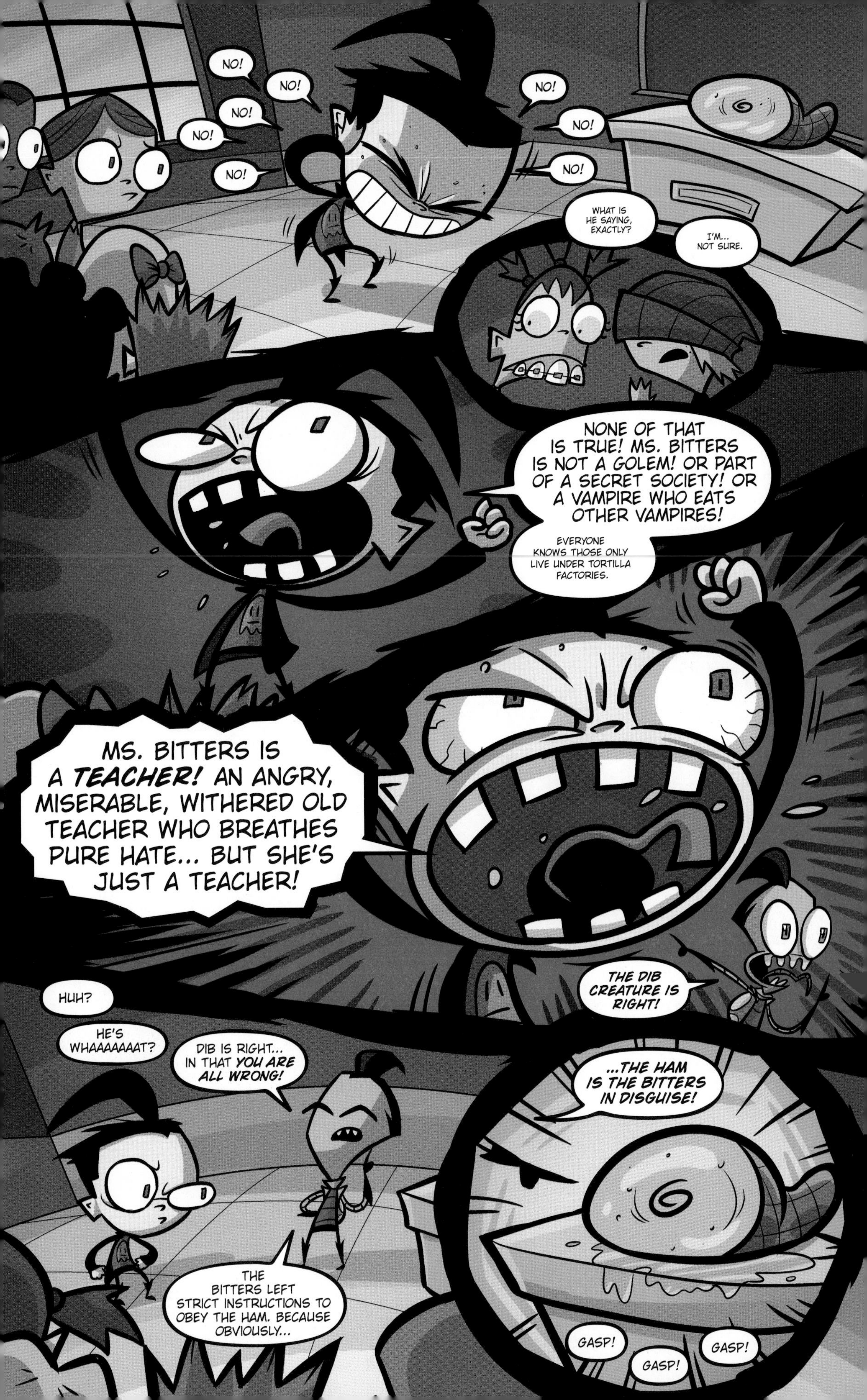
NO!
NO!
NO!
NO!
NO!
NO!
NO!
NO!
WHAT IS HE SAYING, EXACTLY?
I'M... NOT SURE.
NONE OF THAT IS TRUE! MS. BITTERS IS NOT A GOLEM! OR PART OF A SECRET SOCIETY! OR A VAMPIRE WHO EATS OTHER VAMPIRES!
EVERYONE KNOWS THOSE ONLY LIVE UNDER TORTILLA FACTORIES.
MS. BITTERS IS A TEACHER! AN ANGRY, MISERABLE, WITHERED OLD TEACHER WHO BREATHES PURE HATE... BUT SHE'S JUST A TEACHER!
THE DIB CREATURE IS RIGHT!
HUH?
HE'S WHAAAAAAAT?
DIB IS RIGHT... IN THAT YOU ARE ALL WRONG!
THE BITTERS LEFT STRICT INSTRUCTIONS TO OBEY THE HAM. BECAUSE OBVIOUSLY...
...THE HAM IS THE BITTERS IN DISGUISE!
GASP!
GASP!
GASP!

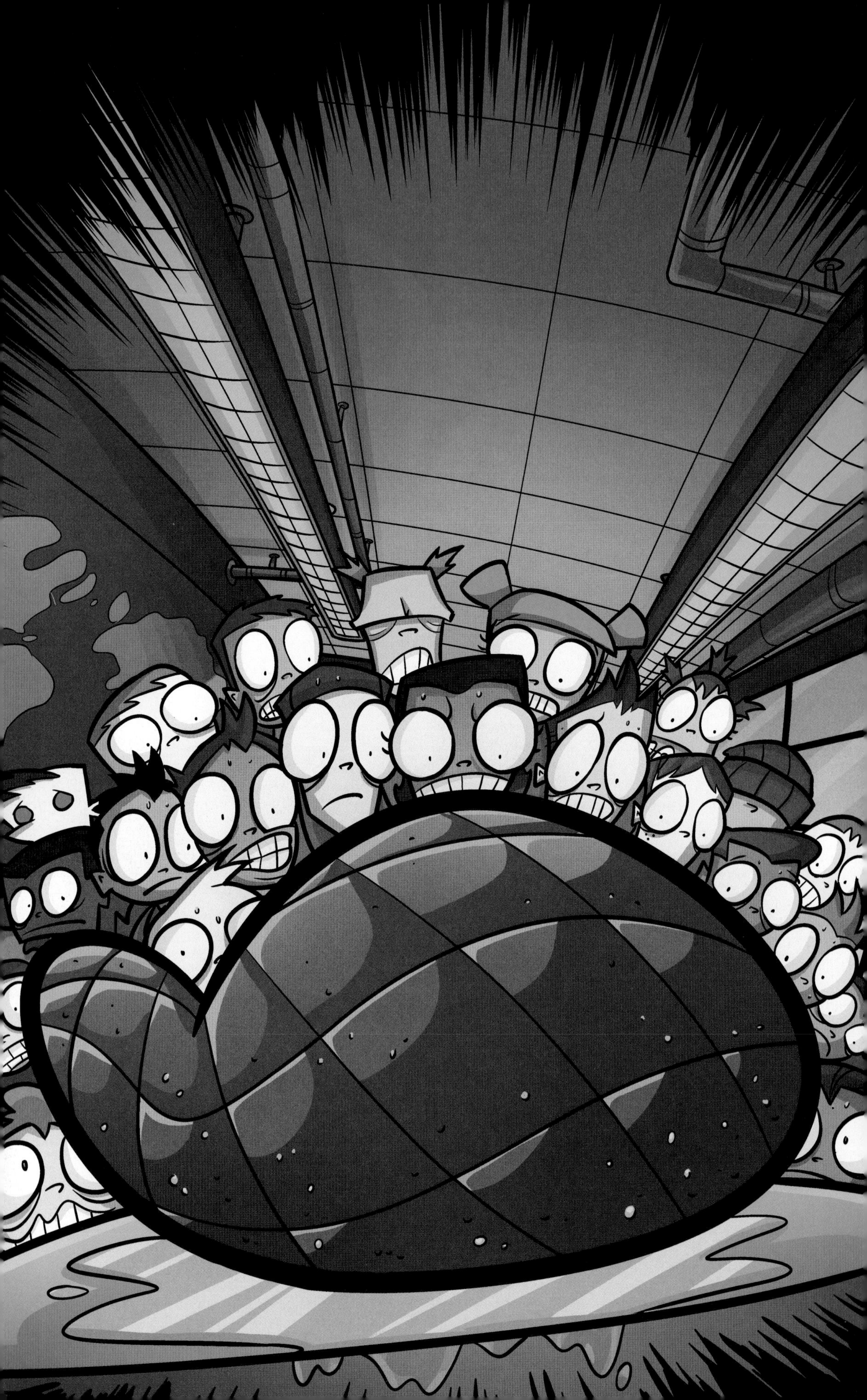

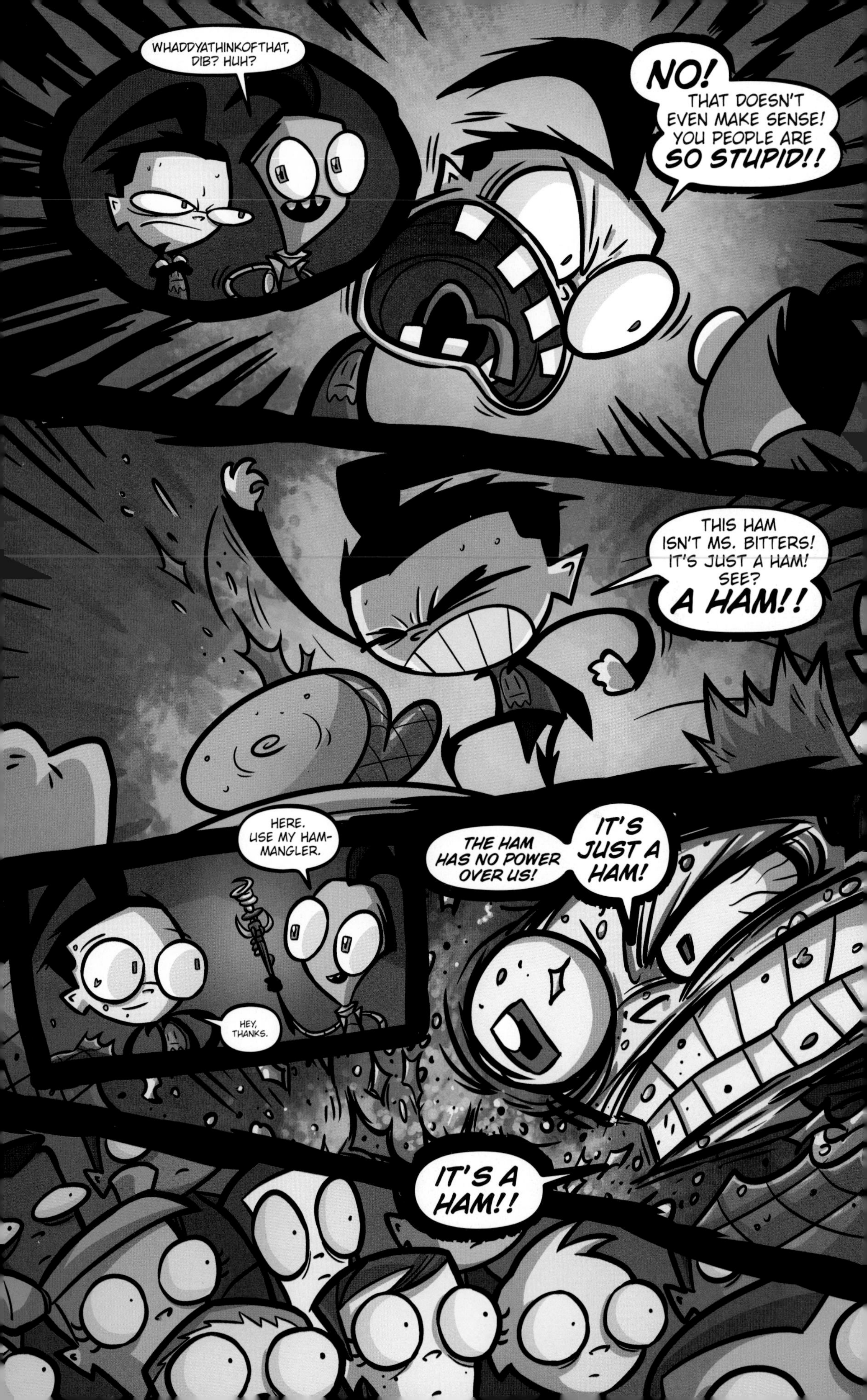
WHADDYATHINKOFTHAT, DIB? HUH?
NO! THAT DOESN'T EVEN MAKE SENSE! YOU PEOPLE ARE SO STUPID!!
THIS HAM ISN'T MS. BITTERS! IT'S JUST A HAM! SEE? A HAM!!
HERE. USE MY HAM-MANGLER.
HEY, THANKS.
THE HAM HAS NO POWER OVER US!
IT'S JUST A HAM!
IT'S A HAM!!

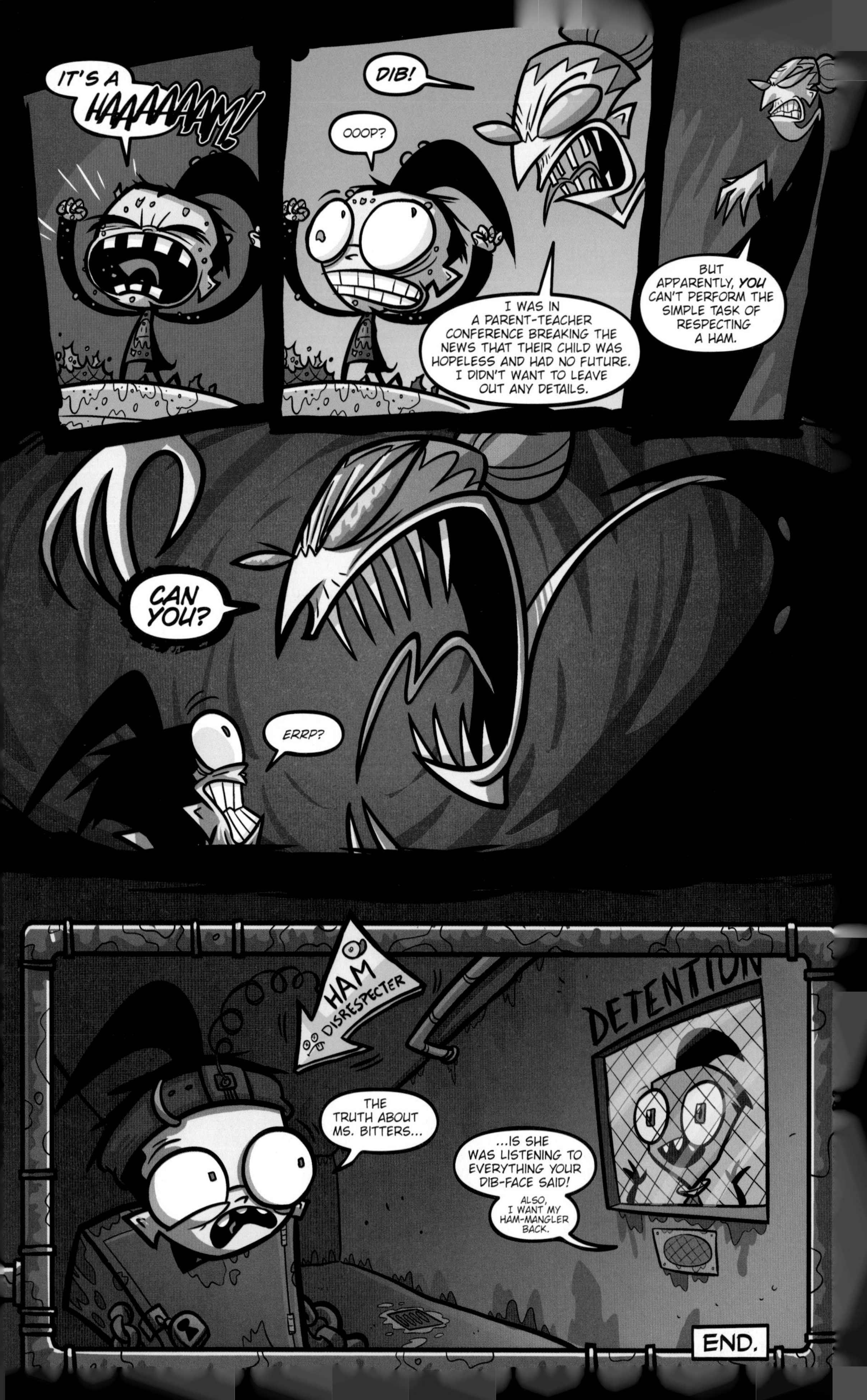
IT'S A HAAAAAAAM!
DIB!
OOOP?
I WAS IN A PARENT-TEACHER CONFERENCE BREAKING THE NEWS THAT THEIR CHILD WAS HOPELESS AND HAD NO FUTURE. I DIDN'T WANT TO LEAVE OUT ANY DETAILS.
BUT APPARENTLY, YOU CAN'T PERFORM THE SIMPLE TASK OF RESPECTING A HAM.
CAN YOU?
ERRP?
HAM DISRESPECTER
DETENTION
THE TRUTH ABOUT MS. BITTERS...
...IS SHE WAS LISTENING TO EVERYTHING YOUR DIB-FACE SAID!
ALSO, I WANT MY HAM-MANGLER BACK.
END.

"INVASION"

Written and illustrated by
DAVE CROSLAND

Colored by
FRED C. STRESING

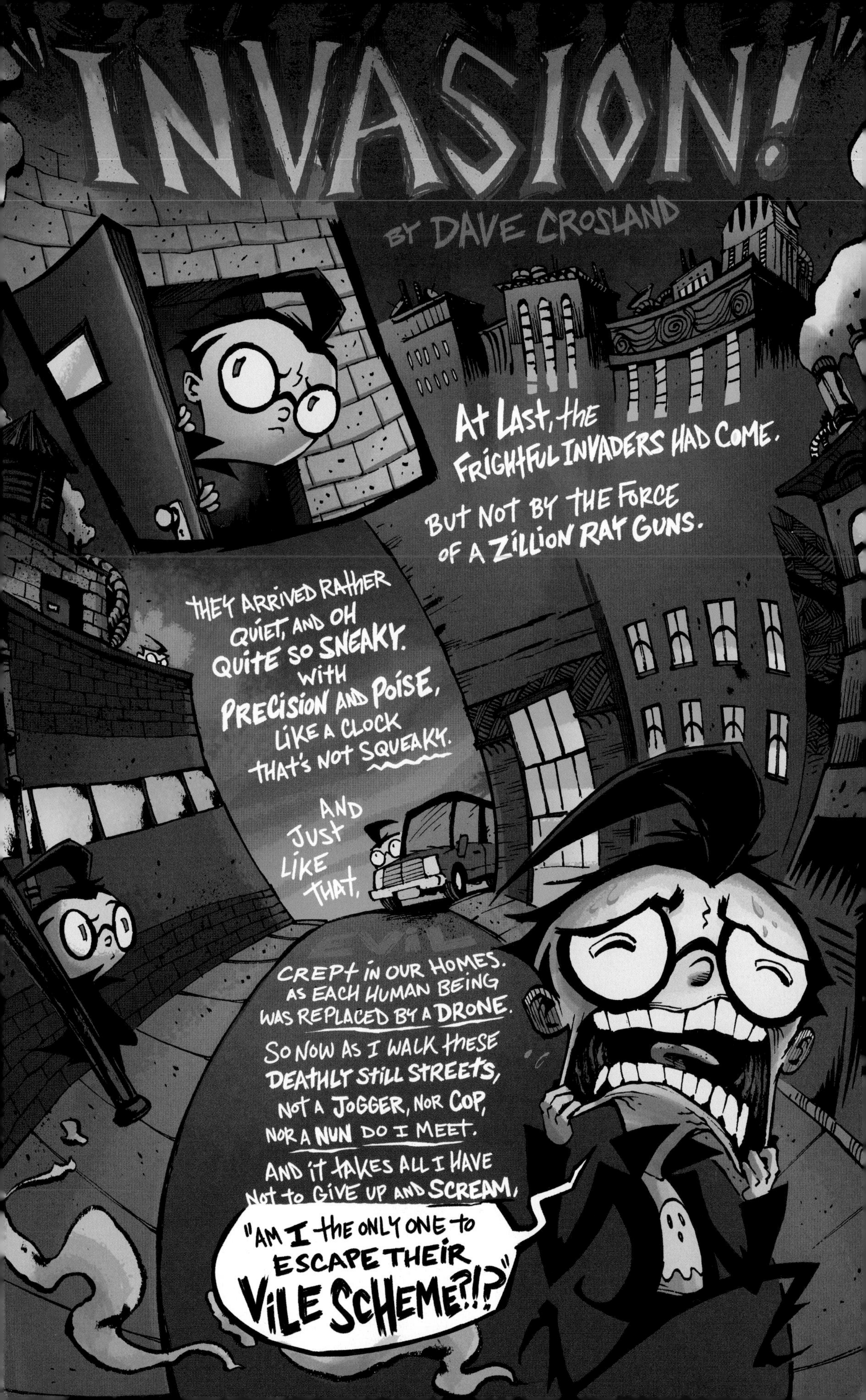
INVASION!
BY DAVE CROSLAND
At Last, the FRIGHTFUL INVADERS HAD COME.
BUT NOT BY THE FORCE OF A ZILLION RAY GUNS.
THEY ARRIVED RATHER QUIET, AND OH QUITE SO SNEAKY. WITH PRECISION AND POISE, LIKE A CLOCK THAT'S NOT SQUEAKY.
AND JUST LIKE THAT,
EVIL
CREPT IN OUR HOMES. AS EACH HUMAN BEING WAS REPLACED BY A DRONE.
SO NOW AS I WALK THESE DEATHLY STILL STREETS, NOT A JOGGER, NOR COP, NOR A NUN DO I MEET.
AND IT TAKES ALL I HAVE NOT TO GIVE UP AND SCREAM,
"AM I THE ONLY ONE TO ESCAPE THEIR VILE SCHEME?!?"

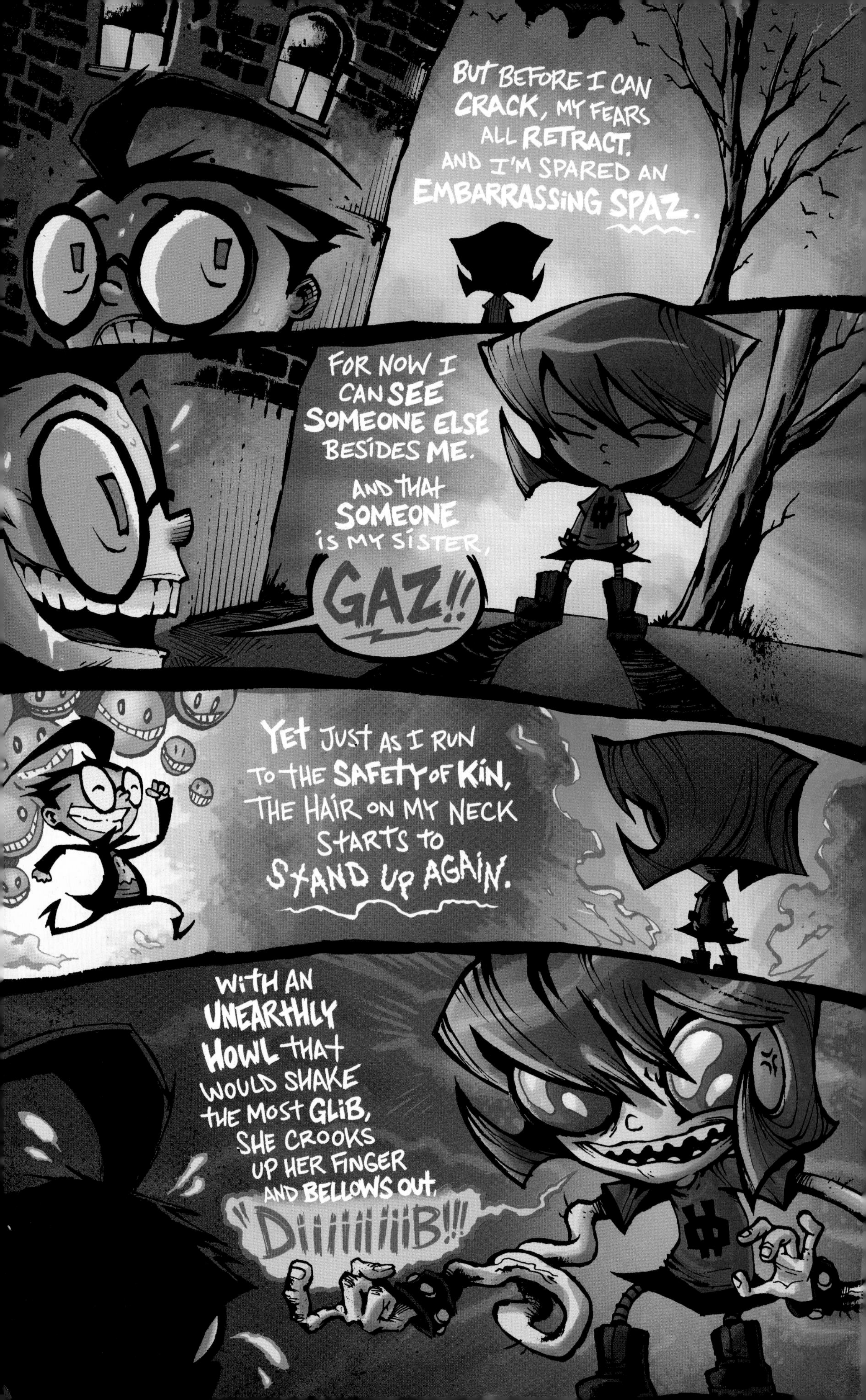
BUT BEFORE I CAN CRACK, MY FEARS ALL RETRACT. AND I'M SPARED AN EMBARRASSING SPAZ.
FOR NOW I CAN SEE SOMEONE ELSE BESIDES ME.
AND THAT SOMEONE IS MY SISTER,
GAZ!!
YET JUST AS I RUN TO THE SAFETY OF KIN, THE HAIR ON MY NECK STARTS TO STAND UP AGAIN.
WITH AN UNEARTHLY HOWL THAT WOULD SHAKE THE MOST GLIB, SHE CROOKS UP HER FINGER AND BELLOWS OUT,
"DIIIIIIIIB!!!

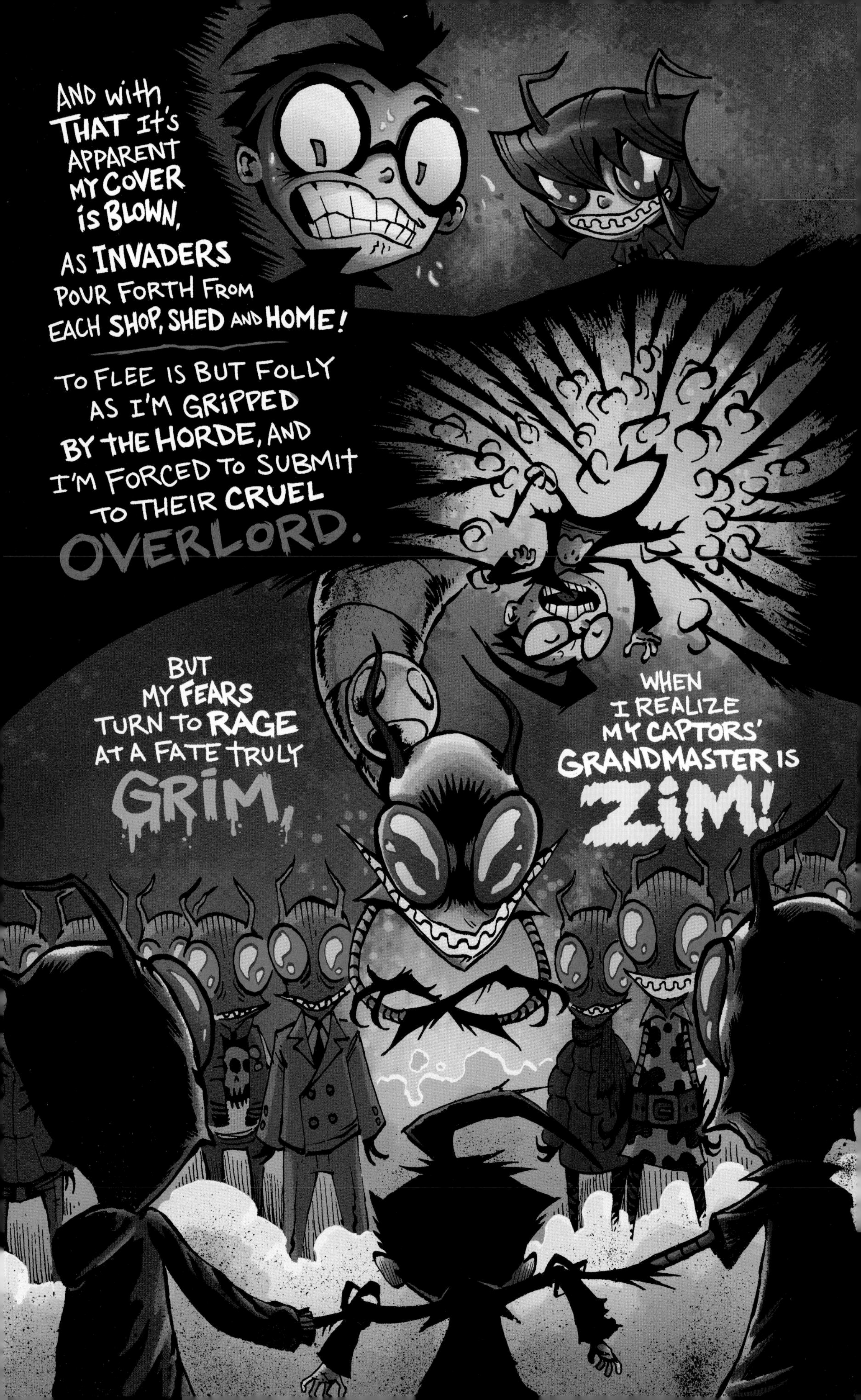
AND WITH THAT IT'S APPARENT MY COVER IS BLOWN,
AS INVADERS POUR FORTH FROM EACH SHOP, SHED AND HOME!
TO FLEE IS BUT FOLLY AS I'M GRIPPED BY THE HORDE, AND I'M FORCED TO SUBMIT TO THEIR CRUEL OVERLORD.
BUT MY FEARS TURN TO RAGE AT A FATE TRULY GRIM,
WHEN I REALIZE MY CAPTORS' GRANDMASTER IS ZIM!

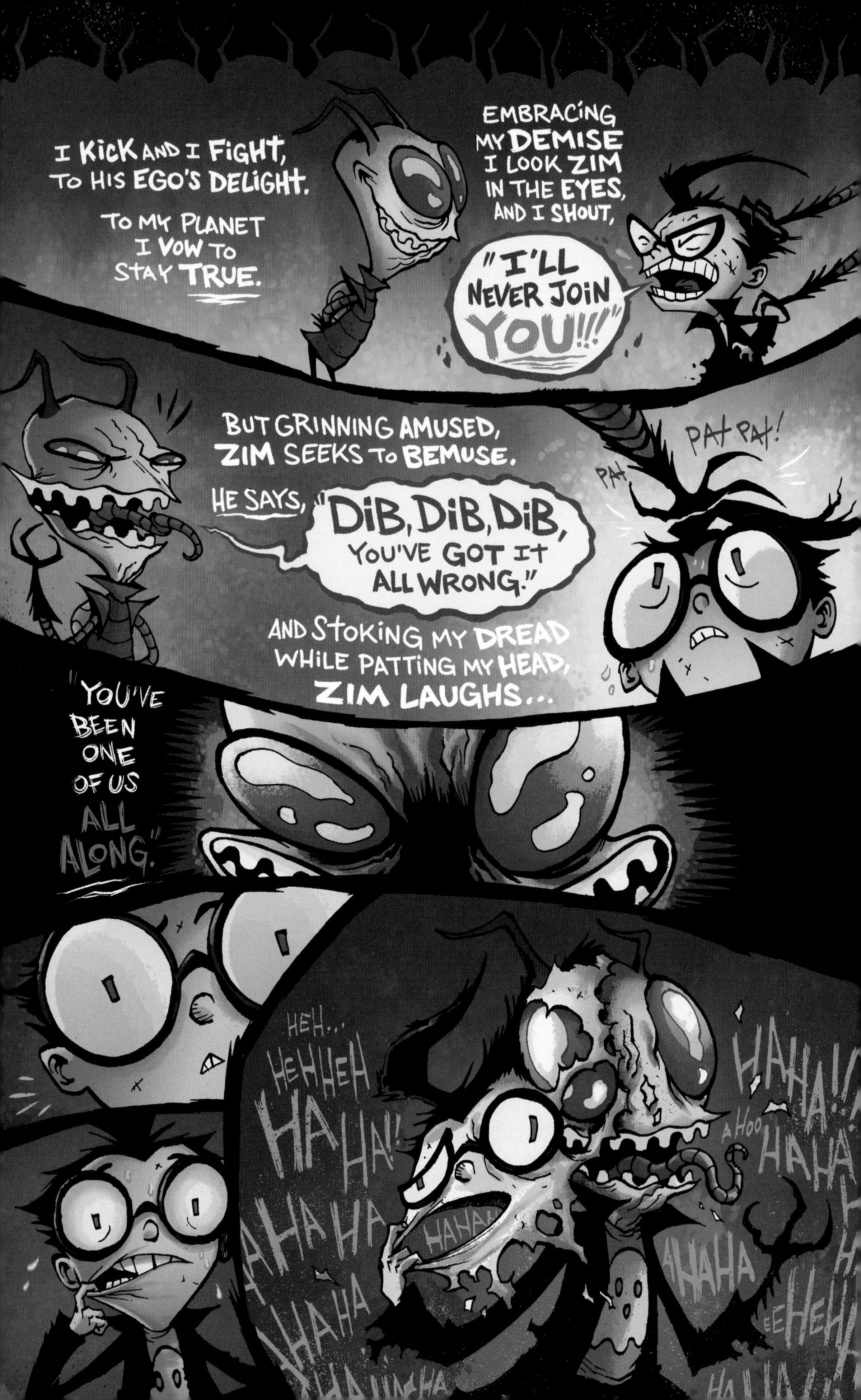
I KICK AND I FIGHT,
TO HIS EGO'S DELIGHT.
TO MY PLANET
I VOW TO
STAY TRUE.
EMBRACING
MY DEMISE
I LOOK ZIM
IN THE EYES,
AND I SHOUT,
"I'LL
NEVER JOIN
YOU!!!"
BUT GRINNING AMUSED,
ZIM SEEKS TO BEMUSE.
HE SAYS, "DIB, DIB, DIB,
YOU'VE GOT IT
ALL WRONG."
PAT PAT!
PAT
AND STOKING MY DREAD
WHILE PATTING MY HEAD,
ZIM LAUGHS...
"YOU'VE
BEEN
ONE
OF US
ALL
ALONG."
HEH...
HEHHEH
HAHA!
HAHA!!
A HOO
HAHA
AHAHA
HAHAHA
WHAHA
AHAHA
EEHEH

"THE SWEAT SPOT"

Written and illustrated by
JARRETT WILLIAMS

Colored by
JEREMY LAWSON

Lettered by
WARREN WUCINICH

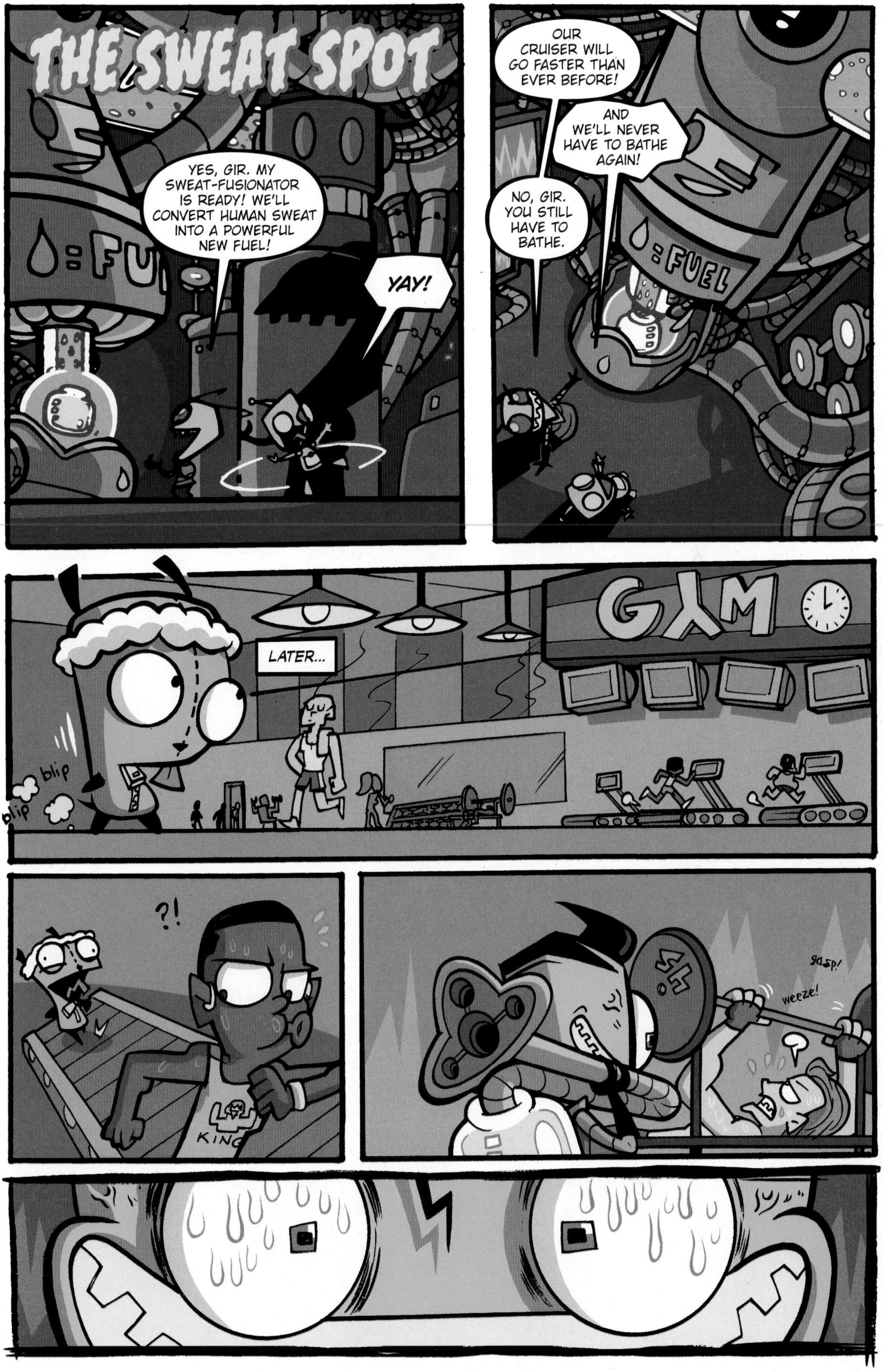
THE SWEAT SPOT
YES, GIR. MY SWEAT-FUSIONATOR IS READY! WE'LL CONVERT HUMAN SWEAT INTO A POWERFUL NEW FUEL!
YAY!
FUEL
OUR CRUISER WILL GO FASTER THAN EVER BEFORE!
AND WE'LL NEVER HAVE TO BATHE AGAIN!
NO, GIR. YOU STILL HAVE TO BATHE.
FUEL
LATER...
GYM
blip
blip
?!
KING
45
gasp!
weeze!

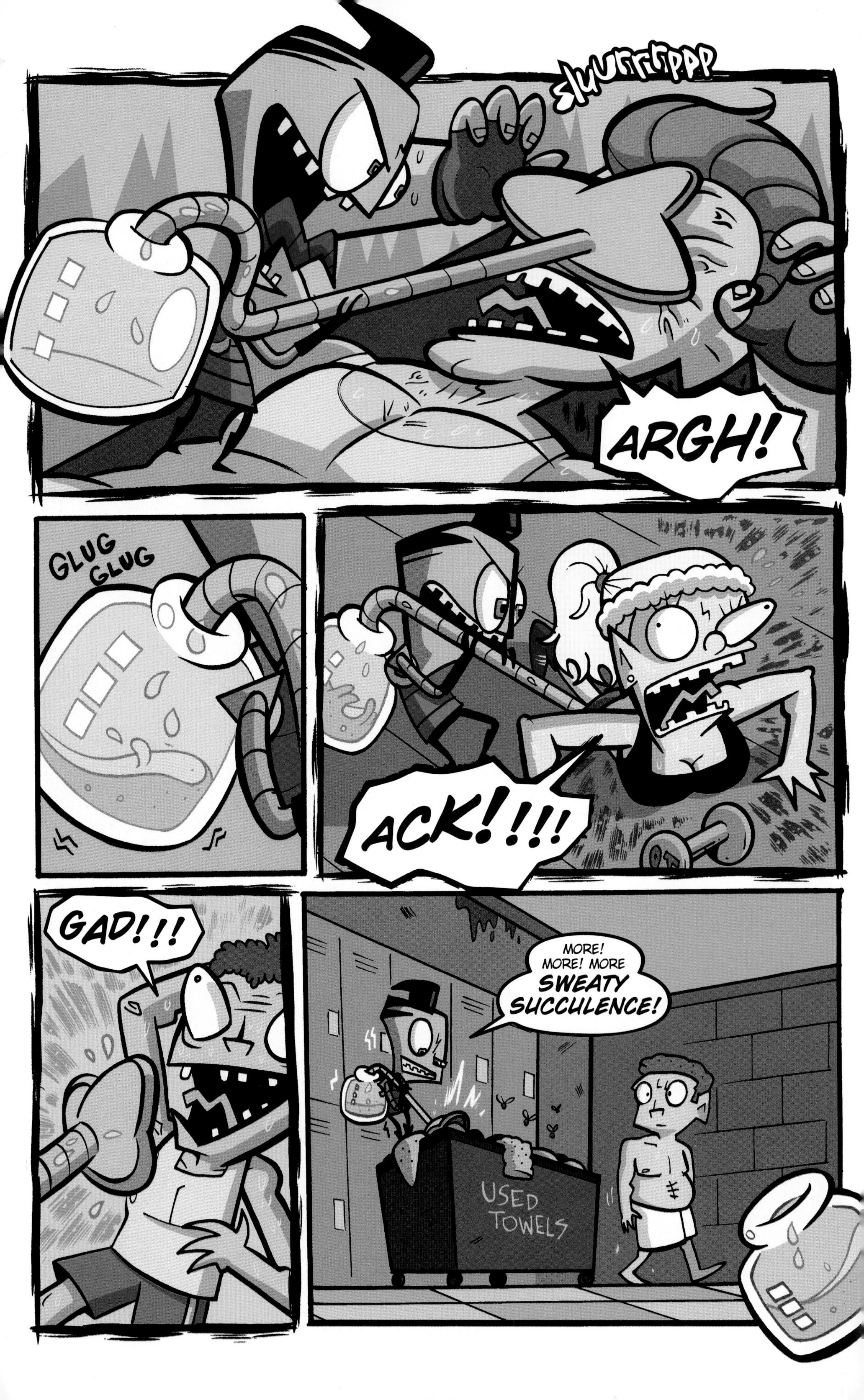
SLURRRPPP
ARGH!
GLUG
GLUG
ACK!!!!
GAD!!!
MORE! MORE! MORE SWEATY SUCCULENCE!
USED TOWELS

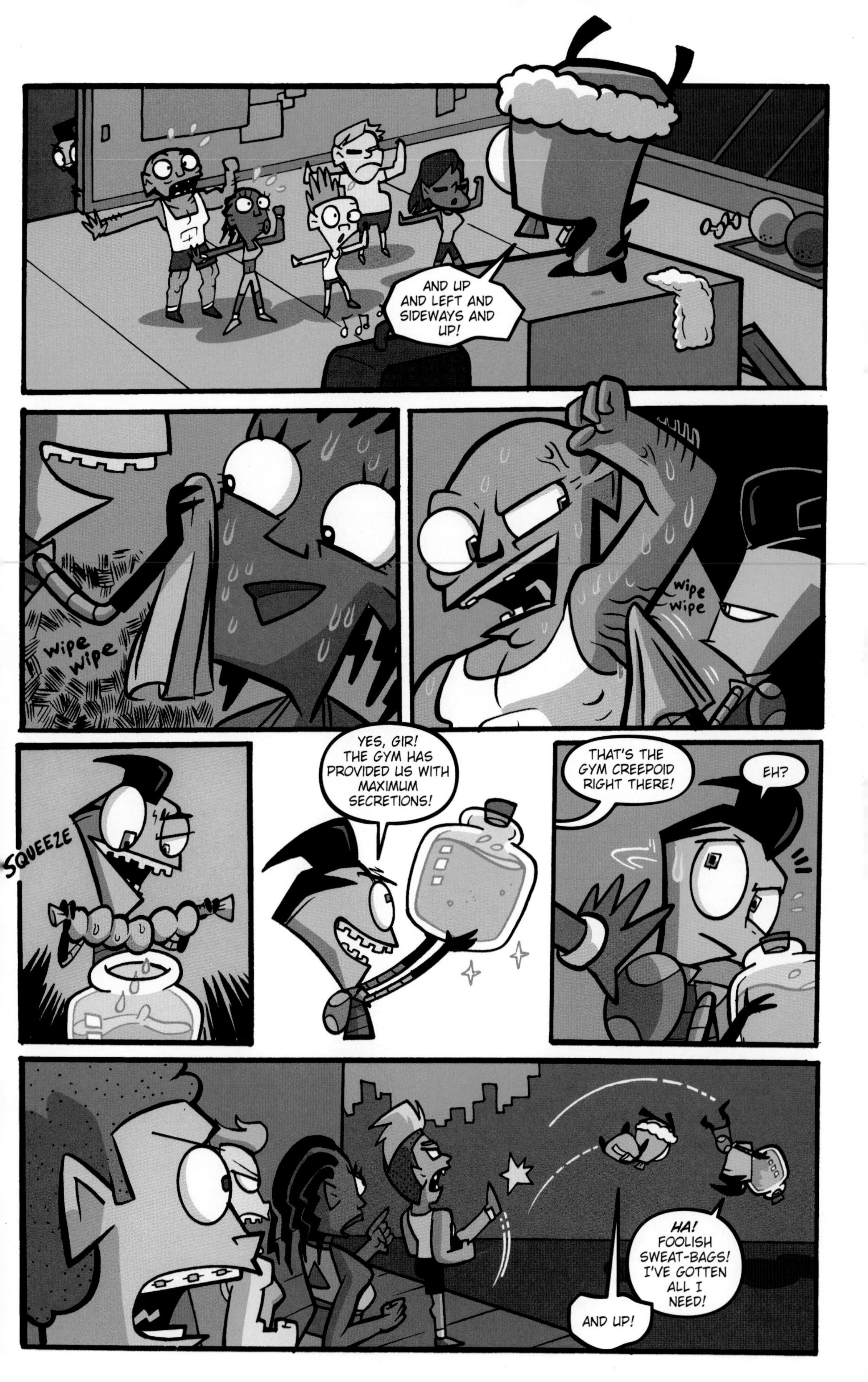
AND UP
AND LEFT AND
SIDEWAYS AND
UP!
wipe wipe
wipe
wipe
SQUEEZE
YES, GIR!
THE GYM HAS
PROVIDED US WITH
MAXIMUM
SECRETIONS!
THAT'S THE
GYM CREEPOID
RIGHT THERE!
EH?
HA!
FOOLISH
SWEAT-BAGS!
I'VE GOTTEN
ALL I
NEED!
AND UP!

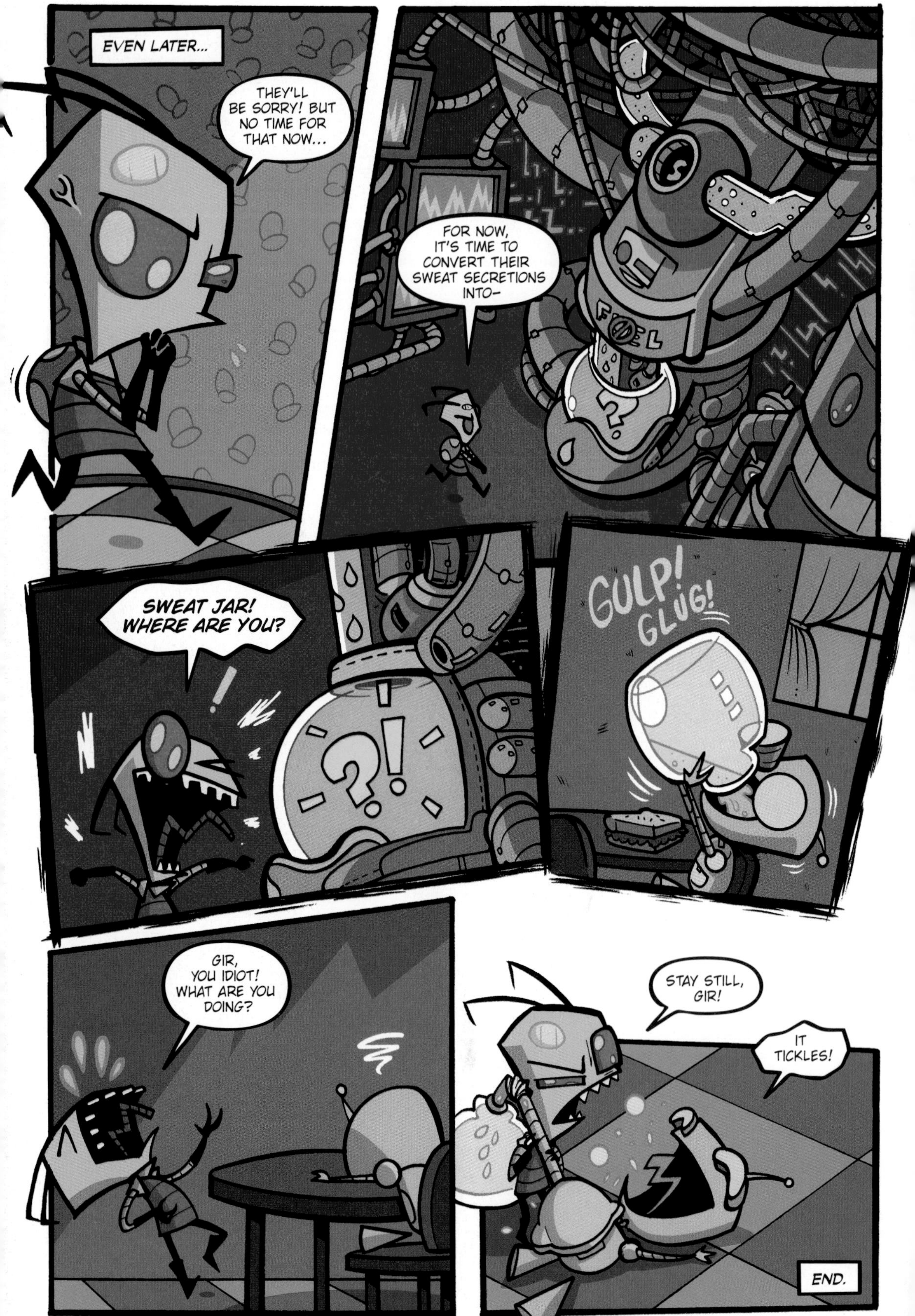
EVEN LATER...
THEY'LL BE SORRY! BUT NO TIME FOR THAT NOW...
FOR NOW, IT'S TIME TO CONVERT THEIR SWEAT SECRETIONS INTO–
FUEL
SWEAT JAR! WHERE ARE YOU?
GULP! GLUG!
GIR, YOU IDIOT! WHAT ARE YOU DOING?
STAY STILL, GIR!
IT TICKLES!
END.

"GHOST AGGRESSORS"

Written, illustrated and colored by
MEGAN LAWTON

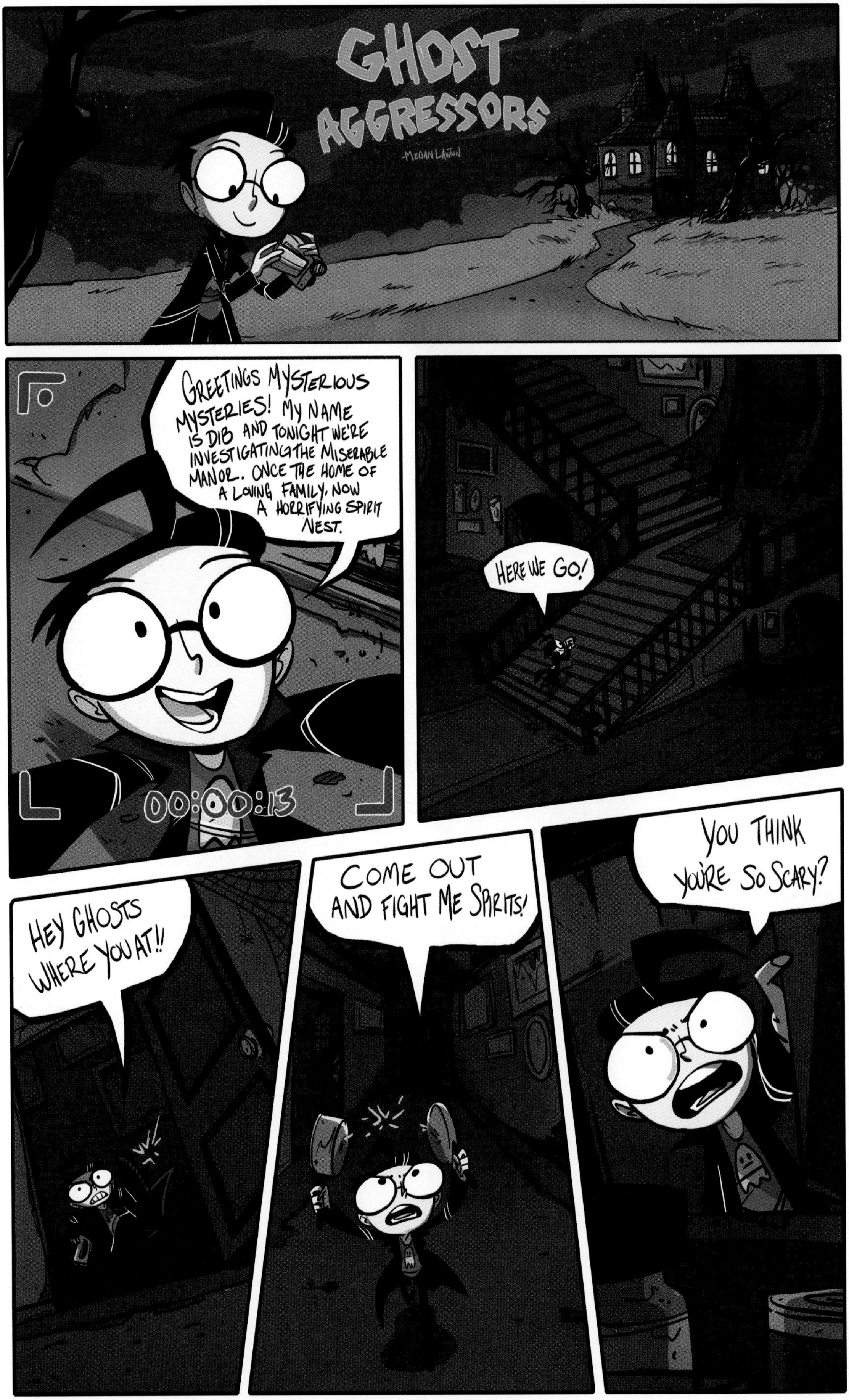
GHOST AGGRESSORS
-MEGAN LAWTON
GREETINGS MYSTERIOUS MYSTERIES! MY NAME IS DIB AND TONIGHT WE'RE INVESTIGATING THE MISERABLE MANOR. ONCE THE HOME OF A LOVING FAMILY, NOW A HORRIFYING SPIRIT NEST.
00:00:13
HERE WE GO!
HEY GHOSTS WHERE YOU AT!!
COME OUT AND FIGHT ME SPIRITS!
YOU THINK YOU'RE SO SCARY?

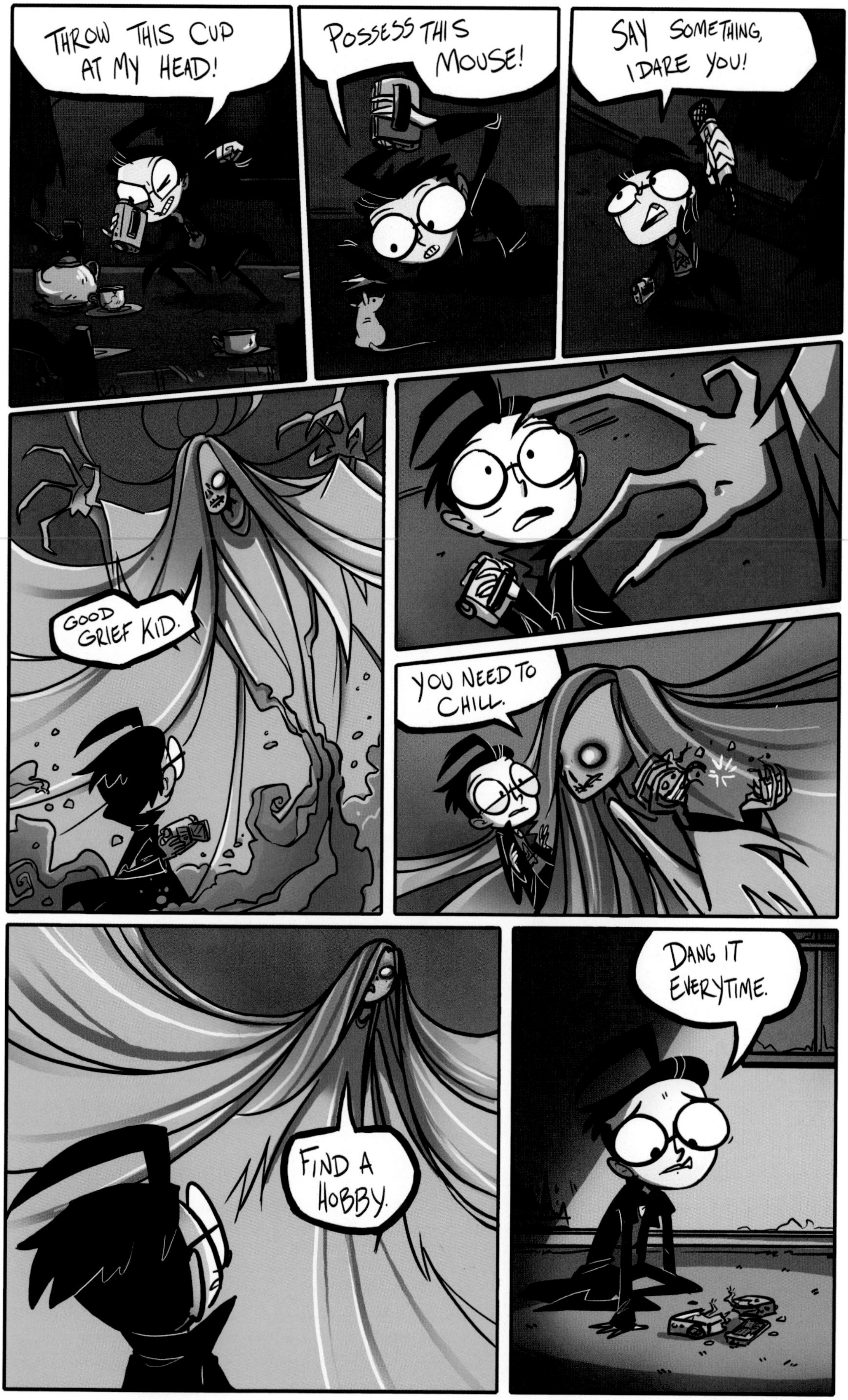
THROW THIS CUP AT MY HEAD!
POSSESS THIS MOUSE!
SAY SOMETHING, I DARE YOU!
GOOD GRIEF KID.
YOU NEED TO CHILL.
FIND A HOBBY.
DANG IT EVERYTIME.

JHONEN VASQUEZ

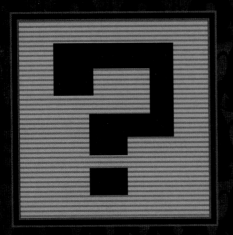

@JhonenV

Jhonen Vasquez is a writer and artist who walks in many worlds, not unlike Blade, only without having to drink blood-serum to survive the curse that is also his greatest power (still talking about Blade here). He's worked in comics and animation and is the creator of *Invader ZIM*, a fact that haunts him to this day.

ERIC TRUEHEART

@erictrueheart

Eric Trueheart was one of the original writers on the *Invader ZIM* television series back when there was a thing called "television." Since then, he's made a living writing moderately-inappropriate things for people who make entertainment for children, including Dreamworks Animation, Cartoon Network, Disney TV, PBS, Hasbro and others. Upon reading this list, he now thinks he maybe should have become a dentist, and he hates teeth.

SARAH ANDERSEN

Sarah Andersen is a 24-year-old cartoonist and illustrator. She graduated from the Maryland Institute College of Art in 2014 and currently lives in Brooklyn. Her comics are semi-autobiographical and follow the adventures of herself, her friends, and her beloved pets.

 @SarahCAndersen

WARREN WUCINICH

Warren Wucinich an illustrator, colorist and part-time carny currently living in Durham, NC. When not making comics he can usually be found watching old *Twilight Zone* episodes and eating large amounts of pie.

 @warrenwucinich

KATY FARINA

Katy Farina is a comic artist illustrator based in Charlotte She graduated from the Minr College of Art and design in with a BFA in illustration, an although that's what she did exclusively for several years sweet siren call of comics ha telling stories in no time!

@Kate_Farina

FRED C. STRESINC

Fred C. Stresing is a colorist, writer, and letterer for a var comics. You may recognize h from *Invader ZIM*, the comic are holding. He has been ma comics his whole life, from th of six. He has gotten much b since then. He currently resid Savannah, Georgia with his and 2 cats. He doesn't know the cats got there, they are r

@FredCStresing

AARON ALEXOVICH

Aaron Alexovich's first professional art job was drawing deformed children for Nickelodeon's *Invader ZIM*. Since then he's been deforming children for various animation and comic projects, including *Avatar: The Last Airbender*, *Randy Cunningham: 9th Grade Ninja*, *Disney's Haunted Mansion*, *Fables*, *Kimmie66*, *ELDRITCH!* (with art by Drew Rausch) and three volumes of his own beloved horror/comedy witch comic dealie, *Serenity Rose*.

@essrose

Aaron was born and raised under seventeen beautiful miles of ice in Chicago, IL, but currently lives in Southern California, where the bright light makes him sneeze for mysterious reasons.

THESE PEOPLE HELPED TOO!

DAVE CROSLAND

JARRETT WILLIAMS

MEGAN LAWTON

DANIELLE KOENIG

JAMIE SMART

KC GREEN

IAN MCGINTY

JEREMY LAWSON

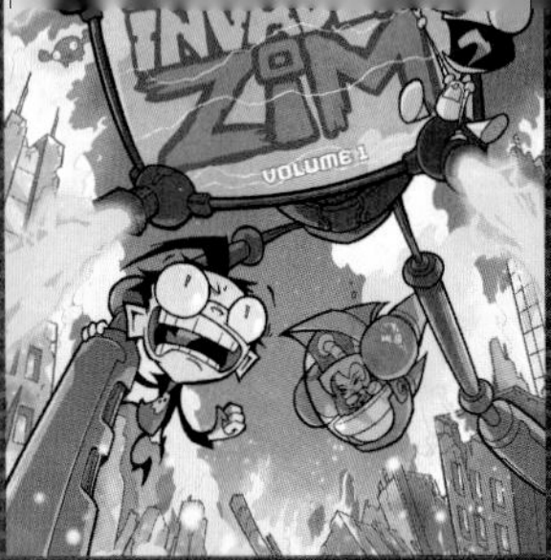
INVADER ZIM
VOLUME 1

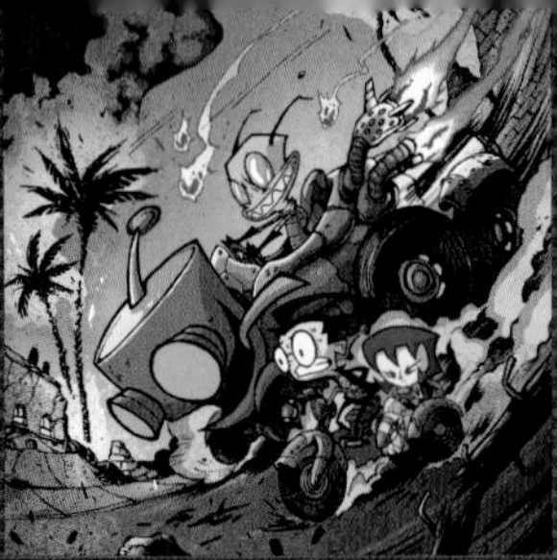

136 pages, softcover, color
ISBN 978-1-62010-293-0

INVADER ZIM, VOLUME 2
Jhonen Vasquez, Eric Trueheart,
KC Green, Dennis & Jessie Hopeless,
Kyle Starks, Savanna Ganucheau,
Dave Crosland, Aaron Alexovich,
Warren Wucinich, and J.R. Goldberg
136 pages, softcover, color
ISBN 978-1-62010-336-4

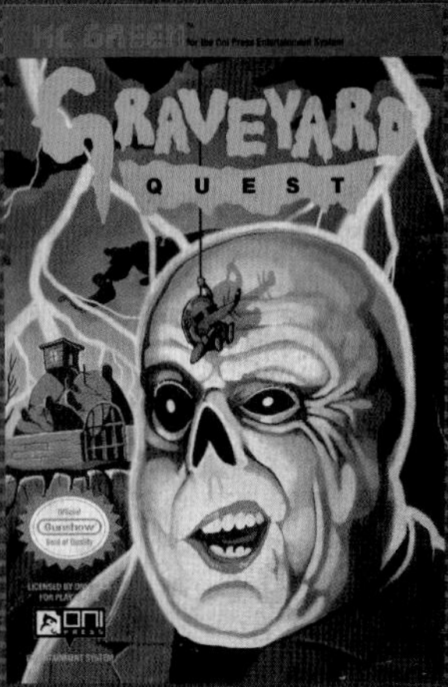
KC GREEN
GRAVEYARD
QUEST

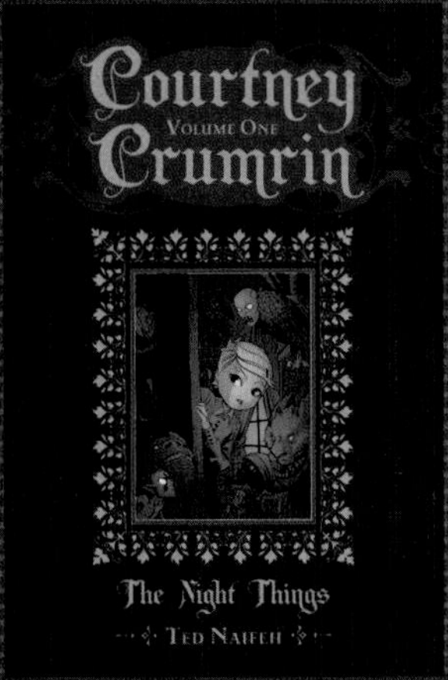
Courtney
Volume One
Crumrin
The Night Things
Ted Naifeh

GRAVEYARD QUEST
By KC Green
192 pages, softcover, color
ISBN 978-1-62010-289-3

COURTNEY CRUMRIN,
VOLUME 1: THE NIGHT THINGS
By Ted Naifeh
136 pages, hardcover, color
ISBN 978-1-934964-77-4

JUNIOR BRAVES OF THE APOCALYPSE,
VOLUME 1: A BRAVE IS BRAVE
By Greg Smith, Michael Tanner &
Zach Lehner
216 pages, hardcover, two-color
ISBN 978-1-62010-144-5

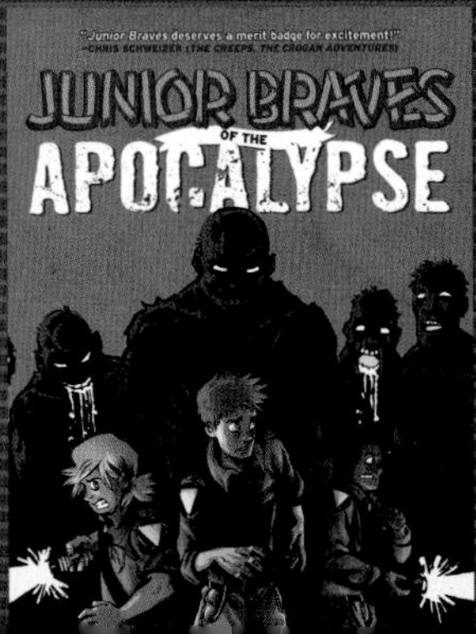
"Junior Braves deserves a merit badge for excitement!"
—CHRIS SCHWEIZER (THE CREEPS, THE CROGAN ADVENTURES)
JUNIOR BRAVES
OF THE
APOCALYPSE

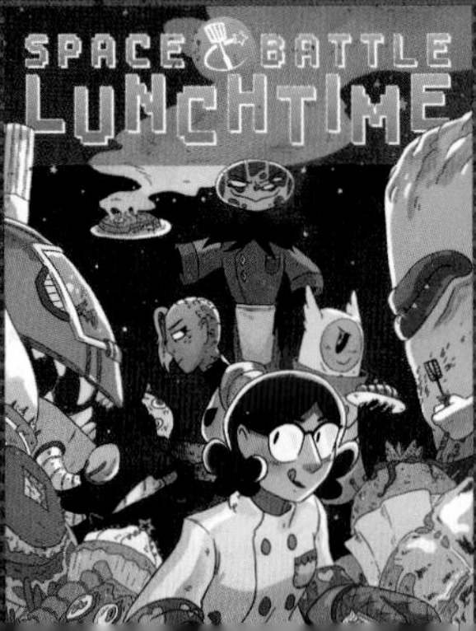
SPACE BATTLE
LUNCHTIME

SPACE BATTLE LUNCHTIME, VOLUME 1:
LIGHTS, CAMERA, SNACKTION!
By Natalie Riess
120 pages, softcover, color
ISBN 978-1-62010-313-5

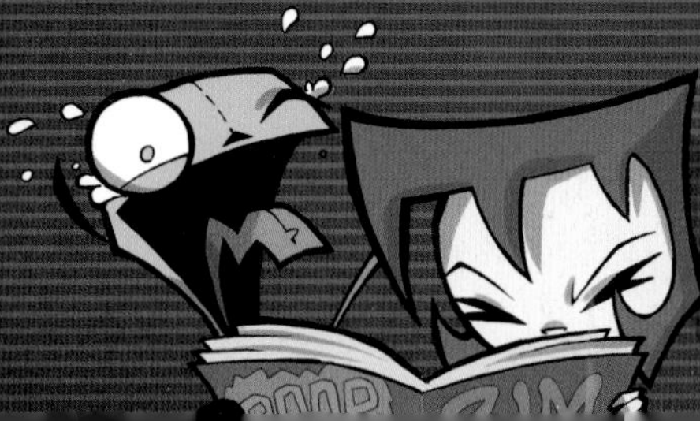